fP

ALSO BY DAVID SOSNOWSKI

Rapture

DAVID SOSNOWSKI

Vamped

A Novel

Free Press

NEW YORK LONDON TORONTO

SYDNEY

FREE PRESS
A Division of Simon & Schuster, Inc.
1230 Avenue of the Americas
New York, NY 10020

FREE PRESS and colophon are trademarks
of Simon & Schuster, Inc.

For information about special discounts for bulk purchases,
please contact Simon & Schuster Special Sales:
1-800-456-6798 or business@simonandschuster.com.

Manufactured in the United States of America

1   3   5   7   9   10   8   6   4   2

Library of Congress Cataloging-in-Publication Data
Sosnowski, David.
Vamped : a novel / David Sosnowski.
p. cm.
1. Vampires—Fiction. I. Title.
PS3569.O716 V36 2004
813'.54—dc22   2004046956

ISBN 0-7432-6253-0

For my parents,
with gratitude
(again)

If God didn't want us to eat animals,
how come He made 'em out of meat?

—Seen on a bumper sticker,
just outside Detroit

Vamped

-1-

THERE'S A SUCKER BORN EVERY MINUTE

Here's a tip:

When you give the world one last chance to save your life, be specific about the *how*. A selection of A, B, or C would be good, along with a couple of "nots"—to clarify the answers you *don't* want. This is especially important if you're a vampire and don't really need to have your life saved, *unless . . .*

I've come up with this advice by not following it. Which is to say, I began this night—possibly my last—with some vague notion of letting the world take one last shot at keeping me on board. And so I got the answer you get when you leave the world to its own devices.

This:

Me, with a kitchen knife sunk up to the hilt in my guts, while the little brat who's plunged it there looks on—shivering, hoping, waiting for me to die. The two of us are in the middle of a very big, pine-thick nowhere. She breathes and you can see it; I breathe and you can't. Neither of us is saying anything at the moment. The pines sigh. Creak. My car, with its door ajar, bing-bings away while the wipers ticktock back and forth under an on-again, off-again rain.

That's something that hasn't changed, even if everything else has. It still rains. Snows. Tornadoes still blow houses apart, still drive pieces of straw through two-by-fours. The sun? The sun hasn't changed, either, as far as I know. It still sets on the just and the un-just alike— even though its rising is only a rumor for most of us.

The knife looks kind of funny stuck there, bobbing up and down with my breathing. Not that I mention this to the kid who stabbed me. She's just a kid, after all. A *real* one, not just a *face* one. Five, six, tops. And she's just standing there, squeezing her pink-and-white fists, making fog but nothing else. Not even a peep. Not anymore.

I guess it *is* a little weird for her. Scary, even. Being stuck in the middle of nowhere, covered with your mom's just-spilt blood, waiting for some stranger to die. A stranger who happens to be a vampire. Not that being terrified and expiration-dated is any excuse for what she's done. Not that being cute and blood-covered is going to save her from what she's got coming. But they do buy her a few more minutes of me letting her sweat as I lie here, not dying.

"That wasn't very nice," I say, finally.

And that's all it takes. Just my saying it is all it takes to make my little fog breather flinch.

And as for me? I guess her flinching will have to do. Her flinching at the sound of a voice that hasn't scared *anybody* in God only knows how long. If that's what the world's offering, I'll take it. For one more night, at least.

Maybe I should back up.

I've been feeling a bit down lately. Edgy. Out of sorts.

Suicidal.

I'd call it a midlife crisis, but what does that mean when your life doesn't have a middle? A lot of vampires go through this sort of thing, right around the time we should be dead from natural causes. I'd say it feels like the flu, but vampires don't get the flu; they don't get sick, period. What they get, instead, is bored. You start feeling bored, then moody, and then your skin doesn't seem to fit, even though it hasn't changed a bit since you were vamped. Your friends, the ones you personally made immortal to keep you company throughout eternity, are *boring*. They bore right into your soul, like boll weevils of predictability. You know what each one is going to say before they say it, and when they do, you start thinking about how long forever really is.

But it's the missing that gets you most. All the things that are no longer part of your life. Like sunlight. Of course. Like chocolate. And cigarettes. A peach—even one of those syrup-embalmed canned ones. The excuse of a bathroom break to get away from your stupid job, or any other part of your stupid life. The feel of the seasons on your skin and in your bones. The sweet relief of stepping out of the cold and into a restaurant, its windows fogged with the warm embrace of different-flavored needs being met. Watching the steam rise from your name, written in yellow in a fresh snowbank, lit blue by a full moon, way past the middle of a night clocked in vodka tonics and shots with dirty names.

And coffee. And coffee. And coffee . . .

When I'm feeling like this, I find that tits usually help.

Pert and spotlit, naked and alive and bouncing just slightly to the beat of whatever the DJ happens to be playing. It's a habit I got into long ago, back before the ratio of mortals to vampires flipped—back when some of my benevolent buddies and I decided to help the flip along. We were missionaries of vampirism, and strippers made good apostles. We'd vamp them, they'd vamp their customers, their customers would vamp their wives and loved ones. The whole six-degrees-of-separation thing. Johnny Appleseed, but with fangs.

We called ourselves the Benevolent Vampire Society and our goal was pretty simple: we wanted a little company for our misery. We wanted to vote the other guys out—to be normal, to fall in love again, to live for something other than the next meal. We didn't want to watch the others around us growing old as we stayed young, reminding us of our open-endedness, and the pitiful little we'd filled it with.

Our motto was pure hubris: "There's a sucker born every minute." The problem was, the closer we came to making that true, the more obvious it became that *we* were the real suckers. "Normal" meant "tamer." Vampirism became . . . *domesticated.* Industrialized. Commercialized. The hunt for victims and benefactors was replaced by the sorts of jobs we thought we left behind. We had to work for a living again—or after-living, as the case may be. We went from slipping our fangs into nice, juicy necks to filling up grocery bags with name-brand plasma, grown in a vat instead of a vein, made from stem cells and other lab-fresh ingredients. And just like that, we went from being the perfect predators to the perfect consumers—ones with a perfectly understood need that could be perfectly met, forever and ever.

Amen.

*S*o, *this vampire walks into a bar . . .*

He doesn't fly, doesn't pad in on wolf's feet, or skitter across the sad linoleum with clicking little rat nails. He doesn't steam in through the keyhole, or crawl foggily under the door. *Real* vampires don't go in for such special effects—partly because we *can't*—and so a bipedal entrance will have to do.

He's decided to give himself up to the night—maybe his last—with an open (but empty) heart.

That's the way my evening started. In that kind of mood, making those kinds of decisions. It didn't take long to see the error of my ways.

By the way, if you want to get a feeling for how much the world's changed, just go to a vampire strip club. If it wasn't for the poor lighting, the bouncers, and the half-naked women, you'd swear you'd stepped into a grade school from before. They're not really kids, of course; some of them are older than I am, and I'm not just talking about my face age. We call them Screamers, and you'll know why if you ever set one off. Each one is a frozen tragedy, their vamping coming before their bodies reached the right age to spend forever in—kids with leukemia or some other fatal disease for which vamping was the only hope. And now they're stuck, and pissed. You'll see them sulking around the malls at midnight, children's bodies carrying their adult-sized souls, the wrinkles on their foreheads never quite setting, but not for lack of trying. I like to think of them as munchkins from the bad side of Oz—ones with very rich vocabularies when it comes to your anatomy and the many painful uses to which it can be put.

Strip clubs are one of the few places where Screamers don't—

scream, that is. They *smile,* instead, trying to look cute, trying to kiss up to whatever vague, maternal instinct the dancers may harbor in their wholly vestigial (though fetching) breasts. They come in with bankrolls bigger than they are and blow it all on reverse lap dances, straddling the dancer's leg with their stubby little ones, bouncing up and down, slapping their stunted manhood against bare thigh over and over again in a very adult game of horsey.

I look at the horny grade school surrounding me and feel even more depressed than I did before coming in. I look up and see myself in one of the bar's many mirrors. You know that thing about vampires not having a reflection? Myth. Vampires reflect all the time. In mirrors. In chrome. In their lonelier moments. Like me. Like now.

What a face I've got. What a mug I've been saddled with for all eternity. It always looks a little sad, a little tired, a little like it's been through the wringer a few too many times. It's the sort of face that women find compelling, I've been told. I think it's because I look experienced, like I've been through that wringer and survived. It's my eyes, that's what does it. They're standard-issue vampire eyes— all black, matching my short-shorn hair, my mood. What's different is their prominence, their hyperthyroid eagerness, as if my mere skull were having a hard time keeping them in. They're the eyes of someone who listens, sympathizes, bleeds with every tragedy that's related to him across candlelit tables. The rest of my face is baby smooth, innocent, deceptively safe—the perfect face for a vampire who needs to get in close before dinner.

The other baby faces—the ones with shorter legs—are starting to get rowdy. I check out the glasses on the table next to me, fogged with condensation. That's another big difference with the vampire version of these kinds of places—the heat. While the old clubs cranked up the AC to keep the dancers' nipples hard, our kind work just the opposite. We're cold-blooded, just like lizards, which really means that our blood's not *cold* so much as room temperature. And like a lizard basking on a sunny rock, the way to get us *hot* is to get us hot. That's why vampire sex usually starts with a trip to the shower, or a good crank of the thermostat to the right. That's also why the air swims around our apartment buildings on cold Saturday nights. The excess heat of steaming showers and cranked thermostats coming from dozens of apartments makes the air watery, makes the moon behind it ripple like a reflection in a puddle. If you're quiet, you may hear the moans and groans, the occasional howl or bark of vampire delight, but these are just the grace notes. It's the heat that tells the story, all that vampire love shimmering in the cold night air.

Like they say, all's Fahrenheit in love and war.

Being good businesspeople, the owners of vampire strip clubs take full advantage of their clientele's biological predictability. Steadily throughout the evening, they turn up the heat as the customers get more and more worked up, spending more and more money on blood and lap dances. By last call, the place is like a sauna. Already warm glasses of blood begin to sweat. Watch crystals go blurry. And every time some bowlegged munchkin goes stumbling for the exit, a steamy swirl of fog follows him out.

And then there are the bartenders.

Or rather, there's the *lack* of bartenders. I've never gotten over that, there being no actual bar or bartenders in vampire bars, whether strip, gay, sport, classy, divey, or whatever. No one to chew the fat with, to spill your guts to, to cut you off when you've had too much. Oh, they've got bouncers, and video cameras, and someone at the door to check your coat, charge you the cover, point out a table if one's not obvious, but no actual *bar*, or anyone tending it. No need, really. There's only the one drink—the "house *vin*"—and self-serve is just more cost effective. So, instead of bartenders or waitresses, each table has a metered tap that's pretty useless when it comes to spilling your guts. But they *do* accept coins and bills and credit cards, all for your convenience.

When they're working, that is.

When you don't try feeding them a twenty that's been out of circulation since before the change, only to find out, now that it's too late, that it's all you've got. And so you keep shoving it in and the slot keeps spitting it back, Andrew Jackson's too-small face mocking grimly. You flatten it out, straighten the corners, crease it down the middle, and still you get that mechanical whir of rejection.

The other patrons begin turning in their seats, their stubby little legs not reaching the floor. They look at you with their black-marble crow eyes. They look at you like *you're* the loser. They don't know it's a last-straw night. They don't know that you're one of the people who's responsible for what they are, for where they are, for what the world's become.

Shove. Whir.

Please. Fuck. Dammit. Shit . . .

And so there you are, in a vampire strip club, surrounded by nonscreaming Screamers, shouting at a machine that won't listen to reason. The half-naked women onstage have stopped dancing and are looking at you with that no-chance-in-hell look, that not-worth-the-trouble sideways stare. And out of nowhere, you find yourself thinking about Paul Newman in *Cool Hand Luke.* No, not the "failure to communicate" scene, but the one right at the beginning where he's cutting the heads off parking meters, just before all the trouble starts. And that's when you get the idea, the one that makes you smile to yourself. The one that makes you think:

A man's gotta do what a man's gotta do . . .

It's not until after things start getting broken that it occurs to you—perhaps too late—that libido is not the only thing that rises with the heat.

I'm asked to leave.

I'm cut off before I was even on.

On the night I've given the world one last chance to save my life, I'm asked by a bouncer who'd be dust now if it wasn't for me and my benevolent brethren. I—Martin Kowalski, Vampire, Esquire, founding member of the BVS and cocreator of the world, such as it is—I am *asked* to *leave.*

Okay.

Okay, and fuck you. *Fuck this.*

After the steam of my exit dissipates, I notice that it's raining. That's one thing that hasn't changed, I think. It still rains. Snows. Tornadoes still . . .

The valet brings my car around with the wipers already going. He looks at me like I'm one of those guys who pops his cork a minute and a half into his first lap dance. He lets the keys drop into my palm to avoid any accidental contact. He exits the vehicle with hands retracted, full of second thoughts about having touched whatever I've touched. He's judging me. I can see that by the way he holds his lips, the little bit of fang he lets show. I'm being judged by someone who'll probably be making minimum wage for all of eternity.

Great. Lovely. Jim-fucking-dandy.

I make the car roar. It's a sporty little number—bloodred, natch—and is worth more than the valet's entire life, counting tips and multiplying by forever. I had the heater on all the way up here, to get me in the mood. It's still on, and I'm still in the mood, but for something else now. I let it drop to a throaty purr, then rev it again, and decide to see how fast I can make it go. Peeling out of the parking lot like a bat out of a cliché, I rip down side streets, jump sidewalks, slip, slide, skid, screech. I endanger my fellow citizens, treating stoplights like suggestions, recklessing my way to the nearest unlit two-lane.

Where am I going? That's easy. Out. I'm going *out*. Preferably, with a bang. I've already disabled the air bags and removed the safety belts because, well, I've been going through this little midlife crisis for some time now. So far, I've been leaving it to chance, but . . .

Sometimes, when it's raining, when the heater's cranked up all the way and I'm really going fast, I'll let go of the wheel. It's exciting. It's an attention getter. It feels like *something*, instead of the nothing I usually feel. It feels like the Hope and Promise of Death as opposed to this night after night of longing for all those things I've given up to be bored forever. It's the *out* I'm going for; it's a plan, an exit strategy.

And then I see it.

Her.

Sizzling along in my bright red crisis, looking for something I can't name because everything I *can* name bores me senseless, I see it. A wisp. Just a single white wisp coming out of the darkness along the road. I skid to a stop, fishtailing into the oncoming lane. I look in my rearview mirror. Wait. And there it is again—another clean white puff swirling away in the cold and rain. I put the car in reverse and crawl slowly back to what I imagine is just a wounded dog, breathing out its last breath at the side of the road. I park and get out, waiting for another frightened plume to point me in the right direction. I say "frightened," because it seems that whatever the breather is, it's been holding its breath ever since I stopped the car.

The road I'm on passes through woods—evergreens, mainly. Pines. My crisis prefers rural settings, what with their narrow lanes and no lighting, no police, no pesky Samaritans, should the not-unforeseeable happen. It's definitely *not* the trees that have brought me out this way, whether evergreen or never-green or whatnot. Except for the antisocial demands of my crisis, I'm basically a city vampire. But I *do* know a thing or two about pines. And one of those things is:

No feet.

Pine trees do not have tiny bare feet with tiny toes curling, trying to get a better grip on the muddy earth. They don't have blotchy pink legs, either, trembling from the cold, speckled here and there with something dark—mud, maybe, or . . .

"Hello?" I say, brushing aside the branches of the pedestrian conifer in front of me. And there she is, my little escapee from statistics, a still-warm-inside, mouth-breathing fog maker. A mortal, which is rare enough, but a child, too. A *real* child—not the freak show kind I stumbled here to escape. She's plump in that baby fat way. Good veins. Farm raised, I'm guessing. From one of those farms that officially "don't exist" but do. A free-range bleeder who's gotten a bit too free.

And all for me. A little going-away present from the world, on this, my maybe-last night.

She's wearing one of those retro "Got Milk?" T-shirts. The ones the Screamers think are funny, or sexy, or appealing to a maternal instinct that's also retro, and getting more so all the time. She's got blond hair. It's been gathered up into a pair of asymmetrical ponytails that look like they were done quickly, and mainly to get the hair out of her face and into a couple of manageable clumps. A few loose strands hang down, heavy from the rain, clinging to her face and shoulders. Her thumb's in her mouth, her eyes squeezed tight, her whole body shivering. The dark stuff on her legs speckles the rest of her as well. And now that I'm closer, I can smell it:

Blood.

Plasma and platelets and coagulating coagulants, but not hers. There aren't any wounds big enough, nothing fresh gurgling out. Still, she was standing right next to whatever bled like this. Judging from the spatter, I'd say it was an arterial bleed, some major trauma that this little one apparently just walked away from.

Gently, I pull her thumb from her mouth, uncorking another plume of white. "Hello," I say. Again.

"Don't eat me," the little girl cries.

Now, I hate to quibble, but this is one of my pet peeves. Vampires do not eat little girls. We don't eat people, period. At least not in the chewing sense. We relieve them of their blood supplies, which involves biting, or cutting, or puncturing, but we don't bite anything *off*. We don't masticate, or grind with our grinders. Not that I'd mind feeling my teeth click through a pinched inch or so of well-fed neck flesh, especially now, but that'd be gratuitous; it'd be showing off and it's just not something that's done. Not anymore. Not in polite society. It's like that bumper sticker I hate—"Chews Life"? No—a *proper* vampire never *chews*. A civilized vampire *sucks*—get it straight.

Of course, I don't imagine that these distinctions will mean much to the little mortal quivering in front of me. The difference between being eaten or just sucked dry is pretty much semantic, especially if you're the one on the menu. And so I don't quibble. Instead, I ask, "Why not?"

"I don't taste good," she says.

As if drinking blood is something you do for the taste! I have to smile, and so I do. "Oh yeah," I say. "Why's that?"

"I'm spoiled," the little girl cries. "Mommy says . . . ," followed by sobs in place of whatever it is Mommy says. Or *said*, I assume—past tense. I also assume that Mommy's being past tense explains all that blood covering her frightened little girl. The one who's too old to be sucking her thumb but is back at it again, sucking and sobbing, sobbing and sucking.

The word for "human female parent" in almost every language on earth starts with an *m*. Mom, mater, madonna, madre. It's usually the first word spoken by a child, and is rooted in the sound made while suckling. And that's what it's all about—our language, our relationships, our being at its very core; we suck, therefore we are. And the world is forever divided into the suckers and the sucked upon. It's always been that way; we—me and my vampire friends— just made it a little more literal.

"So, you're spoiled, eh?"

She nods her head. I pull out her thumb.

"Is Mommy dead?"

She looks at her feet. Her thumb, like a heat-seeking missile, starts heading back for her mouth. I stop it in midtrajectory, my big cold hand cupping her tiny warm one. "Don't," I say.

A minute goes by with nothing much to fill it but the sound of rain steadily shushing through the needles of the trees surrounding us. I still have her hand in my hand, can feel its borrowed heat invading my fingers, crawling just a bit up my wrist, and then stopping. It's when my hand starts feeling like a human's—when my hand starts feeling like her own—that's when my pleasant little surprise finally looks up at me with something less than terror in her eyes.

"What's your name?" I ask.

"Isuzu."

"No, your *real* name," I say. And that does it; that's what makes her snap.

"It *is*," she demands. "Isuzu Trooper Cassidy," she repeats—*recites*—pulling her hand away from mine, her thumb folding back into its fist. "Like it or lump it," she announces—quoting, I'm sure, whatever brain thought of naming a little girl after a gas guzzler.

I laugh—I can't help it; this little human is just so . . . *human*. Even soaked to the bone, even covered in blood, and standing next to a vampire twice her size, there is only so much shit she's willing to put up with, and getting grief over her name is at the top of the list.

"What's so funny?" she demands, about two seconds away from stomping my toes or kicking my shins. Or so I think.

"You are," I say, casually preparing myself to fend off whatever pathetic attempt my little sport utility might make at defending her mortal dignity.

Of course, it hasn't been my night for making the right call. So:

She nails me.

Right as I'm reaching to tousle her blood-clotted hair, the little brat whips out a twelve-inch bread knife with faux ivory handle and plants it in my solar plexus. Where the knife came from, I have no idea. Somewhere behind her. Somewhere I wasn't looking. Maybe the more important question is why I wasn't expecting her to be armed. Did I imagine that baby bees don't have stingers? She's a mortal in a world full of vampires, for Christ's sake. In her shoes, I'd be packing every kind of heat imaginable. Silver bullets, garlic, holy water—you name it. Not that any of that stuff would do any good. Real vampires can't turn into bats or fly, but we're also not a crucifix away from turning into bone and ash. No, if you want to kill us, you've got to get the head, or the heart, or trap us outside when the sun comes up. And that's it. That's your *A, B,* or *C* when it comes to vampires and our killability.

But back to Isuzu and her kitchen knife. Out it comes, and in it goes—slurp-thunk—like that first good stab into a ripe melon. That's the noise we vampires make when we get stabbed where I'm stabbed—just below the belly button, and just above the fun stuff. Isuzu's just so high to begin with, and even when she's holding the knife over her head with both hands and going up on tiptoes, my belt line is as close to my heart as she's going to get.

Fortunately, there's not much down there anymore. The virus or whatever it is that makes vampires cold and bloodthirsty, that turns our skin pasty white and our eyeballs midnight black—the same thing rearranges our indoor plumbing. We don't have much of a digestive system, especially below what used to be our stomachs. The blood is absorbed directly into the bloodstream by the tongue, the membranes of the mouth, and the esophagus. As a result, a vampire taking in blood isn't so much like a mortal drinking coffee as like a cocaine addict doing a line. It's just a matter of biological efficiency—a way of mixing the old and new blood as quickly as possible without actually poking holes into our veins.

Not that getting stabbed where I'm stabbed doesn't hurt. It does. It does for *me*, at least. Whether through dumb luck or the regular kind, Isuzu's managed to find my last scar, the site of my last, very nearly mortal wound. Every vampire has such a scar, and it's one of the few places on any of us where you can still inflict for-real *pain* pain without killing us. Some call it a vaccination scar, others, their second navel. But the flesh remembers and we don't give up the location of our last scars easily—if we've any choice in the matter, if we can hide it with our hair or cover it with a turtleneck.

So, when I wince pulling out the knife, it's for real. I'm not play-acting. Not about that, at least. Where the real acting comes in is my acting like I don't mind, like I don't plan on getting even. But I do. My little Happy Meal stabbed me with every intention of doing grave bodily harm, and it's the thought that counts. And what I'm thinking is this:

Later.

Not now. Not when it'd be easy for me to snap, and for her neck to snap right along with it. No. Immediate gratification is overrated, anyway. Plus, her adrenal gland's probably wrung out. The fact that a five- or six-year-old mortal girl who's only so high could get a knife to stick into me all the way to the hilt . . . yeah, there was some adrenaline working overtime. But she's on the downslope now. I can tell that by the way her breath puffs are coming out, by the way she's just standing there, letting her skin hang on to her bones like a marionette hanging on to its strings. And I *hate* stale adrenaline; it's got that scared-past-being-scared aftertaste.

So, no. Not now. Later's better. Later, when she'll least expect it. Later, when I can scare out something fresh, when it'll be more . . .

Fun.

And just like that, it hits me. *This* is why I've been depressed. *This* is what I've been missing. The coffee, the chocolate, the peeing, and canned peaches—red herrings. You want a *real* clue to the psychology of the modern vampire? It's this: we're cats. We're feral cats who've been forced inside. We need to play with our food before killing it, but can't. The world's full of kibble—no problems there—but there are no birds, no mice, not even small lizards to hunt, catch, play with, and kill. Nothing to kill, not even to save our lives. Nothing *legal,* at least.

That's kind of where I am—*have been,* for years.

And the whole rest of the world's been there with me, whether they know it or not. We've been taken care of. We're well fed. We suck on bottles of blood, sip it from snifters, tip back mugs and cups and glasses—and not a damned one of them ever puts up a struggle. Not a damned one ever feels quite right. Sure, they spike the bottled stuff with adrenaline, but lab-grown versus the real thing is like Tang next to fresh-squeezed.

And look at me—Mr. Lucky. I just found myself a real live orange.

Not that I say anything. Not that I let that particular cat out of the bag. Nope. Instead:

"I believe this is yours," I say, handing over the knife like a maître d' the wine list.

-2-

THE TARP GUY

The problem with delayed gratification is, of course, the delay.

And the problem with not harvesting Isuzu right away is having to take care of her in the meantime. Take care of, and keep safe, and fed, and hidden from my no-longer-benevolent brethren. It occurs to me that this may be a bigger slice of life than I'm ready to chew at the moment. Or suck dry, for that matter. But then again, not too long ago, I was ready to chuck it all. And it's not like I don't have plenty of time to kill. So:

"Sorry," I say.

I get the feeling I'll be saying that a lot. I get the feeling I'll be learning a whole new vocabulary of regret, penitence, contrition. I see a lot of flubs and oopses in my future. This time, the apology is for stopping Isuzu while she was trying to make a run for it.

We're in my car at the time of the attempted escape. I figured that being inside with the heater running beats being out there, in the cold and rain. Not that the cold and rain were bothering me, but I figured it might get Isuzu to stop twitching—or, you know, shivering. Chattering. Stop her blunt little teeth from click, click, clicking away. It's surprising how quickly that kind of thing can get on your nerves.

So we get into the car and she goes back to the rag doll routine, resting her head against the passenger window, making it fog. I think about reaching out, reaching over, placing a hand on her bloody little shoulder—to comfort, to reassure, to lull into a false sense of security. My own security's secure; I've locked the knife in the glove compartment. No surprises, this time. But I hold back on my reassurance. The no-surprises thing works both ways, and I'm worried about the coldness of my skin. I don't want to startle her. I don't want to keep reminding her about our differences. About our respective places on the food chain. So I rest a hand on the dash first, borrowing a little heat before continuing on.

She glances. She sees it coming. But she flinches anyway. Just a quick twitch, and then it's back to Raggedy Ann. I pat her limp shoulder. She lets me. I pet her hair, trying to soothe a frightened puppy. She could care less. I keep it up until it feels stupid, and then I pull my hand away, damp now with you-know-what.

You-know-*whose.*

What I do next I really shouldn't, but it's been a stressful evening. Lots of drama. Lots of gratification delayed. And really, it's such a little thing. Just a matter of bringing my fingers to my lips, a quick run of the tongue. Just a taste. Waste not, want not. And Isuzu? Hell, she's busy looking out the window at all that nothing out there, making a big show of *not* looking at me, so why not?

This is why not.

I've already told you that vampires reflect all the time. In mirrors. In chrome. In their lonelier moments, and over there, in the unfoggy corner of my passenger-side window. Isuzu's been watching me all along—staring at me, at my reflection. Watching every move, every idle gesture. She's seen me lick her mother's blood from my fingertips. And that's all it takes. Her little hand goes unlimp, darts for the door handle, yanks up.

No.

Oh no you don't, my little dumpling. No, no, no . . .

I flick a switch on my driver's side armrest, and all the locks thunk down together. The once-and-future rag doll keeps on yanking pointlessly, jiggling the handle with one hand, two hands, working a foot up and kicking at my fine leather interior.

I should probably say something. This is when one of us should say something, and it looks like I'm it.

"Sorry," I say, because every iceberg starts at the tip.

The problem with not harvesting Isuzu right away is having to humor her. I'd forgotten how kids can be. How they can get a thought into their heads and just fix on it, beating it like a dead . . .

Well, in this case, mother.

Here are the terms of the deal: if I'm a "good guy," if I'm not "like them," I'll save Mommy Dearest. I'll presumably do this by vamping her. Do I really need to tell you how bad an idea this is? The blood on Isuzu is already drying, or at least gluey. And there are bits of . . . *tissue* . . . in her hair. By the time we get to wherever her mom is, there isn't going to be anything left to save. It's like I'm some TV repair guy and here comes this kid, holding nothing but a limp cord, asking, "Can you fix it?" Where do I even start?

"Um," I say, and then immediately worry that it might sound like "yum," like the sinister noise it isn't. Or at least not yet.

"Listen," I add, to interrupt—to derail, defuse, deflect. To put something other than a maybe-yum out there between us.

"Sweetheart," I continue. It just slips out without me thinking. Until after it slips out, after which I think plenty. Like: Taste-related endearments are probably just as bad as "yum." But when I try to think of ones that aren't, I get stuck.

Honey—no.

Sweetie—no.

Honey- and/or sweetie pie—no.

Kiddo?

Kiddo might work. I give it a try. "Listen, kiddo," I say, starting over.

But Isuzu—my new sweetheart, my save-it-for-later yum—has already fallen into a kid trance, muttering the mantra "Please" over and over again. She knits her little fingers together so tight, her knuckles blanch. And then that praying, pleading knot of fingers starts to shake.

"Oh please, oh please, oh please . . ."

Her little two-tone eyes well up with tears. Clear ones, not the pink kind my kind squeeze out every so often. For show. Once in a blue moon. When hell freezes over.

I guess she and her mom must have been close or something. Go figure.

"Point," I say, finally, when I can't think of anything else.

When we get near to where her mother was last seen, I have Isuzu get out of the car and into the trunk. "Just in case," I say, and she gets in without a peep. She's good at that—at not making peeps. I guess that's just one of those things you get good at, being a mortal in a world full of people like me. I guess you get good or you get gone.

Along the way, we've worked out a code of knocks, so she'll know it's me when I get back. Nothing elaborate—me: *shave and a haircut;* her: *two bits*—but at least it's something. A little just-in-case, just in case.

It doesn't take me long to find the mom or to confirm what I already know. It's stopped raining and the full moon has slid out from behind some clouds, making the woods around me stark and skeletal. There's a mix of trees—evergreens, never-greens, and sometime-greens—the last two leafless and bony-knuckled. Until tonight, Isuzu and her mom had been living in a hole in the ground, by which I do not mean some really run-down place or hermit's shack, but a *real* hole dug in the *real* ground, covered with a sheet of plywood and some AstroTurf that's been painted brown, in honor of the season.

Inside the hole—which opens out into a decent-sized mud cellar, once you get past the bottleneck of the entrance—are two air mattresses, one large, one small, a bricked-off pit full of charred twigs, a laundry basket full of laundry, and a five-gallon jug of what turns out to be boiled rainwater. Shelves are dug into the walls and on some, tin cans stand with candles inside, while others sport small collections of books, the wizened spines bearing names like Stephen King, Anne Rice, Clive Barker.

If this were a sitcom, this is where I'd do the obligatory double take. *Horror stories?* Living in the middle of her very own tale from the crypt, and what does Mommy Dearest pick to read? Jesus! I guess you can't stop human beings from being human, but still.

The rest of the hole is filled with cans of cat food, stacked in pyramid after pyramid. Isuzu and her mom were apparently living on the stuff, but before you rush to judge—stop. The dietary options for mortals are exceedingly few nowadays. For one thing, we don't have grocery stores anymore—or rather, the grocery stores we have really don't carry groceries, per se. We still have Kroger, A&P, and even Farmer Jack, as double-edged as that name is nowadays. But you can't get milk in any of those places. You can't get lunch meat or hot dogs or cans of Campbell's soup. What you can get is soap, laundry detergent, moth balls, bug spray, lint rollers, the *National Enquirer*, and lightbulbs, though nothing much above twenty-five watts.

And you can get pet food—Dog Chow, Cat Chow, Iguana, Spider Monkey, and Ring-Tailed Lemur Chow.

Vampires love their pets to death, and sometimes even farther. Of course, vamped pets don't need Cat Chow; vamped pets share the same boring diet as their owners. But more often than not, we prefer our pets to stay disposable. They die right around the time we get bored with them, and then we get something else, working our way through the natural kingdom ever more exotically. Hence the iguanas, the spider monkeys, the lemurs of the ring-tailed kind.

I should add that it's a pretty good time to be a pet, especially a disposable one. It's a pretty good time because of all the leftovers from when mortals ran things. Canned food, for instance. Canned *human* food, that is. After the change, a lot of it just got relabeled and sold as pet food. And all the cattle that were slated to become Big Macs and steaks became Alpo instead. Eventually, they'll go back to grinding up horses, but for the time being, pet food's not a bad way to go, if you're a runaway human trying to keep yourself and your daughter alive.

Which brings me to the saddest part of the Cassidy hole, other than the dead mother outside it. On one wall, mother and daughter have created what I can only think of as the Shrine to Chocolate—a mosaic of empty Snickers and Mounds and Hershey wrappers tacked into the bare mud. Needless to say, candy bars do not make good pet food and aren't something you can just buy or shoplift at the grocery store. And it's this that confirms where Isuzu and her mom came from, before the hole in the ground, out here in the middle of what turned out to be not nearly nowhere enough.

Chocolate is what they use on the black market farms that officially "don't exist," but do. The farms where they breed little bonbons like Isuzu for wealthy, discriminating vampires with a taste for blood au naturel. Chocolate doesn't enter the equation until just before the end, during the last stages of market prep. The story is that it does something "special" to the blood, lends it a little sweetness, cuts down on that rusty-salt aftertaste. I don't doubt it. Force-feed someone into becoming a borderline diabetic and it's bound to do something "special" in the blood department. The only problem is, messing with glucose levels works against the rush that comes when your blood's container knows it's going to die. Personally, that spurt of adrenaline is why I'm humoring that little blood donor locked in my trunk. But apparently, the rich don't mind a little passivity. Apparently, they like the idea of the blood fighting against itself, instead of the little tidbit's fighting against his or her "ultimate purchaser." So much for roughing it. Killing a farm-raised kid after a week's worth of nothing but chocolate is like hunting animals that have been drugged. Like shooting fish in a very small barrel.

I'm guessing that when Isuzu and her mom escaped, they left with as much chocolate as they could carry, knowing it was going to have to last them a lifetime—hell, *two* lifetimes, however long those were going to be. I imagine the original plan was something like "only for birthdays" or "only for Christmas and Easter." I imagine that plan lasted about as long as a vampire swearing off blood. And so here they were, the bones of that failed plan pinned to the wall of their root-cellar home like old pornography. Here they were, the souvenirs of all life's sweetness, chewed up, swallowed, gone.

•   •

It's the sound of the tape, that first, long rip—that's how they'd announce themselves, in the dark, where they could see her but she couldn't see them. Before that, I imagine them sitting in the hole in the dark, waiting for Isuzu and her mom, waiting with their duct tape and tarp, their thermoses of lab-grown to tide them over. They're ready to wait till hell blows cold. It doesn't matter to them. They've got nothing but time, and a taste for blood when it's laced with human fear. They've already exchanged stories about other kills from way back when, the look in this or that one's eyes when she crawled into her hiding place and found them waiting for her in the dark, where they could see her but she couldn't see them. One of them will say it's worth it—it's almost *always* worth it—for the looks on their faces alone.

They'd laugh over that. Nod. Wait. Consider this the delay between themselves and the gratification heading toward them, aboveground, wholly unaware that it's on the menu tonight.

As far as what's left goes, I'd say it was gory, except "gore" implies "blood," and there really isn't any. Oh, there's the blood that got on Isuzu before she got away. And there's the blood that managed to stain her mother's clothes before they'd been ripped off and hung, almost neatly, from the naked branches of a nearby tree. But that's it. They didn't even leave enough to leave a bruise on the various parts of her, lying here, lying there. Her skin—the torn bits of it hanging in shreds, or folded back like a flap, exposing this or that ball joint—her *skin* looks like cold pastry dough. Apparently, nobody ever told these bozos that *proper* vampires don't need too chew.

But all I can think of at the moment is how pristine the savagery is, how spotless and bloodless, like a white china plate licked clean.

I say "they" because there are half-moons from three different sets of fangs stamped here and there on her pastry dough skin. Three dogs worrying over the same sad bone—until it breaks, and everybody's happy. Except the bone, of course. Except the bone's daughter, locked in your trunk praying her white-knuckled prayers not to God anymore, but to you. Her last hope. Her "savior."

Oh please, oh please, oh please . . .

Spare me.

Like you ever listened to them when they pleaded.

Do I really need to tell you I wasn't *always* benevolent?

I think I've been just about every kind of vampire you can be. During World War II, I was a patriotic one, limiting my feedings to German cuisine. A little later, I went through a monstrous phase, limiting my feedings to pretty much anything with a face. Then there was vegetarianism, with its strict diet of coma victims, followed by a streak of vigilantism, when I went around killing those folks who just needed killing. Eventually I got tired of coming up with excuses and let hunger and opportunity decide.

But then there came this time when the guilt seemed to back up on me and I started hunting in packs as these jokers have done here. The pack thing was so I wouldn't feel personally responsible for the murders we were doing—kind of like the government, or a corporation. Everybody's guilty, so nobody is.

The pack thing can be done with as few as two. You can make a game of it—flip a quarter, heads for throat, tails for thigh. You each take your turn, the flow of blood seesawing back and forth, your victim's eyes ticking left and right along with it, until they begin flickering and finally roll back, waving those two white flags of surrender.

That's the fifties malt shop version. The vampires sit across from each other, their victim in between like an ice-cream float with two straws being sipped at during that chaste first date. Sure, it's still murder, but murder of the daintiest sort.

There are less dainty versions. More aggressive ones. Versions where you don't say "Pardon me" and "Please" and you don't take turns. Versions where it's a tug-of-war played with blood and arteries. You suck, they suck, and you can feel the pull of the other. Pause to swallow and the blood in your straw reverses course. You have to fight against the current to get it back. Eventually, one of you takes his ball and goes home. Or really, one of you rips the part you're sucking on free from the rest. This can be pretty wasteful, what with blood leaking out at both ends, like a hot dog with too much relish on it or an ice-cream cone with the bottom chewed off.

In situations like this, it's best if someone has the foresight to bring along a tarp. Back before I was benevolent, when I was still hunting in packs, *I* was the tarp guy. Somebody else would sniff out the victim; somebody else would duct tape their wrists and mouth. Me—I set the table, shaking out the tarp with one good snap, laying it down, smoothing it out, straightening the corners.

Now, it might seem kind of wimpy, being the tarp guy, but that's the part that always got the strongest reaction. Okay, you duct tape his wrists and mouth, the victim knows he's in trouble; but when you start laying down the tarp, that's when everything clicks. The tarp foreshadows the mess they're in—and about to become. And that's when their eyes start screaming from the tops of their lungs; that's when their chests start heaving and their nostrils flare in and out. And if it's cold, that's when the steam starts chugging, hard and heavy, like the Little Train That Could.

I *think* I'm dead. I *think* I'm dead.

I *know* I'm dead. I *know* I'm dead.

Chew-chew . . .

Have you ever tried walking in a woman's shoes? Even sensible ones, like the tennis kind? If you're a guy with big feet—which I am, thank you very much—you're lucky if you can squeeze your tippy toes inside. And walking! Just try walking so you can leave a clear set of prints leading away from some fake-grass-covered hole, through the mud right up to this patch of ground cover that could lead—frankly—anywhere. Just you try that. After hiding the bloody dress. After covering up its owner's various parts. After scribbling "Mom" on a sheet of blank paper you fold in half and leave behind. The one you'll say includes the telephone number of the place you're both going back to—for when it's safe again, and your orphan's mom comes looking.

That's right. I've decided to lie. Or really, I've decided to keep on lying. When you've got a little kid locked in your trunk, thinking you're there to save her, instead of just saving her for later . . . well, lying's the easiest way to go. Lie big. Lie bold. Lie like a cheap rug on the big bald head of a big lying liar.

Shave and a haircut, I knock.

Two bits, Isuzu knocks back.

"She got away." It's the first thing out of my mouth.

Isuzu looks at me. She blinks those two-toned eyes of hers, weighing what I've just said. She still has arterial blood caked in her hair. She's been hiding out in a hole in the ground and eating cat food all because of guys like me. She's been locked in the trunk for over half an hour, just in case guys like me were still hanging around, waiting for the prodigal daughter's return. And now here I come with my lame attempt to keep the emotional baggage down to a single carry-on. What else can she say but what she says?

"Liar."

If it's possible for a vampire to get paler than he already is, I do.

"No, it's true," I keep on lying. Once you start down that path—even when you're called on it—you just have to keep on going. "You can see for yourself," I add, helping her out of the trunk.

Standing there next to her, staring at the evidence of her mom's miraculous "escape," even if I had the sort of insides that made my breath show, you wouldn't see anything. Not coming out of me. Not until Isuzu says something. Or makes a peep, at least. *Any* kind of noise. Even another "liar" will do.

But she doesn't say anything. Instead, she gets down on her little girl knees, reaches out her little girl fingers, and feels the craters I've made. Not looking at me, she says, "I can read."

She says, "My mom taught me."

"That's good," I say, wondering why I thought this particular lie was a good idea. Sure, it'll cut back on the weepy stuff, give her something to hope for, a distraction. And it'll make getting her back to my apartment, where the phone is, easier. But eventually, when that phone doesn't ring—eventually, other bells will, and when they do . . .

Jesus!

Like it's ever going to get that far! I'm delaying gratification, sure, but I'm not sending it off to college.

Meanwhile: *"K,"* my delayed gratifier says.

Followed by: *"E, D, S,"* she reads.

"That spells 'Keds,' " she announces, her finger underlining the word stamped there in the muddy earth.

"That's right," I say. "It does."

And it keeps on spelling "Keds," in every footprint she investigates, leading right up to a patch of grass that could lead anywhere—but back.

-3-

THE PITS

I'm thinking about my dad.

I haven't thought about my dad in—*Christ,* ages. And I haven't thought about my dad as a "father" . . . well, I don't know that I ever *really* did. He was just the guy around the house who paid for stuff, who got teased about funny things he did when he was younger, and smoked like a chimney until the fireplace went cold, way too soon. He was my whole life, and as kids will with things as big as life, I took him for granted until he was gone.

It's Isuzu and her mom that have got me thinking like this. Thinking *parentally.* Mortally *and* parentally.

I suppose I'm trying to imagine what might be going on inside her head—or at least what *was* going on, before I decided to fabricate the miracle escape of the century. I'd like to know whether that was a good thing or a bad thing—taking that grief away. It's a successful thing, I know that. Isuzu seems to have perked right up. Not knowing how much she may have seen before escaping, I've embellished, suggesting semiplausible theories, like maybe one of the vampires did what *I* was asked to do.

"Was she pretty, your mom?" I ask.

Isuzu nods.

"And were any of the vampires *boy* vampires?"

She nods again.

"Well, there you go. Maybe they thought she was so pretty that . . ." I trail off without finishing, but Isuzu gets it. It sinks in as a concept, and I catch the reflection of a smile in my passenger-side window.

"Like Cinderella," she whispers, filling in the blank I've left.

I nod.

So I'm inclined to think it was a good thing. A *kind* thing. Just like, sometimes, you have to be cruel to be kind? I'm guessing that you have to be kind before you can be a real success at cruelty. At least some of the times. At least as often as the other way around.

And I'm thinking this now because of my dad. And what it was like for me when he died too soon. I'm thinking this now because of what it was like for me later, when I didn't.

Even though he was a mortal, my dad loved blood. He loved it in all its coagulated forms: in blood sausage and duck-blood soup, in the shit brown drippings under broiler pans, and in the vein of marrow running through a chicken bone. He loved the last best, cracking the shaft against his big back teeth, leaving translucent shards blooming around the ball joint like a ruptured party favor with a bony fist at one end. He'd have made a wonderful vampire, but he never got the chance. He died, instead, too awfully and too young, of lung cancer brought on by those *other* bones he loved to suck, at a rate of three packs a day. Eventually, they had to cut a hole in his throat, followed by the bigger hole they dug for the rest of him.

I was just thirteen-dammit. (I can never talk about how old I was when my father died without adding a "dammit"—the age and curse are like one word in my head, hyphenated.) Other loved ones had died before—aunts, uncles, grandparents, a girl my own age the other kids called Fuzzy after the hair she didn't have because of the leukemia that killed her—but none of their deaths hit me the way my father's did.

I didn't know how much I loved him until he died, and the only good thing about his dying is that he did it before I got a chance to treat him like shit. He died before I could act embarrassed about the way he talked or dressed in front of my oh-so-much-cooler friends. Sure, he wasn't the hippest guy in the world, didn't dig jazz or swing or big band. Sure, he had that funny little Charlie Chaplin mustache and pronounced his *th*'s like *t*'s— turty-tree and a turd— but he had a good heart that he put to good use.

I'll tell you a story my uncle used to tell.

He and my dad were in the war together—the first "world" one, from before they started numbering them. And they found themselves staying with a family on a farm in France. On their last night there, they get invited to dinner, and dessert is cherry pie. My dad takes one bite and—click!—bites right down on a cherry pit. Here he is, "overseas," having dinner with a nice French family while people all around are dying, and he's sitting there with a cherry pit in his mouth. Not wanting to embarrass his hosts, my dad does what a guy like my dad does: he swallows it. Another bite and— click!—another pit. So, down the hatch it goes. As does the next. And the next.

And then, suddenly: "Where are your pits?" their host asks, alarmed.

That's when my dad finally looks up and sees all the plates around him ringed with cherry pits like so many freshly yanked teeth. It's local custom, it turns out, to cook cherry pie with the fruit whole, to preserve the flavor.

After hemming, after hawing, my future dad confesses that he's swallowed all his pits.

"In America, they do this?" his host asks.

No, my dad admits, explaining that in America we take the pits out before cooking a cherry pie. He's swallowed his here and now because he thought the cook had made a mistake.

And his hosts splutter with laughter, followed by assurances to my father's reddening face that, no, they're *impressed,* they're *touched.*

They're the old world, patting the new one on its polite, naïve little head.

•   •

My uncle used to tell the Pit Story while my dad was still alive, to embarrass him, to get his goat, to tease. And he always ended it the same way. "Pretty *pit*iful, eh?"

Except for the last time, that is.

When my uncle told the Pit Story for the last time, it was at my father's funeral, and my uncle left his punch line off. He choked up, instead, his Adam's apple working hard as if he were trying to swallow a cherry pit of his own. Finally, he spit it out:

"And that's the kind of guy my brother was," he said. "Kind. He was the *kind* kind of guy. A *gentle* gentleman. It took a lot of swallowing to be that way—pride, mainly, other people's sh . . ."—we were in church; he edited—". . . stuff." He looked up from the podium he'd been staring at. "You know," he said, and we did. Almost everyone around me was working hard at swallowing something. For me, it was tears.

I was just thirteen-dammit and had just started to become the jerk it is our pubescent destiny to become. I was a boy, too, trying to become a man in pre–World War II America, way back when, before people couldn't shut up about their feelings. So I choked back, and swallowed, and toughed it out, at least long enough to make it to the men's room and the stall next to the wall. Once inside, door bolted tight, I used a big wad of toilet paper to muffle whatever flushing didn't mask.

I didn't think it was possible to hurt that badly again. I was wrong. I started hurting that badly just about every Christmas. My dad died on December 24, just in case I was in any danger of forgetting the exact date. So every year I was reminded and every year I resurrected my grief. I missed him. I kept thinking about all the things he was missing by being dead. I wondered what he was like when he was whatever age I'd be turning in the coming year. I wondered what he'd do and what he'd make sure to do *more* of if he knew what I knew about how long he had left.

What would *I* do in his shoes, with the same number of years?

At fourteen, on the first anniversary, I decided I'd take more baths. Not for hygiene, but to relax. To make my back stop hurting like Atlas all the time. More long hot baths, with a cup of coffee within reach and a slice of cold pepperoni pizza. I'd arrange it so that during these baths there wouldn't be any noise except the sound of the gurgling water rushing out of the faucet. And it could run and run, without going cold or overflowing the tub, for as long as I needed it to. My mother—here was the *real* miracle—*wouldn't* come knocking at the door, asking if I'd drowned, or what was wrong, or did I think she was made of hot water. And when I started thinking about my dad, and all the hot baths he'd never take? That magical tub that never over-flowed would know what to do with those tears.

At fifteen, the something I'd do more of also involved locked bathroom doors. Ditto for sixteen. And seventeen.

And when it finally looked like we'd be going to war because of a guy with a mustache just like my dad's, I imagined him giving his hand a rest and signing up. If he knew what I knew about how long he had left—sure, he'd sign up. After all, if he knew *that,* he'd know he'd come through it okay. He'd know he'd be around long enough to have a son he could leave too soon. You just had to do the math.

And so I signed up, thinking war was mainly a matter of knowing what to swallow and what to spit out.

I've already mentioned about vampires and their last scars and Isuzu's uncanny aim when it came to mine. That's another part of this little carjacking down memory lane. Like a lot of my benevolent buddies, I got vamped during World War II. That's how far back mine goes; that's the bit of history my second umbilical loops around. You'd think that as scars go, it'd be as dead and hard as a horse's hoof by now. But no. All it takes is a little twelve-inch blade to retenderize everything.

So there I am:

My last sunset has sunk and I'm sinking fast, right along with it. I've taken some shrapnel in the breadbasket and I'm dying, looking toward my last moon, a turd of cloud scudding across its face. There's a bombed-out farmhouse in the distance, and in the delirium of my dying, I become convinced that it's the same one where my dad swallowed all those pits, all those years ago. I try to crawl to it. I'm Catholic, so I'm praying, too—*Hail Mary* (stretch, grab, pull) *full of grace* (groan, grab, pull)—getting my soul ready for the Great Whatever. And that's when she appears out of nowhere, a woman in a trench coat and Marlene Dietrich sunglasses, speaking French. I can't really understand her, just little bits and pieces.

Mort—I catch that one. Something about death. Dying.

Yeah. Right. I'm dying. Leave me alone, please . . .

Then: *Bon*. That means "good," I think. Like in *bon voyage*.

So now she's being sarcastic? It's good I'm dying? Fuck you, you French . . .

Not that I say any of this. Not with my mouth. Not out loud. The thing that's killing me is sending blood gurgling up my throat the wrong way. But that's a good thing, my not being able to speak. God only knows what would have happened if I said what I was thinking—and if she understood. As luck would have it, all I can say is "Fuck you" with my eyes. And I never was very good at speaking with my eyes, even back when I still had pupils to dilate and whites to show interest or contempt.

Don't hurt me.

That's what my eyes usually seemed to say—back before they went all the way black. Back before they learned the look that forever says "midnight" and "snack."

So there I am, the moon and me, a hole in my belly, my life bubbling out at both ends in a gory red gush, my eyes going squinty, trying to pay this Frenchwoman back for saying she's glad I'm dying.

And then she smiles.

You know the smile I mean. The one that changes everything. The smile that raises the curtain on those big dog teeth of hers.

Surprise!

And that's when she tucks into me like I'm a steak. A *mistake*, probably, but a juicy one. And it's incredible. It feels like she's giving me a blow job through my stomach. I go from going to coming, just like that. My toes curl in my GI boots and every beat of my heart is another orgasm . . .

That lasts for about as long as that sort of thing lasts, but then: *Oh-oh* . . .

Here comes the dying part. I can feel it. I can feel my heart giving up. I can feel my . . . *everything* . . . going cold from the inside out. She's got her hand on my chest. She just worked her little fingers between the buttons of my uniform, rests her already-cold flesh against my going-cold flesh—not squeezing, not tweaking, not trying to arouse. Just *checking*. Even though I'm delirious by now from lack of blood, I know she's counting my heartbeats. I know she's decided to do something other than kill me—something other than leaving me here to die.

Something wrong. Something unnatural. *Something I want more than anything else in the world.*

She stops sucking just before my last heartbeat. She squeezes the halves of my wound together, places her lips on my lips, and spits a little bit of me back into me. A little bit of me, mixed with her. I don't know it at the time, but she's bitten her tongue just before darting it into my mouth. Different vampires do it different ways, and this is hers. A French kiss from a French vampire.

Pulling back, she closes my mouth with the tips of her fingers and makes an exaggerated swallowing gesture. So I swallow, and when I do, I can feel the skin of my stomach tug in around where the gash is. Or was. I can feel the skin going tight, stitching itself back together.

She finds some water in the moonlight. It's not that hard. There are puddles everywhere—all of them suddenly on fire to my new vampire eyes. She washes her hands, and then washes what will be my last scar. My new belly button. The bull's-eye Isuzu found with that bread knife of hers.

And after that we play charades.

In the moonlight, in the middle of France, in the middle of World War II, with mortar flashing in the distance, an old French vampire and her new American calf play guessing games. First word, two syllables. She points toward the east, and then mimes "sunrise" by raising a fist in a slow arc above the horizon of her opposite arm. She mimes "death" by choking herself with both hands.

"Hide"—my borrowed jacket, hitched over her head as if to shield her from the rain. "Sleep"—head tilted to a pillow of pressed hands.

I nod, and nod, and then nod, again.

Sunlight will kill me. Got it.

"Am I like Dracula?" I ask, and she nods her head: Yes. She holds up a finger: But. She shakes her head: No.

So I'm a yes-and-no Dracula and one of those yesses is the part about being killed by sunlight. "What about crosses?" I ask. "What about garlic?"

But she just smiles those big dog teeth of hers and brushes the hair off my forehead. Leaning in, she places a kiss there, still stained with my own blood. She lifts her sunglasses, revealing those black-black eyes, winks, whispers a *Bonsoir,* and then disappears into the same French nowhere she came from.

And that's how she leaves it—that's how she leaves *me,* not-dying in the middle of World War II. *Not-dying*—but filling up with a thousand different questions.

Can I turn into things?

Do I still have a reflection?

Why does everything seem so bright when it's still night out?

Can I pray if I still want to? And who'll answer me if I do?

My savior taught me the bare minimum I needed to know to survive my first daybreak; the rest I had to figure out for myself. She wasn't being cruel, just economical. I needed to know what would kill me for sure, and she told me. The rest was really about what *wouldn't* kill me, despite Hollywood and its myths. And so I worked my way through a series of pleasant surprises. Being immune to bullets? That brought a smile to my face the first time it came in handy. Garlic? Crosses? How was I supposed to avoid those things in Europe, of all places? So it was nice to know I didn't have to, finding myself staring at my former savior without going poof. And that's how my vampire lessons usually went—an Oops, followed by an Oh, followed by an Okay.

As far as the rest of the rest of it, like learning how to feed myself? The movies got that part right. Not that I needed a movie to tell me what to do. You get hungry enough, and your body lets you know. After all, even a newborn can find its mother's breast.

I forgot about the calendar.

I gave up days, and I gave up counting them. I was immortal; what was time to me? And anyway, I was too busy learning all the rules and privileges that came with my field promotion up the food chain. When the weather grew cold, my breath didn't do anything special. It came out just as invisibly as when it was warm. And when the snowflakes started falling, they rested on my skin, unmelted—which was a little disconcerting—but I didn't read into it any further than that. I didn't see it as a reminder. I didn't take it as a clue to what was coming.

And so those first few months as a new vampire went smoothly, in blissful ignorance. We were—thank God—at war. I had a clearly defined enemy that the U.S. government sincerely wanted me to kill. The fact that killing also meant a free meal? Well, two birds with one stone. And war really is much more fun when you don't have to worry about the bullets—when all you have to stay out of the way of is the big exploding stuff. Oh, sure, I had to stay away from *hails* of bullets; one good sweep from a machine gun and you could just tear me along the dotted line. But all in all, my attitude toward war had lightened up considerably.

Until . . .

I'd been technically AWOL but still doing my job, at least at night. And I was sneaking up on my soup *du jour*—my little Sauerkraut—who'd been cut off from his troop. He just sat there, shivering in his foxhole, wearing his dick-shaped helmet, whispering to himself in German. I figured he was probably cursing himself for being stupid and getting lost, but doing it quietly. Too quietly for mortal ears, but . . . this wasn't his lucky day.

Or night. *Nacht.*

I was thinking to myself, This is not your lucky *nacht,* when out of the whispered gibberish I heard the very word I was thinking:

"*Nacht.*"

It was being sung—quietly, again, but . . .

It was being sung to the tune of "Silent Night." And just like that, I remembered what day it was.

Or night. *Nacht.*

So I put a little moonlight between his body and its head.

And yes, I know, I've already told you: that's not the proper way. It's not necessary, and it's not practical. For one thing, it makes everything much more difficult, like trying to drink from a garden hose that's running too fast. But I couldn't help it. If he'd been a radio, I would have thrown him across the room, or smashed him to bits with my fist.

"Acting out."

That's what the crowd that's always talking about their feelings would say. They'd say I was really beating myself up, or ripping off my own head. And they'd be right. Kind of. I *was* furious for having forgotten about Christmas while this stupid *Nazi* remembered, even though *I* had more reason for remembering than just about anybody.

And so I started thinking about my dad and how he died, and how I didn't, and wouldn't, and there was nobody there.

Nobody except for me and a dead Nazi, lying on the snow-covered earth under a star-crowded sky. So when my eyes started leaking, I let them. I let my tears turn the snow red—at least where my dinner hadn't stained it already. And when my bloody tears started freezing to my face, well . . . *that's* why I didn't cry at my father's grave. *That's* why I saved it for the bathroom, flushing and flushing over the sound of me bawling my eyes out. I just didn't want to get frostbite.

That's all.

Now it didn't matter. Bullets didn't matter, so frostbite sure as hell didn't. Which is when I started thinking about it—my warmth, and how foolishly I'd wasted it while I still had it. Now the snow wouldn't even melt on my skin, and my breathing left the cold night air unsmudged. Now I was just a reptile, cold-blooded, and cold-hearted, and left out in the cold.

"I was just thirteen," I whispered to the dead Nazi, the stars, and snow.

"Dammit," I added to the no one who listens to vampire prayers.

Some critics think *Frankenstein* is autobiographical. They point to Mary Shelley's mother, who died giving life to her daughter. They suggest that Mary was raised to feel like a monster herself. A monster who'd killed her creator and grew to despise her own existence, the unfixable past, the unpayable debt.

That's a good theory. Here's another:

Maybe *Frankenstein* is just about growing up. Puberty. Maybe it's about suddenly having the power to create life and not knowing what to do with it. That's the Dr. Frankenstein part of growing up. But there's the monster part, too. The part where you feel pulled together from mismatched parts. Shelley wrote about her monster when she was still a dewy young girl, not yet twenty. And who among us wasn't a little monstrous when we were going through all those changes, our voices splintering, hair sprouting in the oddest of places, full of strange new desires?

A monster.

That's how I felt, there and then, under those mute, judging stars. I felt like a monster. I hadn't up until that point. I felt like a war hero. I felt like a good guy doing good guy stuff, taking a literal bite out of the Nazi war machine. I was a regular Sergeant York with fangs. But then Christmas came, and nearly went unnoticed, unmarked, un*grieved*—and bingo:

I'm Frankenstein. I'm Dracula. I'm the fucking Wolf Man.

Every vampire goes through this. It's all about dying. Dying, and who has to, and who doesn't have to anymore.

Feeling monstrous is just what happens, when you're distracted by watching death shrink in the rearview mirror and don't notice that Mack truck full of grief barreling right for you. Vampires know this. Vampires *learn* this, sometimes sooner, sometimes later. But we've all gone through that period of retroactive grief. It goes by different names—the vampire blues, the mourning after, vampire survivor syndrome—but it all comes down to the same thing. Imagine mourning—again, and all at once—every loved one in your entire life who's ever died. Imagine each hitting harder than it did the first time, because *this* time you know better. You don't buy the inevitability of death anymore. Now you know that life and death are choices.

So choose . . .

I look over at Isuzu, leaning her head against my passenger window like a see-through pillow. See-through, but for the fog she's breathing on it, snoring her little-girl snore. Sawing teeny-tiny balsa-wood logs. Dreaming her Cinderella dreams of a mother's miraculous escape, and the unimaginable, mud-free palace I'm whisking her off to. As promised. Along with the phone that'll ring, once the coast is clear.

Watching her, I remember a bumper sticker I used to see. This was back when I grew my hair long, so it would fall over my eyes, hiding them from all the two-toned ones trying to get a better look at what made me not quite right. The bumper sticker was about one of those arguments we don't have anymore. One of those arguments that people with two-toned eyes got all bent out of shape over:

"I'm a child, not a choice."

That's what the bumper sticker said, the one that's just popped into my head, watching Isuzu as she sleeps. And you know, I've just got to smile to myself.

That's what you think, kiddo . . .

Choices.

That's what going crazy is all about. Choices and not making them. When you go crazy, you lose the ability to discriminate. Good from bad. Love from hate. Giving a fuck from *not*.

I went a little crazy after my not-so-silent night. And when I did,

I stopped caring about the sorts of helmets my victims wore or if they wore any helmets at all. I also stopped caring about the difference between moderation and excess. And I began to kill, not for the cause of democracy, or freedom, or food, or even to stop some greater evil. No. I killed because my victims were killable. They harbored inside them the ability to die rather easily, and I wanted to see what I'd given up. It was research. A survey of mortality. I wanted to see the faces it made—this being mortal—when it fulfilled its destiny. And like any good survey, mine was demographically diverse. It included Germans, Americans, allies, enemies, men, women, children, a dog, a few horses. Pretty much anything with a face I could look into, and a pair of eyes in front of a brain that could shut down.

I think I was looking for someone who could tell me what I needed to know. I had a few questions I wanted answered. And the person who could answer them would be the one who made the same face while dying that my father made. I was on a quest, like Prince Uncharming, looking for the foot to match the glass slipper. And when I found that face, we'd have our winner. I'd take them all the way in to my father's dying face, back them out again, and ask my questions.

Are you sorry I brought you back?

If I were your son and didn't bring you back, would you ever forgive me? Would you haunt my dreams, given the chance?

That's what I think the plan was, but what do I know? I was crazy.

I never did get to ask my questions. Instead, my victims were the ones doing all the asking—assuming I didn't bite into their voice boxes just to keep them quiet. And the questions they asked were really just one:

Why?

The one who stopped me being crazy was the one who didn't ask, "Why?" She didn't plead for her life or even seem terribly surprised. When I revealed my fangs and intentions, she merely said, *"Danke,"* and tilted her neck to give me a clearer shot.

We were in a nightclub in a little Bavarian nowhere. The town hadn't been bombed yet because of the limited military applications for chocolate and porcelain. I was wearing the uniform of a German officer who didn't need it anymore and entered the nightclub with no questions asked.

My condition had taken a turn for the decidedly worse. At the moment, it was leading me to take bigger and more public risks. Why? Who knows? Maybe I was that famous criminal who really wants to get caught; maybe I was just crazy, like I said before. But there I was, in a room full of Germans, unable to speak the language beyond a few essentials like *Scheisse, Nacht, danke, auf Wiedersehen*. And what was I planning to do? Nothing much—just public murder. That, and watching the faces of all those polite Nazis when a geyser of arterial blood sprayed across their crisp white tablecloths. For a grin. A smile. A chuckle.

But she spoiled it all with her *Danke* and willingness.

She was seated toward the back, lit only by a globed candle. I picked her, I think, for the whiteness of her skin. It leapt out at my vampire eyes, overexposed—more real than real. A flashbulb sitting in a room full of dim bulbs. Plus, it reminded me of me. Her skin was nearly as pale as mine and I almost skipped her, figuring it must be cabaret makeup. Biting through makeup always feels weird—greasy—like you're doing a clown. But then I noticed the lacing of blue veins showing through, and the matter was settled.

Her. I'd do her. Here, now. In full view.

There was an empty chair next to her, but she didn't check her watch, didn't fidget or look around like she was expecting someone to join her. Instead, she seemed to be looking at the backs of her own hands as if they were suddenly as mysterious as street maps from Mars. There was a singer up front singing some awful German torch song, but my chosen didn't seem to care, or even notice. Her own mysterious hands were of far greater interest.

I approached her table with a drink and my not-nearly-enough German. When she looked up, I mimed introducing her and the drink to each other and then placed it down between her dead-white hands.

"*Danke*," she said, picking up the glass and tilting it back, clearly intending to down it in a single gulp. When she looked at me over the rim, I smiled, letting my fangs show, and then winked. I already had one of her hands in mine and was ready to yank her forward, ready to cup a hand to her mouth before she could scream or plead or ask, "Why?" like the others. But no. She winked back, placed her drink down, and said, "*Danke*," again, but as a sigh this time.

And then she tilted her neck. That's when her hair slipped slightly to one side. For a second, I imagined she was wearing a mask, one she was about to pull off with a "Ta-da!" to reveal a grinning skull underneath. The truth was a little different, but not much. It was a wig she was wearing, not a mask, and the skull underneath still had skin on it, but little else. She had what my friend Fuzzy had, but the adult version, and was pretty close to the finish line. As I later learned, she'd come to the club with a small pharmacy of sleeping pills in her purse. Her parents were dead, her soldier husband recently killed, and there was no one else.

Her biggest fear wasn't dying alone; it was going undiscovered until the smell gave her away. She knew it really didn't matter, but she couldn't stand thinking about the flies and the bloating up, her skin splitting open like overripe fruit and being remembered only as *that stink*, the one that lingered in the hallway for days until someone finally broke down the door.

So she came here to die, where she'd be found promptly, or at least by last call.

As a way of dying, I was as good as an overdose, with the advantage that my way left less to chance. Or so it would seem. She smiled eagerly and I . . . I just *couldn't*. I guess this must be how women feel about men when it's painfully obvious how much we need to get laid. There she was—wanting it, needing it—and I just couldn't. I tried miming around my lack of German again, covering my fangs with my hand, shaking my head.

"*Nein*," I said.

"*Ja*," she said, pulling my hand away. She tapped the artery running down the side of her white, white neck. "*Ja* . . ."

"Fuck," I muttered out of frustration.

Her eyes widened. She made an "okay" with her thumb and index finger before darting another finger into the *O*. *"Ja?"* she said, as if she hadn't considered this alternative to public suicide, but now that she had . . . sure, she was game. A last tumble before dying? That sounded just dandy. She smiled again, in that too-needy way, as I clapped a hand to my forehead. I almost said "Fuck" again, but didn't need to. My "no" was clear. My aim perfect. Her head dropped and shook.

And then everything changed.

I started thinking about Fuzzy, who sent all her classmates sympathy cards before she passed. And then I went back to looking at this pleading, dying woman who'd gone back to looking at her hands. That's when it happened. That's when a thought—just a word—popped into my head:

Choose . . .

You get to choose. What you hold on to, and what you let go. What you kill, and what you save.

And so I tapped the hand of my Fuzzy here-and-now.

She looked up, her eyes shiny with this latest insult—she couldn't even get a vampire to kill her. To kill her *or* fuck her.

I pointed at my heart. "Me," I said. I pointed at hers. "You," I said. I made a swirling motion in the space between our hearts.

"We," I said. *"Auf Wiedersehen, ja?"* I walked two sets of fingers across the tabletop toward an uncertain future.

The dying woman looked at me, her eyes both sad and bemused. I imagined what she was thinking: *Of all the vampires in all the gin joints in the world . . .* She sighed. Shrugged.

"Ja," she said, pulling her wig straight. "Okie-dokie," she added, using the English she had with the vampire she got.

I've never done this before," I said, later, in the apartment she didn't want her corpse stinking up. "So, if you die . . ." I might as well have been talking to the wall, but I was nervous, so I kept on going. ". . . well, it's not like that wasn't Plan A, right?"

By this time, I already knew about the pharmacy in her purse, and even understood about her fear of being found too late. The first was just a matter of letting me look inside; the latter involved sign language—her hands crossed over her chest, posed for death, followed by pinching her nose, making a face, fanning the air.

My intentions were somewhat more difficult to communicate, but I gave it a shot. First, I mimed fangs, crooking two fingers and holding them in front of my real fangs. I then placed my fang fingers to the side of her neck.

"*Ja*," she nodded, followed by crossing her hands over her chest again.

"*Nein*," I said.

I wanted to let her know not only that I wasn't going to kill her, but that she would never die. I noticed a calendar on the wall. The month was in German, but the year—we had those in common. So I ripped off a page and turned it around to the blank side. I drew a little tombstone with two years on it and X-ed it out. Next, I drew another with just a birth year and a dot, dot, dot. I underlined this one.

"*Nein*," I repeated.

"*Nein?*" she echoed, a little confused by the concept. I was going to bite her—*ja*, she got that—but she *wasn't* going to die? She shook her head and I could tell she was having a hard time with the not-dying part. I suppose if you've accepted your own death to the point of planning the where, when, and how, the idea of immortality is a little hard to buy. For me, when I was breathing my not quite last, death was the thing I was having a hard time buying. So when my death got vetoed, it kind of made sense to me, seeing as I really hadn't believed in it to begin with. But for her, death had been bought and paid for; she'd taken it for a test drive; she'd driven it off the lot. What the hell did I mean, no?

"*Nein*," I nodded. "*Ja. Nein.*"

She let her head drop, shook it doubtfully, but then looked up again. She shrugged. "Okie-dokie," she said.

And then she stood there.

And I stood there.

She looked at me.

I looked at her.

We were like a shy young couple, meeting each other for the first time on this, our wedding night. Because that's what vamping's like. Sure, it's not exactly the birds and the bees—more like bats and mosquitoes—but it *is* the way vampires increase their numbers. It's intimate. Bodily fluids are exchanged. Life-changing decisions are made.

And for the vampire doing the deed, performance anxiety becomes an issue.

Sure, if you're vamping somebody they are, by definition, a virgin. And that usually helps, except for that first time when it's the first time for both of you. And when you're the product of a hit-and-run vamping like me, with no mentor to show you the ropes, that first time at bat makes murder seem like the better idea. At least with murder the victim doesn't smirk at you when you're done. She doesn't blow smoke in your face, either, or act like she's been killed by much better killers than you.

So I decided to keep murder open as an option, should things turn ugly—or sarcastic. That lifted a good part of the burden. The rest was just a matter of getting started with those calm, death-accepting eyes trained on me.

I began by touching her face without benefit of preheating. She flinched ever so slightly at the cold. Her eyes flickered the briefest *Nein.* But that was enough. I lunged, unhinging my jaw like a snake opening up for a rabbit. I clamped on. She whimpered. I took her all the way down to hell's parking garage, and then I stopped.

I disengaged. I stepped back. Looked at her. She was pale before; she was practically translucent now. This was the time to do it. I remembered the kiss that brought me squalling into the dark. And so I reset my jaw and wiped my mouth free of any residual gore. I bit my tongue and placed my lips on her barely warmer lips. I let my bleeding tongue slip between, and into. After that, it was up to her. She'd know what to do, just like a baby knows what to do with its mother's breast.

And boy, did she ever know!

Golf balls, garden hoses. Gerbils, drinking straws. Whatever tasteless comparison you can think of—that's how hard she could suck. Like her life depended on it. Which it did, of course.

At one point, I worried about my tongue coming out by its roots. I worried that she'd tear that little flap of skin underneath. It didn't, and she didn't. She *did* bite a few extra holes in my tongue, but they healed over quickly enough.

The humming didn't start until about midway through. It started as a moan, then became a hum. Mmmm. Just like one of those Campbell Soup kids. She'd thrown her strengthening arms around me, one cupping the back of my neck, the other wrapping itself around my waist, pulling me closer. I was wanted and I wasn't going anywhere. And then the humming started. Mmmm. This was good, this thing we were doing—that's what the hum was for. That's what it meant. This thing we were doing was good enough to hum about.

So she did. And I did back.

Eventually, our hips found each other. And when they did, they ground a bit. The humming continued. It got louder, and then softer, in waves. Even after, it continued, our new, shared language.

"Mmmm," she mmmm'd.

"Mmmm," I mmmm'd back.

That was my first benevolent vamping. And I liked it. I liked it a lot.

I liked it so much I did more in the evenings to follow, all women, all attractive, all very grateful afterward. The hard part was holding back the smile that seemed permanently stitched to my face.

Eventually, I had to leave that music box of a city. I'd started to get known. A set of black marble eyes would show up with a two-toned pair, explaining in German that I was the guy she'd been told about. When I heard my name shouted one evening from across the *Strasse,* in an accent that rhymed it with "Marseilles," I knew it was time for Marty the Vampire to leave.

About a week later, the music box was incinerated. The chocolate vaporized. The porcelain, pummeled. And all my little immortals were reacquainted with their mortality.

I sighed after hearing the news. If that's what being good got you, what good was being good? And so I decided to put benevolence aside. There was a war on, after all. There was a war on, and it would still be going on long after this silly world war was history.

Isuzu stirs. She turns her sleeping face and breathes out a bubble of spit. It jiggles there, capping the O of her lips, catching the shine of the moon coming through the windshield.

I have to. Sometimes, a man's just gotta do what a man's gotta do.

I pop it.

I reach over with my smallest finger—the pinky. Dart in, out. Smile. Mischief accomplished, I go back to driving us to my apartment, feeling much less mature, and much better for it.

But then, suddenly:

"Mom?"

The word's just there in the car with us and I didn't say it. When I look back at Isuzu, her eyes are still closed. I'd forgotten that people can do that—can talk in their sleep. When everybody you know sleeps at the same time, you tend to forget what it looks like from the outside.

It looks nice, and I wait for more words, but none come. Instead, Isuzu stirs again. She wrestles with something in her sleep. Her brow furrows; her teeth set. Her lips begin moving as if she's chewing on something tiny. Like a seed, perhaps. Or maybe a cherry pit. She seems undecided whether to spit or not. Her throat just keeps working at it, going up and down, until it works something clear out of the corner of her eye. That's when I begin to wonder about my little POW, her mom, and my story. That's when I start to think about what it is we swallow when there's really no other choice.

-4-

WHAT DIED?

Isuzu shits.

This occurs to me later than it should, but I've got an excuse. Shitting's not something vampires do, and I just forgot. There were no reminders back at the hole—no foul bucket, no means by which wiping could be achieved, no flatulential air clinging to the muddy walls. Of course, they *were* living in the woods, which are notorious for being shat in by everything, from popes to bears. So no. It didn't occur to me that Isuzu might need to shit until we're already in the car, headed back to my apartment. She's still asleep, grinding her blunt little teeth, when suddenly it becomes obvious that not all the noises coming from her side of the car are benign.

"Jesus Christ, kiddo," I whisper, rolling down my window. "What crawled up your ass and died?"

That's my dad talking. That was his favorite saying anytime any-one farted. Or floopsed. My dad would never say "fart." Floops—that was his word. "Who floopsed?" he'd ask, followed by the dead-ass line. Followed by "Light a match" or "My eyes are water-ing" or "What you been eating, boy?"

But there's no need to ask who floopsed this time. There's only one floopser in the car, and it isn't me. And if there's floopsing being done this early in the game, it's only a matter of time before some-thing more substantial follows.

Which brings up another problem with this whole delayed gratification thing—having to deal with all the shit that comes along in the meantime. I'm tempted to just admit defeat, pull over to the side of the road, and dive in with both fangs.

"Sorry, kiddo," I'd say, "but I forgot how nasty you things can be."

But I don't.

I don't because the stink is still pretty heavy and it stops my appetite from rising to the task. So I roll down my window a little more and keep on driving, wondering what else my little shit factory is going to spring on me between now and mealtime.

After the last war—the one my benevolent buddies and I "won" by flipping the odds—after that, the world seemed like one big broken heart. It was like everybody had just broken up with somebody else, all these things vampires didn't have uses for anymore just sitting there, making our eyes leak, reminding us of what we'd given up to live forever. And so, like jilted lovers, we went through the Big Purge. Bonfires were involved; ditto, wrecking balls; and pits, and landfills, and tankers dumping ton after ton of our ex-world into the deeper ends of the deeper oceans. Plates were flung like Frisbees into brick walls or shot out of the night sky like skeet. Forks and spoons were melted down. We recycled what we could, and brutalized what we couldn't, taking out our heartbreak in increasingly creative, increasingly violent ways, until it looked like we might actually succeed.

That's when some of us started getting nostalgic. Started hoarding. Started boxing, shrink-wrapping, slipping into specially made collectors' bags. I once saw a friend handling a greasy french fry sleeve with tweezers and white cotton gloves. "Breathe deep," he instructed. "That's lard, buddy boy. Not peanut oil. Not oleo. *Real lard* . . ."

Old restaurant menus—back from when the variety of things to eat had to be written down to keep it all straight—menus are *très* retro and *très* hot. I saw one from Big Boy go for $500 on eBay—and that's with half the lamination missing.

An actual Big Mac, set in a block of acrylic as a paperweight—a grand, easy.

An unopened can of Diet Coke . . .

A fifth of Seagram's . . .

A frying pan . . .

A potato peeler . . .

Salt, pepper, thyme, oregano.

An aspirin. A single, generic aspirin: twenty-five bucks; name brand: thirty.

I'm thinking about all this now, because of a fart and what it foretells. And I'm thinking eBay and I are going to be very good friends. I can see that already, listening to Isuzu grunt out another one next to me. I can see my future, and the hundred different things that'll break my heart just taking them out of the UPS box, with their Styrofoam peanuts, their certificates of authenticity.

"Look, Isuzu," I imagine saying in that not-too-distant future. "Toilet paper."

I imagine pausing, listening.

"Yes, of course." I sigh an imaginary sigh. "The *soft* kind."

Bathroom-going is *not* something my apartment is ready for. I have the bathroom, yes, with a sink, a shower, and even a toilet, but the last has been turned off for decades. I use it as a planter now—a lot of vampires do. We used to just rip them out, but that got to be more trouble than it was worth. For one thing, the sanitation department charges to haul them away and then the landfill tacks on a monthly storage fee, like you'll be asking for it back anytime soon. They used to dump them into the nearest river, but you dump enough of anything into a river and it gets a little higher than it should. Which is when the flooding starts. Which is when the dumps start charging storage fees and toilets start making good planters.

Me, I've got Venus flytraps in the tank, and a small cactus garden in the bowl. It mirrors my personality—predatory and prickly.

Or *mirrored*. Past tense.

If Isuzu's going to be spending any time in my apartment, she's going to learn to use a toilet. This ain't no woods, missy; you can't just take a squat wherever you feel like it. Which is why I find myself kneeling before my toilet-turned-planter, turning it back into a toilet after all these years.

It's while I'm pulling up traps and cacti that I start wondering if I'm letting a golden opportunity go down the drain. Nostalgic vampires collect more than just menus and saltshakers. Some collect shit. No, not kitschy crap, but honest-to-God *real* shit. I understand pricing is driven by two main criteria: size, and the presence of identifiable . . . *elements*. Corn, blueberries, a bloated bit of french fry—these all contribute to making one piece of shit worthier than another. To their collectors, at least. And it occurs to me that this "delayed gratification" business is bound to get expensive. So why not put Isuzu's little butt to work?

The smell of fertilizer tells me why not.

It's because selling shit means doing business with the sort of people who *buy* shit. It means getting into arguments with shitkickers about whether your shit's for-real *people* shit, and not just some dog shit or cat shit or—who knows?—*horse* shit you're trying to pass off as the gen-you-wine article. And that's just bullshit, man. *Total* bullshit.

And so I finish cleaning out the bowl and the tank. I scoop out sand, and fertilizer, and potting soil by the handful. I tap the pipes to break up any dirt that may have gotten caked there, go over it all with the vacuum hose, tap some more, suck some more, scratch at a stubborn clod with my thumbnail. I squirt a little WD-40 on the rusty knob under the tank. It squeaks like something small and rodential being strangled, but then the water starts giggling out, filling the tank.

Straightening up, I brush some dust off my knees and pronounce it good to go. So to speak.

It's after the float valve closes off that I make the mistake of flipping the handle. It's just a test run. I'm just making sure everything still works the way it's supposed to. And it does. Dear God Almighty, does it ever. It works like a bastard.

The noise!

The noise of a toilet flushing in an apartment building that hasn't had a toilet flushed within its rusty-pipe-hiding walls in a couple of decades is the kind of noise that kinda . . . stands out. It's different from the sound of water going down the drain from a shower. It's . . . *throatier.* More percussive. Pipes grown accustomed to polite dribbles and drabs rattle in protest, banging their coppery joints against the plasterboard as if to say, What *the fuck* were you thinking?

As if to join that other banging, coming from your front door.

"Hey Marty, didja hear that?"

"Where the hell did *that* come from?"

"Was that what it *sounded* like?"

And me—what do *I* have to say?

Nothing.

I just tiptoe around my apartment, switching off twenty-watt bulbs here and there. I sit then, nice and still. I hold my breath in the dark, listening to the sluicing of water behind my too-thin walls. And I . . . *don't* . . . *say* . . . *shit.*

I moved Isuzu from the front seat to the trunk for the last few miles of our trip. It's a safety precaution. Again. And she's still out there, in the trunk, while I'm inside the apartment, getting things ready. If it wasn't so cold, I would have tried passing her off as a Screamer.

"Just say 'fuck' a lot," I'd tell her, if it wasn't so cold.

"Add a few 'bastards,'" I'd add, if her all-too-seeable breath wasn't such a dead giveaway.

I've thought about having her take a deep breath and then just making a run for it. But that won't work and I know it. My neighbors are a curious bunch. All it takes is the sound of a car pulling into the parking lot, and there go all those heavy sunproof drapes, parting like the Red Sea. They see me walking toward the building with Isuzu and they're stopping us, steam or no steam.

"So, who's *this*?"

"Niece."

"*Really* . . ." They'd pause. Look Isuzu up and down, trying to catch a glimpse of her eyes, her teeth. Was that a blush rising in her cheeks? Why wasn't she shouting? "Why . . . ?"

"Leukemia," I'd say.

"*Really . . .*" And they'd just stand there, tsk-tsking in their vampire heads, letting the clock run until Isuzu either passes out or lets go. And after that . . . *snap!* Life sucks, and then you die. There wouldn't be any negotiation; there wouldn't be any "May I," "Please," or "Thanks." Delayed gratification? Fuck that. They'd just dig right in. Isuzu would be off her feet and horizontal in a heartbeat, her ankles squeezed together in one hand, the top of her head eagle-clawed with the other, her neck bent just so and already clamped between those greedy fangs. And afterward—after the body was drained and the cob picked clean—my neighbor, whichever one it was, would look at my scowling face, sincerely confused.

"Did you want some?" they'd ask, now that it was no longer an issue. They'd blink their innocent shark eyes. "You should have said something if . . ."

"Skip it," I'd say, pissed, but partly to blame. What was I thinking, waving around a stack of hundreds in the bad part of town?

No. The only way to get Isuzu inside safely is to do it under the cover of daylight. So that's the plan. I've already showed her how to kick out the backseat from inside the trunk. I've already promised to leave my door open.

"It's on the fourth floor," I've told her. "Do you know how many that is?"

She's already nodded her head.

"Show me."

And she did, holding up the appropriate number of fingers. "Good." I wrote the apartment number on a slip of paper and handed it to her. "Look for this on the outside of the door," I said. "Turn the knob with both hands and push hard. It sticks a little sometimes. I should probably oil it, but . . ."

"What if my mom calls before it gets daytime?"

"Huh?" And then I remembered. "Oh, yeah. I'll take a message, okay. I'll write everything down. I promise." I paused. "But I don't think she'll be calling tonight, kiddo. She's gonna be pretty busy doing vampire stuff."

"What kind of vampire stuff?"

"Well, toothpaste, for one. She's gonna have to buy a brand-new tube of special vampire toothpaste. For her fangs. And a new toothbrush, too."

Isuzu smiled. She knew I was pulling her leg.

"And mouthwash for her bat breath," she added, all on her own, following it with the flattest, most restrained little tee-hee laugh I've ever heard. It was a don't-let-them-hear-us-laugh laugh. If I wasn't planning to kill her anyway, it would have come dangerously close to breaking my heart.

"Good one," I said, and she tee-heed again. "Sleep tight, kiddo," I added. "Don't let the bedbugs . . ." I didn't want to say "bite," and so I didn't. I just left the bedbugs hanging there.

"Don't let them *what*?" Isuzu asked, not ready to let me off the hook so easily.

"Um," I said, stalling, and then:

"Tickle your toes," I said, tickling with all my might, trying to raise the volume on that stifled little laugh. But all I got was more of the same.

"Tee-hee," she went, as steady as a pacemaker, as quiet as a frightened little cliché.

*W*hat were you thinking?

That's what my heart wants to know, as I sit in my darkened apartment, trying not to squeak. Just like that little girl in my trunk. The one who shits. The one who must be prepared for. The one who's already tried to kill me, who'll be padding around my apartment all day long, while I'm just lying here, unconscious, defenseless.

This is your definition of smart? my heart asks.

It's been a half hour since the toilet faux pas. The pipes have stopped banging, and so have my neighbors. Now there's just my heart, banging against my rib cage, trying to knock some sense into me, from the inside out.

What? it mocks. *She needs you alive to answer a phone?*

So I click on the lights again and try to see everything fresh, through maybe-still-vengeful, mortal eyes. Okay, the kitchen knife is taken care of. I've locked that in my glove compartment. That's a good start.

Now, there's just everything else.

All the stuff in my apartment that might be turned against me, given world enough and plenty of daylight. My hammer, for instance. The hammer and various hammerable things. Like my sex toy knives. Screwdrivers. The longer nails. Hell, even a pencil jammed up my nostril with a good whack. The matches have to go. Same for flammable liquids. My hacksaw. The nastier power tools. My bowling ball. Other heavy, skull-crushing, droppable things. Wires of any appreciable length and something to use as a spindle— something to loop around my neck, twist, and tighten like a garrote, cutting my head from my body like a cheese cutter cutting through cheese . . .

The casters on my bed!

Even the casters on my bed could be used against me. And so I remove them a post at a time, to make wheeling me toward an open window less likely. I locate my handcuffs, too, just in case she tries dragging my sleeping body out of bed and into the path of some heavy-duty sunshine.

And if you should die before you wake? my heart tap-taps.

I look at all my stuff with my own eyes again, wondering if this is the last time I'll be seeing it. My books and CDs. My stereo, TV, and computer. My gliding rocker and sofa. My so-called coffee table, stained with overlapping rings of dried blood like some logo for the vampire Olympics . . .

Not good, my heart says, and my brain agrees.

So I fan out some magazines to hide the stains—no need to incite my little guest with careless reminders. And then I go back to looking at my apartment, this time with a different set of mortal eyes. Not vengeful so much as wary. Leery. On guard.

There. That. That's a no-no.

The framed poster of Bela Lugosi, his cape in full spread? What seemed so retro hip before now seems a little tasteless. And so down it comes, and behind the sofa it goes, Bela facing the wall as if he's being punished for all my vampire sins.

Ditto the old Red Cross poster, beseeching all to "Give the Gift of Life."

And the IV stand turned into a reading lamp.

And the pens made to look like hypodermics; the hypodermics made to act like pens.

The unopened box of Count Chocula I got off eBay.

The postcards featuring old crime scene photos, the blood leaking out black as oil onto the flashbulb-bleached pavement, soaking through the sloppily draped sheet, each with some variation of the same message scribbled on the back:

"Mmmm. Tasty . . ."

My, how witty we vampires are, in our one-track, one-note way. And how pathetic it all seems now, looked at from the other side of the tracks.

And then there are all those reminders of the death we no longer fear—the bones of my little necropolis scattered here and there. The human skull. The shrunken head. The mummified hand, palm up and waiting for my pocket change and keys. The casket handles on my kitchen cabinets. The funeral-procession flags reduced to washcloths. The toe-tag bookmarks. The halved rib cage used for sorting my mail. The death certificate coasters. The collage I made from dozens of different poison labels, the skulls grinning more and more ironically the closer they get to being contemporary. The laminated obituaries of famous dead people held to my blood-filled refrigerator by magnets in the shape of bats, tombstones, skulls . . .

I get a garbage bag and begin grabbing. This, this, this, and that. That, that, that, and this. It takes nearly an hour to re- (or rather un-) vamp my apartment, by which time the sky has started growing pink in the east. The ten-minute warning siren begins whooping, calling all suckers back inside their variously blinkered apartments. Rush hour. Last call. Bedtime . . .

The graveyard shift.

I can hear sports cars just like mine screeching into the carport, footsteps running down the hall, front doors opening and then slamming shut. I check the lock on my front door—still open, as promised.

If I should die before I wake . . .

I pull the heavy drapes closed, and then head to the bedroom. It's as I'm closing the door that I notice it—a skeleton key. I'd never paid much attention before—never really needed to. I live alone. Always have. The only door I've ever bothered locking is the front one. If you had asked me before if there was a lock on my bedroom door, I would have asked for a minimum of two guesses. But there it is. A skeleton key. Of course.

Which means I can lock the door, ensuring for myself an extra margin of safety. If I want to. If I want to play it safe. But if that's how I wanted to play it, I'd have drained Isuzu back at the hole. If I wanted to play it safe, I'd still have my air bags, and never would have found her in the first place.

I look at the key in its hole. Should I?

Of course you should.

But . . . *should I?*

On the plus side, leaving my bedroom door open could create the illusion of trust. Isuzu can't see the fact that I've hidden the more obvious implements of destruction, but if she checks my bedroom door and it's locked . . . that'll say I'm hiding something, that I don't trust her, and that I can't be trusted in return.

I look at the key in its hole.

I close my eyes and try to picture Isuzu, lying there in my trunk, waiting for the last siren to die down, waiting for the metal over her head to warm a few degrees before pushing out the backseat, crawling through and up and out. I imagine her clicking across the asphalt in her little-girl plastic-soled shoes, the ones we've brought back with us from the hole, along with her deflated air mattress, her "cat" food, and a few pieces of clothing, still reeking from her farting, sweating humanity. She blinks in the bright sunshine, but doesn't start blistering, doesn't start smoking, unlike yours truly. Unlike everyone else yours truly knows. There are probably birds in the sky. Isuzu probably stops to look up at them flying by. Her little heart probably beats fast, even though she knows sunlight is her guardian angel, looking out for her, keeping her safe while her mother's away, dealing with her bat breath. She opens the front door to my building and sees all the darkness inside. Her little heart probably beats a little faster. She probably wonders if there's such a thing as vampire insomniacs, and whether I'd tell her if there were. She looks at the sunlight, and then back at the dark. She runs up the four flights to my apartment as fast as she can. Checking the scrap of paper I gave her, she locates the door, grabs the knob with both hands, twists, pushes in, click-clicks across the hardwood floor. She starts checking doors—the spare bedroom, the bathroom, my room.

Unlocked. Unlocked. Locked.

Her heart starts knocking some sense into her. She remembers me licking my fingers. And if she wasn't thinking about killing me before, she starts to now. She fills a glass with water—it's something she's seen her mom do—and uses it like a magnifying glass to catch some old newspapers on fire. She runs out and down and sits on the hood of my car, watching a whole building full of vampires go up in smoke. I'll bet she laughs then. I'll bet she busts out of that flat little tee-hee and laughs her floopsing ass off.

The two-minute warning blows and I open my eyes, still aimed at the keyhole in my bedroom door. I reach over and remove the key. Place it on my nightstand with a click.

"Fuck it," my mouth says.

And my heart? My heart can't be reached for comment.

-5-

JESUS WEPT

When I wake up, nothing's sticking up out of me that shouldn't. Nothing's smoking or crushed either. There *is* the sound of something being crunched, however. And when I turn my head, there they are—those two-toned eyes, floating above a pair of cheeks, chipmunked around a hundred dollars' worth of very stale chocolate cereal.

I have no idea how long Isuzu's been standing there, just watching me. Vampire sleep is more like hibernation or a coma than sleep. To mortal eyes, we appear dead. Respiration drops to less than one breath per minute, and our heart rate slows to the bare minimum needed to prevent our blood from turning to sludge. When we're asleep, you could take a Black & Decker to our eyeballs and we wouldn't flinch.

Isuzu crunches another handful and then notices that my too-pale eyelids have been replaced by the shiny black of the night before. And before I can say anything—before she even swallows—she wants to know if I know him, pointing at the box, the cartoon fangs.

"Do I know Count Chocula?" I echo, wondering how I'd forgotten to include that with all the other stuff I've hidden away. I think about lying to her—think about reinventing Count Chocula as some vampiric Santa Claus—but then I think better of it. The lie about her mother still being alive is plenty.

So: "Nope," I say. " 'Fraid not."

"Oh," Isuzu says, accepting the information with utter neutrality. She just had a question and wanted an answer, but wasn't vested in the response either way. Pure curiosity. No agenda. I'd almost forgotten that such a thing was possible.

Isuzu grabs another handful from the box, cups it to her mouth, chews. She stares at me with her big, still human, still part-white eyes. She blinks. But it's not a normal blink. It's a blink that's been thought about and willed. She stops chewing, swallows, does it again.

"My mom says this is how cats smile," she says, blinking a third time.

Oh.

Okay.

I blink back. Isuzu smiles with her mouth, but then covers it, stifling a giggle. She blinks again. I blink back.

She blinks. I blink.

She. I.

She. I.

She. I.

She giggles. It's the flat tee-hee from before, but a little looser, a little faster, a little louder.

Before, I used to wonder how it is one spends eternity. How do you kill its numberless minutes, hours, nights? Do you tinker it away? Do you putter it to death? Or do you just give up and disconnect your air bags?

No.

No, the answer's as simple as being a kid. Remember what it was like to be a kid, when forever was just a given, and doing something over and over again just made it funnier each time?

While she's still laughing, I blink, three times, fast. I, I, I.

She matches me, blink for blink. She, she, she.

Followed by: I, I, I.

But when she laughs this time, I make the mistake of laughing, too. I make the mistake of letting my stupid fangs show without even thinking. That's when Isuzu's blink muscles get stuck on open.

It lasts only a second, but it's a *long* second—longer even than the several seconds I sat staring at her knife plunged into my guts. It feels like the longest second we've shared so far. I put my hand across my mouth. I blink. She stares.

I blink. She stares.

Finally: I *stare.* I make my bug eyes bug a little more, letting more of those shiny black marbles show. I take my hand away from my mouth, my fangs hidden now behind lips set for the new game. The challenge.

The stare-off!

Ready, set . . .

Isuzu understands and props both elbows on the edge of my bed. She settles her chin between cradling fists. And stares. *Hard.*

I ignore the handful of involuntary blinks she blinks before deciding to lose. And then I blink. I blink *big.* I blink *huge.*

She smiles with more than just her eyes as I groan and throw a melodramatic hand to my heart.

"Ya got me," I say, not the whole truth, but not exactly a lie, either.

It's midnight—vampire lunchtime—and Isuzu's yawning by the kitchen table as I stand by the counter, my Mr. Plasma clicking off its degrees (ninety, ninety-one, ninety-two . . .) followed by the tenths (98.1, 98.2, 98.3 . . .). I've opened one of the cans of "cat" food we brought back from the hole, the label underneath the label reading "SpaghettiOs." We've been having "discussions" all evening, laying down the ground rules. The things she has to wait until daytime to do, like go outside, like flush the toilet. Followed by the facts of vampire life:

"Yes, I *do* drink blood."

"No, from a bottle. Not from people." I say this with a straight face even as I'm watching the light blue squiggle at the side of her neck. It branches right around where her jaw hooks into the rest of her skull, and I can't decide whether it's a lightning bolt, a naked tree in autumn, or maybe a river the way it looks to God, and satellites.

"Because not all vampires are as nice as I am," I go on.

"Yes, sunlight is good for plants and little girls and birds, and yes, I miss it, but no, not even for a little, no."

"Because I *said* so."

"No, I can't eat chocolate."

"No, not chicken, either."

"No, not beets—are you *kidding*?—yuck."

"Yes, 'no chocolate' includes chocolate cake."

"*And* chocolate milk."

"*And* Count Chocula."

"Just because I *do*, okay? A person doesn't have to eat something just because they've got a box of it lying around."

It's Isuzu who suggests we have a secret safety song. She and her mom had one, and if either one got into trouble, she'd sing it, so the other would know and stay away, or get help.

"Okay," I say, humoring my little gratifier-to-be. "Let's hear it."

Isuzu pauses, perhaps wondering if it really *is* okay. Maybe I'm smiling too much. Maybe I'm trying too hard to sell this Marty-as-good-guy sham. I've got this closed-lip, fang-hiding smile I've been wearing ever since we stopped smiling by blinking our eyes. Every so often, my teeth grind behind these fixed and curving lips. But I keep smiling. I staple it on both ends. I spot-weld it. And now she's looking at me like she wonders if it hurts, smiling like that for so long. She looks at my smile like it's a crack in the ice that might spread underfoot with the slightest misstep. She's not that far off.

Or maybe I'm just projecting. She blinks an ordinary blink, and then, for some reason, she goes up on her tiptoes. She goes up on her tiptoes and opens her mouth, and this is what comes out.

"You are my sunshine," she squeaks, most of the syllables hitting most of the right notes.

I flinch. I swallow my smile.

"My only sunshine," she goes on. I shake it off. I try joining her.

"You make me hap-py," we continue, "when skies are gray." I can feel myself warming to Isuzu's secret safety song. Warming, or something like that. There's something inside me that's getting bigger, spreading.

"You'll never know, dear, how much I love you," we go on together, right up until I almost can't. The something bigger inside me is choking me. It's the next line, coming up like a brick wall. My voice, already croaking, cracks a little more.

"Please don't take," I sing around the cracks in my voice, my life, my *world* ever since . . .

I stop. Isuzu stops, too. We go back. I start again, without her.

"Please don't take . . . my sun . . . shine . . . a . . . way."

Isuzu's looking at me funny. The smile's gone, replaced by something like worry. I look down and she's holding out a wad of tissue—the most worried-over, overused wad of tissue I've ever seen in my life. It's practically just a handful of tatters, held together by little more than will. She seems to be offering them to me, though for what reason, I have no idea. When I don't accept them, she goes up on tiptoes again, stretches the hand holding the tissue scraps over her head, and goes right for my face. I catch her wrist in my hand; a thumb-and-index-finger "okay" is all it takes to encircle the whole thing.

"What is it?" I ask.

"You're crying," Isuzu says.

"I *am* not."

"Are too."

And then a drop hits the floor.

Plish!

I touch my face and it's wet. I pull my fingers away, and they're pink. Jesus Christ. I *am* crying. And over a stupid song about somebody taking my . . .

Well, you know what the stupid song's about. And they're coming out bloody, by the way. My tears. Of course.

Jesus H. Christ . . .

Or maybe I should make that "Jesus wept."

Because he did, in Gethsemane—that's what the nuns told us—and it was blood that time, too. Jesus wept blood because he could see the future. All the atrocities of history. Back when I was just a kid, what this meant was the tortured martyrs and the various wars, up to and including the "world" one. Not World War I, per se; they hadn't numbered them yet. No, Jesus wept blood because of the kaiser and Lincoln's assassination and the Reformation. The Crusades and the Spanish Inquisition weren't mentioned by the nuns, and Hitler and Hiroshima were still waiting in the wings. Needless to say, there also was no mention of vampires, benevolent or otherwise, or of little girls living in dirt holes, or coffeemakers rewired to warm up factory-grown blood. And yet, even without all that, in grade school when I was a kid, we nodded our heads. Understood. Agreed that history counting backward from where we sat was enough to make God's son weep blood.

Funny how we keep moving the line on what that sort of thing takes.

Funny how, nowadays, all it takes is some sucker like me, and some stupid, sentimental song. But we've already gone over that. No use crying over spilled blood.

Not anymore.

-6-

BAD LUGOSI

I try.

Note that word choice: "Try." Not "succeed."

I try to kill Isuzu. I really do. Honest. After that whole weepy-weepy number over that stupid song, the time feels right, if not for a meal, well, at least for getting rid of the one witness to my . . . *softer side*. It's her feeling sorry for me, for my tears—that's what does it. That's the trigger. That's the last straw blown through the last two-by-four.

That's it!

That's your death warrant, you little shit factory!

Perhaps, as a line, that would have come off better spoken. Out loud. Out loud, and not just thought to myself, inside my frequently overcrowded head. You need something like that, I think, in retrospect. Something bad-ass. Something to sell the visuals. Lacking a sinister sound track to reinforce the emotional expectations of the scene to come, all you've really got to anchor things is the dialogue and the tone in which it's delivered. Without the dialogue—without the spooky music or the kick-ass, badass line—all you're left with is this:

Me, poised like a vampire going in for the slow-motion kill, fangs exposed, mouth wider than wide, my lower jaw unhinging, my hands turned to claws, my fingers shocked all the way open—every tendon stitching every digit to the rest of me, tight, tight, tight—my fingers doing their crawling-tarantula impersonation, creepier than creepy. In other words, what you've got is *me*, doing bad Lugosi, with the sound turned down.

I vant to suck your blood . . .

Yeah, I leave that little gem unspoken, too. Which is probably the only good call I've made so far. Not that it does any good. Isuzu reacts in exactly the way my overly earnest attempt to terrify deserves:

She giggles.

Tee-hee. It's the loosest and loudest one so far.

"Oh, Marty." She laughs, pushing me back with her little hand. "Quit teasing."

And just like that, a six-year-old mortal has successfully ripped my vampire balls off and handed them to me. Nice try, guy. Too bad, so sad. Better luck next time.

"I'm *not* teasing," I insist, and even as I do, I know it's a lost cause. Anytime you have to explain that you're not teasing . . . well, you might as well hang up that shovel, gravedigger, 'cause the hole's deep enough. Going deeper's only gonna get you closer to hell.

And oh, I have gone to this hell before . . .

You know that point in a relationship where you just *know* you've screwed up and you're never going to get laid? That point where you've played the nice guy for just a bit too long, and the would-be love of your life becomes convinced that you're too nice to take to bed? She doesn't want to "ruin the friendship," blah, blah, blah.

Yeah, that's the hell I'm talking about. Relationship hell. Dating hell. And I've been there more times than I can count, which is why Count Marty remains a bachelor well into his—what?—hundreds. It's why Marty the Predator sucks when it comes to playing Marty the Dater, and why Marty the Benevolent Vampire prowled strip clubs before the flip, a habit he hasn't quite been able to shake.

And now it seems that Marty the Predator can't even pull off Marty the Predator anymore.

Not judging from Isuzu. Not judging from that tee-hee laugh of hers, which has been loosening progressively, going from flat to rounder and rounder the longer she's around me. Without meaning to, I seem to have lulled her into a completely accurate sense of security.

Shit . . .

I've played the protector for too long, and she just doesn't believe in my fangs anymore. I'm a puppy now; I'm a kitten. I'm a pet and a playmate with pointy teeth that don't mean her any harm. They're just-for-show fangs, that's what they are.

Shit . . .

And the kicker is:

A very big part of me doesn't mind.

If I'm being honest with myself, a very big part of me is relieved. It concurs in her casual dismissal of me, and the threat I represent.

When Isuzu placed her little hand to my chest and pushed back at my presumed teasing, I could have grabbed her wrist and snapped it like a twig. That would have turned her head around on the whole "just teasing" thing. That would have cracked a little sense into her. I could have sipped at the blood spurting from the ripped skin of her compound fracture, could have run my tongue along the jagged bone sticking out until it glistened white. I could have done this while she screamed and thrashed about, and by the time my hungry neighbors broke down the door, I'd be done. I could have tossed her limp body aside like a spent bottle of beer sent shattering against a curb.

I could have done all that. And my apartment could have gone back to being as quiet as it's always been. The floorboards that always squeak between the living room and bedroom could go back to making their predictable, solitary noise. And me, I could go back to challenging this evening and the next and the next to show me something worth living for.

Go like this," I say, pushing my nostrils up like a pig's snout, and Isuzu does.

"Go like this," I say, making a snorting noise, and she does that, too.

"Say, 'Th-th-th-that's all, folks.' "

"Th-th-th-that's all, folks."

I laugh and she laughs. I scramble her hair and she scrambles mine.

And I'm getting that feeling again—that feeling that forever isn't that long, after all. Not with a kid around to show you how to spend it. With a kid around, forever doesn't seem so scary anymore.

And as far as delaying gratification goes, well, that works only when the thing that gratifies is expected to stop. To run out. Expire. If the thing that gratifies has to be rationed, sure—defer, delay, postpone, hold off. But what if the gratification could go on? A little mortal girl has only so much blood to give, and when it's gone, it's gone. But laughing! Jesus Christ, *laughing*. A little girl's giggles—even muted, even held a little bit back, and down, and hushed. Keep a little girl in food and water and the giggles could keep on coming. And your heart could keep on doing that zinging thing it does when she does, and . . .

And that's the good thing about delaying gratification, I guess. Getting a second chance at a second chance. Having the time to find what you didn't even know you were looking for, before it found you.

"Say, 'Isuzu's a stinkbug,' " I say.

"Marty's a stinkbug."

"Close enough."

I'm thinking about my dad again.

It's just a snapshot this time. He's in the basement, at his work-bench, under a cone-shaded lightbulb. A curlicue of smoke ripples up from a half-spent cigarette in the ashtray perched on the edge of the bench. The smoke collects in a hazy halo, circling the light overhead. His tools are spread out on the bench before him: the wishbone of his needle-nose pliers, his Phillips and flat-head screwdrivers, the socket wrench set, a half dozen C-clamps, the tin snips, a clawed hammer, some steel wool, a rat-tail file. There's a yellowed bar of soap, gouged from the threads of all the bolts that have been drawn across it, to make screwing them into wherever they're being screwed easier. There's an open jar of blackened Vaseline for the same purpose, and an oil can for squeaky wheels. And the rest of the bench is taken up with the parts of a bike I'm not supposed to know I'm getting for Christmas.

Bikes for Christmas in Michigan? Talk about gratification delayed.

I'm hiding in the shadows at the top of the stairs, by the way—holding my breath, waiting, watching. My dad takes up a socket wrench, and I can see his wing bones shift under his shirt, followed by the click-click-click of things being tightened. When the clicking stops, my dad reaches over for his cigarette, the long ash breaking off in powdery clumps. He inhales deeply and begins to let it go when my foot shifts and the plank I'm standing on groans. The blue needle of smoke coming from my dad stops. He turns on his work stool, letting out a slow, skeletal squeak, the flashlight already in his hand, already aimed and ready to blow the shadows back behind me. I blink there, spotlit and waiting for him to say something, to scold, to send me off to bed—something of a disciplinary nature. But he just winks instead, and lets the rest of his smoke go. He smiles, presses a sssshhhh finger to his lips, and winks again. And then he just turns back to his workbench and the scattered bits of my future happiness, awaiting assembly.

So, yeah.

I'm thinking about my dad. Again. Still.

And I'm thinking parentally, too, but not in the what-it's-like-to-lose-one way. I'm thinking about parenthood in a way I never have before. I'm thinking about what it might be like to *be* a parent. How do you know what you need to know? How do you know when to yell and when to wink? How do you *become* the sort of dad who knows those sorts of things?

And what would it be like to be one of those dads for a little girl in a world that's not built for little girls anymore?

Isuzu and I are sitting in the living room where I haven't killed her. And it's been maybe a half hour since either one of us has made a peep. I'm sitting on the couch, my arms stretched across the back, my legs stretched out in front of me and crossed at the ankles. I've been watching her for that peepless half hour, while Isuzu's been lying on her stomach on the floor, drawing with some colored pens I've given her. Her ankles are crossed, too, but her legs are crooked up behind her, ticktocking at the pivot of her knees, buttward, floorward, buttward, floorward.

"Isuzu?"

It's been a half hour. Maybe more. And I need to hear her voice.

"Yeah?"

"What's your name mean?"

"Dunno."

"Didn't your mom ever tell you?"

"Yeah. I guess."

"And?"

"And what?"

"What did she say?"

"She said Isuzu was because I was an 'accident waiting to happen,' " Isuzu says.

"And Trooper?"

"Trooper's 'cause I got big feet."

Isuzu hasn't bothered looking up during this entire exchange. And I'm embarrassed to say it, but this thrills me utterly—the fact that she's ignoring me already. Kind of ignoring me, at least. There's a taken-for-granted quality to how she's responding to me that feels . . . parental. It feels like how a kid treats his parents when there are no birthdays coming up.

"That's pretty cool," I say. "My name isn't that cool."

"Marty?"

"No. The last one. Kowalski," I say. "It means 'lunch meat' in Detroit." By which I mean, it was the name brand of a lunch meat made in Hamtramck, a mostly Polish community surrounded on all sides by the city of Detroit. Assuming the same loose standards for translation, I guess Kowalski could also mean *A Streetcar Named Desire* for people *not* from Detroit, but I spare Isuzu that footnote.

"What's lunch meat?" she asks.

"It's a kind of meat people used to eat for lunch," I say. "Before," I add.

"Before vampires ate 'em?"

I decide to let it slide.

"Yeah, kinda," I say, before changing the subject back to lunch meat. "There were all kinds, back then. Ham. Bologna. Salami, which I used to call 'spot meat' when I was your age."

Pretty slick, eh? How I just slid that little equalizer in there. Sure, I used to be a kid. I was even your age once, kiddo. We're practically the same person, practically.

"There was kielbasa, too," I go on, "which is Polish, like me, and hot dogs, and . . ."

"Mom used to make dog," Isuzu observes casually. "And squirrel, rabbit, water fish and can fish, duck, a possum once, SpaghettiOs, Snickers, blueberries, dandy-lion salad, yucky beetles, her special chicken à la can opener—that tastes like snake—and . . ."

And I guess that makes two of us in the slick department. Me, trying to remind her how much we have in common underneath the superficial differences of fangs, cold-bloodedness, and my hundred extra years, while she casually reminds me of what people like me have driven people like her and her mom to do.

Clearly, it's time to change subjects. Again.

"What do you think of this place?" I ask. It's a cheap ploy for a little positive affirmation on my part. My apartment isn't a palace by any stretch of the imagination, but I'm pretty sure it beats living in a hole in the ground.

"I dunno."

"Well, do you like it?" I prod.

"It's okay, I guess," she says, her knees still opening and closing, like a door hinge.

"Just okay?" I ask, my delight at being taken for granted waning steadily.

"It don't smell like worms."

Well, call me crazy, but that's something. And I'm pretty sure I can continue to have my apartment not smell like worms for the foreseeable future. Yep. This parenthood thing's going to work out just fine.

"That's why I decided to live here," I say. "The ad stipulated, 'No worm smell,' and I said, 'Where do I sign?'"

I wait for the giggle I've developed a fondness for. But none comes. No. All of a sudden, she's become like a drug dealer with these things. The first few were free, but now that I need them . . .

No giggles. No tee-hee, either. Instead, what I get is:

"You talk funny."

And all of a sudden my heart feels like a fish in a barrel, the water *ping*ing up around it, calamity just a matter of time, and marksmanship.

I used to worry about the way I talked all the time. This was back before, when I was hanging out at places that matched my face age (twenty-one) instead of my mind age (eighty-something). I was self-conscious about how age-apparent my word choices were to the mortals I was trying to survive among, and seduce. I didn't want to sound like some fifties sitcom kid, spouting dialogue written by adults trying too hard to sound like kids. And so I listened to college radio; I shopped where the pierced and tattooed shopped. I eavesdropped on the chatter coming out of night classes, and followed it into bars where people got into shouting matches about Nietzsche and Tori Amos. Bars where I had to constantly translate my first thoughts into second and thirds: "black" or "African American," not "colored," and *really not* the other one; "fridge" or "refrigerator," not "icebox"; "PC," not "horseshit" or "Give me a fucking break."

But I thought I was past all that. Apparently not.

"What do you mean, 'funny'?" I ask, realizing too late how close being taken for granted is to being made fun of.

"I dunno," she says, casually checking the chambers of her twenty-two, taking a bead on the barrel of my chest, the guppy of my heart.

"Well that sheds a ton of light on the subject," I snap. "I'm clear as tapioca now."

She cocks. Fires.

"Yeah," Isuzu says. "Like that."

Okay, so maybe I *do* talk funny. But that doesn't mean she has to *say* it. Show a little diplomacy. A little *gratitude* for my deigning not to kill her. Ah, but she's already seen through me and my mushy feelings.

Fucking sunshine . . .

Fucking song.

Not that I say any of this out loud. It's already been proven that out-loud words and I can't be trusted around my little judge and jury. So, no. All I say is, "Oh."

Just "Oh," while the guppy of my heart floats on its back, waiting for the next round.

I screw up about fifty-seven more times before it's time for Isuzu to say good night for the night. We've set up her air mattress in the spare bedroom that I've been using as a junk room. The latest argument is about the practicality of having a separate thing called "a pillow." When I hand her one, she looks at it strangely and begins turning it in her hands, until the pillow slips from its case. She looks at the empty sheath in her hands, then at the lump on the floor, and then up at me. The expression on her face tells me that she doesn't get this joke either.

"It's a pillow," I explain. "It's for resting your head on when you sleep."

But Isuzu has already recovered the pillow and is inspecting the seams, looking for a way inside. She finds the zipper and opens it, only to find wads of useless cotton batting. She gives me the sort of look I'd expect if I'd given her a box of dog shit for Christmas. And as far as resting her head goes, that's what Mom's clothes are for. You just roll them into a ball and dream about how much your mommy loves you. Everyone knows that. Why don't *I* know this?

"Only hoboes sleep on their clothes," I say, falling back into that funny way I talk. "I mean 'bums.' No, wait. That's not right, either." Pause. "Only *the homeless* sleep like that."

My little Bambi blinks once. She doesn't say "duh," though a "duh" is surely justified under the circumstances.

"It's more hygienic," I try again, and then consider the likelihood of her knowing the word "hygiene." Clearly, this talking-funny business is something I'm going to have to work on. "I mean 'clean,' " I say. "A nice fresh pillow's cleaner than a bunch of sweaty ol' . . ."

"It's *soft*," Isuzu announces out of the blue. And just like that, she begins hugging the once-dismissed pillow with a sincerity that makes me jealous. Of both it and her.

"Yeah, that's another reason," I say. "And it doesn't smell like worms, either."

This makes her smile. Again. And finally. And thank God.

I say good night, rushing to end our first full evening together on that smile. But before I can switch off the light, Isuzu says:

"Tell me a story."

I freeze. My brain fills up with four-letter words and exclamation points. My stuck smile is the only thing holding them back.

It's not that I don't have stories. I'm a vampire who's helped change the course of human history! I've got *plenty* of stories. It's just that I don't think a six-year-old kid should be hearing about vamped strippers or ripping the heads off Nazis—even a six-year-old who's eaten dog and lived in a hole in the ground.

"Um," I say, and Isuzu hugs her new pillow in front of her, settling in to full story-listening mode.

"Once upon a time," I begin. That's the easy part. They all start that way. Now what?

"There was a beautiful girl," I try—and Isuzu perks up—"who . . ."

And here's where my head hits the wall. Once upon a time there was a beautiful girl who *what*? Wore a little red riding hood and found her grandmother eaten by a wolf? Ate too much gingerbread siding and ended up in an oven? Pissed off a troll? Ran afoul of a wicked witch? Ate the poisoned this, drank the drugged that? Found the magic shoes that made her legs fall off? Turned insomnia into a sign of royalty? Grew her hair as thick as rope as a means of escape? Only to save the day—at last!—by burning up the witch, cutting open the wolf, handing the giant over to gravity . . .

Isuzu squeezes the pillow tighter—the one that doesn't smell like worms but doesn't smell like her mother, either. She waits. Blinks like Bambi, or a cat, smiling.

"On second thought," I say, beginning again. "Do you know what a cherry pit is?"

-7-

WINDOW-SHOPPING

I embellished the Pit Story for Isuzu's sake. Her face made it obvious that a little dramatic license was called for, lest my selection of bedtime story confirm my status as weirdo. I suppose she *is* a little too young. And I suppose a lot of what I liked about that story was knowing that it really happened, and that it happened to my dad, who was sitting right there. I loved that story because I loved watching his face go red while his brother told it, loved the play between him and my uncle, and how they seemed to become kids again. The poking. The teasing. The laughing! The great, booming laughter that always came as part of the overall package.

And so, for Isuzu's sake, the cherry pits turned out to be *magical.* By swallowing them, the prince was able to fly to where the princess was, and where she *wasn't* being terrorized by an evil step-anything. No, nor held captive by a wicked whatever, or threatened by anything with fangs and a taste for the pea-bruisable flesh of princesses. She was just bored, our princess. And yes, of course, she was beautiful and he was handsome. You kidding? He was the handsomest pit-swallowing flying prince you ever saw.

Please note that nothing in my modest revision of the actual facts involves the act of breaking and entering. The flying prince took nothing away, other than the princess's boredom. No castle windows were broken. No alarms were tripped. The castle's TV and stereo were left untouched. All the prince did was tell knock-knock jokes, swallow pits, and fly. At the time the crime was committed, the prince was sound asleep, along with everybody else in the kingdom.

Except . . .

Perhaps I should back up a bit.

I wake up. This is the second evening I've woken up to find I haven't been killed in my sleep. It's the second full evening I'll spend with Isuzu, returning the favor. At least that's the plan at the moment—the me-not-killing-her part. But if the last forty-eight hours have proven anything, it's that plans are made to be broken.

Not that I *plan* on breaking the not-killing-her plan. I just like to keep my options open. I'm over a hundred years old and still a bachelor. If that's not about keeping your options open, I don't know what is.

But going back to where I was going back. This is the sunset immediately following the flying prince story. And the night breaks with the sound of shouting. As a general matter, my neighbors are not particularly noisy. Nosy, yes. They'll pull back a curtain in a heartbeat, but unless someone decides to set off a bomb or flush a toilet, they keep as quiet as the thinness of our shared walls demands.

But not this sunset.

This sunset begins with my neighbors loudly demanding to know Who the fuck, What the fuck, and Where the fuck, followed by louder requests for God to damn "it" and/or "them." These shouts are coming from the hallway a few floors down. They echo up the stairwell, booming through the ventilation system into my bedroom. Behind them, I can hear the whimpering of home security systems dying, their batteries coasting on fumes after running all day long.

Isuzu's done something.

I don't know if it's fair of me to jump to this conclusion, but jump I do.

Isuzu's done something and she's in trouble and it's already too late for safety songs about sunshine. She's dead. She's dead, or too badly bled to bring back. And if she's not . . .

Well, that's not saying she *won't* wish she was, once I get my hands on her.

Swinging out of bed, I bolt for the door, only to feel my arm pulled back as I walk my head into the wall, thanks to the handcuffs I clicked on last night, just in case. Just a bone to keep my paranoia happy. A modest concession to the possibility that I'm not the only one selling false security around here.

Just a really good bang, right to my head, and right between the eyes.

Shit!

I scramble for the key, unlatch myself, and step into a living room, where the elves who don't sleep when I do have been very busy. Stuff. Everywhere I look, I see my stuff and other people's stuff, stashed, and stacked, and squirreled away for a year's worth of rainy days. Where once I had one, I now seem to have *two* notebook computers. Ditto, for flat-panel TVs. Plasma makers? Yeah, there are three now. And stacks and stacks of new CDs, DVDs, and books. There are at least a *half dozen* lamps from a half dozen different decors, none of them quite matching the one I've chosen. And cans! The stashes of several dogs and cats and at least one spider monkey have been stacked in pyramids in my kitchen, on my coffee table, on the cushions of my sofa and love seat. There are boxes of laundry detergent, too, and bars of soap, some new, some open, some still slimy from the showers they were taken from.

And mortal girls?

It seems I still have only the one. And she's standing right there in the middle of all this loot. She smiles when she sees me and stuffs her hand deeper into the box of Count Chocula. She blinks—a happy little cat burglar, with a full mouth.

"Isuzu?" I say, pulling my bathrobe more tightly around myself. "Where did all this come from?"

She's still munching, so she points. Down.

"Downstairs?" I say. "All this came from downstairs?"

She nods. Chews. Reaches for another stale handful.

"What *is* this?" I say, actually shaking both hands in a beseeching gesture I've never used with anyone my own height.

Isuzu swallows. "Shopping," she says.

" 'Shopping,' " I repeat.

"Window-shopping," she adds.

And all of a sudden, I can see it. *Them.* Isuzu and her mom going shopping, holding their own little Daylight Madness sale. Fagen and the Artful Dodger, that's how I see them, ransacking vampire homes and grocery stores with the help of sunlight, and bricks. Not that they're not entitled. But . . .

"Isuzu," I say, struggling hard to maintain my calm. "I have to *live* with these people."

"They're not people," Isuzu says, and I can just imagine the motherly lectures that must have started that way. "They're vampires."

"Like *me*?" I point out.

And my Artful Dodger just shrugs. It's a yeah-sure-whatever shrug. The kind of shrug that says it's a mortal thing, and I don't count.

Maybe the handcuffs were a good idea, after all.

I continue to not-kill Isuzu.

This is after I've locked her in the bathroom. And after I've gone downstairs to put in a little face time with my first-floor neighbors, to look shocked and sympathetic regarding their shattered windows and vandalized apartments.

"How is this possible?"

That's pretty much what they all want to know. And I shake my head with disbelief, but don't offer any answers. I've seen enough cop show reruns to know that once you start offering theories, even a blind man can see you're deflecting. So, no, I just look at the jagged holes in their plate glass windows and mutter a "Fuck," with which pretty much everyone concurs.

I also case the various crime scenes, casually, reassuring myself that Isuzu hasn't left any obvious clues behind, and especially not anything that would tie any of this to me. And there's nothing, except for the timing, of course, which screams "mortal." Fortunately, that's pretty much as good as screaming "Sasquatch," nowadays. The investigation will focus on trying to figure out how whoever did this made it *look* like a mortal did it.

But surely Isuzu and her mom aren't unique. Surely other mortals have escaped from these "farms" that everyone knows about but no one mentions.

No.

The reason farms are allowed what license they're allowed is partly the wealth of their well connected clientele, but also absolutely rigid product control. Biological weapons labs weren't half the sticklers for containment that the farms are. Nobody leaves the farm with their little mortal morsels. No. Everything's done on a strictly in-call basis. You go to them. You use their rooms, or their hunting preserve. Because the last thing anyone needs is some band of feral mortals running around out there, living in holes at night, ransacking our homes by day, and figuring out the where and when of their getting even with the rest of us. No more vampire hunters. We've been there, done that. Won. And the last thing any of us needs is to lose our hard-won peace.

So, no. I just tsk-tsk, shake my head, and leave my neighbors to speculate about how Sasquatch made off with all their stuff. Back at my apartment, I resume not-killing Isuzu, and start laying out a few extra dos and don'ts of non-hole living.

In the end, I treat Isuzu's haul like a dead bird.

With the exception of the extra pet food, which *will* come in handy, the rest is just stuff I don't need or want, but which has been presented to me, nevertheless, as a bizarre token of affection. Like a cat bringing its owner something dead. Sure, I'd just as soon she didn't, but now that she has, I have to admit that this is a good sign. She's thanking me. She's bringing me gifts. She's treating me like an accomplice—just like her mom.

Unfortunately, my switch in perspective doesn't come until I've already started speculating out loud about what I might do to punish her. Isuzu stands her ground, though—a real trouper—but she can't stop her lip from trembling. She sucks it in, tries to hold it with her blunt little teeth, but it's no use. And once the trembling starts . . .

Well, everybody knows that the lip muscles are wired directly to the tear ducts. And so her eyes start getting shiny, start brimming, run over by a single tear's worth, which snails down her cheek to catch a corner of the trembling lip that started it all. And tears are like oil to the tremble muscles, which tremble more, which squeeze out more tears, more trembles, more tears, more . . .

And there I am, getting it all wrong.

I'm using a hushed, keep-it-within-these-walls kind of shouting that can be more awful than the louder kind, especially when you're on the receiving end. And snap! I *realize* I'm getting it all wrong. I *understand* that this—all of this—*isn't* about Isuzu's being a vampire-hating mortal. It's not about her being a postinfantile delinquent, either. It's not even a veiled attempt to get me beaten up by my neighbors and possibly arrested. No. This is about my sunshine, my only sunshine trying to let me know, dear, how much she loves me.

I think.

I hope.

Maybe "loves" is too strong. "Likes," maybe. But definitely *not* "hates."

That's what all this is about. It's about how much Isuzu *doesn't* utterly hate my guts. And *that*—you've got to admit—*that* is definitely *something*.

So I stop yelling. And I start scrambling for a quick route into unscolding her. If this was before the flip, we'd be on our way to the toy store in a guilty heartbeat. If this was before, we'd go from the toy store to the ice-cream shop, to the candy store, and whatever fast food restaurant served the nastiest, greasiest crap she was forbidden to have under any other circumstances. That's what I'd do, if this was before. But it's not. This is the new world, not the old one, and this one isn't built for assuaging the guilt of bad parents, foster, step-, or otherwise.

It's as I'm thanking God that my own parents aren't around to see how badly I'm messing this up that it occurs to me that Isuzu's mom couldn't have been perfect. Mistakes must have been made, and she must have had a way of dealing with them. I remember the hole and its Shrine to Chocolate, and wonder how many Snickers something like this would have cost.

I decide to ask her price. After apologizing, of course.

"Isuzu," I say, letting my voice go back to its normal pitch and volume.

She flinches anyway. Lets go of a few more drops of lip muscle oil.

"I'm sorry," I say. "I . . ." Fucked? Screwed? *Messed!* ". . . messed up."

Isuzu sucks in a sniffle. She's listening. Waiting.

"I didn't get it," I say. "I thought you were being bad. But I know you were trying to be nice, and I'm sorry I yelled. I'm really, *really* sorry."

Isuzu looks at her shoes, but before she does, I catch a little bit of a smile.

And for a split second, I feel conned. I feel reverse-psychologized. But I swallow it down and move on. "Did your mom ever not get it?" I ask.

Isuzu looks back up.

"Did she ever mess up and yell when she shouldn't?"

And like a last-minute reprieve from the governor, Isuzu rolls those two-toned eyes of hers, and I want to hug her and kiss her and thank her and swear I'll never do it again. Just that hint of a smile and the eye roll, and I know that Mommy Dearest was at least partly the same kind of fuckup I am.

"So I'm not the only one?" I say, and Isuzu does something in the laugh department she hasn't done outside of the one pig imperson-ation I coaxed from her—she snorts. Just once. The nasal equiva-lent of an eye roll. An olfactory "Are you kidding?"

"I'll take that as a yes," I say, and she snorts again. And then I ask her what her mom did to make up for messing up. I hold my breath against the near certainty of chocolate. *Real* chocolate, and not this Count Chocula crap. And if chocolate's the answer, then it's going to be Isuzu's turn to delay gratification. Because even with eBay and FedEx, chocolate's a few days from here.

But Isuzu doesn't say "chocolate." She doesn't snicker "Snickers."

Instead, she pulls a deck of cards out from that improbable bounty she's bestowed upon me. That's when I notice the other packs, still boxed, lying here and there, shuffled among a stack of books or CDs, or all by themselves. They're everywhere. As a separate category of stolen things, packs of playing cards are second only to food. Funny I hadn't noticed that in my original inventory.

She hands me the deck with just one word, or maybe two. Just saying it makes her smile.

"Slap," Isuzu says, cranking that smile up to its full wattage, "jack."

Before, when there were still children, concerned parents used to complain about how violent video games were corrupting them. Being the occasional practitioner of for-real violence, I was always amused by these protests. After all, the same people blaming video games for Columbine would be shocked if you pointed out that nobody ever got their arm broken playing Doom, unlike, say, football. And don't you dare suggest that watching the latest war for oil on CNN is surely more damaging than joysticking a couple of cartoons to death.

I mention this to put my little Trooper's selection of parental penance into context. From the hundreds of card games out there, Isuzu's picked the one that actually requires physical violence during regulation play. Slapjack. If I had to pick a game that could potentially trump bad parenting as an explanation for something like Columbine, I think I'd pick slapjack. Unlike Doom or Mortal Kombat, slapjack isn't slapjack if the players don't hurt each other.

For those unfamiliar with the game, it works like this: Two players split the deck and take turns throwing down one card at a time, until someone throws down a jack. After that, it's a race to see who can slap the card first. Whoever does captures all the cards underneath, and also gets to slap the wrist of his or her opponent. The winner is the one with the most cards (and the fewest rope burns) after you've run out of jacks. It's a competition of reaction times and pain thresholds, and not a very fair game for an adult to play against a child. It's especially not fair when the adult is a vampire and the child's not. Our reaction times are just too unequal—the forever-stacked deck of predator versus prey. A vampire who chooses to can be like lightning, while his victim is the mere afterthought of thunder. In the old days, before I was benevolent, I could snap my dinner's neck before it even saw me coming.

In other words, if I want to, I can kick Isuzu's little ass.

But that's not the point. I'm sure Isuzu's mom could have beat her, too. And I'm betting she never did. Instead, slapjack was the game she played to lose, whenever she messed up and needed to make up, like Isuzu and me now. It's an excuse to let the child spank the parent.

And my little ray of sunshine is *beaming* at the prospect.

So I open the deck, get rid of the jokers, split it, shuffle the halves back together, and then do it again. I hand the twice-shuffled deck to Isuzu, who spreads them out on the floor, smushes them around, and then scoops them back together. Clearly, she takes this business seriously. And trust—always a shaky proposition at best—is a luxury she can't afford. Especially considering my recent behavior. Especially considering I'm playing this game as a kind of punishment for my recent untrustworthy behavior.

So Isuzu deals, we collect our piles, and begin tossing down cards. As luck would have it, I throw down the first jack. It seems to lie there for an eternity before Isuzu notices and then shoots her slow-motion hand to cover it. *Slap!* She giggles, delighted with herself, and the prospect of giving yours truly what for.

And so I roll up my bathrobe sleeve and surrender my wrist. Isuzu folds in all the fingers of her right hand, except the first two. She raises her hand as high as she can, even arching a little bit backward to squeeze out a few more foot-pounds of pain. She holds it there for a second, letting me anticipate. Letting me sweat. And then, like the arm of a just-sprung catapult, she throws everything she's got forward, teasing out two quick red stripes on my white, white skin.

I look just like a candy cane, I think, and Isuzu reads my mind.

"You look like a candy cane," she says.

And I think: Candy canes, lollipops, bad parents, and old vampires—we're all suckers when it comes to kids.

-8-

THE LUCKIEST VAMPIRE ON EARTH

I found Isuzu on a Friday evening after work. We passed each other's trust tests, did our cat-smiling and our rule setting on Saturday. And then came today—Sunday—the day of surprises and new rules and slapjack. I've tucked her into bed a few hours before sunrise, and afterward, it occurs to me that Isuzu does more to keep herself alive and unkilled asleep than awake. Awake has proven dicey—lots of mines, eggshells, opportunities for yours truly to screw up. But asleep, the *idea* of her surfaces and fills my heart with the missing of it. Of her. Asleep, during these few hours before sunrise, while I'm still awake, her absence creates a dead space in my life—a warning. A reminder. With Isuzu asleep, snoring her snores behind that closed door, my apartment goes back to the too-quiet I never recognized before—before it was gone, that is, and only after it returns.

And all that's left in this dead space at the end of our weekend is this: me, staring down the barrel of Monday, and the reality of what I've elected to do. Over the weekend, I seem to have become a father. Or at least a foster father, and of a mortal, to boot. Just like that—*snap!*—I'm a dad. I'm the dad of a kid everyone I know—and most of the people I *don't* know—would love to kill. I'm a dad with no mom to speak of— not even one in the wings—and even if there *was* one, how could I trust her?

And then there's my day job. Or *night* job, really. Vampires don't have day jobs; we're all moonlighting in one way or another. But come Monday evening—*tomorrow*—I've got a job I have to go back to. To bring home the pet food. To earn some blood money. A job where day care is not part of the benefits package. A job where I can't just call in sick.

So the question naturally arises:

How?

How am I going to do this thing I've decided to do? How am I going to raise a child and hold down a job and not screw up both beyond recognition?

You know that *Twilight Zone* episode, the one called "To Serve Man," where the title refers to an alien cookbook? In a lot of ways, we're living that joke. This occurs to me as I'm surfing the Web, looking for "historical" information on how to prepare a child for life. And all I can find is advice about how to prepare a child for a meal in which they're the main course.

It's the farms again, hawking their wares on password-protected Web sites demanding credit card numbers and other vital stats before they'll open their cyber doors. They have digital photos of their "product line"—hundreds of little Isuzus with chocolate-smeared faces and headlight eyes. Under the photos, the current bid. I sit and watch as the numbers click up. Some of the faces have yellow "Sold" signs X-ing them out. I imagine my Isuzu among them.

I get angry.

I turn off the computer.

I go to the window and pull the drapes aside. I look at the apartments across the way, the yellow rectangles of their windows. There are silhouettes in some, actual people in others, and still others are just empty boxes of low-wattage light.

I've looked at this same view a thousand times before. It's never meant much of anything to me. Ground clutter. Just some stuff in the way of my view of the horizon, that point where night and day breaks, our lowest common denominator. But I've never looked at those windows like this before. I've never looked at my neighbors with such a powerful desire for a machine gun of some sort. Something to riddle and strafe, rapidly and with too many bullets to ignore. Something to help me draw an X through those yellow boxes across the way.

"What made him do it?" the talking heads would ask afterward. Heavy metal? Video games?

Nope.

Slapjack made me do it. Slapjack and a little girl who's never going to wear a "Sold" sign. Not if I can help it.

I have to keep reminding myself that Isuzu escaped. She and her mom, both. And I start wondering yet again how she did it—how Isuzu's mom raised her on her own, at least up until the point where I found her. How will my parenting skills compare? I know I can lose at slapjack as well as she, and my apartment definitely beats living in a hole, but . . .

But maybe not.

"What do you think of this place?" "It don't smell like worms."

Hardly a ringing endorsement, and nowhere near the enthusiasm I expected.

So maybe Isuzu's living arrangements were broader than the root cellar she called home when I found her. I'm guessing the hole is what they did *at night*, when they had to hide. It was just for sleepovers. Strictly no-frills. But during the day, they could hang out anywhere they could get into with a brick.

So what was it like—an average day for Isuzu and her mom? It's not likely the mom had a job to go to. Raising Isuzu was probably all she had to do, all day long. She could devote time to it. Make it a specialty. Earn best-mom-in-the-world points for no other reason than the fact that she was always around, and not off working some pointless job to earn money to buy stuff that's just as easily stolen, what with the whole world being asleep when you're not.

I'm guessing window-shopping played a big part of most days. Let's say they start rising and shining at about eight o'clock, maybe nine, find a rock, steal breakfast from the nearest grocery store, grab some newspapers on the way out, but not for reading. Instead, they head to the nearest park, find the dog path, let their shit blend in with all the dog shit already there. Look for another rock so they can break into somebody's place to wash up, maybe do laundry, maybe steal some stuff for the hole that doesn't involve electricity. Books, say, or candles, or whatever clothing's been left lying out that fits.

I don't see them rifling through closets. Or at least not any that involve going into the owner's bedroom to get to. Why tempt fate? Why tempt your own highly understandable but risky thirst for revenge? Plus maybe—while you're not looking—maybe Isuzu decides this crypt of a bedroom is just too gloomy for words. And so maybe she throws open the sunproof drapes, and maybe a shaft of light pours in. And maybe this shaft of sunlight finds the world's unluckiest vampire, just lying there on the bed, out like a light. And as quick as you can scream "Fire!" that long overdue corpse just goes up—ignites, combusts, immolates itself right there, burning itself down through the padding and the mattress to the box springs, which glow cherry red as other things start catching fire. And it's all you can do to get you and your kid out of there—unscorched, unsinged, and all in one piece.

Plus, God only knows what kind of kinky vampire sex stuff you might find in some stranger's bedroom, so . . . no. No need to be meddling in any vampire bedrooms. Which probably explains why Isuzu has never seen a pillow before, but recognized TV even though there wasn't so much as a Sony Watchman back at the hole. But why should there be? The hole's no place to be making unnecessary noise. The hole's all about talking in whispers, reading by candlelight, breathing in that rich earthy *worm* smell. That, and sleeping on each other's old clothes, the better to keep each other company, even in your dreams. The hole's no place for laughing at vampire sitcoms, listening to the vampire nightly news, watching vampire cops bust vampire perps. The hole's all about dust-to-dust, us versus them. It's the place for lying low, and making plans for tomorrow.

Plus, why add batteries to your shoplifting list if you can do all your TV watching during the day? Except . . .

Except there *is* no TV to watch during the day. The broadcast day ends with—*the day*. Which leaves TV as pretty much just a box for playing DVDs and video games, and that's it.

Maybe that explains something else that didn't make sense at the time. After making me cry with that stupid song, Isuzu toddled over to the couch and plopped down in front of the TV. She reached over to the coffee table and snatched up the remote control like a regular pro. But after taking aim and hitting the power button—just as the picture flicked on—she flinched.

"It's not blue," she said.

"What do you mean?"

But she couldn't explain. The lack of a blue screen was just wrong, but it wasn't like it was broken. It was like it was working super good. *This* TV made pictures *without* having to load something first. But that's not how TVs are supposed to work. When you turn them on, the screen's *supposed* to be blue—it was always blue when she did it before, during the day, in some stranger's apartment. You switch it on, get the blue screen, drop in a disc, and stay away from that door until mom gets back. And when mom gets back from doing whatever needed doing without a six-year-old tagging along? That's when they tidy up, and leave maybe one piece of furniture in front of the bedroom door for when the monsters wake up.

Sssshhhh . . .

Tee-hee . . .

Smile like cats.

And after that, after the window-shopping and videos, I imagine a day full of Frisbee in the park, and dress-up tea parties, and silliness. Just hours and hours of silliness in the bright, sheltering sun. I imagine them staring each other down, repeating everything the other one says, getting into tickle fights. I imagine nonpunitive games of slapjack, just for the fun of it. I imagine a pocket full of chocolate, even though they shouldn't, even though they've sworn to save it. But when she smiles like that . . .

"Here you go, you little con artist."

I try imagining how it happened. How they were found out. Did the mom just get tired of always being so careful all the time? Or did she maybe want to treat Isuzu to something special—for a birthday, or as a reward for being good, or as an apology for some maternal failing beyond the cleansing violence of slapjack? What was she trying to do when she slipped up for the last time?

Maybe it was something stupid, like hitting the same place too many times. Using too much electricity when the world was supposed to be asleep. Too many volts being used during the daytime would be a dead giveaway. Not that the cops could do anything about it when it was happening, but they'd get involved, sooner or later.

It starts with the owner complaining about an unusually high electric bill. The utility company checks its records. And there's Isuzu and her mom, translated into kilowatt hours. That's when it becomes a police matter. That's when the police break out the bloodhounds, who have no problem distinguishing the stink of human sweat from the next-to-nothing vampires leave behind. The dogs bellow and yelp, straining at their choke chains, dragging some K-9 squad rookies all the way back to Isuzu and her mom and . . .

I look at my front door.

I didn't hear any barking during the commotion earlier this evening. Or at least nothing I couldn't write off as coming from the pets whose food Isuzu had liberated. And I haven't heard any panting, or yelping, or yipping since everything else quieted down. There have been no heavy paws thumping down my hallway, no big nails clawing at my front door . . .

Yet.

I panic, which feels appropriately parental—but also extremely unhelpful under the circumstances. I need pepper, not panicking. Or pepper spray. I have neither. Ditto, coffee grounds. And rosemary. And thyme. I *do* have a vacuum cleaner. I do have a vacuum cleaner that hasn't been emptied . . .

. . . well, *ever.* I'm a bachelor; cut me some slack. The point is, the vacuum cleaner's got a vacuum cleaner *bag* chock-full of dust and allergens. And it'll have to do.

So I break out the vacuum and pry out the bag. Gray stuff poofs and sprinkles everywhere. I take the bag out into the hallway, trying not to spill any more than necessary. I don't want to leave any evidence in my attempt to hide the evidence.

Which is how I find myself on my knees, outside my front door, carefully sprinkling a meticulous line of highly stirrable dust between the welcome mat and doorway. A long, thin, manicured line, like a line of gray cocaine for any snuffling bloodhounds that might happen by. Something innocuous, something a casual observer wouldn't notice, but which a ground-level snout would Hoover up before exploding in a fit of sneezing. And just like that—the trail, the case, their noses—all would be equally blown.

That's the plan. And that's why I'm kneeling outside my front door. Or why I *was*. But why am I still on my knees? Why can't I get up?

I think the answer goes back to my being raised Catholic. That kind of thing gets in your blood worse than being a vampire. It doesn't take much to make it flare up. Just a little life flashing before your eyes. Just a little panic. Just an overwhelming sense of how much you've got to lose, and how easily you could lose it.

Maybe that explains the little voice inside my head, the one suggesting something it hasn't suggested in a long, long time:

Pray.

With an *a*, not an *e*.

Pray for forgiveness. And help. And like you mean it.

A mortal kid and a vampire dad? Are you kidding?

Pray like *both* your lives depend on it.

Webcams—this is what I'm thinking.

Lots and lots of webcams, and rules, and locks . . .

Not that this occurs to me originally. What originally occurs to me is duct tape. Or maybe a harness and tether. Or one of those electric dog collars that zaps 'em if they try to leave the yard. And, truth be told, I haven't ruled out any of these, especially given this evening's little surprise, but . . .

I check the clock on the DVD player. There's still time to go to the computer store and get things set up before sunrise. Not that I want to leave Isuzu in the apartment by herself, but . . .

I grab my phone. The tethered one—the landline. I switch off the ringer, and then call the number with my cell. I tiptoe to where Isuzu's still snoring away, the jack all slapped out of her. I open the door a crack, just enough to slip the receiver through. I attach the headset to the cell, slip it on, and step away from the door, listening to Isuzu snore through the tinny static.

I grab my keys and wallet and step out into the hallway, trying not to disturb my line of bloodhound repellent. It's weird, having her in my ear like this, the sound of her snoring undiminished, even as I put more and more distance between us. It's weird, but reassuring, too.

I get into my car, and Isuzu's still there. Still there, in the store. Still there, coming back.

It's not great, this ad hoc baby monitor. It goes out under bridges. I lose her, panic, get her back, sigh. It's not great, but it will have to do. Just like the webcams, and the warnings, and the locks.

Just like yours truly, in the parent department. When all is said and done, I'll just have to do.

My job—the thing I do when I'm not figuring out how to raise a mortal in a revamped world, the thing I do to make money to make the raising possible—my job is . . . well, I write memos. Memos for someone else's signature, someone higher up the bureaucratic ladder, someone too busy to do their own writing, or—I suspect—their own signing. Someone who has no idea who I am, or the role I played in making the world what it is. The Benevolent Vampires were anonymous, and given the dubious nature of our results, we like to keep it that way.

I write reports, too, and rewrite the reports the technical staff have managed to render entirely in Martian. I also do briefings in PowerPoint, write position papers, and have even published the occasional *Federal Register* notice, revising this or that regulation to comport with whatever the political flavor (or favor) of the month happens to be. In short, I sell time-shares on my brain and try not to think about it when I'm off the clock.

The organization I do all this scribbling for is the Bureau of Blood Quality—BBQ, for short. You've probably seen our mascot, the Hemogoblin—our version of Smokey the Bear. The Hemogoblin's mission is "to warn the public regarding a number of blood quality issues." That's what we say, at least. Really, he's pretty much a guardian of the status quo and a capitalist tool, offering aid and comfort to the mega-super-multinational bleederies while demonizing the mom-'n'-pop microbleeds.

"Consider the source," the Hemogoblin advises.

"Stick with names you can trust."

Meaning, of course: Corporations good, independents bad. After all, it's the microbleeds who water down their product line with horse, cow, and pig blood. It's the microbleeds who lace in vampire blood, which acts like a tapeworm on heroin, consuming the consumer and making you buy more and more, trying to quench a suddenly unquenchable thirst. It's the microbleeds who doctor expiration dates, skimp on quality control, let stock thaw and refreeze over and over again, and still have the balls to call it "vein fresh," "just tapped." "If it were any fresher, the bottle would have a pulse."

Yep, that's exactly who it is—the little guys. The guys who have absolutely nothing to back them up, except their reputation among satisfied customers and good word of mouth. It's the microbleeds cutting corners with impunity, knowing the Hemogoblin's just itching to lose all that corporate tax revenue by shutting down, say, the blood-bottling equivalent of a Coca-Cola.

As the Hemogoblin says, "Do the math, sucker."

And don't bite the hand that feeds you.

I suppose you could say I'm the cynic of the office, though I prefer the term "realistic." I find that cynicism, as an operating principle, makes the evil we do easier. It helps clarify what would otherwise be as inscrutable as Zen koans.

Like: The job of the Recall Division is to *not* initiate recalls.

Like: "Oversight" means closing your eyes, looking the other way, seeing no evil—at least when it comes to the macros.

Ah me. Oh my. Your tax dollars at work.

Do you know what I like about my office? By which I mean, do you know what shocks me for no other reason than the fact that it doesn't seem to shock anybody else? All the corporate logos on pens, pocket protectors, scratch pads, baseball caps, what used to be called "coffee" mugs. The coworker in the cube next to mine, for instance, sips all night long from a mug hawking Sneaky Pete, the Sleepytime tea of bloods, while another glugs from a sports bottle advertising Xtreme Unction, the vampire's Jolt Cola.

"Get some Unction in yer junction if ya wanna function in da . . . Xtreme!"

The last word is pronounced like two: "ex" and "dream."

Adrenaline.

That's why I almost killed Isuzu. And that's why her mom was killed, in all likelihood, by a band of bottle-feds looking for a little taste of old school.

Adrenaline is also the big thing in the blood biz nowadays. That's the thing they add (or withhold) to simulate various long-gone "blood acquisition modalities." Sneaky Pete, for example, includes almost no adrenaline at all. It simulates blood gotten by way of the sneak attack, after the victim's been seduced into acquiescence and mistakes the pressure at his or her throat as an arousing (but not fear-inducing) love bite. In the midadrenal range, there's Head-lights, named after that deer cliché. Headlights simulates the short shock of realizing you're dead just before you are.

And then there's Xtreme Unction and its imitators—Death Rattle, Little Seizure, Chest Cracker. All have roughly *twice* the adrenaline needed to instigate a heart attack in your average mortal. Having tasted the real thing, I can assure you that these last don't simulate anything. They're aimed at the pumped-up imaginations of bottle-feds, dreaming about what hunted blood must have been like. And it's these bottled, romanticized lies that get my adrenaline going, whenever I think about all the damage they've meant for the likes of Isuzu and her mom.

Hell, I almost fell for it myself, even though I know better. Sip at the same lie often enough, and you start to believe it. The bar gets raised, the exaggeration becomes the baseline, and all we can remember—those who think we remember what real blood is like—is that "real" was *always* better than "bottled."

Of course, without those myths, Isuzu would never have been born. And I wouldn't be sitting here in my cube, using my email window to hide my webcam feed, clicking back and forth whenever someone passes. I wouldn't be sitting here, catching glimpses of Isuzu napping, watching TV, offering some of her pet food to some invisible someone.

"Whatcha got there?" my supervisor asks as I click back to my email and try not to look guilty.

"Lab says the sample from that Tucson microbleed's clean as a whistle," I say. Just like all the samples always are. Your tax dollars, et cetera.

"Okay, okay," my supervisor says, nodding before bending to sip from his "Got Blood?" mug. He screws up his face like a clean lab report is some kind of a problem. Which it kind of is—especially when it's for a micro that's started cutting into a macro's share of the market. Macros don't get lab reports. We've already discussed this. The math's been done; the feeding hand left unbitten.

"Okay," he says, deciding it. "Bust 'em on that licensing technicality and have enforcement destroy their inventory." He smiles in that midmanagement way, with his fangs denting his bottom lip.

So much for free and open competition in a market-driven economy.

"Will do," I say, as he returns to his office, clicking his Xtreme Unction giveaway pen—just a nervous habit, or so he claims.

Isuzu stands framed in her little window on my PC. I click Expand and she fills my screen, maxing out the pixels, turning into a pointillist version of herself. A face behind stippled glass. She's mugging in front of the mirror I've hidden a camera behind, pressing her nose into a pig snout just like I showed her, tugging down her lower lids, experimenting with various tortured mouth shapes. Now she's cupping her forehead with her hand, hiding her hair. She squeezes down and makes furrows, followed by a stern setting of the lips. She pulls her brow smooth again, followed by a grin almost maniacally wide.

I glimpse my own reflection, notice my expression matching hers, smile for smile, frown for frown. I check the clock at the bottom of my screen. Two more hours. Two more hours here instead of there. Two more pointless, non-Isuzu hours before I can walk in through that door behind her there, scramble that hair, ask her what she did while I was away, nod, nod, smiling away like the luckiest vampire on earth.

"No watching TV on the company dime," a voice says behind me.

I flinch and turn. It's a coworker with less seniority and a sense of humor that manifests itself in the form of barked orders, as if she actually outranks me.

"I'm on break, Cindy."

"I know. I was just kidding," she says. "Hey, is that a new one?"

At first, I don't know what she's talking about and don't know what to say.

"I'm a Little Bobby Little fan, myself," Cindy says, and then I get it.

KidTV.

On the opposite end of the spectrum from the farms, there's KidTV. After all, vampires are as prone to nostalgia as anyone else, and the thing we're nostalgic about is the thing that's impossible to get back: our childhoods. Unlike before, we can't use kids as an excuse to buy toys and relive our own childhoods. So while the farms raise little Isuzus for private slaughter, the Little Bobby Littles of KidTV are raised like celebrities. Instead of being hunted on some secluded preserve, the KidTV kids play before the cameras in their idealized 1950s bedrooms, their nostalgic cuteness beamed from some undisclosed fortress to sterile vampires all over the world.

"Caught me," I say, trying to put myself between Isuzu and my coworker.

"Hey, she's cute," Cindy says, peeking around behind me. "Looks a little like me when I was that age." Pause—and I already know what's coming. "Have I ever shown you the pictures of me when I was a kid?"

God, what a pathetic bunch we are, reliving our childhoods by watching strangers grow up on TV. Strangers a lot of us would make into fast food, if we knew where the hell they were being kept, if they're even real in the first place, and not some computer-generated fiction or some old videotape being passed off as live. And if it's not KidTV, then it's our own childhood photos, passed around, cooed over, bragged about, displayed on our desks as if we were somehow our own parents.

"Yeah. Yeah, Cindy, you have."

"Oh . . ."

She seems disappointed, and normally I'm not this rude, but I'm still a little shaken over being caught, mooning over my very own personal version of KidTV.

"You were a real cutie," I say, making nice, clicking off the web-cam window.

Cindy unzips a smile in this weird way she has, showing first one fang, then the other. "Thanks," she says.

And then she winks. "P.S. ," she says. "Your secret's safe with me."

At the sound of the word "secret," my heart clenches like a fist. It tries a knock-knock joke on the inside of my rib cage. *How does she know?* it wants to know. *What do we do now?* it demands.

But Cindy continues. "Just don't let the big guy catch you. Break or no break, those Web TV broadcasts really put a strain on the network . . ."

Oh. My heart unclenches. She doesn't know a thing. She just thinks I'm hooked on one of those kid shows. Good. That'll be my cover story if I ever get caught again—and Cindy will back me up, saying she warned me, she did, and I'll agree, and apologize, and swear I'll never do it again.

"Thanks for the warning, Cindy," I say, and she unzips that smile again.

"No prob," she says, before leaning in and whispering, "I got busted for the same thing last year. They gave me the 'resources' talk and a slap on the wrist."

"Good to know," I whisper back, thinking: one hour and forty-five minutes to go.

-9-

KKK DAY

Time passes.

That's something new—or something old that seems new again—noticing the passage of time. It's Isuzu who's reminded me, just by being here. Watching what even a few months' worth of it does to her, the changes it makes, the inexplicable pressures it creates. It's made me impatient with my fellow vampires, the way they chat endlessly in the checkout line, the way they tell stories that zigzag in a hundred different directions, one step forward, five back, picking up subplots and background and stream-of-consciousness non sequiturs, taking forever to get to a point or a punch line and frequently forgetting both along the way. They spend their time like drunken sailors spend their money—plenty more where that came from—oblivious to the fact that some of us may not actually *have* all the time in the world.

It's been over a year since I found Isuzu, and I've started wearing a watch. Not one of the new ones with the preset alarm to let you know when the sun's coming, but one of the old kind, with a second hand and everything. I wear a watch, and I find myself watching it—when I'm not watching Isuzu, on my PC or in person.

I have calendars, too. Plural. One of which is prominently displayed in the kitchen, on the wall where we've started measuring the progress of Isuzu's lengthening bones. She's passed a couple of hatch marks already, and I've already told her that at this rate, by the time she's my age, she'll be banging her head against the moon.

She's already giggled at that, and I've already thanked God.

Glancing at the calendar tonight, I notice something new. Or really, something very old. It's a date, one that Isuzu has circled in stars. It's not her birthday; that was a few months ago. And it's not Christmas, either, which was even further back. But each of those days got this kind of star treatment.

It's a holiday, but one the calendar makers have stopped paying attention to, even as a matter of historical interest. These lost holidays are generally the food ones or the death ones—like Thanksgiving or Easter. Something tells me that these holidays were still celebrated in the Cassidy hole, perhaps as a political statement, perhaps in solidarity with things that die and are eaten. Or maybe they were just an excuse to eat some of that chocolate they stole before escaping.

"Boo!"

It's Isuzu. She's snuck up behind me while I was standing here, counting the days between now and the date she's circled at the end of October.

Turning, I find her standing there, a bedsheet pulled over her head, a fresh pair of eyeholes scissored out.

I snap my fingers.

"Ku Klux Klan Day!" I say. "Of course!"

"Huh?"

"Joke," I say. She stares at me through her eyeholes, not getting Marty's funny way of talking, yet again. Which is fine by me. Which is great. Given the choice of which bit of history to forget—the KKK or Halloween—I'd drop the pointy-headed cross burners in a heartbeat.

"Bad joke," I say, as much to myself as her.

Still:

There are some out there—the vampirically correct—who don't see much of a difference between what the KKK and Halloween represent. Both celebrate intolerance, they'll say. Both embrace stereotypes. Both demonize that which they don't understand. And it's for these reasons as well as the irrelevance of its candy-kids-and-death elements that Halloween has fallen off the calendar.

Well, every calendar except mine, it seems.

I look at Isuzu in her sad little retro costume. "Are you a g-g-g-g-ghost?" I stammer, a hand fluttering to my chest. She nods. A giggle leaks out from under the sheet.

"What have you done with Isuzu?" I ask.

"We drank her blood," Isuzu says, mixing not only the type of undead she is, but also her pronouns.

I should probably worry about that—and I plan to, someday. But for now, what I'm thinking about mainly is:

How?

How are we supposed to celebrate Halloween? How are we supposed to make it special in a world that's pretty much one long, monotonous Halloween after another?

How did her mother manage it? The whole door-to-door trick-or-treating thing is out, obviously. Did they keep it simple? Was it just a sheet and a boo, some stale chocolate, a pat on the head, and a "Happy Halloween, kiddo"? Were decorations involved?

And what about a pumpkin?

I remember pumpkins playing a big part, but who grows pumpkins anymore? It's not like we need them for a pumpkin pie or anything. How am I suppose to get a pumpkin in . . .

I look at the calendar. Two weeks? I can't grow a pumpkin in two weeks.

I look at Isuzu. Halloween is still two weeks away, and she's already starred the date. She's already wearing a costume. It's one of those counting-the-days holidays. And that means Big. That means Expectations.

So, what did they do—Isuzu and her mom—in the two weeks leading up to Halloween? I'd ask, but asking means I don't know, which suggests a failing of parental instinct and a lack of knowledge of things so basic as to call everything else into question.

So I don't ask. I imagine. I fill in the blanks. And what I imagine is this:

Serial B-and-E's, in costume, with some petty vandalism thrown in for good measure. "Trick or treat," I imagine Isuzu's mom saying at their last stop, before jimmying open a lock or bricking her way into someplace fun.

Laser tag, maybe.

We've still got those places. We've actually got more than we used to. Vampires *love* laser tag. It fills the hole left behind when hunting became irrelevant. And I can just imagine them—Isuzu and her mom—firing up the fog machines and black lights, donning the target vests, making sure their laser guns work. I imagine daughter chasing mother, mother chasing daughter, scrambling up ramps, hiding behind plywood walls, their hearts pounding their old-fashioned blood around their expiration-dated bodies. I imagine their stereo giggles echoing everywhere while red wires of light slice through the foggy air.

"Ah, ya got me!"

"You got me, too!"

More giggles. More fun than Isuzu and I have ever . . .

They'd steal candles from the hardware store to wax windows with. They'd cut rolls of paper toweling into halves or thirds and fling long streamers into the monster-clawed branches of unleafed trees. They've got some wild duck eggs they found during the summer and didn't use for breakfast, saving them for this. They're quite ripe now, and smell like shit when they smash their runny asterisks against the oh-so-deserving windows of all those places that *have* windows to be smashed into.

"Take that, you suckers!"

"Yeah, and this, too."

"Good aim, baby girl."

And Isuzu would blush and giggle and dig out another rotten egg from their garbage bag full of provisions.

In the treat department, there'd be a few chocolate bars left, saved for just this occasion. And they'd have some homemade sweets, too. Rock candy made from maple sugar Isuzu's mom boiled down from the sap she's tapped. There would be honey, too, the getting of which accounted for the swelling that was still going down, but worth it—when you factored in that smile.

Apples from an abandoned orchard.

Wild berry jam, bottled when they were still in season.

A fruitcake that actually *did* outlive mankind—confirming the suspicions of fruitcake haters everywhere.

And then, later, back in the hole—after the mischief and sugar are done—they'd exchange a couple of whispered "Boos." They'd curl up to sleep then, while the rest of the world was just getting up, oblivious to what the day used to be and wondering who put all that shit in the tree.

Through her eyeholes, Isuzu's eyes are posing a question:

"So?"

It's the So of Great Expectations.

The So of, "So, now that you know Halloween is coming, what are you going to do about it?" There may also be a "sucker" in there, somewhere, to clarify who the So is aimed at, not that I need clarification. Tag, I'm it. Let the competition begin. And may the better parent . . .

"I see you're all ready for Halloween," I say. When in doubt, state the obvious.

Isuzu nods her head, and even though the sheet is hiding her mouth, I can tell she's smiling.

"That's the one with Santa Claus, right?" I tease, and Isuzu goes, *"No . . ."*

"Sure it is," I say. "Santa comes down your chimney and steals your TV and . . ."

Isuzu is not amused. She puts her foot down. "No. No. No. *No,*" she insists, shaking her head so violently, her eyeholes slide around to the back.

"Okay, then it's the one with the Parsnip Man," I say, tugging her eyeholes back around, lining them up so I can see her reaction. She is—I'm happy to report—both shocked and appalled.

"Who?" she asks, her eyes saying "laser," her eyes adding "aim to kill."

"The Parsnip Man," I say. "He flies around in his magical Coup De Ville, bringing parsnips to all the good girls and boys." I pause. Isuzu shakes. "Don't tell me you never put out an old pair of shoes for the Parsnip Man?"

She stops shaking long enough to say, *"No,"* so derisively I almost want to check for ID. She sounds like an eighteen-year-old girl turning down a sixteen-year-old boy for the prom. I think about mentioning this comparison to her—not the whole thing, of course. Just the part about sounding older than she is. If I remember anything about being a little kid, it's this: Little kids want to be big kids, and the sooner, the better.

"How old *are* you?" I ask.

Isuzu holds up one hand, full open, and then adds two fingers on the other hand. "Seven," she says.

"Wow! You seem *a lot* older."

And no matter how ham-handed the compliment—no matter how obvious you are about telling somebody something they want to hear—if it's the right thing, they'll believe it, even if everybody else within earshot is making the puke gesture with their fingers.

And so Isuzu smiles.

She even blushes. Oh, sure, vampires are sensitive to that sort of thing, and can see blushes where others can't. But it doesn't take black marble eyes to see that flush of pride. Hell, you could practically read by the glow she's giving off. You could use it to land aircraft.

And just like that, I'm forgiven for my Parsnip Man faux pas.

"So," I say, "what's a big kid like you do on this—what is it again?"

"HALLOWEEN!" Isuzu shouts, going up on her tiptoes so she can reach the top of her lungs.

I flinch.

This is the first time since I've known her that Isuzu has made so much noise. Her little in-hiding, tee-hee laugh—though less flat than before—remains a tightly leashed thing. She knows better. I know she knows better.

"Shshshsh," I shshshsh. "Keep it down, will ya?"

And the ghost Isuzu's playing at just *dies*. It's kind of like watching a hot air balloon deflate. All of a sudden, the sheet she's wearing goes heavy, her tiptoes go flat, and the ghost sinks back to earth, almost apologetically. She starts staring at her shoes, and I can see the part in her hair through the eyeholes.

The hum of electric things fills this quiet space we've entered.

It goes on for a minute. Almost a whole minute's worth of me being quiet, Isuzu being quiet, me staring at her, her staring at her shoes. And then, suddenly, her eyes grow back behind her eyeholes. They begin to sparkle again with seasonal mischief.

"Ha-a-a-a-l-l-l-l," Isuzu whispers, drawing the word out, keeping her voice down.

"O-o-o-o-o-oh," she adds, bouncing up and down on her tiptoes again, a happy little ball.

"*We-e-e-e-n*," she concludes, using all of her hushed breath. She marks each extra syllable with a bounce—my happy, restrained ball of pure kid joy—ping-ponging between heaven and this other place.

A lot of our Halloween decorations are really just my old decorations, returned to their rightful places, now that they're more seasonally correct. All the little funereal knickknacks I hid away, trying not to scare Isuzu on her first evening here—the bone things, the cemetery things, the various homages to Dracula, Nosferatu, Lestat—out they all come. Safe now. Acceptable. Expected and required. I could put them out as Halloween decorations, maybe spray them with some Silly String cobwebs, and then maybe just forget to ever put them away. Maybe then my place would start feeling more like my place again.

Not that I'm complaining, but ever since Isuzu came into my life, everything's been . . . *different*. Different in good ways, sure. But also different in "just different" ways.

Like?

Well, I feel like a visitor to my own life. I feel like I'm always on-stage. Always on guard. I can't really be *me* around her. Instead, I've become the me-I-am-when-I'm-around-her. More careful. More worried. More *mortal*.

More inside my head, trying to see things through her eyes, hear things through her ears.

Usually, at least.

Sometimes I forget myself. Or, really, sometimes I go back to the me I was before I was under constant surveillance. It's the little things that usually do it—bring out the old, real me. The one with a Screamer's patience—and vocabulary. The one so easily frustrated over something as simple as, say . . .

. . . a jack-o'-lantern.

How are we supposed to have Halloween without a jack-o'-lantern? We can't, obviously. So, obviously, I have to get one, which means I have to *make* one, which means I need a pumpkin, which is when I start swearing.

"*Fuck*," I mutter under my breath—but not far enough under for Isuzu to miss it. Not that this requires much volume. When it comes to hearing things she shouldn't, my little Trooper has the receiving capacity of a larger-than-average satellite dish.

"That's a *bad* word," she calls out, not bothering to look up from the drawing she's doing, sprawled on the floor, a peacock fan of colored Magic Markers spread next to her. "You're gonna go to *h-e-double-hockey-sticks*," she adds—echoing, I'm sure, what her late mother probably said whenever her daughter made the mistake of echoing her own swearing.

"Sorry," I say, smiling at the thought of a vampire's being told he's going to hell. And her spelling my damnation out—it's almost too cute to bear.

H-e-double-hockey-sticks.

And so I start thinking about playing hockey in hell—perhaps when it finally freezes over. Which gets me thinking about what other games might be played in hell. Bowling, for some reason, seems likely. Followed by . . .

"Wait a second," I say, my pumpkin dilemma suddenly dovetailing into my mental riff on sports in hell and then blossoming into a full-blown Eureka.

I snap my fingers and tap at the air. *"Yes,"* I say. "That's it!"

"Yes, yes, yes," I say, adding a tap per "yes."

"What I do?" Isuzu says, snapping to and freezing, like a dog startled by a sudden noise.

"A basketball," I say, bending to scramble Isuzu's hair, before disappearing into my bedroom closet and returning with the object itself.

"Orange," I say, before letting it go, letting it pang on the hardwood floor, and then catching it with the fingertips of both hands.

"Round," I say, letting it go, letting it pang, catching.

"Say hello to our pumpkin, Pumpkin."

The first eye pokes out just fine.

The basketball is still rigid with the air inside it. It pierces neatly with a single hard stab from the pointier half of a pair of scissors. It exhales one long sigh, the air coming out stale and rubbery, with a hint of talcum. The rest is just a matter of cutting out from the hole, following the Magic Marker triangle I've outlined.

The second eye—that's another story.

The basketball keeps its shape easily enough when the only thing pressing on it is the outside air, but when I try stabbing it again, it caves in. Clearly, I need to re-create the resistance of that first time. And so I work two fingers in through the first eye, squeeze the ball so I can prop the second eye up from behind, and then press in with the scissors again. The idea is that the tip will poke through and pass safely between the V of my fingers.

Ideas. Plans. Wishful thinking.

Perhaps the better idea would have been to stick a funnel in the first hole so I could fill the basketball with sand. That would have kept the whole thing rigid and my fingers in clear view. With the basketball full of sand, I could just poke, poke, poke—eye, nose, mouth—shake the sand out, and then cut, cut, cut.

That would probably have been the better idea.

And this is probably a good place to mention that vampires, when we bleed, do not bleed well. Where a mortal might have to squeeze a pricked finger to tease out a single shiny bead, vampires *gush*. We gush at the slightest provocation. We gush like a teenage girl meeting her favorite celebrity. We do not gush *long;* we're not talking about hemophilia here. But we do gush hard for a second or two, the blood flung out in a syrupy red spurt that can travel pretty far, provided it doesn't hit something along the way, like, say, the eye of the bleeder or some innocent bystander.

The first time you see it, it's always a little weird, a little embarrassing for both parties involved—worse still if the nonbleeding party is the one who catches a round of friendly fire:

"Oh *jeez* . . ."

"Sorry . . ."

"*Shit* . . ."

"Let me get a handkerchief."

"Better make it a towel."

"Sorry . . ."

And *that's* how it goes if the parties involved are mutually consenting vampires who are not—as a general matter—squeamish about all things bloody.

Unfortunately, Isuzu is not an adult. Or a vampire. Or immune to the sight of blood, even though she'd seen quite a lot of it in her short life—most of it coming from the woman I've just stabbed myself trying to outdo.

Unfortunately, too, my vampire reflexes, sensing they're being attacked, react with all their true vampire speed. My heart doesn't have time to get off a single beat between the scissor point piercing my fingertip and me yanking my fingers out of the eyehole and into the open.

Right out there in the open—and aimed at where Isuzu lies sprawled, innocently coloring away at a yowling black cat, her legs crooked up behind her and crossed at the ankles. To me—to my vampire eyes—the spurt seems to take forever to trace its arc from my throbbing fingertip to the sheet of paper she's been working at for the last half hour.

And then: *Splash!*

A great bloody red Rorschach.

Isuzu looks up, already disgusted as a second spasm sends another bit of me sailing smack dab into her already scrunched forehead. She looks both shot and shocked. Her eyes blink and the red splotch on her forehead begins running, slowly, down between her eyes, along the bridge of her nose, to the jumping-off point at the tip. Her eyes dart down to where another drop has splashed on the floor, and then back up at me, just in time to see the last few drops dribble out before the wound closes up like a tight-lipped smile.

I tense, prepared for anything—a crying jag, a screaming fit, a flashback to the night her mom was killed. Anything, that is, except for . . .

"Gross, Marty," she says, looking at me like I did it on purpose. She brushes her arm across her forehead like she's wiping her nose. "Totally gross."

It's not until she looks back at her drawing, the red Rorschach and black cat having bled together to the improvement of neither. It's not until I look where she's looking that I notice the clear little drops of nothing pat-patting to the already ruined page. Her back is to me, and she does her crying silently, but it's crying nevertheless.

I wait for her to turn. She doesn't. And I don't make her.

"Sorry about your picture, kiddo," I whisper, and she shifts her little wing bones in a shrug.

I really should have used sand.

By the time Halloween arrives, I've actually done some of the things I imagined Isuzu's mom doing. Like tapping maple trees for sap to make sugar to make rock candy. Like finding an abandoned orchard where apples still grow. I've even scared up some chocolate on eBay, and found a maker of scented candles who grows and dries her own fruit for the fragrances. I talked her into FedExing me some dried apricots, peaches, and cranberries at an exorbitant cost, and under the pretense that I was a small-scale perfumer experiencing a temporary supply chain glitch.

"Ya, sure," she said over the phone, all the way from California, by way of Maine. "Waddever."

Renting out the laser tag place for the night wasn't cheap, of course—but at least I've got my grand finale for the evening.

On the issue of costume, we've had to compromise.

I had my heart set on turning Isuzu into a princess, one of the several I've created for her bedtimes over the last several months. A princess whose skin is made of tougher stuff than fabled—pea-proof stuff. A trouper. A princess who can take care of herself, but doesn't have to, because she isn't being held captive by a mean, or wicked, or evil step-anything. I'd even gone as far as buying the necessary yard goods—the gauze and glitter, the needle and thread, the pipe cleaners and some sparkly blue Liberace cloth. The rubber sword. The too-big army boots. But Isuzu prefers the classics. Her heart's vote was cast for that holey old sheet she'd sprung on me two weeks earlier.

In the end, we morphed the two. For Halloween, Isuzu would become the ghost of a warrior princess—a clear sign that even princesses who can take care of themselves are living on borrowed time.

As it turns out, we never make it to the laser tag place.

And as far as my basketball jack-o'-lantern? Funny thing about that. Seems a basketball that can hold its shape even when the air's let out won't keep that shape once you put a lit candle inside.

I've cut the candle down, so I can slide it in through the biggest available opening, which in this case is Jack's zigzaggy mouth. And then I push the face gently in, bending an eyehole over the wick, so I can light it before pulling the face gently back into shape. Isuzu is still getting ready in the bathroom, and so I dim the lights so Jack can shine in all his flickering glory.

The effect, I must admit, is magical. For a while, at least.

Isuzu sees it the first thing upon emerging from the bathroom, the candlelight hitting her princess sequins, sending dozens of blue-tinged blobs of light dancing across the walls like a mirrored disco ball. She turns one way, watching the little blue lights swim up-stream, and then the other, watching them retreat. She looks at Jack, and then at me, smiling as broadly as either of us. And then she claps, holding her hands off to the side for a quick, polite pat-pat-pat. The applause of an art patron's understated appreciation for her up-and-coming's latest effort—the "bravo" assumed, but not the air kiss to either cheek. It's one of those gestures that make me wonder about Isuzu and her mom's life together, before me, before this. Did her mom clap for her this way after some long-forgotten accomplishment? Was this the language they'd developed? And did Isuzu's heart feel like it might break or burst the first time her mother praised her this way—like mine's feeling now?

"Thank you," I say, taking a bow. "Thank you. Thank you . . ."

Air kiss. Air kiss.

"You're welcome," Isuzu says, courtly, still her mom for a second longer, before settling back into being Isuzu, a little girl dressed up as the ghost of a warrior princess.

"Trick or treat," she says, her little pink hand darting out suddenly from underneath the sheet, palm up.

I start with a piece of rock candy. The plan is to work up to the chocolate, and then on to laser tag to work off the sugar buzz.

Her fingers close around the rock candy as her hand retracts under the sheet, followed by the sound of crunching and the subtle bobbing of Isuzu's warrior-princess-ghost head.

"Tank you," she says, in between crunches, her mouth full.

"You're welcome," I say, trying to echo her, echoing her mom.

The crunching and bobbing stop, and the little hand pops out again.

"Trick or treat."

"What do we say?"

"Thank you."

"You're welcome."

And so it goes, Jack flickering in the background all but forgotten as I deal out treat after treat to my sole trick-or-treater. At one point, I suggest that maybe it should be trick or *re*treat, and—to my amazement—she actually finds this funny.

"Trick or retreat," she says.

And says.

And says.

Until I'm pretty sorry I got the whole thing started, but pleased, too, because even though it's getting a little monotonous at the moment, that's exactly what we're having—a moment. Time of the quality sort. Good parent points, scored and banked.

And that funny smell? I don't think much of it. Or what I think is this: Herbs. I haven't burned a candle with dried apricots and herbs in it since—well, forever. So yeah. Herbs. Burning herbs. That's what stinks.

Until the smoke detector goes off. Followed by the fire alarm. Followed by my entire building being evacuated.

"Come on, Marty." A neighbor bangs on my door. "It's a fire. We gotta go."

I act like I'm not home. It's not too hard. We've been quiet and the lights are already turned down. And now, with Jack reduced to little more than a smoldering hunk of burned rubber, the place is completely dark. I reach out and find Isuzu's hand—also not too hard, seeing as it's been reaching out to the same place every minute or so for the last half hour.

"Sshh," I say, and she doesn't have to be told twice. We listen together in the dark as doors open and close, followed by footsteps, some running, some surprisingly slow, given that they don't know that it's a false alarm. It sounds like the footsteps of old people—but there aren't any of those anymore—not bodywise, at least. Which leaves the only other explanation I can come up with: reluctance.

But what would make someone reluctant to leave a burning building?

And then it hits me. My reluctant friends and neighbors? They were doing it! They were naked and in the shower and doing it when the alarms went off.

This, I have *got* to see.

So I go to the window, but then stop. Because this is not something Isuzu should be seeing. Not that I'm a prude, but there's only so much honesty a kid should have to put up with to make her parent feel open-minded. Some lines have to be drawn, and this is one I'm drawing. Isuzu doesn't need to be exposed to public displays of exposure.

Me, on the other hand, I'm way past legal and I've known these people forever. And I'll admit it. I'm curious. There are some nicely curved silhouettes from across the way that I've been wondering about for years. And it's not as if opportunities like this drop in your lap every day.

So I part the drapes, but up high and out of range of Isuzu's roaming ghost eyes. I live on the fourth floor and have a halfway decent view of the lawn below where my friends and neighbors are now gathering.

But when I look down, what I see makes me bark with laughter. It makes me want to believe in God again. What I see is not genitalia—tufted, shaved, or swinging. It's not breasts, shapely or otherwise. It's not even secret tattoos or piercings, where and on whom I'd never have imagined.

But it *is* about secrets. It's about a world of secrets I should have guessed, but didn't. It's about perversity and hypocrisy and the delight of discovering we can still count on both.

Four stories below me, huddling and mingling and milling about, are ghosts and witches and Dracula-style vampires, complete with old-time fake plastic fangs over their real ones.

"Son of a bitch," I say to myself, but loud enough for Isuzu, even with a sheet covering her radar ears.

"That's a bad word," she reminds me, just in case I was in any danger of forgetting. "You're gonna go to . . ."

"Ssshhh," I say, cutting her off. "I know," I whisper, still staring at my oh-so-vampirically-incorrect neighbors. And I'm not the only one staring. The ones who aren't dressed up are staring, too. Their disgust is clear from even four stories up. Those who *are* disgusted—that is—which is by no means all of them. Some are just amused, while others seem almost contemplative, as if wondering why they let themselves be talked into giving this up. Oh, so it's un-VC, eh? It's kids' stuff and we're not kids anymore?

Yeah. Right.

Some of the uncostumed ones are chatting with their made-up neighbors, some of the latter turning to afford them the full view, or fanning out their capes, giving them the ol' Lugosi batwing spread.

Isuzu tugs on my pant leg. "Trick or retreat," she whispers.

"Hey, Pumpkin," I whisper back. "Come here." I kneel so we're the same height, and then spread the drapes again, but lower.

"For you," I whisper as she presses her little ghost face to the glass. "Happy Halloween," I add, wishing I could take her down there, let her mingle, let her play, let her offend the sensibilities of those who disapprove. Because that's what Halloween was all about before—that's what made it such a great holiday.

The only rule for Halloween is breaking the rules.

But I can't. This is as close as we get, this little peek from a distance. Is it enough? Is it a cruel tease?

Isuzu turns away from the window and answers all my questions with a hug. She kisses me on the cheek through her ghost sheet. When she pulls away, I can see the shape of her mouth bleeding through the front of the costume, in chocolate.

"Thanks, Dad," she says, as I try to gulp my heart back down. Try not to leak anything red on her princess sequins, or her little make-believe shroud.

-10-

POPE PETER THE LAST

I still don't know what to do with the dead time between Isuzu's going to bed and sunrise. I've tried synching up our schedules better, so that she sleeps for a good part of the time I'm at work. And I've pushed back on her bedtime, a little bit each week, trying to shrink that dead space, trying to encourage her to sleep through as much of the day as possible. But you can push that sort of thing only so far. She's growing like a weed, now, and mortals, like plants, need sunlight. There are vitamins in it, or something.

I still use the cell phone to listen to her snore. It helps. I've bought a separate phone, just for under her bed, which is a real one, now, and not just the air mattress. But sitting in the living room while she's in her bedroom, snoring over a wire plugged into my ear . . . this seems weird. It's too close. Too creepy.

So I go for a walk. The moon's out, and full, and it's drawing those inky black shadows of everything across the sidewalk. I still have Isuzu plugged into my ear, just in case, and to keep me company.

Before Isuzu, this would be the time I'd head out to a strip club, in search of noise, distraction. Breasts. But that doesn't seem right, now. Not with a child at home. Not considering the fact that the last time I went, I got kicked out. Plus, I wouldn't be able to hear my cell over the music.

So I just walk to walk, following my shadow, no particular destination in mind.

It's after I've walked for a few blocks that I see it, up ahead. A church, all lit up for midnight mass, which isn't just for Christmas anymore. It's Sunday. The dead time's always worse on Sundays. And the stained glass is throwing rainbows to the sidewalk, along with the moon's inky shadows. Catholic vampires (and yes, there *are* Catholic vampires) stroll in through the yellow rectangle of the wide open double doors—singly, doubly, in small groups that almost look like families. There's a sign outside, lit up, with a question mark in it.

"CH __CH," it says, followed by, "What's missing?"

I have to go around to the other side—the side closer to those open doors—to read the answer.

"UR," the other side says.

Normally, something that corny would make me groan, or slap my forehead, or shake it, at least. You see, I gave up being religious back when I gave up dying. But every so often lately, ever since Isuzu's started living with me, I hear a little voice.

"Psssssttt . . ."

I flinch. That's *not* the little voice I was thinking about that just went *psssttt*. The little voice I was thinking about usually comes from inside my head. The *psssttt* is coming from just behind me.

"What's the score?" the voice asks.

When I turn around, what I see is the same bucktoothed collar that hovered over me as a child, all throughout the school week, and every Sunday. He's got a German shepherd on a leash. It's not vamped. I can see its hot breath chugging out in puffs.

"Father?"

"What's the score?" he repeats, tapping his ear.

I've never been much on sports, especially now, when the hockey players heal so quickly. There doesn't seem to be much point in it.

"Aren't you supposed to be in there?" I ask, pointing.

"Not my shift," the priest says. "And Judas wanted a walk."

"Judas?"

"What else would you name a son of a bitch?"

"Good point."

"Plus, I like the idea of keeping Judas on a leash, if you get my meaning."

"Cute."

We stop. The conversation just runs out of gas. Instead, we stare at each other for a second or two, black marble eye to black marble eye. This never works with vampires, this trying to size each other up by looking into the onetime gateways to our souls. But we keep on doing it anyway, until one us blinks.

"Father Jack," Father Jack says, offering me his unleashed hand.

"Marty," I say, taking it.

"You look a little lost, Marty, if you don't mind me saying."

Yeah, it's that kind of talk that's kept me away from these kinds of places. Usually. But lately . . .

I sigh, Isuzu still in my ear. She makes one of those grunts she sometimes makes, when she's dreaming and the dream's turning badly.

So I don't tell Father Jack to go fuck himself. But I don't bite, either. Instead, I change subjects. And the one I'm talking to.

"Hey, boy," I say, scratching Judas's head just behind his spired ears. He leans back into it and lets his big dog tongue loll, dripping saliva onto the sidewalk. His fog production goes up. "Attaboy, Judas."

"You got a dog, Marty?" Father Jack asks.

"Yeah," I say.

"What's its name?"

"Um," I hesitate. "Trooper."

"Were you in the army?"

I nod.

"Vietnam?"

"World War Two."

"Oh yeah?" Father Jack says. "The greatest generation, eh?"

"Soitney," I say.

"So you're a Stooge man, too," Father Jack says.

I nod.

But he's doing the math under the cover of this chitchat. He's still trying to size me up, place me within my historical context. Could I be . . . *one of them*? Could I be one of the ones who . . . *did this*?

Not that anyone linked to the Catholic Church has any reason to get judgmental on that account. Not considering the role they played . . . *doing this.*

Father Jack continues, preparing his exit strategy. "So, anyway," he says, "Judas and I are usually around this time of the night. Out walking." He pauses. "In case you and Trooper ever need any company," he says. "Or, you know, someone to discuss Stoogiana with."

"I'll keep that in mind," I lie. "'Night, Father."

"'Night, Martin, pater *Trooperis,*" Father Jack says, letting Judas lead the way.

Perhaps I should back up.

All the way back, to before.

It all started because the strippers weren't cutting it. I mean, they were good. They worked their little fangs off to drum up recruits for the Benevolent Vampires. But we were still miles away from reaching critical mass. We needed something *big,* something to push us over the tipping point. And so I had this great idea.

Here I was, living in the home state of Henry Ford, father of mass production. What the Benevolent Vampires needed was a way to vamp en masse, to give up on the onesies and go straight to the hundredsies.

So I got myself a job with the local blood bank, and slipped a little bit of me into every pint.

I just didn't think it all the way through. I survived a mentorless vamping, why wouldn't they? Seems I conveniently forgot that I was actually present and witnessed my vamping, got winked at by the vamping party, and even *bonsoir*ed. I conveniently forgot about our little mortar-lit game of charades out there in the middle of World War II. Sure, I didn't get mentored *much*—but the most important stuff had been passed along, along with whatever it is in our blood that does this to us.

I remember waking up that first night into my "great idea," the air stinking with the smell of combusted hemophiliacs, smoldering hospitals and homes and apartment buildings. Sirens wailing wearily in the distance. Lawns and sidewalks scorched with the silhouettes of fallen bodies. City garbage trucks on overtime, beeping and clattering with the leftover bones.

All the TVs in all the bars, diners, and department stores are tuned to the news, some with actual footage of flameouts, played in slow motion, zoomed in, digitally enhanced, trying to pinpoint the point of ignition. Is that smoke—or just a shadow? Other stations are interviewing witnesses and loved ones, showing faces in profile, sunburned on one side, pale on the other, or unwrapping bandaged hands to reveal blistered palms that had held on for just a bit too long.

Everyone thinks it's the end of the world—and it was supposed to be, but I got it wrong.

Another station is doing street interviews and I recognize a few familiar faces—a few familiar *malevolent* faces—fighting to hold back smiles.

"Awful," they say, shaking their milk white heads, wearing baseball caps to shield their black, black eyes. "Simply awful." They talk like fish blowing kisses, not wanting their fangs to show.

No one makes the blood connection. Nobody but those air-kissing fish, my nonbenevolent brothers. The mortal media are still busy babbling about the Rapture and UFOs and whether or not there's a terrorist link. Fortunately for vampires like me, the crime has destroyed its own evidence, but sooner or later we're going to be forced out of our shadows.

The plan from the beginning was to go public only after we had the numbers in our favor. But my little fuckup put the whole thing in jeopardy. Instead of being "this close" to success, we're suddenly "this close" to total exposure, and disaster.

Needless to say, I am talked to.

I am advised to "stick to the strippers, Marty," to take it "one neck at a time."

"They have to be hand held," I am reminded. "They need to know the rules."

Me, I nod. I agree. I swear I'll do better.

And then I go around, bumping into things for a while. Crying inexplicably. Going blank. Going to the strip clubs, but not to vamp. I go there for the noise, the distraction. A shoulder to cry on.

"What do *you* got to cry about?" a mortal stripper asks me one night.

And when I look up, it's her—the tipping point. I don't know that, yet. I don't even know who she is outside of a stripper who's a little too white for a mortal and too tattooed for my taste.

"Marty," I say, not interested, but not impolite.

"Lizzy," she says, sitting her bony ass down. "The pope's sister," she says.

I laugh, despite my mood.

She doesn't.

And she's not kidding, either. She *is* the pope's sister. His little sister. They come from a big old-fashioned Catholic family that wasn't planning on going to hell for using birth control. Over a dozen, give or take, a good chunk of them still in Detroit—a better-than-thou chunk of them wearing funny hats in the Vatican. She's the black sheep of the family, a junky living on the streets of Detroit, doing a little stripping, then a little prostitution, and then a little dying, when all the bills came due. At the ripe old age of twenty-six, she woke up with full-blown AIDS playing Pac-Man in her veins. At the time I met her, she'd gone back to stripping, hoping to earn funeral expenses, at least.

Like the woman said, what did *I* have to cry about?

Hey, Petey sweetie. This is Lizzy. I'm kinda fucked. Call my cell."

That's the message she leaves on the pope's—her brother's—voice mail. I was there to hear it; I was there to make her make it. But even *I* didn't know that crude little message would become the Benevolent Vampires' "one small step for man."

My goal was much more modest. I was just trying to do something about another little problem we vampires were having—benevolent and malevolent both—namely, the Vatican death squads. I was just trying to get Lizzy's brother's kind to stop killing *my* kind. To earn my way back into the good graces of the Benevolent Vampire Society. To help balance out my karma, at least a little. I had no idea it was going to work out the way it did.

I'm with her when the pope calls back. We've been waiting on a crumbling door stoop in one of Detroit's crackier neighborhoods. It's raining, and windy, and judging from her shiver, probably cold, though it could also be a fever from her disease, or withdrawal. I watch her breathing; it leaks out in wisps. She's wearing a black leather suit jacket, no padding, no special lining to keep her warm, and so she isn't, even though she's got both arms wrapped around herself. Her phone starts bleating in her pocket so she takes it out, flips it open, says, "Hello?" but all she hears is the local wind, blowing in the mouthpiece and coming out in her ear, rewired and staticky.

"I can't hear you," she shouts, switching hands because the first one is already freezing. "Let me get out of this shit for a sec," she says, looking up the street and noticing an old phone booth, the phone long since busted out. The dome light still works, though, backlighting the squiggles and scrawls of gang graffiti. She closes herself inside, but I force it open again. I play windbreak while she slumps to the floor of the booth, still hugging herself with one arm, holding her phone up with the other.

"Hey, Petey. Long time no—"

"No. Yeah. No. Same ol' same ol'. Like you care. No. No. *Money* I can get. Like you care. Friends. Just *friends.* Yes, *guy* friends. Listen, I got it. What do you mean, 'Got what?' 'Got milk.' *It.* The bug. AIDS." Pause. "Hello? Petey?"

I imagine the pope all alone in his bedroom, brocade this, velvet that, gold everywhere, even on the edges of books, the threads of his clothing, his whole world heavy with gilt. The hand with the ring holds his secure phone, while the other hand—the one that's just old and heavily veined—cups across his eyes. "Lizzy, Lizzy, Lizzy," I hear his tinny voice say, all the way from the Vatican to crack land Detroit. She was just a baby when he entered the seminary; he watched her grow up in Polaroids his mother sent him, along with clippings of articles from the *Weekly World News,* with penned-on notes like "Ain't this a stitch?" or "Thought you might need a tickle." The photos and the clippings are what his mother sent instead of letters. He didn't take it personally.

"Have you told anyone else?" he asks, meaning their other, less important siblings, the ones who looked at Lizzy as a good source for black sweaters.

"No."

"Do you have a plan?" he asks. For as long as he's known her, his little sister has always had a plan, generally one he disapproved of, but which he could do nothing about. She seemed to specialize in surviving in ways aimed at horrifying and embarrassing her older brother.

Family, it's a wonderful thing.

"Don't know as I'd call it a *plan*," Lizzy says. "It's more like the me-not-dying option. It's kinda the last card in my deck."

I imagine the pope, her brother, taking his hand away from his eyes. "Meaning?"

"Do you believe in vampires?" Lizzy asks. This was back when belief in my kind was still optional, when the Vatican's budget for its vampire hit squad was hidden under the line item for landscaping. This was the time when the official answer to Lizzy's question was no, when mysterious disappearances were just left mysterious, or written off as your run-of-the-mill serial killings.

And let me assure you, we vampires didn't have to work all that hard, covering our tracks. There were plenty of folks on the other side only too willing to make up excuses for us. So maybe it wasn't so surprising that no one had made the link to my little goof-up. You don't generally find what you're actively avoiding. In fact, the vampire hunters were just about the only reason we had to be careful at all. As far as local law enforcement went, nobody ever lost their job for pulling out the ol' drug-hit stamp. The Vatican was well versed in this "Don't ask, don't tell" charade, having cut its teeth on pedophile priests, lesbian nuns, priests and nuns living together like married couples.

But none of those things stayed covered up forever.

"Are you talking to *me,* or the papal 'we'?" her brother the pope asks.

"You, Peter," Lizzy says. "It's just me, and I'm talking to just you."

"No," her brother says. "I don't *believe* in vampires. I don't have to. I *know* they exist. I've *seen* them. I've seen them explode in the rays of the rising sun. I've looked in their dead eyes, touched their crypt-cold skin, listened to their devilish lies."

If I ever die, I'll probably go to hell for this, but while the pope's speaking, I'm making that yackety-yack gesture with my hand. Lizzy rolls her eyes and nods in agreement.

"Um," Lizzy says. "Yeah." She pauses. "About that, you see. That's kind of my future you're dissing."

"Meaning?"

"I've got two choices, brother dear. Dead or undead. And I'm not liking that first one."

"I see."

"Which brings me to my reason for calling."

"You mean you didn't just call to tell me you're dying of AIDS, but have decided to become a vampire instead?"

"Well, that was part of the reason, sure," Lizzy says. "But there's this other thing." She pauses. "The guys tell me you've got like this special-ops team or something, cutting off heads, torching 'em, chaining 'em up while a boom box plays 'Here Comes the Sun.' "

" 'The guys,' " the pope, her brother, repeats. "You mean your bloodsucking friends?"

"I don't recall saying anything about lawyers."

"Cute."

"But seriously, Petey," his sister says. "If these people are gonna be my buds, it's kinda not cool, you having 'em offed and all. 'Thou shalt not kill,' remember?"

"*They're* the killers," her brother insists.

"Not all of them," Lizzy insists right back. "There are some good ones. Remember stem cells? Yeah, I know. I know. Sore subject. But, hey, they're making fake blood now. No need to . . . *you know.*"

The pope, her brother, doesn't say anything.

The junky, his sister, waits for a second or two before telling him she can hear him crossing his eyes—which he doesn't believe she can, even though, at the moment, he is.

"So, whaddya say, Petey sweetie?" Lizzy wheedles. "Ix-nay on the eath-day ad-squay?"

There's a pause on the other end. More wind. More static. Finally:

"What death squad?" the pope says.

The short version is, the Vatican stopped murdering vampires forty-eight hours later and a delegation of my benevolent brethren met with His Holiness the following week. And after that, Pope Peter the Whatever became Pope Peter the Last. It seems immortality without killing had a certain appeal to the aging pontiff. Seems there was something in the Bible about drinking somebody's blood and getting eternal life in return. And if you didn't have to kill people, then so much the better.

Eventually, the wealth was shared. Arrangements were made, adults-only midnight masses scheduled, and for the next several weeks, Communion was standing-room-only.

A mass distribution system. That's what we needed, and that's what we got.

The sick and dying got preferential treatment, followed by the Knights of Columbus, the Altar Society, the ushers, and the rest. Each stuck out his or her tongue, already numbed with oil of cloves, and a deacon drew a scalpel down each, after which the priest offered the chalice and another deacon handed out pamphlets of dos and don'ts.

In Safeways across the land, clerks on the graveyard shift wondered at the sudden popularity of tinfoil and duct tape, and when these sold out, spray paint. The blacks—flat, glossy—went first, followed by the darker shades of blue. Followed by tumbleweeds blowing down the empty aisles, followed by flies drawn to the Dumpsters full of rotting produce, followed by customers again, but all wearing sunglasses after dark, all smiling oh so pointedly.

"Pssst, kiddo. Have you heard the good word?"

"No."

"*Excellent . . .*"

Followed by, "Cleanup in aisle six."

So, yeah, Father Jack's got a lot of nerve, judging me. And I plan to tell him so, the following evening, after putting Isuzu to bed.

"Where's Trooper?" he asks.

"Excuse me?"

"Your dog," Father Jack says.

Oh yeah. "Busy," I say.

"Busy?"

"Doing dog things," I say.

"Yeah, same with Judas," Father Jack says, having come to a halt. He waits as Judas squats on his hind legs, quivers, strains. "Which is generally why we take them for walks, no?"

"Oh, Trooper's not into that."

"Trooper's not into relieving himself?" Father Jack says. "So . . . Trooper's been vamped?"

"Um. Yeah."

"Why?"

"I never really liked dogs, per se," I say. "No offense, Judas. But I love puppies."

"Tell me about it," Father Jack says, and the way he says it so wistfully, it's clear there are a lot of other things he's *not* saying. It's clear he wants me to notice him not saying these other things. He wants me to ask. I think I probably already know. I guess this really was an invitation to talk, not to be talked at, or recruited back.

"Oh yeah?" I say.

Father Jack nods.

"Occupational hazard?"

"Curse." Father Jack sighs. "Karma. Or destiny. I was as a kid. And I promised myself I'd never. So, of course . . ."

I stop. Dead. Isuzu's still in my ear, keeping me company. And I'm younger, stronger, and bigger than Father Jack.

"Important question," I say, my teeth and fangs clenched.

"Shoot."

Yeah, if I had a machine gun, maybe.

"Did you ever," I say, "and I mean *ever*—practice?"

Father Jack weighs this question. "Almost," he says. "Which is how I found out. But no. No. I just suffer all the joys of not practicing."

Wind. Trees. You know the routine.

"I don't know if I would have stayed that way," Father Jack goes on. "But then I got lucky, I guess. The world changed. No kids, no problem." He pauses. "Timing's everything, I guess."

More wind. More trees.

"On the plus side," I say, "I guess I don't have to kill you or anything."

"Thanks . . . ," Father Jack says.

"You're welc—"

". . . for nothing."

Normally, a semisuicidal, nonpracticing pedophile priest with fangs would not be my first choice as confidant. Surely, there must be less appalling hyphenates to pick from. A Nazi-Quaker shaman, for instance. Or an obsessive-compulsive, anal-retentive hair stylist. Or even a chitchatty mail carrier ticking like a time bomb and committing postal fraud with a fake ID and a rented post box from Mail Boxes Etc. All of these would seem less dubious, less trouble, less risky.

But lately, I've been finding myself in the same boat as Father Jack. Not *the same* the same. But a sympathetic boat—a boat that can relate to Father Jack's boat. I'm a vampire living with a mortal I've decided to watch grow up, instead of killing, and even though I dearly love my little sports utility vehicle, even though my life would be a wasteland without her, in the right light, I can't help but notice that vein pulsing slowly in her neck. She'll be lying on her stomach, coloring, and she'll brush back some hair that's fallen in her face, tuck it behind her ear, and there I am, looking at her young neck, exposed.

"Where you going?" Isuzu asks.

"Forgot to get a paper," I say. "Hold down the fort."

And then I follow my shadow around to Father Jack's place. Ask after Judas, whose ears are always up for a vigorous scratching.

"How ya doin', boy? How ya doin'?

"Attaboy.

"Good boy."

"Having an urge to gamble, are we?" Father Jack asks.

Gambling. That's my euphemism. That's the surrogate addiction I've confessed to, the boat that can relate to Father Jack's boat. No need to make this any more complicated than it is.

"Yep."

"Have a seat," Father Jack says. "I'll warm something up."

-11-

THE PERFECT PET

W hy'd ya give it *my* name?"

This is the first thing Isuzu wants to know after the introductions have been made. And it's a fair question, though not the reaction I expected, bringing home a black Labrador puppy, freshly vamped and wearing a bow. I was expecting something more in the hug department, but she's been rationing those lately—just like her giggles. Nowadays, the only thing she doesn't seem to be skimping on is sentences that sound vaguely accusatory and tend to end in question marks.

"Because he's got big feet, too," I say, letting Trooper's paws prove my case.

"But it's *my* name," Isuzu insists.

"I swear I won't get you guys confused. Deal?"

"But it's *my* name," she repeats, her little fists clenched tightly in front of her, as if trying to hold on to one of the few things that is hers.

"Your middle one, yes," I say, frustrated by this sudden territorial turn. "The one that never gets used anyway."

"But it's still *mine.*" Her little fists start shaking; she starts going up on tiptoes, as if preparing to launch into a yell.

"And Trooper's going to be *yours,* too," I say, pressing down on the top of her head, returning the soles of her feet to ground control. "See the bow? He's a present." Pause. "He's a present for *you.*"

"I hate him."

The suddenness of this pronouncement knocks me back, and I'm not sure what to say. I check to see if I have any telepathic powers that might help.

Trooper, I think, *lick the kid's face. Now.*

Nothing.

Trooper? Are you receiving? Your life may depend on this.

But Trooper just spreads his big puppy paws out in front of him, letting them slide forward on the hardwood floor. He settles his big puppy head between his paws, and then hikes up both eyebrows—a gesture that makes me wonder if *he's* trying to send *me* a message. Something like: *Leave me out of this.*

"Can we call him Troop?" I ask. This seems like a fair compromise.

"No."

"Tru?" I try.

"No," Isuzu says, crossing her arms over her chest.

"Pooper?" I float. Sure, having rhyming names might get a bit confusing for the poor thing—one for inside, another for when we're walking with Father Jack and Judas—but the poor thing's immortal. He'll have plenty of time to get used to it.

Isuzu seems to be considering the Pooper alternative. I try to imagine the gears turning in her head, the criteria she might apply to picking an appropriate name for . . . *what*? My *other* pet? Is that it? Does Isuzu feel threatened by Trooper? Is Trooper the equivalent of a new baby as far as she's concerned? A competitor for my affection?

In retrospect, I regret rolling on the floor with him when we got home.

"Surprise!" I said, opening my coat to reveal what I thought was the perfect pet. I let him gambol across the floor, his nails clicking on the hardwood as Isuzu watched, overjoyed into silence. Or so I thought.

"His name's Trooper," I said, just before all the scratching and belly rubbing and rolling around the floor like an idiot.

I was just trying to show how much fun the new puppy was going to be.

I guess what Isuzu saw was how much more I seemed to like this new puppy than her. And then, to add insult to injury, I let him have her name, too, like an oblivious parent who lets the new baby play with the older kid's toys.

So, what kind of name do you give your rival? One that will serve as a constant humiliation, perhaps? Pooper. Or Crapper. Or, maybe, Li'l Ass Wipe?

"Okay," Isuzu concludes.

"Pooper's okay?" I confirm.

Isuzu nods, grimly, arms still folded like a judge.

"So, do you still hate him?" I ask, hastily, while she seems to be in a conceding mood.

Isuzu looks at her brand-new vampire puppy and Pooper looks back. The puppy in question is a chocolate Lab, the cutest breed of puppy on the face of the earth. They have to be; they grow up to be one of the worst kind of yapping beasts your next-door neighbor could ever own. They grow up in dire need of killing. Fortunately, Trooper will never get any bigger or less cute than he is right now— staring at Isuzu with those big puppy eyes, his nose flaring slightly, already learning his new master's scent.

"I guess not," Isuzu says, perhaps realizing that this will be something to play with while I'm at work.

The way I figure it, a dog was going to happen, sooner or later. A dog was going to be required, if only to justify the grocery bags of pet food I brought home, and the empty tins the sanitation department hauled away every Monday. I'd already had a few close calls with neighbors in the hall. And the vamping? Well, that was just a corner I backed myself into, trying to explain why my imaginary dog didn't join us that first night back to where Father Jack and Judas took care of business. Not that the vamping seems like a bad idea. I wasn't kidding when I told Father Jack I'm not particularly fond of adult dogs. But a permanent puppy who doesn't shit around the apartment—this, I think I can handle. Just let a little of whatever I'm heating up for me end up in Trooper's bowl. And that's it. The ultimate in low-maintenance pets—like a cat that doesn't even need a litter box. And Pooper could serve multiple functions, coming with me on my dead-time walks, and also keeping Isuzu company while I'm at work. As far as I'm concerned, I'm thinking that getting Trooper is *still* a great idea.

"Why don't you pet him?" I suggest. "It's okay. Petting's allowed."

Yep, a "great idea." That's what getting Pooper was.

Do I need to remind you about my track record with "great ideas"?

"He's cold," Isuzu says. This should be my first clue. It's not.

"Well, yes, Isuzu," I say, being parental, and a wee bit patronizing—if that's not redundant. "He's a vampire. A cute, furry, four-legged vampire, but he's *still* a vampire."

Yes he is. He *is* that.

And he seemed so friendly at the pet shop. And I *did* ask. I asked at the pet shop if he was a biter. Maybe I should have listened a bit more closely to the shop owner's reply.

"Bite?" he said. "*You?* No . . ."

Fortunately, all he's got are those pinprick puppy teeth and they'll never get any bigger or sharper than that. But that doesn't mean they don't hurt. Especially when he chomps down with all he's got. Especially when your fake dad has just assured you that it's okay, with those big puppy eyes and that stupid bow lulling you into letting your guard down, just before those pinpricky teeth catch you completely by surprise.

I will not try to replicate the exact noise Isuzu makes. It's part "Ow," part yelp, and I think she may have borrowed some of my hell-worthy words along the way. But there's also something else—a tone of betrayal, and helplessness, a tone that seems to wonder aloud why everything in the world lets her down like this.

Pooper, meanwhile, is squeaking out this hell-puppy yip-yip-yip—another talent he kept hidden back at the pet shop.

And me? My hands have found my head and are holding on to it by the temples. They move along with it when I shake my head back and forth. They're safe there. There, they won't grab Trooper by the throat and start squeezing out bagpipe noises. And I don't really need them, anyway, to slide our little guest across the hardwood floor with the toe of my shoe.

This is not kicking. I do not kick the dog. At no time does he become airborne.

This is scooting. The floor is waxed. Slick. The fur of his butt and the pads of his big puppy feet don't offer much traction. The mechanism by which the scooting is accomplished just happens to be the toe of my shoe.

And I keep on scooting Pooper until we hit bathroom tile, at which point I give him one more boost and then shut the door. For a moment, I consider going in after him and closing the door behind us both. But I've got a feeling it doesn't really matter which side of the bathroom door I'm on. I'm in the doghouse, either way.

Trooper and I have to go get the paper. *Now.* Only one of us will be returning.

This is fine with Isuzu.

She suggests leaving him outside for the sun to get. I think I have a better idea.

See: Marty. Track record. Ideas.

"Father Jack," I say when he answers the door.

"Is *this* the infamous Trooper?" Father Jack asks, reaching out a hand to scratch behind Trooper's ear.

"Yes, it is," I say. And for a second, a weird lightness blows through my chest—a sense of relief at making at least one of the lies I've told Father Jack retroactively true.

"Why's he got a bow on him?"

"That's his thing," I say, feeling the lightness evaporate. "He likes to dress up."

"He's told you this?"

"Not in so many words." I slip the bow off, over and around his big puppy ears. "Somebody dared me. It was kinda like a . . ."

". . . *bet?*" Father Jack says.

I shake my head, and then let it hang.

"Marty, Marty, Marty."

"I know, I know, I know," I say, and the remorse in my voice is not all an act. Or *just* an act. It's just not over gambling.

"Did you win, at least?"

"Crapped out," I say. "Total disaster. I don't know what I was thinking."

"If our *inclinations* were about thinking, Marty."

"I know, I know." I pause. "You need a dog? He's way beyond housebroken. Extremely low maintenance. Just let a little spill into a bowl when you're making something for yourself and . . ."

"I don't think he'd get along too terribly well with Judas, do you?"

How come everybody can figure this out but me? Vampire puppies are good pets *only for vampires*. Duh!

"I didn't think of that," I admit.

"We've already discussed thinking," Father Jack jokes. "Next subject."

"Do you know anybody who might like a puppy? A vampire, chocolate Lab, world's cutest puppy, guaranteed to stay cute forever."

"Why are you trying to get rid of your dog?"

Good question. Why *am* I trying to get rid of this dog that theoretically I've had for at least the last several months? What could have changed that would all of a sudden require me to get rid of my dog?

"It's complicated," I say.

Father Jack looks at me with a smirk on his lips. "Marty," he says. "This is me you're talking to. Complicated's my middle name."

"I thought it was Joseph," I joke. Deflect.

"I'm gonna give you such a slap," Father Jack says, glancing the side of my head with the side of his hand, knocking my cowlick out of place. "I'm serious, Marty. Confide. Confide."

Okay, I've been lying to you all the time you thought I was confiding in you. I don't have a gambling problem. The truth is, I've been raising a mortal from scratch and that's more complicated than it might sound. Case in point: tonight. Trooper didn't get along any better with her than he's likely to get along with Judas. Which means I get rid of either the pup or the kid. And seeing as I just bought Trooper, I'm not emotionally invested on that side, so . . .

Comments? Feedback? Input?

"I need the money," I say. "Gambling debt."

"Have you thought about taking him back where you bought"

him?" Father Jack asks. "I mean, he's vamped, right? He's still good as new. It's not like he's some stereo with an expired warranty or anything."

I guess that could work. Either that or I could chain him to a tree and let the sun do my dirty work, as Isuzu recommends. It occurs to me that I should probably be concerned about how quickly she came up with that particular suggestion. As if she'd been thinking about it in another context. Fortunately, my capacity for denial and self-deception is even greater than my ability to delay gratification.

"That could work, I guess." I pause, sensing that this counseling session has drawn to a close. "By the way," I say, and I really don't need to say any more than that. We've developed a routine.

"Today's paper?"

I nod.

"Why don't you ever buy one of your own?" Father Jack asks, going to fetch his copy. "This is most of it," he says, returning. "Sports is missing."

"That's okay," I say. There's always a section missing. This is also part of the routine.

"Judas is still reading it," Father Jack says; it's what passes for good-bye. Or the first half of good-bye, at any rate.

I wait.

"If you catch my meaning," he adds.

Which is when I reach over my head with an empty hand, still open. I close it like I'm catching a fly.

"Bingo," I say.

"Parcheesi." Father Jack waves.

The pet shop guy looks at me like I'm crazy.

"He not hurt a fly," he says. "Look. Look." He rubs his wrist under Trooper's nose. "See?" He rubs his wrist so hard it pulls back Trooper's upper lip, exposing those pinprick fangs. "See? No bite."

He eyes me, trying to read me in that way I've already mentioned never works.

"Did you feed?"

Yes. I did that. I'm not stupid. In that way, at least. We stopped for a drink on the way home to surprise Isuzu. It's just that Trooper hasn't gotten the hang of delayed gratification, that's all.

"Yes," I say. "I feed."

"Before bite, or after?"

"Before."

He looks at me. He looks at the vampire puppy I'm trying to return. He looks back at me.

"So what?" he says. "Show me this big, bad bite." He laughs. *At* me. Not *with* me.

And I guess it *is* a little funny, a vampire complaining about being bitten—by a pinpricky little puppy, no less. Even if the poor thing managed to break the skin, the problem wouldn't be the wound. The problem would be getting his fangs *out* before the wound healed around them. The big problem would be not sticking to his vampire victim like he's been Super Glued there.

I think about just leaving Trooper on the counter and making a run for it. What would they charge me with? Not shoplifting. More like shop *dumping*. I paid cash. There's no address on file. And he'll just resell Trooper to somebody who isn't living with a breathing chew toy. He'll laugh all the way to the bank.

It's not hard to imagine him doing that. Laughing seems to be something he's good at.

"You want I should get you a Band-Aid?" he asks, before exploding again.

"Fine," I say.

He laughs.

"Fine," I repeat. I remind myself the alternative involves a chain, a tree, and sunlight. And my being stupid isn't Trooper's fault. There's no reason he should suffer for it.

So I run. I leave Trooper on the counter as the pet shop guy laughs even harder. And I run.

I run like hell, all the way back to my other pet. Back to the one I'm emotionally invested in. Back to the one I couldn't give back, even if I wanted to.

•   •

Alll gone," I announce, walking in the door, empty-handed.

Isuzu's sitting on the couch, watching TV. *The Little Bobby Little Show*. She's got her elbows on her knees, her chin cradled between the knuckles of both fists. "Good," she says, not taking her eyes away from the screen.

I sit next to her on the couch, smooth a stray hair away from her forehead. "So, what's Bobby up to today?"

"Singing into his hairbrush," Isuzu says.

"Is he any good?" I ask.

But Isuzu just shrugs and goes on watching.

-12-

SLAPJACK

We're playing Isuzu's favorite card game when my world is blown apart by a sneeze.

(aaaahhh-chooo)

No caps. No exclamation points.

Isuzu has an elfin nose, and the noise it makes is a polite little excuse for a sneeze. It might be dust, stirred up by our smacking the table over and over again, trying to slap those darn jacks. Or maybe a strand of her hair, undone, has spilled out from the exertion of slapping and giggling and scraping all the cards over to her side of the table when I let her win again. Maybe that errant hair has brushed her nose, tickling the sneeze nerves along the way.

Or maybe this is the first sign of how my heart will pay for all its presumption. I won't lose Isuzu to my friends or neighbors. No. I'll lose her to the thing we don't have the things to stop anymore: disease. The plague. The flu. A common cold, which is by no means common anymore.

Vampires don't get sick. We don't need doctors or medicine. The things that kill us do so quickly; we don't linger in some reversible biological limbo. To stay healthy, we practice prevention, avoidance, abstinence. We drive just slightly under the speed limit—those of us not suffering from midlife crises. We know exactly when the sun sets and when it rises. In a pinch, we can sleep in the sunproof trunks of our cars if we cut it a little too close some night. And that's about it. That's our wellness plan. That's our exercise routine and heart smart diet.

Isuzu rubs her arm under her nose, sucks a sniffle back in, tosses down another card. It's a jack. Of course.

Distracted, I forget to pull my punches this time, forget to hold my vampire reflexes in check. So my hand goes out and covers the card several heartbeats before Isuzu's hand covers mine. Her eyes go wide; she didn't even see me move. And then her eyes scrunch closed, her head tilts back, her mouth Ohs around a series of prefatory Ahs . . .

And then the other Choo drops.

Our hands are sprayed, along with the cards fanning out from under them. I look at the little beads of warm moisture scattered like diamonds on the back of my surreal, too-white hand. In the center is an absence—a silhouette in the shape of Isuzu's hand, left behind when she took the real one away, to swab at her nose again.

"You're supposed to say, 'God bless you,' " she informs me.

I'm still shaking off the brick that's just hit me.

"I'm sorry," I say, because I am—so incredibly, desperately sorry that my heart feels like it might stop.

Isuzu's sick.

Isuzu's sick in a world that does not suffer sick little girls gladly.

"I'm sorry," I say again, overwhelmed by my sudden uselessness. Isuzu's sick, and I have no idea what to do about it.

" 'God bless you,' " I say, at Isuzu's prompting, hoping he hasn't stopped listening to me. Praying he hasn't stopped taking my phone calls.

I *know* I've done wrong. I *know* I've been bad.

I know I've broken your stupid commandments. I know I've stopped going to your stupid weekly get-togethers. But your big threat hasn't been such a big threat, lately—you know? Why would you do this to a little kid? Getting at me through her?

Oh, that's *mature!*

Why don't you pick on someone your own size?

I look over at Isuzu, who's doing something she's never had to do before. She's shoving all the damp cards I've won over to my side of the table. She gets about half of them over there before stopping to sniff and rub again. And then she rolls up her snotty sleeve and turns her wrist to me, preparing to accept her punishment for losing.

"Wait, wait," she says, hurriedly. She closes her eyes.

"Okay," she says. She holds her arm out as straight and stiff as she can make it. It's almost like it's a single piece of bone—no joint, no elbow. She holds it there without me doing anything long enough to begin shaking. She holds it there long enough to finally open her eyes again. First one, then the other.

"Marty?" she says. "What's wrong?"

She's scalding, of course. Burning up. When I place my cold hand to her warm forehead, all I register is "hot." But that's how all mortals feel to my vampire hands at first touch, before the heat exchange, before I feel like them to them, and they feel like an extension of me. But is Isuzu's "hot" *too* hot? That's the question. And me, I just sit there like a dope, staring as my heat-pinked palm goes back to pale.

And then I have an idea.

I drop a pint into the reservoir of my Mr. Plasma, slide the carafe into place, and tap the warm-up button. The little red numbers click up and then stop. There's a rocker switch on my model so I can raise or lower the temperature to suit my preference, but the preset is always the same:

Ninety-eight point six degrees Fahrenheit.

Those are the numbers I'm staring at now, terribly pleased with my ingenuity, terribly frightened of what it might tell me. Cupping my hands around the carafe, I wait until they don't feel like my hands anymore—or separate from what they're touching. It's always a weird sensation, this warming up to the dissolving point. You can feel each degree as a throb or wa-wa in the blood. In your temples. In all your pulse points. They come fast, at first, but then slower and slower until the wa-wa's stop. That's when the background hum of nothing special—nothing different, distinct, separate—reasserts itself and you find that you've become one with, say, the cup of coffee you bought to avoid startling your next victim.

Before, borrowed heat was always a big part of any seduction of a mortal by a vampire. We'd rest against registers, lean against warm car hoods, cradle cups of coffee, anything with the heat we needed to camouflage our own chillier disposition. And then we'd cup the cheek, caress the neck, run a warmed finger along this or that length of exposed skin. They never knew what was going on. They never suspected that by touching, we were borrowing their heat, too, reflecting it back to them, degree for degree, so that our touch felt like their own to them, the touch of the perfect lover.

But now the thermodynamics of vampiric seduction have become the fuel of parental dread.

So this is what karma feels like. So this is how I am to be paid back. I've been running away from my life ever since I didn't die, but now—now my life has caught up with me, and it's getting ready to take it out on the only thing it still can, my sunshine, my innocent bystander, my too-easily-killable . . .

I take my hands away from the carafe and it feels like what it must feel like when an amoeba splits—that momentary sense of doubling, then loss. Before their borrowed heat can fade, I place one of my hands to Isuzu's forehead, praying for the background hum to continue, uninterrupted. That would mean that she's the same temperature as my plasma maker—98.6. That would mean she's normal, which would mean it's probably just a cold, probably just something that'll come and go on its own.

Probably nothing to worry about. Probably something to just ride out.

But the hum doesn't continue.

I can feel a distinct waaa as soon as my skin touches hers.

Okay, okay, I tell myself. No need to panic. A degree or two of cooling between pot and forehead. That's to be expected. My hand will warm back up to that point, and then stop, and everything will be okay. Right? Right.

Except they keep coming—wa-wa-wa—and I start counting them, like Mississippis after a lightning strike. Granted, this is hardly as precise a measurement technique as even counting Mississippi, but . . .

By my reckoning, Isuzu has a fever of around 110.

I turn a whiter shade of pale.

"Marty," Isuzu says, though it's harder to hear her this time, through the rushing of other people's blood in my head.

"Marty," she repeats. "What's wrong?"

The highest fever I can remember having was 104, when I was six years old. My mother made me get into the bathtub, which she'd filled with cold water and bags of ice from the drugstore. I cried from the cold and she cried from having to make me bear it. At the time, I had no idea how serious the fever was, had no idea that children like me were dying. All I knew was that I was sick and my mother seemed to be punishing me for it.

"Please," I pleaded, grabbing the edge of the tub, trying to pull myself out of the icy water.

"No." Followed by a hand to my forehead, pushing me back down.

"I'm s-s-s-sorry," I apologized, a feverish little Catholic boy, guilty since birth, periodically called upon to pay for it.

I tried getting up again.

"No."

The water closed in so cold, I could feel my bones inside my skin.

"B-b-b-but . . ."

"No." My mother wept, pushing back. The strings in her neck were pulled so tight, they seemed ready to snap.

"I w-w-w-won't d-d-d-do it a-g-g-gain," I said. "I s-s-s-swear . . ."

Which is when my mother slapped me and I stopped crying. Stopped pleading. Stopped trying to get out of the bath. I just went numb, and from the look in her eyes, my mother had done the same.

I didn't know children like me were dying. I didn't know that the ones who did were sometimes luckier than the ones who didn't—the ones who ended up inside machines that breathed for them. I just knew my mother had finally figured out the truth about me, and was going to get even. Even if it killed us both.

Obviously, Isuzu did *not* have a fever of 110 degrees.

That's brain-cooking temperature. That's "This is your brain on drugs" territory.

That's the "too" in "too late." At 110, she'd have gone past delirious straight to spontaneous human combustion. And there I'd be, scooping up handfuls of oily ash from the kitchen floor. Maybe I was counting wa's when I should have been counting wa-wa's; maybe the pace of the wa-wa's had something to do with my own frantically beating heart. But she *did* have a fever—my little experiment proved that much—which meant it wasn't just a cold.

I could draw a bath for Isuzu, but lots of luck finding ice in a world where there's no use for it. No drinks that are drunk on the rocks. No frozen foods section. No use for it but chipping it off our cars when it's that time of year, and it's not that time of year.

I've seen aspirin on eBay, at twenty-five bucks a tab, but with the bidding, the back-and-forth with the dealer, even with FedEx, it would be a couple of days before I had anything I could offer Isuzu. Assuming it wasn't counterfeit. Assuming it was even still good. And even if it *was* still good, what's the proper dose for a kid Isuzu's age? I remember something called "baby aspirin." "Baby" according to whom? The mothers who insist, "You'll always be my baby"? Or is there a specific cutoff? Are baby aspirin and adult aspirin even the same thing at different doses, or are they completely different? And isn't there supposed to be some disease where you're not supposed to give kids aspirin?

Plus, if there's a fever, doesn't that mean there's an infection? And doesn't that mean antibiotics? I haven't seen those on eBay. I think about calling Father Jack, asking him if Judas has ever gotten antibiotics from the vet, if he's got any leftovers. But how would I explain the need? Maybe I could get a mortal puppy from a different pet store, cut it, let it get infected, and then take it to the vet so I can get a bottle of antibiotics for Isuzu . . .

But what am I thinking? Even vets don't carry antibiotics anymore. That's partly because vets aren't really vets anymore. They're more like glorified dog groomers, nail clippers, the runners of pet hotels for when the owners are away. Maybe they spay and neuter the unvamped. And that's about it. An owner whose pet is in bad enough shape to need the services of a for-real, old-fashioned vet either can deal with the problem himself by vamping the thing, or else he was really looking for a disposable pet in the first place.

What about penicillin? Penicillin is an antibiotic. The first one. And wasn't that just made out of mold? But what kind? How do you find it? How do you grow it once you find it, and how do you get penicillin from it, once it's grown? And then we're right back in aspirin territory. How much is too much, too little, just right? And what if Isuzu's allergic? A lot of people used to be, proving yet again that every miracle has another side.

And it's not like I can't think of what to do. It's not like I don't have a one-cure-fits-all choice to consider. To choose. To decide.

Vamping.

That's the thing I have in my back pocket, worst-case scenario. Just like the do-it-yourself vets out there. If things get out of hand, I can always cure Isuzu by turning her into one of those howling midgets. It wouldn't be so different. Not right away. We could stop hiding. That's a plus. I could stop worrying, turn my toilet back into a planter, and never write another check to someone I met on eBay.

But eventually, things would change. As her face and age grew further apart, she'd realize what was stolen from her. That's when the fun—and screaming—starts. That's when my misery finally gets the company it deserves.

Ever since the change, History has become the largest section of most bookstores, at least those that didn't sweep their Cooking and Health Care sections into the bargain bin right from the start. Almost everything that's no longer relevant to the current context has been deemed "of historical interest," and reshelved accordingly.

And so it isn't too hard for me to track down a copy of *The Merck Manual Home Edition.* The hard part is explaining why.

Sex, blank, and rock 'n' roll, I decide.

That's my excuse. Fill in the blank. Drugs. Getting high.

It's long been rumored in the vampire world that certain diseases produce an inebriating effect when the vampire's immune system fires up to combat them. AIDS, anthrax, hepatitis—strains of these viruses are rumored to still exist, and can be purchased through the same dark channels through which cocaine and heroin once flowed. You know a guy who knows a guy; you meet someplace; you exchange newspapers. And then you go home with a postage-stamp-sized Ziploc bag full of fuzz or slime. You add a little to your bottle of lab-grown, keep it warm for a few nights, let the buggies cook, and voilà! When the BBQ's Enforcement Division isn't busy hassling microbleeds, these are the guys they go after. The bug dealers. AIDS, anthrax, and hepatitis—these are the pot of bug culture. But then there's the higher-end, exotic stuff—dengue fever, Ebola, typhoid, SARS.

I pick the clerk who looks like she might understand. Punky, cropped hair. Black T-shirt, "Bite Me" in white military-style stenciling across the front. Black plastic, dark-lensed cat glasses. I bend close to the counter so she has to lean forward to hear. I mutter my cover story into my fist, explain that I'm a bug head, looking for something new to pique my hemo- (cough, grin, sell the pun) *philia....*

Not that the clerk cares. It's midnight; my attempt at humor is cutting into her lunch break.

"Yeah, whatever," she says. "Don't forget your receipt."

I thank her and leave the child care books for another night, and a better excuse.

W hen I get home, the TV is on and Isuzu is asleep on the couch. Her blanket is kicked to the floor, her already-shiny face is shinier still, thanks to the sweat the fever has brought out of her. While watching her sleep and watching her breathing for signs of its getting shallow, I list her symptoms in my head.

Fever—check.

Sneezing, runny nose—check, check.

Cough—yes, okay.

But then:

Irritable? Fussy?

These are *symptoms*? Do they mean more than how she is normally? Is there some sort of scale or examples or something? Calling me a "poophead," say, versus threatening hara-kiri if I won't let her watch *The Little Bobby Little Show*?

And then there's this whole thing about spots—on her tongue, in her mouth, on her face. Red, white, brown, or worse? Regular or irregular? Plain or pus-filled? Carbuncular. Scaly. Leprotic. Open and oozing.

Flesh-eating!

I'm supposed to be the vampire, here. *I'm* supposed to be the one who sucks the life out of things, makes them feel hollow and exhausted and like parts of them are dying. But all it takes is a few sniffles from a mortal half my size to trump anything my fangs and I can pull off.

When I was vamped, there was a point when I'd been nearly drained, when I'd been taken to the bottom, the brink, to as low as a living thing can get and *not* be dead. It was a hole. A hole into which I'd fallen, only to discover that *I* was also the hole into which I'd fallen. It was a point of utter despair and emptiness. Before, I always imagined that the feeling was fear. Now I know better.

It was love.

Before, back then, it was my love of self. It was the love that gushed out of me when I saw my life ending, when I saw *myself* going away forever. This time . . .

I turn the pages. More contagion, pestilence, plague. More obscene illustrations of what to look for, lit clinically, lit with a sad, cold, slightly jaundiced light that reminds me, somehow, of pornographic films from the 1970s. All that's missing is the wocka-wocka background music.

No more.

I just can't take it. I just can't handle this Chinese menu of heartbreak anymore. And so I slam the book closed like a movie assistant marking a scene.

The noise makes Isuzu stir. She stretches. Rubs her eyes. Looks at me. I try not to stare at the whites of her eyes, try not to wonder what qualifies as jaundiced.

"How you feeling, Pumpkin?" I ask.

"Poopy."

"Poopier than before?"

She thinks about this as she checks whatever she needs to check inside that dying-since-birth body of hers.

"Nah," she says.

And then the word that puts my world back together again:

"Better," she says.

Sure, there's a few pieces missing, and it's a shakier place, for damned sure, but the Band-Aids are in place. Ditto the nails, staples, chicken wire, and twine.

"Better?" I ask, making sure.

"Yeah," she says, sucking in a sniffle before looking around her, toward the kitchen. She looks back then, at my face, at the pure sense of relief that's made its home there. Sensing a winning hand, she asks:

"We got anymore Count Chocula?"

Yes, I nod. Yes, of course we do. A hundred dollars a mouthful? No problem.

She smiles then, but doesn't say it. She doesn't have to.

Slapjack!

It's understood.

The funny thing about dodging bullets is the more you dodge 'em, the more convinced you become that the next one's got your name on it. So you start taking precautions. You duct-tape over the open outlets. You slip-proof the shower. You padlock the poisons. You fill a big tub with dirt, grow potatoes, build a still, cook up some moonshine, and disinfect every nook, cranny, and cubic foot of this pestilential sponge you call an apartment . . .

Welcome to Hypochondria by Proxy 101.

I figure it like this: whatever Isuzu had, she picked it up from somewhere and it wasn't from me. By which I mean, vampires don't *carry* anything—not typhoid, not influenza, not the common cold. Our blood's the bug zapper to beat all bug zappers. Period. Which is why the bug heads have to buy their supply of contagion, and why they have to keep coming back for more.

Which meant that something bacterial, microbial, or viral got tracked into the apartment from out there to make Isuzu sick. And it was probably still clinging to the drapes, the sink, her pillow, the clothes in the laundry hamper. Which meant the apartment and everything in it had to be disinfected. Which is where the potatoes came in. I couldn't cook penicillin on my own, but moonshine is just high school chemistry.

And so I dip and redip everything in my apartment, scrub everything down to the bone with homemade alcohol. Isuzu starts laughing a little too loud, just from the fumes. But even after I'm done, even after every bone glistens, there's still one other place to worry about:

Outdoors.

The place where the sun, and germs, are.

So the short version is: Isuzu and the outdoors are history.

She needs sunshine, I understand that. And she can stand by the window all day long as far as I'm concerned just so long as it's on the *inside* side of it. After all, the inside can be sterilized, but the outside? Are you kidding? The cubic footage alone is just *not* doable.

An ounce of prevention, that's what this is. Tough love. One of those things we do for the other's own good. Like a dunk in cold water. Like a slap in the face. Anything to keep them in the tub and out of the iron lung.

And it's not like it's a prison. I have a view. Isuzu can look at it during the day. Watch the weather. The birds. Whatever. We just don't have a front door that opens anymore. Not without the key I've hidden where the sun don't shine.

-13-

AN OUNCE OF PREVENTION

Growing up, I remember this cross over my bed. The beams were as thick as the dining room table's legs, and nearly as elaborate, looking more like fancy molding than some primitive instrument of execution. But the cross was the cross was the cross. It hung over my head every night for years, and when I wasn't kneeling before bedtime to pray to it, I really didn't give it much thought. At least not in terms of the object itself.

And then one day—the first day of spring that year— my mother opened all the windows and issued the eleventh commandment: Thou shalt dust! And dust we did, every nook, every cranny, every piece of fake fruit in the fake fruit bowl. Inside, we coughed and sneezed, while outside, the birds chirped and trilled, laughing their birdy laugh at all our silliness.

It was as I was dusting the cross from over my bed that I noticed it. I'd taken it down to make sure I did a good job, and was dismayed to see its ghost still there on the wall, outlined in grime I wouldn't have noticed if I just left the cross alone.

But the ghost cross isn't the point of this memory.

It's the real one, the one I took down to dust. It's as I'm dusting the *real* cross that it happens. The Jesus moves. I'm using cheesecloth and it's gotten snagged on the nail poking through Christ's crossed feet. I pull the cloth up, and Jesus rises; I lower it, and he descends. His body, it seems, is affixed to a smaller cross that fits into the larger cross in a kind of tongue-and-groove arrangement. There are secret compartments underneath the smaller cross—compartments containing candles, a vial of holy water, a vial of blessed oil, and a piece of paper printed with the words for the Last Rites. On either end of the crossbeam there is a socket inlaid with brass—holders for the secret Last Rites candles.

That cross had been hanging over my bed ever since the ice bath when I was six. There was a similar cross over my parents' bed, and over the beds of all my Catholic friends. A spiritual first-aid kit—or last aid, maybe, waiting. Every ready. And just in case.

Sweet dreams.

Germs, of course, are just the messengers. And Isuzu's sneeze was just a warning shot over my bow. I know what this little scare was *really* about.

Godlessness. Mine.

I can sterilize my corner of the world if I want. I can lock Isuzu away like a fairy-tale damsel for her own good. I can keep telling myself that I've always got vamping in my back pocket, as a last resort. But who knows what might come home on my shoes one night, or tag along with the Styrofoam peanuts in some box of eBay provisions?

"Look Isuzu, the soft kind . . ." And a side of plague.

What if she catches something fast and fatal while I'm asleep? Or while she's asleep and I'm not watching or listening in? What if I'm at work, where there's no such thing as sick days, or family leave, where annual vacations have to be negotiated months in advance, planned around, not easily changed without raising more questions than I care to answer? What if I wake up or come home and she's already dead, or so close there's nothing I can do?

What then?

For me, ever since I didn't die, I've been a member of the Two H Club: hell or here. I get to choose. So far, I've stuck with here. It seems like the smart choice.

Before not-dying, I would have thrown in a third *H*: heaven. But

I'm too Catholic to believe I've got a chance at redemption after everything I've done. I was raised before Vatican II and remember scapulars being pinned to my underwear. I grew up over a hundred years ago, in a house where every wall seemed to have its picture of Mary or Jesus, their hearts exposed and on fire, and circled with blood-dripping thorns or pierced by fierce short daggers. I was never molested by any of Father Jack's less conscientious brethren, but I got knocked around by nuns who could have put Joe Louis to shame. I was taught the cruelty of kindness, and vice versa. I really did believe I could go to hell for eating meat on Friday.

But since not-dying, I've eaten a lot worse things on Friday and every other day of the week. Or night, *Nacht*. I've killed. I've killed plenty, and with some enthusiasm, for quite some time. I saved a lot, too. And I did a lot of gray area stuff in between. And before Isuzu—before the possibility of losing her—I felt pretty much untouchable in both the retribution *and* redemption departments. I was a lost cause, sure, but I didn't care because there wasn't anything he could do to me anymore. At least not until the asteroids hit, or the nukes start going off, or the next ice age comes grinding glacially along.

But all that has changed. And even though I don't feel particularly salvageable myself, I have to think about Isuzu. *She* still has a soul to lose; all the *H*'s are still open to her. It's up to me to see that she gets into the right *H*.

And no, I'm not talking about Harvard.

Isuzu," I call. "Come here."

"What I do now?" she asks, and I wonder if this presumption of guilt is a good thing or a bad thing, given the task at hand.

"Do you remember Christmas?" This seems as good a place to start as any.

"Yeah?" she says, already suspicious, like I'm setting her up to take something back. Which I kind of am—in this case, Santa Claus. She's eight. She's eight with extenuating circumstances, sure, but it's way past time she knew the truth about Santa versus Christ.

"Do you know why we celebrate Christmas? The *real* reason, I mean?"

"Because that's when Jesus was born," Isuzu says.

I blink.

We've never discussed this, and I just assumed she didn't know. Sure, she *did* have a life before me, but I've listened in after putting her to bed, and I've never heard her praying. No, all there ever was, was her saying good night to the things in her room, followed by that sweet snore of hers. Maybe she prayed silently. Living in a hole in a world full of vampires, she'd learned to do a lot of things quietly, so maybe praying was another one.

"Yes," I say. "We celebrate Christmas because that's when Jesus was born." Pause. "And who *is* Jesus? Why do we care about him?"

It's Isuzu's turn to blink. She scrunches up her face. "I think he's one of Santa's elves," she says. "The one who wanted to be a dentist."

I imagine Pope Peter the Last, covering his eyes, talking to his dying sister long distance, the tips of his fingers rubbing his temples in little circles.

"No," I say. "That's Hermey, and he's just a puppet on TV. There aren't any elves. Not for real."

Isuzu looks at me with renewed suspicion. Clearly, I'm changing my story from even a few months ago. Clearly, I'm not a man to be trusted.

"So who makes my toys?" she demands, already ignoring the middleman. *My* toys. Not *Santa's* toys, not the ones he brings to all the good little girls and boys. There's no such thing anymore. There's just Isuzu and KidTV and *The Little Bobby Little Show.* That's probably where she learned about Hermey, the dentally inclined elf. She probably watched Little Bobby Little watching it on TV—*on TV.*

I wonder what she must have thought, unwrapping the homemade crap I labeled "From Santa" and then seeing what Bobby Little got on TV. Did she think that Santa just didn't love her as much? Or maybe the problem was Jesus-aka-Hermey. He was too busy thinking about teeth, and so the stuff he made didn't turn out as good as the stuff Little Bobby got. All Jesus' stuff went to the Island of Misfit Toys or maybe to little girls named after trucks, who used to live in holes, who used to have moms, who used to not know what the other kids got, and who used to be happy.

"*I* make your toys," I snap, a little angry. Not at her, but at her situation. "The elves on TV are fake. The kids on TV are fake. Santa Claus is a fake." Pause. "But you and I are real, and I really want you to—"

"Does this mean I won't get any more toys?" Isuzu asks, cutting to the chase.

"No," I say. "I made them and I'll still make them."

"Okay," Isuzu says, and begins to walk away.

"Wait," I call out. "We didn't finish talking about Jesus."

"I thought he was a fake," she says, turning back around.

"No."

"But he doesn't make toys?"

"That's right. He doesn't."

"And he doesn't pull teeth?"

"It'd probably be easier than this, but no."

"So why do we care about Jesus?"

"Funny you should ask," I say, patting the sofa cushion next to me. "Once upon a time, a way, way long time ago . . ."

So, was Jesus like the first vampire?" Isuzu asks. "Is *that* why we celebrate Christmas?" And I can already see her being troubled by this possibility, seeing as her mom used to celebrate it with her, too, and her mom wasn't exactly crazy about vampires.

"No," I explain for the third or fourth time. "Jesus was the Son of God, and he died for our sins."

"But you said he drank blood and didn't stay dead. And he made other people not stay dead, too. And he didn't get *old* old, and he cried blood, and . . ."

And I want to tell her to just trust me on this one. Sure, Jesus had a lot in common with vampires, but he wasn't one. If anything, maybe he was the first vampire *victim*, in the metaphorical, sacrificial lamb sense. Problem is, I can't think of a way to explain the idea of a metaphor without making it sound like a lie.

"Jesus was just Jesus," I say, trying to hide my exasperation. "He wasn't like anyone else. He was special. He was a gift from God— you know, like a present, for Christmas, but this one was for everyone, even the bad boys and girls, because Jesus was going to help them be good. Jesus was mortal, like you, but he was immortal, too, like me. But unlike you *or* me, he was holy. His holiness is what makes him special and—"

"Were the holes in his neck?" Isuzu asks.

"What?"

"You said his holes made him special," Isuzu says. "Did a vampire give him the holes? Did God do it? Is *God* a vampire?"

"No, no, no," I say, my exasperation right out there in the open. "'Holy' doesn't mean 'with holes,' it means—"

"Oh, wait," Isuzu cuts in. "You mean the holes in his *hands.*" As if to call attention to the limb in question, she nails her forehead with the heel of her palm. "Duh."

" 'Holy' doesn't mean 'with holes,' " I repeat, trying to plug whatever holes I may have created. "If anything, it means 'without holes.' " Pause. "Do you know what a 'sin' is?"

"Something bad," Isuzu says. "Being naughty."

"Yes," I say. "But sin can be like a hole, too. The bigger the sin, the deeper the hole. Some sins are hardly deep at all, and it's really easy to get out of them, but other sins are so deep, there's almost no way to get out without somebody's help. Some sins are so deep, when you look up, you can't even see the sky."

I'm feeling pretty proud of how well my analogy's extending itself. But then I look over at Isuzu.

I stop talking.

She's pale.

She's pale, and her lip is trembling. Her eyes are beginning to well up.

"Me and Mommy *lived* in a hole," she sobs. "A long, long time." And she doesn't say it, but I can tell she's thinking it, that the people who helped them out of that hole for the last time were vampires like me, like maybe this Jesus guy with holes in his hands, but none in his soul, and for sure, none in his history of former residences. Mangers. That's as bad as it ever got for Jesus H. Christ, D.D.S. , mangers, and maybe a cave here and there, during that fasting-in-the-wilderness gig and later, during that three-day aboveground dirt nap he took between Good Friday and Easter. And that's it.

And somehow, all of this is the real meaning of Christmas!

No wonder the toys she got sucked. She'd been living in a hole, which is a kind of sin, which is naughty, for most of her life, and then her mother had to go away, because naughtiness has to be punished. Little Bobby Little—he's on the good list. And Isuzu . . .

Well, Isuzu is crying that spooky, almost silent cry of hers. There was math to be done and she's added it up. And the bottom line is this: she's on the wrong list. The bad one. And she doesn't know why, just that she is.

"I'm sorry," she says, followed by more slow-leak sobs.

And me?

I'm thinking that parenthood is like a hole you dig a little deeper each day, until eventually it's so deep you can't throw the dirt out anymore, and it just keeps falling back on you. At the moment, I'm about ankle deep, I'd say. But there's more coming, and that's the scary part.

I still have my Last Rites cross. It was packed away in a box of my mother's old things. It still has the candles, and the oil, and one empty vial of what used to be holy water, long since evaporated.

I figure I can postpone most of the sacraments until after Isuzu's an adult and vamped. After that, it'll be safe to bring her fang-to-fang with Father Jack—safe on at least two counts. For confession, sure, she'll be looking at a lot of Hail Marys by the time she hits twenty-one, but I've already started keeping a list of her sins and she's promised to do the same. When the time comes, we can compare lists, debate, negotiate, compromise, and then book a couple of nights on Father Jack's schedule. Communion? Let's just say Communion has changed a lot since the change. It's become a lot more . . . *literal*. Strictly nonmortal fare.

Confirmation?

Confirmation's just a booster shot for Baptism, only with the additional complication of adding a vampire bishop to the mix. Matrimony? Yeah, *right*. Like I'm ever going to have a dead body for that to happen over. And the same goes double for Holy Orders.

But I can't risk Isuzu's soul should anything not unforeseeable happen between now and her vamping. Which means Baptism is still on the table. Fortunately, you don't always need a priest to get baptized. In an emergency, if someone's dying . . .

And I still have that cross. It still has the candles, and the holy oil, and one empty vial in need of some water, freshly blessed. Lucky for me, I know a guy. I've got a connection.

So, when do you go on?" I ask Father Jack, during our next dead-time walk.

"Go on?"

"Perform," I say. "Say mass. Um, officiate."

Father Jack smiles wide enough to actually show fang. If it weren't for the black eyes and the clown complexion, you almost wouldn't know Father Jack's a vampire for as often as he lets his fangs down. Of course, Father Jack's an old pro at hiding what he really is. Not that it matters much now, but still.

I like knowing, by the way. I like knowing about Father Jack's . . . *inclinations*. It helps keep me quiet about Isuzu—just in case his being a vampire isn't enough. Plus, it helps in the holier-than-thou department. Father Jack isn't holier than anybody. He's a priest like I'm a blood inspector; we're both just moonlighting.

"So, you're interested in attending a service," he says, the fangs still denting either end of his smile.

"For old times' sake, I was thinking," I say.

More smiling. More fang.

"Jack," I say. "Turn it down, will ya? I forgot my shades."

"Kill me for being happy," Father Jack says. "Or, wait, no. Not happy. *Amused.*"

"Oh yeah? What's so funny?"

"You," Father Jack says. "Could this finally be the mighty Kowalski, admitting he needs a Higher Power to deal with his gambling?"

"Don't bet on it," I say.

"Cute."

"But not like 'altar-boy cute,' right?"

"Touché."

"Say," I say, changing subjects, or getting back to the original one.

"Yes?"

"I haven't been in a while," I say. "Do people still cross themselves with holy water when they come in?"

"It's almost all the same," Father Jack says. "The holy water. The liturgy. Communion's a little different, but I'm sure you already know that. The fish are different."

"The fish?"

"The symbol of the early Christians," Father Jack says. "They've monkeyed with it. Now it's got a little grin with a fang poking out." Pause. "It looks like a G.D. piranha, but I didn't get a vote."

"Tell me how you *really* feel," I say.

But Father Jack just goes back to smiling at the prospect of having netted another one. The fangs poke out at either end of his smile. He looks like a goddam piranha but at least he's a happy one.

I figure it like this: Isuzu *is* dying, not quickly, but quicker than anybody else I know. *And* there *is* no priest available—no *safe* priest, at any rate. So I did it myself. Just like Halloween. Just like the crappy Christmas presents. I baptized Isuzu just before her ninth birthday. I promised God that I'd get something more official done, once it was safe.

"It's cold."

That's all Isuzu has to say, as I pour the holy water over her head as she leans over the sink.

"That's to remind you of the pain Jesus suffered for us," I say, making it up as I go along. Just like always.

"Oh," she says, gritting her teeth—my brand-new Christian Trooper.

"Okay," she adds.

"From your lips," I say, making the sign of the cross with my thumb.

-14-

KID STUFF

Super Glue and a ten-year-old is a bad combination.

Ditto, paint and a ten-year-old. Not to mention twine, duct tape, screwdrivers, thumbtacks, rubber bands, idle hands, and guaranteed unsupervised time locked inside, all day, every day. It doesn't matter that she's being kept inside for her own good. It doesn't matter that you're trying to limit her exposure to germs and your own bad karma. It doesn't matter how many trees there are out there she could fall out of, breaking God only knows how much, how badly. What matters is that she blames you, and has plenty of time to think about it, because you—you vampire wannabe dad, you—you sleep the same sleep of the dead that all vampires do.

And so waking up becomes an adventure—especially waking up after punishing Isuzu for some infraction or other. Will I wake to find that my wrists and ankles have been bound together? Or will it be my eyes and mouth that have been duct-taped closed? Will I get most of the way to work before glancing in the rearview mirror to notice the raccoon mask painted around my eyes? Or perhaps the back of my chair will just fall off when I rest against it, sending me tumbling backward while my glass of warm blood splatters against the wall like some shotgun suicide's P.S.

Tonight I wake up with my hands glued to my face, one per cheek, bracketing my mouth like some real-life version of Edvard

Munch's *The Scream.* Or maybe she was going for the cover of one of those *Home Alone* movies (a birthday present I now regret). The thing is, I haven't even punished her this time—or rather, I didn't punish her last night. All I did was refuse to cave in to her latest whim.

It occurs to me to scream, to yell, to blow my top and read Isuzu the riot act. It occurs to me, too, that she knows I won't—*can't,* really, not with our thin walls and nosy neighbors. The system we've worked out to get around this problem is to use a normal voice to say whatever it is we'd like to scream, but snapping our fingers before and after, like quotation marks.

(Snap.) "Go to your room." *(Snap.)*

(Snap.) "I hate you." *(Snap.)*

That's how it normally works. Under the current circumstances, however, my fingers are busy getting to know my cheeks better, making the snapping alternative to screaming a bit difficult. Sure, I could rip my hands free, which I'll have to do eventually, but I'm saving that. And yes, I could *say* the word "snap," but the word itself and the bone pop of actual snapping fingers are at least an octave apart—an octave in which lies all the difference between "I mean business" and Rice Krispies.

And so I walk into the living room, my hands still stuck to my face, saying nothing. Isuzu's lying on the floor with her back to me, coloring, when I find the right floorboard, step on it, and watch her little wing bones tense. The hand she's holding the crayon with stops, waits. Still saying nothing, I find another squeaky floorboard, and smile to myself when the crayon she's holding snaps in half.

I don't say "snap." I don't *say* anything. Instead, I walk right up to her, lean forward a little bit, and muss her hair in a friendly, paternal way with the bony knob of my elbow. Her flinch is all I'd hoped for, and more.

Moving on to the kitchen, I pinch the refrigerator door's handle between my elbows and pull. The gasp of the door's rubber gasket underlines all the breath holding going on in the next room. Inside the refrigerator—inside my part of the refrigerator—is blood, bottled, jugged, IV-bagged. Invariably, the surface surrounding the fluid, whether glass or plastic, is smooth. Slippery. Decidedly *not* elbow friendly. Well, maybe a pair of *bare* elbows might pull it off with a little friction and luck, but mine are swathed in designer silk pajama sleeves. And it's not as though I can just roll them up. Even gravity's no help. All gravity does is gather all that slick fabric at the crook of my arm, where it's least needed.

No matter. Succeeding is not the measure of success for this particular task. Failing is. Failing as loudly and as messily as possible. And so I go for the glass.

Isuzu comes running at the sound of the crash, her bare feet stopping short of one of the farther-flung shards. Me, I'm barefoot, too, standing on the other side of all that broken glass and cold blood, hands to cheeks, the gesture finally seeming appropriate to the circumstances. I can practically see her heart beating in her chest. I can definitely see her pulse throbbing in her neck vein, straining against the muscles and strings, swallowing, working very hard at keeping quiet until *I* stop being quiet.

Which I don't stop doing, even after ripping both hands free of my face, taking a little cheek away with each. The resulting blood sprays out in a mist like a perfume spritzer, the tiny droplets hanging in the air—those that aren't speckling Isuzu head to foot.

I have only a second or two before the clotting starts. So I snap my blood-slicked fingers, spraying Isuzu anew. I take a step forward through the broken glass. The next snap is a little harder, a little stickier, while the third is harder still. I take two more steps through the broken glass. By the fourth, fifth, sixth step the blood is completely dry, and snapping my fingers is a snap again. With my last step, I clear the glass and am standing right next to my daughter, the practical joker.

The wounds on my cheeks—still stitching themselves together, bright pink—look like clown makeup against my death-pale skin. I look down, she looks up. I grin with every tooth in my head.

And when Isuzu finally hugs me about the waist, blubbering her muffled apologies into my stomach, I figure I've played it just about as well as it can be played.

•   •

Maybe the problem is me.

I come from a generation that really doesn't believe in the so-called cry for help. We figure that if a kid is acting like a brat, it's because he's a brat and not because he's nursing some find-me-if-you-can emotional trauma. Half the kids I grew up with were pyros, and the other half were petty thieves. And on Devil's Night in Detroit, we'd pool our talents, steal some matches, and leave burning bags of dog shit in front of every door we could knock at and run away from. We were kids—that was our explanation. I mean, sure, I was raised Catholic, but that whole part of the Bible about kids being innocent and "Suffer the little children," yeah, *right.* Pull the other one. *The Lord of the Flies* was old news before it was even written. My friends and I were little whooping savages. And we knew this simple fact better than our own names:

Being bad's just more fun than being good.

So, Isuzu's pranks? Kid stuff. Blowing off steam. I went through the motions of disapproval, but it wasn't like I could threaten her with being grounded. She already was. Had been pretty much since that first sneeze blew our world apart. If she didn't deserve to be cut a little slack, who did?

But then the pranks just stopped.

There were a few halfhearted attempts after gluing my hands to my face—a couple of thumbtacks that tickled, more than anything else, in my slippers, a bottle of blood with the cap Super Glued on. But after that nothing.

And then she started doing this thing with her neck. She'd be walking across the apartment, stop, tilt her head back, and then crank it, left, then right, popping vertebrae like knuckles. Other times, she'd complain about her jaw hurting, just under her ears, right where it hinged into the rest of her skull. And sometimes, she said, she could feel the veins at the side of her head. She'd just start thinking about them, and then she could *feel* them, could feel them *pulse.* After that, it wasn't too long before she started wondering if her pulse was going too fast or too slow. She'd stare in the mirror, her head tipped slightly, trying to see if she could see the vein in her temple moving the way it felt like it was moving.

And then there were the movies. *The Diary of Anne Frank. The Great Escape. Home Alone. Cool Hand Luke. Birdman of Alcatraz. Anne Frank*, again. And again.

"Izzy," I say, when Anne's decided that people are basically good for the third or fourth time, "is there anything you want to talk about?"

"Huh?" she says, her face lit blue by the screen.

"Is anything wrong?"

Shrug.

"Are you okay?"

Shrug.

"I was thinking of setting the apartment on fire." Pause. "Whaddaya think?"

Shrug.

She talks to her socks.

She talks to them and begins staging hand puppet shows before putting them on her actual feet. And then, one night she *stops* putting her socks on altogether. She also stops changing out of her pajamas.

"Why?" she asks, after I ask her the same question.

"What's the point?" she adds, clarifying the point.

The Diary of Anne Frank is a good movie," Father Jack says, holding on to Judas's leash. "Lots of people watch it over and over. Sure, six times in one week *is* a little much, but I don't think it's a sign you're going crazy." Pause. "I think it's a sign you should get out more. Which you're doing now, by talking to me."

Judas stops to take a dump.

"Do you ever wonder what might happen if Judas ever turned on you?" I ask.

"Turned?" Father Jack says. "You mean, accidentally became a vampire pooch? How would something like that happen, Marty?"

"Not that kind of turned," I say, transposing Judas and Isuzu in my head, trying to keep the pronouns straight. Trying not to let anything slip. "What if he started hating you? You know, started biting or taking a shit in your shoes when you're asleep."

Judas finishes, drags his ass a few feet across somebody's lawn.

"Well, I guess I'd start watching for foam," Father Jack says, eyeing Judas like maybe I know something he doesn't. "I guess I'd lock my shoes in the closet when I'm asleep."

"But what would you do to him?" I ask. "Would you . . . ?" I fake two fangs with crooked fingers in front of my real fangs, mime biting down. Not that I'm thinking about killing Isuzu, or vamping her. It's just that things are going badly and I don't know how bad "bad" is going to get. This is the little girl with the bread knife, after all. The little girl who wanted to chain up her own dog for the sun to get.

Father Jack has stopped, and he's looking at the leash, crossing the back of his hand. He looks a little sad, like he'd just as soon not talk about what we're talking about. "Why would I kill my own dog when he's having trouble?" he says.

I shrug.

"Maybe if he was in a lot of pain," Father Jack goes on. "Maybe if he was suffering and there were no other options." He squeezes Judas's shoulder muscles through a handful of fur. "This dog has saved my life on more nights than I can count," he says. "I couldn't let him down when he's doing everything he can to say he needs me."

"Biting you is saying he needs you?" I say.

"If I'm keeping him well fed otherwise," Father Jack says. "Of course."

"And how would you help him?" I ask. "Assuming it's not rabies or something like that."

"I think I might consider finding him a friend," Father Jack says, after a slight pause. The word "friend" does something to his face, even in profile. Makes it seem more serious. More sad. More in need of a little friendly teasing.

I think.

"Not a puppy, I hope," I say, teasing him with the cross he bears. "You know what they say about owners and their pets," I add, figuring it's fair; he teases me about gambling.

But all Father Jack says is, "Don't go there," not in much of a joking mood. He pauses. "I don't," he says, tugging at Judas's leash a little impatiently.

-15-

THE PRICE OF EVERYTHING

A vacation.

That's what we need. A vacation from everything. A vacation from our lives. This place. This routine. Someplace totally different, where we're not known, where I wouldn't have to worry about germs. Someplace where it would be possible for Isuzu to pass.

Someplace like Fairbanks, Alaska.

I've picked up the brochures. Fairbanks is "the vampires' Miami." During the winter, the sun barely pokes its head above the horizon, for maybe three, four hours a day. The rest is glorious night, with stars everywhere and auroras hanging overhead like the ghosts of rainbows. During the winter, the night air fills with the whoops and giggles of vampires living it up—way, way up—past their astronomically imposed bedtime.

"Say Yes to Fairbanks," the brochures say, "for Moonlight, Midnight, and More . . ."

One of those "mores" is the fog. At forty degrees below zero, the temperature difference between the land and the surrounding air makes the entire landscape steam like an ice cube tray fresh from the freezer. The ice fog gets so thick sometimes even vampire eyes can't see two feet in front of them. It's like how I used to imagine purgatory: a place teeming with the souls of the almost lost, each seemingly alone in the crowd, individually wrapped in swirls of blinding, perpetual fog. I've always liked that idea—the idea of being able to disappear with just a few steps in any direction. And with Isuzu in my life, I like it even more.

"Hold my hand. Follow me." Poof!

Another "more" is coats. In Alaska, even vampires need something to keep them warm. It's not that we'll feel cold otherwise. Just the opposite. We won't *feel* anything. We won't notice that our blood is slowly turning to slush in our veins. It's like the frog and the boiling water. If you toss a frog in boiling water, it'll thrash about trying to escape, but if you put it in cold water and raise the temperature slowly, it'll just sit there, letting you cook its brain.

They're wired, these coats we wear in Alaska. That's because we don't have any body heat that can be trapped to make a regular coat work. Trying to keep us warm without a little electrical help is like trying to heat a rock by wrapping it in a blanket.

On the plus side, being wired for heat lets us see our own breath again. It's a little thing, this breathing steam, but it's one of those things that's become a symbol of our being alive, back before we were simply not-dead. Seeing your own breath again, for a vampire, is like some old guy's first hit of Viagra.

So let's add it up. Easy invisibility? Coats and fog breath no longer causes for suspicion? Plus an average outside temperature that kills more germs than Listerine ever did, back before everybody's breath smelled like a rusty old can?

Yep, I'm thinking vacation. That's what Isuzu and I need. A vacation from everything.

I buy her parka from the Screamer department at JCPenney, the down pillows from Coffin, Crypt, and Beyond. All it takes to get the wires out is a good tug, but getting the feathers in? That's another story—especially after Isuzu plops down on top of an open pillow, poofing a small blizzard of plumage across the room.

"Hey, Pops," she says in this slow, too-deep, rusty-hinge voice she's started using. Just in case I haven't noticed she's depressed. Just in case I haven't heard her cry for help. "What's up?"

I sputter a feather away before saying, "The price of everything."

That's half of a joke my father used to love. The other half is, "Even the price of down is up."

Isuzu's chewing a rubber grape, yet another weird habit she's developed lately. There's a hole on one end where the grape was once attached to a rubber vine. She can make the thing smack and pop like bubble gum and frequently does because she knows it bugs me. Other times, she gets it stuck to the end of her tongue and then exposes it to me, just for the fun of rattling her old man.

She does the latter now, and I snatch it off with a quick pop.

"Nasty cold sore you got there," I say. "You should see somebody about that."

"Yeah, right," she says, pulling another from a pocket in her pajamas. "But seriously," she says, smacking away again, "watcha doin'?"

"Me?" I say. "I'm getting ready for a little vacation."

Isuzu looks like I've just slapped her. She stops chewing. As much as she loves bugging me, I'm still all she's got. And it's clear from the expression on her face that the idea of me leaving for any length of time scares the hell out of her.

"Where . . . ," she begins. "Wh-wh-where you going?"

Oh, I *do* love this section of the parent-hood. The part where I get to torture the sprout with impunity. I let it last a little longer.

"Fairbanks," I say. *"A-K."*

"Jeezus."

"Language!"

"Sorry," Isuzu says. Pauses. *"Alaska?"*

"Twenty-hour nights, kiddo," I say, brushing away a few feathers that have settled on my shoulders. "Serious party town." I pause before adding, "Woo-hoo!" along with the fist pump of a much younger vampire.

Isuzu's eyes say, *Who are you and what have you done with Martin?*

Her lips decide to plagiarize the sentiment. "Who *are* you . . . ," she begins.

"Why don't you see if this fits?" I say, shaking out the parka and stirring up a brand-new blizzard.

Isuzu's eyes say, *Mine! Mine! All mine!* Or something to that effect.

"Are you kidding?" is what her lips actually say, using her regular voice, not the depressed, rusty-hinge one.

"Nope."

"You're for serious taking me with you?" She says this with an excitement and urgency I haven't seen in way too long.

So I pause before answering, letting her wait. Letting her stew. I give her parka another shake, smile, and let the duck feathers drift down around us, like easy puns.

One thing that's gotten worse since the change is flying. Not the service—the service was always pretty bad—but the fares. One of the fringe benefits of being a vampire was you always got the cheapest fares because you always flew the red eye. Now, the red eye's all there is, and you end up paying extra to offset the money the airlines are "losing" by not meeting their prechange profit levels.

Okay, I'll admit that the logistics of flying *have* gotten a lot more complicated. For example, something as simple as flying east to west demands the sort of rigid adherence to schedules that, frankly, most airlines aren't known for. Depending on the time of year, a plane leaving from New York and bound for Los Angeles might as well not take off if it misses its departure by as little as a half hour. Not that the flight itself takes all night, but flying time alone is not the only thing you have to squeeze into your sun-free window. You also have to factor in the time it takes the passengers to get to and from the airport on both ends of the flight, the time for baggage check-in and collection, the time it takes security to humiliate every third person in line, et cetera, et cetera. Throw a monkey wrench into that and the friendly skies start looking not so friendly, with planes landing on autopilot full of crispy critters.

On the upside, hotels in and around airport hubs have seen their business rise dramatically. Seeing as the only safe way to fly from coast to coast during the shorter nights of the year is to take off and land a couple of times over a couple of nights, any place with a room to rent is bound to make out. As an example, our trip to Fairbanks took four nights and three hotels. The only real problem we ran into was the toilet situation. Food I handled the way I usually do by making a run to the nearest pet store. But my food processor's bathroom needs called for a little creativity with the sink I'm pretty sure the Red Roof people wouldn't approve of.

As far as Isuzu's mortality goes, I've got that covered. On her hands, she wears gloves; on her head, sunglasses and gauze à la Claude Rains in *The Invisible Man*. On the morning before our departure, I make an exception to the no-outside rule and have Isuzu burn some of the leftover feathers.

"Get them going good and smoky," I tell her.

I tell her to take the clothes she'll be wearing, including the gloves and a whole roll of surgical gauze.

"Let it soak in good," I tell her.

"This smells like shit," Isuzu says later, as I'm mummying her head in smoky gauze.

"It smells like what it is," I say. "Burnt protein."

"Yeah," Isuzu says. "Like I said."

In the taxi, at the gate, at baggage claim, all I have to say over and over is one vampire-chilling word to stifle any further conversation:

"Sunburn."

The word goes through them like an electrical shock. They shake it off, but then they get a good whiff, and begin twitching all over again.

On the plane, we're offered extra servings of plasma by a stewardess who can't stop touching her lips, her throat, her lips.

A Screamer and *this, too*—that's what they're thinking.

Botched suicide—that's what they're adding, inside their tsk-tsking heads.

In Seattle they're going through an unanticipated cold snap, and I notice the wisps of fog leaking through Isuzu's bandages as soon as we hit the sidewalk to hail a cab to our hotel.

"Oh, Jesus," I gasp. "Not again," I add, patting Isuzu down frantically, while half a dozen baggage handlers look at their shoes.

"You're enjoying this, aren't you?" Isuzu mutters.

"Only a little bit," I whisper back, pinching an imaginary seed.

•   •

The automatic doors part and there it is—Fairbanks, Alaska, at five in the afternoon local time, the sunset already hours old, a sky-sized curtain of blue-green light fluttering and flickering in a ghost breeze from outer space.

"Wow!" Isuzu says, craning her mummied head skyward, her breath smoking out of her like the exhaust of the dozen or so taxis idling curbside.

Me, I've been holding my breath for a minute or so, waiting for this moment. As the doors slide closed behind us, I purse my lips and blow. A pencil thin stream of vaporous white trickles out. I blow again, harder, and more fog follows, thicker, a bit longer lived.

"Ha!" I bark, so pleased with myself it's almost embarrassing.

Even with the bandages and her eyes hidden behind sunglasses, I can tell Isuzu's making her "big whup" face.

"Well," I say, "how 'bout this?" I wiggle my tongue as I blow, and the stream comes out rippled and wavy. I extend my gloved hands in a ta-da! "Pretty good, huh?"

Isuzu shrugs.

Okay. Okay. I thumb down the thermostat on the collar of my parka until my own breath disappears.

"Breathe out as hard as you can," I say, and Isuzu does. Sucking her secondhand fog into the now-cold chamber of my mouth, I try to remember my army days, back when tobacco was the fifth essential food group. I shape my mouth from memory, hoping the addition of fangs won't throw the whole thing off. And then I puff out once, fast, as a halo of cold steam slips past my pursed lips. It wavers in the air, traveling outward, growing bigger for a second or two before breaking apart.

Isuzu's applause sounds like a teddy bear being mugged—a barrage of hasty muffled thuds from her mittened hands. "Cool," she says.

I bow and do it again on the rise up. Another teddy bear gets smacked around. I switch my collar back up and begin leaking my own steam again.

And then we notice it.

A pole.

A pole sticking up out of a drift of snow, the snow itself as red as a double-cherry Slurpee. There's no flag, no red-and-white barber stripes.

"Is that the North Pole?" Isuzu asks.

"Doubtful," I say, not sure exactly what it is. The pole itself is some sort of metal—steel, maybe, or more likely aluminum. Little pink bits of something dot the frosty metal, ringing it at three feet, five feet, followed by a half dozen rings between five and six feet, and a few more above that. Behind the pole is a digital thermometer, proudly declaring a bright red minus forty-two. And in front of the pole, wearing a parka plugged into a car battery and holding a camera between gloved hands in his lap, an industrious citizen of Fairbanks sits in a lawn chair. At his feet is a cash-leaking strongbox, and a sign reading, simply: "Get it over with," followed by the cost of getting it over: "$5.00 (U.S.)."

"That's not," I say, remembering all the times I'd been dared to lick a flagpole during the winters of my youth.

"Oh yes it is," our Alaskan entrepreneur smiles. "I can do wallet, eight-by-ten, and postcard. Postcard's real popular. I got stamps, too."

Isuzu fingers the first pink ring through her mitten. "What is it?" she asks.

Our businessman sticks out his tongue, points at it, and winks.

Isuzu tilts her swaddled head slightly, processing the information for a few seconds. Then: "Gross!" she says, pulling her hand away as if the pole itself is electrified. "You . . ." And she almost says it. Almost says, "You . . . *vampires*," but stops, changes direction. ". . . have *got* to be kidding."

"Hey," the pole guy says, raising both hands as if in surrender. "It's just something to do. It heals right back. And then you get to go home knowing a little bit of you's stayin' right here." Pause. "Helluva lot less painful than leavin' your heart in San Francisco."

"Maybe next time," I say, scooting Isuzu out of eavesdropping range before placing my hands on her shoulders and aiming her once again at the Northern Lights.

"Remember," I whisper, to the head underneath the bandages. "You get to pick what you remember."

Isuzu strains to look back over her shoulder, before whispering in return: "Not if it's on a postcard."

They don't make white greasepaint anymore. Either that, or maybe they just don't sell it in Fairbanks. Red, sure. Black, sure. Blue, green, yellow . . . purple, even, but no white. Vampire clowns— *Caucasian* vampire clowns—really don't need a base coat; they can manage just fine au naturel. Which is why I'm in Walgreens, buying Vaseline, chalk, and too many bottles of Wite-Out.

"You must make a lot of mistakes," the clerk says.

"You don't know the half of it," I admit.

Back at our hotel room, I dab, pour, crush, stir. I experiment on my forearm, mixing by sight as Isuzu looks on.

"Way too white," she says.

"Your opinion is very important to us," I say in a mechanical voice. "Please hold."

"No, for real, Marty," Isuzu insists. "I'll look whiter than Vanilla Ice."

Have I mentioned that Isuzu's gotten stuck on a 1980s music jag? She's been downloading stuff off the Internet—MC Hammer, Milli Vanilli, Mr. Ice. And me, I'm seriously thinking of nominating the inventor of headphones for sainthood—or at very least a Nobel Peace (and quiet) Prize.

"Listen, kiddo," I say. "When we're trying to fool two-tone eyes, you can be the judge. But for now, I think I've got a better handle on how vampires are going to see things."

She looks down at my arm, and then up to meet my eyes. She changes subjects. "So, do I get to swear?"

"Yes," I say. "Just for now. Just in public."

"And I can shout?"

"It'll be expected."

"Cool."

"No," I correct. "Sad." Pause. "But that's just how things are nowadays."

"Pretty shitty, huh?"

"Save it," I warn.

But Isuzu just smiles. This is going to be like Halloween for her—without the candy, but with all the "Fuck yous" she's been piling up, finally let loose at the top of her lungs.

There comes a time in the life of every father when he gets a little frightened of his child. And even though I've had a few of those moments already, Isuzu keeps bringing me more. Like this, for instance:

We're walking through the mall with the other tourists, Isuzu in her ad hoc greasepaint, fake fangs, dark glasses. I stop to take a sip from the blood fountain, and Isuzu just zooms in on this poor guy in a Hawaiian shirt.

"WATCH WHERE YOU'RE WALKING, YOU SHIT-FOR-BRAINS MOTHERFUCKING SON OF A BITCH!"

That's my little girl, exploding. The words bang against the high ceiling and ricochet around the enclosed courtyard. Every bloodsucker in the place freezes. Watches. It's not like they haven't seen this sort of thing before. They just always stop and watch every time.

The guy in the Hawaiian shirt looks around nervously, smiles, shrugs. Everybody understands. Everybody's glad it's him and not them.

"KEEP ON SMILING, MOTHERFUCKER," Isuzu screams. "I'LL SUCK THOSE EYES OUT OF YOUR MOTHERFUCKING SKULL AND USE 'EM FOR PING-PONG BALLS, I SWEAR TO—"

"I'm sorry," Mr. Hawaii pleads. "I didn't see you . . ."

"FUCKING RIGHT, YOU DIDN'T," Isuzu continues, her voice starting to break from the strain of using a register it's never used before. "LISTEN, DICKHEAD, IF I WANTED YOUR FOOTPRINT IN MY BACK—"

"Excuse us," I say, swooping in, clamping my hand over Isuzu's mouth, trying not to smear her makeup. "She's—"

"Obviously," the Hawaii guy says, only too happy to wash his hands of the matter. "Understood." He practically runs away, a blur of pasty white skin, hyacinths, and green parrots.

Isuzu bites the inside of my hand.

"Son of a bitch," I snap. The crowd that stopped for Isuzu now stops again for me. I wave a healing but still bloody hand in reassurance. "Nothing to see here," I say. "Continue as you were. Mill. Disperse."

I return my hand to Isuzu's mouth, this time to stop her from giggling. "'Mill. Disperse,'" she mumbles, making my fingers vibrate, followed by her warm, wet tongue, looking for gaps to poke itself through.

"Very funny," I whisper. "I *know* I said you could swear, but where the hell were you raised? A truck stop? No, no, wait. A truck stop next to a navy base next to a . . ."

I don't finish. I don't finish because the back of my hand is getting wet. The side *opposite* Isuzu's tongue, which seems to have stopped. Instead, I can feel her swallowing underneath my fingertips—over and over again. I look at the back of my hand, at the shiny fresh trails of sudden tears.

"Izzy?" I whisper. "What is it? What's wrong?"

Isuzu shakes her head. Swallows again.

Finally:

"What if she calls?" she sobs. "She won't know where we are."

"Who?" I ask, but then I know. "The machine will get it, Pumpkin," I lie. "We'll check it as soon as we get back to the room."

And the look on her face—even with the sunglasses, even with all the Wite-Out, trying to hide my mistake—the look on her face tells me she knows. Knows that her mom is dead. Knows that I covered it up. We haven't talked about it since that night I brought her home. I've wondered about her curious lack of curiosity but didn't say anything. I guess I was too relieved at being spared that conversation.

Had been, at least. Relieved. Spared.

But not anymore.

"Do you want me to say it?" I ask.

"Yes," she says, facing me with those dark glasses, making me look at two little mes staring back at me—tiny, trapped.

"She . . . ," I begin, and Isuzu flinches.

"Okay," she says. She nods as if I've actually said it, or maybe to stop me from actually saying it. "Okay," she says again, still nodding. "I thought so."

"How?" I begin.

"She never called," Isuzu says. "Not even during the day."

And just like that, I saw all my little Trooper's invisible, unimagined days, spent doing whatever, but also (always) listening for a phone call that would never come. You can't see that when you're sleeping through it. You can't see it when you play back the videotape later, or when you're watching from your PC at work. You can't *see* someone listening for a phone that doesn't ring.

And it's all my fault.

"You wanna pick out somebody else to yell at?" I ask.

"Nah . . ."

"You wanna yell at me?"

Isuzu looks up, making me look at me again, shrunk down and in stereo.

"Nah."

After our little mall adventure, the new cover story is that Isuzu's a Screamer who can't scream—or even speak, for that matter. Vampirism cured some physical deficits, some forms of blindness, some forms of deafness, but it couldn't make twisted limbs untwist, and it couldn't make stunted ones grow. So:

Isuzu was born without a voice box. She can hear, smile, or pout, as she seems inclined to do. But she can't speak. My little Harpo Marx, in Wite-Out, sunglasses, and fake fangs. I write out a stack of three-by-five cards for her to keep in her pocket and hand out as needed, each reading: "Fuck you and the bat you flew in on." For verisimilitude.

Of course, the new cover story fits nicely with the fact that Isuzu isn't speaking much at all lately, especially to yours truly. The two "nahs" after I confessed (or almost confessed, was fully prepared to confess) her mother's death are pretty much all I've gotten out of her since.

It's amazing how much of our everyday trivial exchanges can be gotten around without words. Especially when one of you is pouting. Especially when one of you doesn't care. For Isuzu and me, for instance, our post-almost-confession conversations quickly take the following form: me, gesturing a choice of some sort—teeter-tottering two different cans of pet food, for example, one in each hand like the scales of justice, or nudging and pointing at a passing sign—followed by Isuzu's shrugging, and showing me what the back of her head looks like.

Back at the hotel room I sit, painting some leftover Wite-Out on alternating nails—the thumb, the fuck-you, the pinky. Why? I have no idea. Maybe the constant quiet is making me a little goofy. Maybe I'm hoping Isuzu will be forced to ask. I blow, fan, blow again.

Isuzu looks at me idly. She steps up, takes the bottle and my hand. Wordlessly, she fills the blanks—the index and ring—and then goes back to watching *The Little Bobby Little Show* with the mute still on.

Missing the sound of her voice, I've taken to sitting in our hotel room in the dark, listening to Isuzu snore—my little idling sports ute—watching the weird reflections of the aurora play over her sleeping face, watching the weird shadows of hotel things stretch across the walls and ceiling. That's what I'm doing now. I'm sitting in the dark, watching, wondering if you can really call it kidnapping if you kidnap your own kid. What if it's for her own good? What if the only ransom you want is for things to go back to the way they were before you stopped talking to each other?

There's no need to bother getting her ready for outdoors. She's already wearing her parka and mittens, has been sleeping in them since we got here. It seems the hotel we're staying at doesn't make its thermostatic decisions with mortal clientele in mind. If you want it warmer for, say, sex, there's a surcharge. Seeing as I've checked in with what appears to be a four-foot-tall Screamer/burn victim, I thought it best not to bother. After all, there are some things that are even too creepy for vampires.

Those polystyrene ties, by the way, make abduction a lot easier than it was when I was still hunting in packs. Back then, duct tape was the way to go, but any efficiency expert will tell you, there was a lot of wasted motion involved. Getting the roll started, wrapping it around the wrists two, three times, ripping it off, and then starting all over on the ankles. With the ties, you get them started ahead of time, making these big *O*s—or maybe *Q*s, really, factoring in the tail thing. And when it's showtime, you just slip your *Q* over their wrists and yank the tab all the way down, no fuss, no muss, no room to wiggle. Cops have been using these things for crowd control for years, and I can see why. Cheap. Effective. Just painful enough if the joker decides to struggle.

With sleeping mortals of a certain length, you can tighten the ankles and wrists at the same time, provided you don't wake them slipping on your *Q*s. That's how it works this time, with Isuzu—sneak, sneak, slip, slip, stereo zip, and bingo! She's bound and portable before she's even had a chance to open those dead-giveaway eyes of hers. And when she *does* wake, she doesn't scream, or question, or say a goddam thing. Maybe it's because she's still pissed, or maybe this is just the noiseless way she always wakes, the way she was trained to, back when the walls around her smelled like worms when it rained.

I wait. Let her focus. Assure herself that whatever's being done is being done by a face she recognizes. And then I lift her out of bed and throw her over my shoulder like a rolled-up rug. She doesn't struggle. Doesn't squirm. Her body's utterly limp, as if it's so used to the idea of death, it doesn't know how else to be.

This makes me sadder than her being quiet does.

I take the back steps to the rental car a bit harder than absolutely necessary, jostling the trussed-up rag doll over my shoulder, hoping for a peep, burp, fart. A "Fuck you," a "Drop dead," a "Watch it."

Nothing. I respond with the same nothing, lowering her body into the trunk and then closing the hood.

I take the shopping bag full of supplies with me, setting it down on the passenger side before unplugging the engine heater from the parking kiosk. I start up the car and pull out.

None of this is necessary, of course. I could have taken her where I'm taking her without all this creepy subterfuge. What can I say? I'm a Catholic, deep down. Redemption *costs*. Between Good Friday and Easter, there's hell to harrow. Plus, I *am* just the teensiest bit pissed at the way she's been treating me lately. This was *supposed* to be a vacation, but it's become a guilt trip instead.

Sure, I lied about her mom getting away, but there's got to be a statute of limitations, mitigating factors, *something* to let me off this meat hook I'm dangling from. Like my not killing her. Like my raising her from that point on—*that* should shave a couple of years off my sentence. Hell, she's ten and I'm over a hundred. On the basis of seniority alone, I deserve a break.

But none of this is putting me in the right frame of mind for what I've got planned. I should be thinking happy thoughts. I should be thinking about the look on Isuzu's face. And so I drive, imagining her pout dissolving into a smile. Imagining her little arms wrapped around my neck, hugging, forgiving, welcoming me back from hell with an Easter egg and a chocolate bunny.

On second thought, maybe I'm putting too many eggs in this basket. When all is said and done, it's just ice. Not justice. Not payback. Not even just deserts.

Just *ice*.

We arrive. I grab the bag of supplies. Pop the hood. Help Isuzu up, let her take a look.

"Yes?" I ask, my entire world balanced on that pinhead, the first word either of us has spoken in days.

Isuzu blinks, would rub her mortal eyes if her hands weren't bound. I'll snip the ties soon enough, but first, I need an answer. She tries getting away with a nod.

"Not good enough," I say. "I need words. Sonic energy traveling through the air in waves. From your lips to my ears."

"Okay," Isuzu says, softly, so softly.

"Excuse me?" I say. "What was that?"

"Yes," she says.

"Cool," I say, snipping her free and then handing her the face paint, fangs, and glasses.

This just might be what hell looks like when it freezes over. When you think about it, when you think about the kinds of people who are probably there—the party people, the artists, the nonconformists. It's probably heresy to imagine that hell on ice could be fun, could be beautiful, could be a hell of a lot like the Fairbanks Ice Carnival.

To which I say: So what?

I'm an ex-murderer who's started taking Communion again, from my friend the nonpracticing-pedophile priest. We're both vampires, and we're both taking care of mortals—he, a dog named Judas, I, a little girl named for an SUV. Heresy's not exactly something I'm troubling myself about.

I've checked out the carnival ahead of time. In this world of ours—where knives are sex toys and five bucks buys you a postcard of a pole covered in tongue tips—you've got to be careful with anything that sounds that close to "carnivore." But it's okay. Nothing you wouldn't see in a PG-rated movie from before the change. There's skating, ice sculpting, your average rigged carnival games, and rides like that Ferris wheel over there, lighting up the sky, spinning in the dark lenses of Isuzu's glasses.

I'll bet her dead mom never took her any place *this* cool, I think, fishing the skates out of the shopping bag—a pair for her, a pair for me. I offer her my hand.

"Shall we?"

Isuzu takes my gloved hand in her mittened one, and just like that, I'm forgiven.

We pass through the entrance with our skates slung over our shoulders, buy a ribbon of tickets, head straight for the rink. The ice—just ice—is as smooth as a brass casket lid. It's also lousy with Screamers who aren't screaming—just like a strip club in the lower forty-eight. They're laughing, instead, with their tight, prepubescent vocal cords, delighted, utterly delighted—for once, and for the time being.

"Can I talk?" Isuzu whispers.

"You can laugh," I say. "You can have a good time. In fact, that's an order." Pause. "Just don't go telling anybody our life story, okay?"

"Okay," Isuzu says, giving me a quick peck on the cheek before heading out on the ice in her flat-bottomed boots. She's got her arms spread like a bird and seems a little surprised that she's not gliding quite as well as the others zipping around her.

I whistle for her attention. "Hey, Slick," I say, lacing up my own skates. "Forget something?"

Isuzu takes her tinier pair from around her neck and looks at them as if she's wondering what they're for. I finish lacing, and she's still holding them in her mittens, staring at them, staring at the insane thinness of the blades.

"C'mere, kiddo," I say. "Let me help you with those." I sit her on my knee, pull one on, then the other, lace both up good and tight for my little first-timer. Taking both her hands, I lead her out on to the ice.

"Okay," I say. "First thing let's do, let's fall on our butts." I let go of her hands slowly, making sure she's steady, making sure her ankles don't buckle. "Okay. Ready?" I drop to the ice, seat first, spinning a half turn. I screw my face up in an exaggerated grimace—open one eye, then the other. "That wasn't so bad. Now, your turn."

Isuzu looks at me with a face full of serious doubts. Perhaps she was a bit hasty with that whole forgiving-me business.

"Listen, it's not that bad. Your butt's all padding." Isuzu smiles every time I say "butt." "Plus, you don't have that far to fall." Smirk. "If you break anything, we'll get a butt doctor." Smile. "A butt specialist." Bigger smile. "The foremost butt surgeon in the world. He'll do a buttectomy. You can pick out a new butt. Any butt you want."

Isuzu starts laughing, starts hiccuping, loses her balance, and doesn't break her butt.

"Wheeee . . . ," I say, grabbing one of her skates and spinning her like a roulette wheel.

The spinning makes her laugh more, and the laughing fuels more hiccups. And me? I'm already grinning so wide, my fangs almost meet in the back of my head.

If the Vatican could have seen us like this, I think it might have stopped killing us a lot sooner. By "us" I mean vampires, of course, and by "this" I mean skating. No one on skates seems evil; I'm sorry, it's just a fact. You can look evil in high heels and jackboots, in muddy sneakers and centurion sandals, but *skates*? No. Same's true for those Dutch-made wooden clogs, but that's another story (called *Heidi*, I believe). And I know what you're thinking: What about hockey players? Sorry. It's the sticks and the masks and maybe the missing teeth—*not* the skates.

It's taken Isuzu a couple of brushes with the dreaded buttectomy, but she's starting to get the hang of it. Right now, she's doing short glides of a couple of yards, her arms out straight as if crucified, until she loses confidence and starts rotating them faster and faster as if this is the way you stop when you've gone too far. Then she walks back to where she started—bowlegged, using the sides of her feet—and does it again.

Meanwhile, laughing Screamers and laughing non-Screamers zip around her at a respectful distance, doing their figure eights, their arabesques, their pirouettes, axels, and icy rooster-tail stops. Vampires can't turn into anything—not wolves, not bats, not spooky, spooky mist—but here, at least, they can *fly*.

Laughter happens. It spreads like the shaved ice, gathering in random doodles, here and there.

Isuzu spots a smaller vampire who seems to be ice skiing behind a taller one, holding on to the long tails of a ridiculous scarf, being towed around the rink, faster and faster, fishtailing at turns but still hanging on, the steam of the little one's pure joy scratching itself across the cold night air like a jet's vapor trail. Isuzu just freezes there, mesmerized, her breath leaking out in a contemplative trickle. And then, in the snap that decisions are made at her age, she takes both my hands in hers.

"C'mon," she pleads, tugging on my hand with more strength than I remember her having.

"But Izzy," I try, "I don't have a scarf."

Yeah, right. Like *that's* gonna work. This is the guy who also couldn't find any white greasepaint, or a pumpkin for Halloween, who right now, back at their hotel room, has the yellow pages, white pages, and Gideon Bible ringing the bathroom sink, playing toilet seat for her still unbroken butt. *This* is *Mr.* Make-Do, the master of improvisation.

Okay. Okay. You got me. There's jumper cables in the trunk of the rental car. I'm not exactly sure this is what the Hertz people had in mind when they put them there, but what the heck? Anything in the name of reckless joy. And so we trudge back to the car, and then back to the rink, me with the Hertz cables tied around my waist like a towline.

"Hold on, kiddo," I say, making sure Isuzu has a firm grip with both hands and is steady on her feet before moving out to take up any slack in the line. And then we're off. Isuzu laughs. She doesn't giggle much anymore. She laughs, instead. A deeper, older kid's laugh.

At first, she's perfectly happy with the moderate pace I've chosen. This does not last. Of course. Soon:

"Faster," she calls.

Okay. Fine. I was holding back, making sure she had the hang of it, which it seems she does; so, faster it is.

Laughing again, but shorter-lived, this time. This time, the bark of "Faster" comes faster.

Okay. Still doable. You want faster, I'll give you fast.

"Faster!"

You can see where this is going, right? She's developing a tolerance, like a junky.

"Faster!"

Isuzu—I want to say, if I could catch my breath, if she could hear me through the wind rushing in her ears—*Isuzu, there are certain laws of physics we were not meant to tamper . . .*

"Faster!"

Do you know how spacecraft gain the momentum they need to leave the solar system? They use the gravity of Jupiter to slingshot them out. I mention this now because, when I finally decide to stop, Isuzu just keeps right on going, creating slack as she gets closer to me, and then taking it up again, once she passes. There are several things that can happen at this point. For example, once the slack runs out, Isuzu's forward momentum could (1) pull me down on my butt, (2) pull her down on her butt, or (3) pull us both down upon our respective butts.

Or . . .

Isuzu could be stopped before she runs out of cable. This could happen as a result of (1) another skater, (2) several other skaters, (3) an invisible portal to another dimension that swallows her up whole, leaving just the smoldering split end of the jumper cable and perhaps one singed mitten, or (4) a bank of loose snow conveniently located at the edge of the rink.

Now, I know that our experiences up until this point may suggest a bias toward that whole invisible-portal thing, but as luck would have it, Isuzu hits the edge of the rink.

Now the snow in Fairbanks—that which hasn't been trampled into concrete by dozens of Sorel boots—tends to make for poor snowmen. It's not the good, *packing* kind, but the powdery sort that tends to stay loose. So when Isuzu hits the bank, it sends up a puff of snow, just as if she'd hit a pile of feathers. And she lies there, on her back, laughing her older kid's laugh while the stirred-up snow falls back down on her like one of those Christmas globes. She throws out her arms to either side and lets them flop down, kicking up more puffs of snow, more laughter, more feathers, more pieces of Christmas, raining down on her like the grace of a merciful God.

And me?

I just stand there. Watching. Smiling. Catching my breath. Feeling a true father's heart beat inside my vampire chest.

•   •

After the skating rink, there's the Ferris wheel, the merry-go-round, the bumper cars, a quick puke stop, and then, finally, the thing that all the rest of this has grown up around, the ice sculpting contest. Now, you might think that sculpting falls somewhere between fishing and chess, as far as spectator sports go. But you'd be wrong. After all, anything involving chain saws and blowtorches is bound to have a certain amount of crowd appeal.

This is the PG portion of our evening.

Each artist starts with an eight-foot-by-eight-foot block of solid ice and is judged not only on the quality of the final product, but also on the amount of time it takes to produce. So we're not just talking chain saws and blowtorches here—we're talking chain saws and blowtorches being wielded at limb-endangering speed in an effort to produce something beautiful as fast as vampirically possible.

By the time we arrive, the artists have already been at it for a while, the competition area already littered with discarded bits and chunks of ice the size of cinder blocks, bricks, ice cubes, snow-cone shavings. Every few seconds another chain saw bites into a virgin corner of its block, sending a fresh blizzard geysering into the spotlit night. "Oooo's" are followed by "aaaa's." The farting of chain saws. The hiss of propane.

The shriek of a mistake.

The gathering up of fingers. The spurting of arterial blood. The sizzle of the klutz's neighbor as he burns away the spatters that weren't part of his original design.

Over there, a unicorn rises out of its block; there, a polar bear, rearing up on its hind legs. There, there, and there, a totem pole, Rocky and Bullwinkle, the sculptor himself as centaur. Chain saw exhaust and ice fog mix to erase the feet of the artists, so that they seem like moving sculptures of themselves, rising magically out of the landscape.

The ice is as clear as glass, the sculptures acting like weird lenses, twisting the light that falls through them, stretching it, shrinking it, making it balloon. Passing behind their creations, the artists become giants, then dwarfs, then giants again. But it's the torches that make the most of these optics, making the sculptures glow orange and red and cobalt blue, seeming to burn from the inside and out, but coldly. Oh, so, so coldly.

And Isuzu's dark lenses catch it all, her little fake-fanged mouth an *O* of pure awe.

Back in the car, returning to our hotel, I ask Isuzu what part she liked best. I figure it'll probably be skating or maybe the bumper cars, but am crossing my fingers for the sake of art.

She looks at her skates, lying on the floorboard in front of her. The snow and ice have slid off, are making puddles, or dark wet spots on the skates' red leather. She looks up at me. She looks at the frost feathering the inside of her window.

"All the people," she finally says, picking the one thing I can't improvise for her back home—not with all the greasepaint or basketballs or jumper cables in the world.

-16-

CLARISSA

It starts about a month after we get back from Fairbanks. Singing. I can hear Isuzu singing in my ear, during my walks with Father Jack. It's after I've tucked her in, after prayers and lights out, after double locking all the doors leading in or out. She sings in a whispery, lullaby voice and I just assume she's singing herself to sleep. But then the baby talk starts.

And so I make an excuse of looking for some misplaced keys. That's when I find the thing, stuffed under her pillow. Of all the toys I've made her, I've never made Isuzu a baby doll. It just never occurred to me. Out of sight, out of mind, I guess. Now it looks as though Isuzu has decided to correct my oversight for herself.

"Crude" does not even begin to describe it, and neither does "sad." I thought she gave up on the whole sock puppet thing after Fairbanks, but apparently I'm wrong. Instead, the sock puppets have metastasized into this. She's stitched several together, making arms, legs, the trunk of a body and head. The stuffing seems to be a combination of dryer lint and the leftovers from her last haircut. The face is drawn on with Magic Marker, big baby eyes, a perky nose, a tiny bow-shaped mouth. The big eyes radiate big lashes like the rays of some kid-scribbled sun.

"Who's this?" I ask, trying not to sound angry, or jealous, or confrontational.

"Clarissa," Isuzu says.

"And what is Clarissa supposed to be?"

"A baby."

"Are you her mommy?"

"She doesn't have a mom," Isuzu says, before adding, "anymore."

"Oh." Pause. "Am I her daddy?" I ask.

But Isuzu just grunts over my too-needy heart, and goes on coloring.

Am I ever going to be a mother?" Isuzu asks, not too much later.

I wish I could say that this is the first time I've heard that question, but it's not. It's the first time for Isuzu, sure, but back when I was vamping strippers one at a time, the question came up again and again.

"What do you mean I don't have to take the pill anymore?" one or another would ask, after I'd run through the do's and don'ts and can'ts of vampirism. "I can still have kids, can't I?"

"You can have the sorts of kids that don't have to be potty trained, but the other kind? No."

It was usually right after these conversations that my brand-new vamplings got their first glimpse of how fast their fellow vampires can heal. As they watched the slashes on my just-slapped cheek zipper shut, their mouths would inevitably drop open as if *they'd* been slapped, and then the pink tears would start.

"I'm sorry," I'd say, leaving out what for, or for whom.

"Maybe," I lie, now, to Isuzu. "Maybe not," I add, to soften the lie.

Isuzu stands there staring at me, hugging Clarissa to her prepubescent chest. There's more to my yes-no answer, and she's prepared to wait.

"There are all sorts of different ways to be a mother," I say. "Maybe you won't be a mom like your mother was, but that's okay. I'm not a dad like my father was but I wouldn't trade places for anything in the world."

"Is that because he's dead?" Isuzu asks, not trying to be mean, just trying to play it a little older than she is.

"No," I say. "It's because he had to put up with me."

Isuzu smiles. She puts Clarissa's dirty little sock hand on the back of mine. Pat, pat. There, there.

"Plus, he didn't have you," I say, winning two hugs—one from Clarissa, and the other from her maker.

There are all sorts of different ways to be a mother."

That's what I told Isuzu, and it's true. Especially nowadays. Especially with all the non-mommy vampires out there, all the childless vampire couples looking for a little two-legged buffer to put between themselves and each other's throats.

And so the marketplace has obliged a needy demographic yet again, turning children into a special effect. CGI, mainly. Computer-generated infants who grow up at the click of a mouse. A vampire couple who wants to raise a child—a child they won't have to protect from other, less nurturing vampires; a child they won't be tempted to uncork themselves for a special occasion, like a bottle of pricey wine—such couples usually start their quest with a trip to the software store. Several packages are available—SimKid, VirtualTot, and Microsoft's WinKid, among others. All of them work pretty much the same way. Digital photos of the would-be parents are shuffled, recombined, morphed, and then "infantilized," yielding a virtual version of the crapshoot previously played by genetics. And after that it's pretty much *Who's Afraid of Virginia Woolf?* meets the dancing Internet baby.

The level of artificial intelligence used in most programs is pretty crude because most such programs never go beyond the cute years in their basic versions. If you want your virtual child to get past its eighth birthday, you have to buy the upgrades, which are notoriously poor sellers.

It should be pointed out that these programmed children are unlike anything ever known in either the pre- or post-vampire-ascendant worlds. They embody the easiest, most parentally appealing aspects of both the mortal and the vampiric. Like vampires', the child's diet is simplicity itself and never leads to anything as distasteful as changing diapers. Like vampires, these virtual children sleep the sleep of the dead during the day, and during the night cry just enough to suggest the general ambiance of babyness without ever actually trying anyone's nerves. The programmers omit such things as birth defects, learning disabilities, and childhood diseases, although the occasional software bug has sneaked through. WinKid, in particular, was notorious for its frequent crashes, followed by the "Nap Time" pop-up box, which could be cleared only by "rebootying" the computer.

Far more telling is the number of bugs reported that turn out not to be bugs at all, but design features aimed at making these user-friendly tykes more "realistic." Like: It always insists on drinking blood from a special cup. Like: The special cup keeps changing. Like: It doesn't seem to understand what the word "no" means.

More often than not, these non-bug "bugs" get fixed anyway. After all, when Darwin meets the marketplace, only the most customer-friendly survive—and you're only as good as your tech support.

Please hold.

So, who should we have be the father?" I ask, assuming it's a no-brainer. I've already loaded her photo, and am about to drag my own into the program when Isuzu says:

"Bobby."

"Who?"

"Bobby Little," Isuzu says, kicking my startled heart while it's down.

"Why Bobby Little?" I ask, meaning, why not me?

"He's funny."

I'm funny. I *talk* funny. We've already established that.

"He's got eyes like me," she goes on, meaning not like mine. Not all black and vampiric and impossible to read.

"And he knows good songs," she concludes, meaning the happier Beatle ones.

It's probably silly of me to feel jealous, but I do. Hell, I'm still jealous of that collection of dirty laundry she calls Clarissa. What's the point of being jealous if you can't be silly about it?

"Well, I don't have a picture of Bobby Lit . , . ," I begin, as Isuzu reaches past me, clicks a few times, and Bobby's smiling face fills the screen.

"You get that off the Web?" I ask, and Isuzu nods.

"Okay," I say, giving in. I click (sigh) and drag (sigh) and let WinKid mix their too-young faces into the face of my virtual (sigh) grandchild.

"What should we call her?" I ask when the morphing's done.

"Clarissa," Isuzu says. "For my mom."

My hands freeze over the keyboard. She's never mentioned her mother's name before, and I've never asked. Now I don't have to. Now I just have to find something to fill the stunned silence I feel myself falling into.

"Clarissa Little?" I ask, finally. "Or Cassidy?"

Isuzu thinks about it. She mulls the possibilities.

"Kowalski," she says, finally, giving me back my heart like a present for Father's Day.

-17-

THEM

Isuzu seems to be growing out of her clothes a lot faster than before. Her bones seem to be lengthening at an alarming rate. And I seem to be spending more time than usual in the JCPenney Screamers' department, buying new this, new that.

The Screamers' department, by the way, isn't really called that. Not officially. It's called "Just Right" at JCPenney, "Big Hearts" in Kmart, and "Small Packages" at Marshall Field's. Sears has a line it calls "Kenmore-or-Less," while at Target, the sign over the aisle just says, "Reaching for the Stars."

"Who fuckin' sez?" a Screamer shopping next to me wants to know. She tilts her head in the direction of the sign marking the aisle we're standing in.

"Just Right," the sign says, hanging there well over both our heads.

"Fucking adding *fucking* insult to *fucking* injury," she mutters, gesturing toward the other sign, set at approximately eye level for a Screamer such as herself.

"No Shouting, Please," it says. There's a picture of a disembodied pair of lips with fangs, pursed in front of a disembodied hand, a single finger raised, the better to ssshhhh you with.

"Fucking fascist bastard goat fuckers," she goes on muttering. "Oooo, that's cute. What size is it?" She grabs the blouse I'm holding, the one I think Isuzu might like. I let her. I'm not stupid. I'm also pretty sure it's too big for her, seeing as the Screamer in question comes up to about my chest, while the top of Isuzu's head is now just shy of my chin.

"Fuck," the Screamer blurts after checking the tag, and just before throwing the blouse, hanger and all, backward over her shoulder, aiming for the aisle floor.

"Sorry," I say, catching the blouse before it hits tile.

"Fuck you," the Screamer says, waddling around to spread joy on the other side of the rack.

Isuzu's bed is made.

That's the first bad sign.

When I get back from my latest trip to Penney's with a couple of bags full of new clothes, I can see her bedroom door open, and the made-up bed inside. She never makes her bed unless I tell her to. And I never tell her to because I don't make mine, either. The last time she made her bed was just before our trip to Fairbanks—before she knew such a thing was even being planned—and I found her in the bathroom with a full garbage bag jammed into the open window. She'd filled it with everything she could from her closet, her shelves, the cupboards in the kitchen dedicated to all that human food of hers. At the time, she'd planned to make her escape under cover of sunlight, while I was still sleeping. But by sunset, she'd only managed to get as far as getting the bag jammed halfway out the bathroom window.

"Hey, Miss Trooper," I said. "Planning a little vacation?" At the time, I was more amused than worried, partly because the look on her face was so serious.

This time, the look on her face is just as serious as she strolls out of the kitchen, holding the bread knife that originally introduced us in one hand, and in the other, a quart bottle of Xtreme Unction that's been replaced with gasoline. She's got several yards' worth of extension cord coiled over her shoulder, and is wearing every black thing she owns. Her face is smeared with black shoe polish.

"I didn't know it was homicidal minstrel night," I say.

"Funny, Dad," she says. "Ha," she adds, dryly. "Ha."

"You seem to have plans," I say. "May I—"

"I'm gonna go find 'em," she says.

"Who?"

"Them," she says.

"Them?" I say, still not getting it.

"Could you hold this?" she asks, handing me the bread knife. She tries the door as I stand there, looking at my own reflection in the knife's blade. It's about a foot long and serrated.

"Key?" she asks, holding out her hand.

And then I get it. Them. Clarissa's killers. She's going to find and kill her mother's killers; with the help of this knife, that gas, maybe just tie them up with that extension cord and leave them outside for the sun to get. She's older and taller and stronger than she was when she tried and failed with me, but I'm still not very optimistic about her prospects. With a little luck and the upper body strength of, say, an O. J. Simpson, she might send one of them to an (extremely) premature grave.

I decide to change gears. When you're dealing with a twelve-year-old holding a bottle of gasoline and, presumably, matches, it's best to take her as seriously as she takes herself.

"How you planning on finding them?" I ask, and she tosses me a copy of the *Detroit Free Press* Metro section from the night before. She's circled the face of a local businessman being honored for something or other. A hotshot. A bigwig.

Shit.

"Key," she repeats, her hand out.

What I'd like to do is just ignore it. Question her ability to recognize any of her mother's killers, after all this time. Problem is, that excuse won't work. Not anymore. Whatever snapshots Isuzu has shock-flashed into her brain are as good as the night they were taken. There's no need to compensate for age, the passage of time. Clarissa's killers look *exactly* the same as they did when they did the deed—and always will. Unless . . .

Well, say you're me. What's a loving father to do?

•   •

What do you think of capital punishment?" I ask Father Jack. Isuzu hasn't gotten the key. Instead, she's been locked in her bedroom, sans cord, gas, and knife. There are no windows through which she can climb, and even in her current state, she knows better than to make the kind of noise that would be required to break down the door. She *is* giving her Screamer vocabulary a workout, however, muttering under her breath, and into my ear, thanks to the power of cellular technology and a foster father with an increasingly unsavory tendency to eavesdrop.

"Conflicted," Father Jack says. "On the one hand, if it weren't for capital punishment, I'd be out of a job." He fingers the crucifix pinned to his lapel, just in case I missed the point. "On the other hand, you know what Gandhi said about an eye for an eye."

"Refresh my memory."

"It leaves the whole world blind," Father Jack says. Quotes. Paraphrases.

Maybe that's why we don't have the death penalty anymore. Not officially. It's considered too barbaric and too unusual in a world where death is no longer inevitable. What we use, instead, is humiliation. Stockades, for example, have made a comeback. Ditto, tar and feathering and stoning, but with sponges soaked in something awful. Banishment, of course, has never really gone out of style; its use has just been codified now. But the most popular form of punishment by far is leeches.

The number and placement depends upon the severity of the crime, and the penalty schedule looks like an old acupuncture chart, with the arrows running to various body parts labeled not with maladies but with malfeasances. Genital application, for example. Genital application involving a half dozen or more, applied publicly and borne for two or more nights in a row—though rare— is the vampire punishment for rape.

But how many leeches do you think someone who's killed your mother deserves?

Exactly. Fuck the leeches.

"Why this sudden interest in capital punishment?" Father Jack asks: "It's pretty esoteric, no? Just a wee bit *historical*?"

"I'm just thinking about some of the stuff I used to do," I say, and then regret it immediately.

"Oh goody," Father Jack says, rubbing both hands. "Tell, tell."

This is what I contribute to the relationship. I bounce my euphemistic problems off Father Jack as a sounding board and in return, I tell him stories of what it was like, back when vampires still had to hunt for a living. Father Jack's a bottle-fed last-waver, and these stories are like vampire pornography for him. And when he's in one of these moods, he's like an English professor whose one guilty pleasure is cheap pulp noir detective stories, full of bad-news dames and other clichés he'd mock in the classroom or condemn at the pulpit. But here, now, in his off time, he's all goody-goody.

"It was great, Jack," I say, feeling like I used to feel, getting ready to tell Isuzu a bedtime story.

"I remember this one time, I couldn't make the guy die."

"No . . ."

"Scout's honor. He kept on flopping around, holding his neck. Then he starts trying to crawl after me, grab my ankle. I finally had to drop a cinder block on his head."

"Ouch."

"And it *does* sound like an egg, you know. Like a big, thick-shelled ostrich egg."

Father Jack nods. Rubs his hands.

And so we walk, I supplying the gory details, Father Jack all wrapped up in his vicarious reliving of the Wild Wild West of Vampirism. Isuzu's still swearing in my ear. I do it mainly just to monitor now, though I've noticed some changes in the things I've heard. When you're talking to someone face-to-face, you tend to focus on the words, the expressions, the body language. But when you're listening to someone over a wire—someone who isn't talking to you, who doesn't even know you're listening in—you can focus on the things that might be considered rude, face-to-face. Like timbre, tone, pitch, the voice as abstract sound instead of the medium through which the words are conveyed. And what I hear in my ear, over the wire, through the angry muttered "Fuck this's" and "Fuck that's," is this:

Isuzu's growing up.

Her voice is getting deeper, richer, less kidlike. More womanly.

I don't want to know this. I don't want to hear it. And so I rest my hand in my pocket. I keep walking. I keep talking. I find the volume wheel on my cell and thumb it all the way down, trying not to think about what's coming next.

Here's some irony for you. Vampires are wimps when it comes to death. Now that they're immortal, they're more afraid of death than they ever were when it was inevitable. And when one of us dies, the loss is immeasurable, the grief among those left behind immortal in its own terrible way. A widely publicized vampire death—and almost *all* vampire deaths are widely publicized, whether or not the deceased was widely known beforehand—wounds the world for weeks, sometimes years. TV news shows pick apart the deceased's tragically abbreviated biography, from birth to vamping, and they all choke up at that point, no matter the manner, no matter the details. They're all like Walter Cronkite, and every dead vampire's another JFK.

The funny thing is, the media itself has probably gotten more vampires killed than almost any other cause, including car accidents. It's the media that makes suicide an attractive cure for vampire ennui. That orgy of attention is a powerful thing. Just knowing that the entire world will be thinking of *you*, that *you* will be lodged in their hearts and minds, that *you* will be the reason why every raindrop they see for the next several weeks reminds them of tears shed. Is it any wonder some vampire suicides leave behind media kits instead of suicide notes, complete with bios and video ready for broadcasting?

Of course, if you don't know you're going to commit suicide, you take what you can get.

• •

It wasn't hard tracking that first one down. Isuzu provided the main clue—the one the article she gave me euphemized around with references to his "stature" in the community. He was a Screamer and not much taller than she was back then. He was the one they put in charge of holding on to Isuzu while the rest went after the mother. He was also the first one she pulled the bread knife on that evening, before stumbling away in shock to be found later by yours truly.

So how was I supposed to find a rich Screamer of the male variety? Easy. All I had to do was park across the street from the Necropolis, a "gentlemen's club" a notch or two above the places I used to haunt. He'd toddle along soon enough. And after a few nights of me casing the joint, he does.

He steps out of a limo with blacked-out windows, wearing a trench coat that scrapes the ground when he walks. The greeter out front tips his hat, pulls open the door, and gets a fistful of crumpled bills in return.

Following a few minutes later, I find myself tipping a gauntlet of hands along the way to a table just behind him. My victim. My first victim in decades. I can feel something inside rising just at the thought of it and have to remind myself that this is for Isuzu. To protect her and avenge her and *not* for this oh-so-delicious rush rushing through my veins.

He's got a cherub's face, my victim. It's lit by the stage he's craning up at with so much longing and desire I almost feel sorry for the little shrimp. Until he starts mock-fanning himself with a spread of hundred-dollar bills, that is. He smiles at the dancer onstage, winks one of his black, black eyes, and loosens his tie. He's got almost no neck at all—not that that's the way I plan on taking him out.

"Is this seat taken?" I ask, interrupting my victim's reverie just long enough to take the seat next to him.

"Do I know you?" he asks, his piping little voice full of financial compensation.

"Not directly," I say. "But we have mutual acquaintances."

"Do we?" he says, arching a brow with interest.

I nod. "What're you drinking?" I ask. Two guys who know guys doing the quick-bond thing.

"Same ol' same ol'," he says, playing along.

"You don't look like a same ol' same ol' kind of guy." I smile. "You look like you might like it a little fresher than that."

And the shrimp plays it cool. He takes a sip. Says nothing.

So I play it cool right back. Say the same nothing. Look where he's looking, which is back up onstage.

"What must it be like," he says, suddenly, "to have legs that long?"

"It's not that great," I say. "You know, the whole bigger, farther-to-fall thing."

"Don't talk to me about falling," he says, placing his tiny hand to his tiny heart, pat, pat, pat. "I do that every freaking night of the week." He pauses, spins his little butt around on the chair. "So," he says, "what did you have in mind?"

Long legs and bare breasts are one way to keep a Screamer quiet. And duct tape's another.

"Quit squirming," I snap, fishing the munchkin out of my trunk at the top of the parking garage we've driven to.

He kicks at me with his stubby little legs until I pull out the ax I've brought along. "Don't make me make you shorter than you already are," I say, and the kicking stops.

I've left his hands and legs free, by the way, because duct tape would be a dead giveaway when his body's found later. As for the strip over his mouth, I plan on pulling that off right around the time screaming will be the natural thing to do.

"Think of it this way," I say, as we head to the roof of the parking structure. "This is the last falling you'll ever have to do."

Listening to myself, I can't help smiling. I sound like a regular bad-ass. God, I forgot how much fun this could be. And so I remind myself again—this is for Isuzu.

Of course, *this* is just hearsay without proof. That's where the ax comes in. Before pulling off the duct tape, before letting gravity do my dirty work for me, I take a little something to bring back for Isuzu. Proof, and maybe something else. With his tiny hand pressed down flat on the concrete ledge, I heft the ax and bring it down. His thumb rolls away from the rest of him. I stoop, pick it up, drop it into my pocket. He won't be needing it where he's going, even though his vampire biology is already busying itself, trying to restore the damage. It doesn't know how much damage it's got coming.

"Any last words?" I ask, preparing to pull off the tape, preparing to let go of the trench coat I'm using to hold him up.

He nods. I rip.

"Thanks," he says. And then he lifts his unbound hands high over his head. His arms slip through their sleeves and I'm left holding the empty black ghost of his coat.

All the long way down to the pavement below, my Screamer doesn't scream. He doesn't make a peep. The only sound is the ripple of his clothing as his body slices through the night air.

It seems like forever before his skull cracks open against the sidewalk, letting out all of its time. I look down and see his splintered bones jutting up and out of his suddenly ill-draped skin. Even for a vampire, it seems like there's too much blood.

Turning away, I decide to lie to Isuzu. "He screamed his head off." That's what I'll say. "He cried like a baby."

So?" Isuzu says, when I let her out of her room.

"Here," I say, fishing the Screamer's thumb out of my pocket. Its wound has healed over but it's still twitching, looking like nothing so much as a big pink jointed caterpillar—with an impeccably trimmed thumbnail where the head should be. I place it on the table and it inchworms along blindly right up to, and over, the edge.

"Jeezus, Marty. What is that?"

Closure, I think. "Them," I say. "One of them. What's left."

"What am I supposed to do with it?"

"Stick pins in it," I say. "Burn it. Smash it with a hammer. And in the morning, get rid of it."

"How?"

"Oh, I think you know, Sunshine."

And she smiles. She smiles as bright and deadly as the sun itself.

It's not enough, of course. A thumb. A thimbleful of revenge. But it will have to do. Isuzu's still got a soul to lose, and murder—even a justifiable homicide—is a good way to lose it. Fortunately, I don't have that problem. And so I do what service I can.

The media, meanwhile, has its field day. The TV news magazines start running special segments on vampire depression, and the special problems of Screamers, who on TV are called "the prematurely vamped" or "our most special vampires." Friends and relatives of the departing contestant are interviewed.

"Him," Isuzu says, pointing at the screen.

"And him," she says, pointing out number three.

A house fire blamed on bad wiring. That takes care of number two. And number three? "What happened to his air bag?" the TV wants to know. "Why did his brakes fail? What caused the accelerator to stick like that? Should there be a recall?"

An investigation is launched. I'm guessing that they're probably interviewing his friends and relatives, too, just as they did with the others. But Isuzu and I have stopped watching the reports. We've fished our limit.

It's time to let the healing begin.

-18-

EBOLA

Father Jack and I have a little routine we do when we first see each other. It starts with me asking, "How's life?"

"Still taking forever," Father Jack says back, full of vampire weariness.

That joke has never seemed less true.

Not nowadays.

Not with Isuzu in my life to remind me of how fast time can move. Not with Little Bobby Little on the TV for comparison, still little, still cute and bouncing around his little kid's bedroom. He's obviously computer generated, or taped for broadcast later—over and over again, year after year. Why others haven't noticed his mysterious lack of aging, who knows? Childhood seems to last forever when you're a kid, and vampires, with their imperviousness to the ravages of aging, have fallen back into that kid sense of time. Maybe his not aging seems right to them. Maybe it's just because they don't have an Isuzu in their lives to let them know better.

In the old movies, they used to visualize the passage of time by showing a wall calendar, shedding days and dates like autumn leaves. That's how it feels around my apartment nowadays. I sometimes feel like our hair should be blowing back, or some cartoonist should ink in long, straight motion lines behind our backs, to illustrate just how fast things are going, how fast one of us is growing up, while the other one just stands there, blown back by the gust of her passing.

Take tonight, for instance.

I'm in the living room, reading a book about the mating habits of insects, and Isuzu's bivouacked in the bathroom, a place that seems to have become her base camp, from which reconnaissance missions are occasionally launched for a quick snack, a quick "Hey," a quick grab at the clicker to see if there's anything better on TV than the program I've decided to watch, and then back to whatever it is she's doing in there. I've just read that the female praying mantis decapitates the male during sex when Isuzu lets out a scream that chills my already cold blood.

"Marty, help!" she adds, as if I haven't already flung the book aside and bolted for the bathroom in the half a heartbeat it takes between her scream and elaboration. The door's locked, but I'm a vampire on a mission, and the lock was really never more than a symbol of privacy. I'll fix the hinges later.

"Izzy, what is it?" I call, terrified at what I might find. In the same half a heartbeat it took me to get to the bathroom—and the other half a heartbeat it took to rip the door from its moorings—all I can think of is the bathroom window. The glass is stippled, of course; you can't see anything from the outside. But it's obviously a bathroom window and she's been spending *hours* in there lately. Obviously, she hasn't been spending those hours in the dark. And a lit bathroom window that stays lit for hours—that's *not* vampire behavior. An outside observer might come to wonder about that. Might make note of it, keep track. Might come one night to investigate for himself, pulling the window out, smashing it in, finding it unlocked, maybe. He'd be a vampire on a mission, too, and he'd find my little Isuzu.

My already chilled blood starts creeping toward absolute zero.

I set the unhinged door aside and look for broken glass, for any sign of a struggle. I look for the shadow or reflection of an intruder trying to hide just inside the doorway, or behind the shower curtain. I look for the telltale polka dots of carnage on the walls and ceiling.

Nothing.

No glass, no shadows, no blood spatters. Just Isuzu sitting on the toilet with her jeans and underwear around her ankles, a towel draped across her lap, hugging her stomach and rocking back and forth.

"What is it?" I ask, noticing the tears and terror in her eyes.

"I'm dying," she sobs. I notice my *Merck Manual* open on the bathroom counter. "I've got Ebola!" she wails.

"Oh my God!" I say, my hand going to my mouth. That my meaning and purpose in life should be struck down at the age of thirteen by a mysterious virus bent on liquefying her insides seems entirely plausible to me at the moment. I'm a parent, and paranoid, and part of my brain has been living in this moment for years. "Oh my God," I say again, catching a glimpse at what an Ebola victim looks like in the *Merck*.

"Look," Isuzu says, rising from the toilet, wrapping the towel around her waist like a skirt. And I can smell it without even looking—the smell as familiar to me as my own name. There's blood in the toilet—from her.

My "oh my God" hand is still pressed to my mouth and it's a good thing; it's hiding the smile of what I've realized, but Isuzu hasn't.

To satisfy my little girl who's apparently becoming a young woman, I take a quick peek at the primary evidence supporting her diagnosis of Ebola. I work to straighten the grin under my fingers into something a bit more serious, and appropriate. Looking at her stricken face helps.

Taking my hand away and clearing my throat, I say, "Um . . . ," but then stop. God, do I feel like a *male,* all of a sudden. Not like a vampire talking to a mortal. Not an adult talking to a child. No. I'm a man stepping into no-man's-land without a compass or a guide or even an adequate supply of feminine-hygiene euphemisms.

And all of a sudden, I start thinking about dating again. I haven't seen anyone of the adult female persuasion since the night I brought Isuzu home. I've been busy raising her up to this point. We've been busy playing slapjack, misunderstanding each other, getting into rows, and making up. So far, it's been a one-man job, with a little involuntary input from Father Jack, and that's been it. That's been enough.

But not now. All of a sudden, it's obvious to me that raising Isuzu beyond this point is a two-person job. And so I start thinking about dating again. Dating hard. Speed dating. Whatever it takes to find a mom I can hand Isuzu off to in moments like these.

"Um . . . ," I say again.

Stalling for time, I pick up the *Merck*, consult it, study it, tap my chin as if pondering my little girl's diagnosis. "Maybe," I say, slowly, "maybe there's another explanation."

Isuzu has apparently anticipated this. She snatches the book from my hands, and flips to the section on hemorrhagic fever. She hands it back.

"Yeah," I say. "That's a good one, too, but . . ." I close the book and return it to the sink counter. On second thought, I place the book on the floor, and rest a foot on top. "I'm thinking it could be something that's not so . . ."

". . . rare?"

"No."

"Contagious?"

"No." I lock my eyes on her eyes, so she can take whatever reassurances she needs from them. "Fatal," I say. "I don't think this is fatal." Which isn't strictly true, of course. Puberty is a sign of growing up, and growing up is a terminal condition, if left unchecked. Still, the point is, I'm not expecting her to drop dead within the next forty-eight hours or so.

I decide to take a different approach. "Do you know where babies come from?" I ask.

The look this question gets is not the one I expected. I expected either a smirk, or embarrassment, or blank, blinking innocence. I didn't expect a look of horror mixed with a clear sense of betrayal. Still wearing that look, Isuzu nods her head, grimly, indicating that yes, she *does* know where babies come from.

"The farm," she says.

Oh my God! I can see the gears working in her head, the shocking "ah ha's" she's coming to, about why I took her in in the first place, and why I haven't killed her—at least not yet. I feel sick. I feel sick, and I want to cry, but crying blood at the moment isn't exactly going to help matters.

All I can do is say, "No." All I can do is shake my head as vigorously as possible. "No. No. No. No." All I can do is throw up my hands, twin stop signs. "That's not it at all."

The look on her face says, *Bullshit*. The look on her face says, *Convince me, motherfucker.*

"Have you ever heard of a period?"

"You mean like a question mark," she says, "but without the squiggly thing?" She draws an *S* or snake in the air.

"No. A *woman's* period. Her time of the month. Getting a visit from Aunt Flo?"

None of these words are making sense, in the combinations I'm using, in the way I'm stringing them together. And why should they? Vampire women don't have periods. Isuzu herself was too young for the information when she was still living with the only woman in her experience prone to such monthly visits. The only chance of something like this being mentioned on TV would be in a . . . well, a period piece. But period dramatizations on vampire TV veer away from that subject matter just as rapidly as regular TV did, before the change. Sure, menstruation means blood, but more than that, it means reproduction. And that means it's just another reminder of the things we've given up, to live forever.

"It's all natural," I tell Isuzu. "Nothing's wrong." I pause. "This isn't about dying," I lie, because, in the long run, everything about mortals is about dying. But I can't think that way. Not now. Not for Isuzu's sake. "It's about life," I say. "There comes a time in a young woman's life when . . ."

I go on, explaining what needs to be explained, assuring her that I'm not when she insists I must be kidding. The explanation I give is clinical, biologically correct, and anatomically accurate, but I'll spare you the gory details. After all, I'm as adverse to these little reminders as any other vampire. I just try not to show it while rescuing young damsels from Ebola.

-19-

WHO KNEW BUDDHISTS COULD BE SO MEAN?

I'm thinking about my mom.

I couldn't save my dad. I was vamped too late; he died too early. But I didn't have that same excuse when it came to my mom. She was still alive when I got back from the war with not a scratch on me, but pale as a ghost and suddenly allergic to sunlight.

"Mr. Hollywood!"

That's how she greets me, after throwing open the door that first night back.

I'm still standing on the porch, still wearing my uniform, a duffel bag slung over my shoulder, the mesh of the screen door still standing there between her and me. The porch light has been burning all evening, awaiting my arrival, driving the moths and mosquitoes mad, the black flecks of their bashed insect brains dotting the bare bulb in a pointedly pointless way. I shake my head. "Huh?"

My mother taps the side of her head, next to her eyes.

"Oh, yeah," I say, reaching to remove my sunglasses, but then stop. I've been thinking about how to do this, all the long way back from Europe. I never did come up with anything that was worth anything.

"Mom?"

"Yes?"

"Can you open the screen door?"

My mother's two-toned eyes widen with an "Oh jeez" or an "Oh yeah," or maybe both. "Oh honey, I'm sorry," she says, pushing the door open. "I was just so busy drinking you in."

I flinch; she doesn't notice.

"Have you gotten taller?" she goes on. "You've gotten taller, haven't you?" She tries taking my free hand; I pull away, making a big show of struggling with my duffel bag. Maybe after I've gotten a cup of coffee, something warm to hold on to, to borrow from, to render less shockingly cold.

"Oh, Jesus."

I don't mean to say it; I just do. I just step in through the front door, and there it is, staring at me like a shotgun aimed at my head. The dining room table. The dining room table, set, and waiting for me, bowls and platters steaming with the delicious steam of my favorite everything.

My mother doesn't even scold me for using the Lord's name in vain. Instead, she starts reciting the menu like she's running through the guest list for the Last Supper.

"Delmonico steak so it's still pink inside, baked potatoes with butter, corn on the cob, dinner rolls from the Italian bakery, iced tea with lemon and sugar, coffee black, fruit salad, baked beans, chicken soup with just broth and noodles—no carrots, no onions, no celery—and for dessert . . ."

And even though my heart is breaking from the sight of all this love I can't do anything with anymore, by the time my mother hits "and for dessert," I just start laughing. And it's a big laugh, one of those throw-your-head-back-and-roar-at-the-moon laughs, the kind that comes on all of a sudden, after too much fear and anxiety and tension, tension, tension, followed by the sudden release and relief of knowing nothing's really changed. Everything's just where you left it, even the people.

My mom hasn't said what's for dessert yet, and I imagine her staring at me—*glaring* at me—pissed at me for laughing at God only knows what. She'll be doing that thing with her fists and her hips; she'll start tapping her foot impatiently; if I wait long enough, she'll say, "What's so funny, mister?"

That's what I expect to find when I finally stop laughing and look at her again. Instead, what I get is a glimpse at what my mother might look like if she wound up on display at the wax museum. Her expression is frozen, as is the rest of her. And just like that, I know she's seen them. She's seen my fangs when I laughed.

"Mom?" I say.

No answer.

"Mom, are you okay?"

Silence.

And so I do it. The damage has already been done, so I might as well damn it the rest of the way. I touch her hand with my cold hand. She flinches. Stops. I remove the shades from my obsidian eyes.

"Mom," I begin. "I've got something to tell you."

"Peach cobbler," she says, pulling her hand away from mine.

"What?"

"Peach cobbler," she repeats, by the table now, taking the place she's set for herself. "Peach cobbler for dessert."

"Mom . . ."

"It's getting cold," she says. "Sit," she adds.

I close the space between her and me, think about touching her shoulder, don't. Instead, I pull out the chair by the place she's set for me.

"Looks great," I say, drinking it all in with my eyes. "You shouldn't have gone to all the trouble," I add, staring at the part in her hair, hanging there in front of me, over her plate, over her Delmonico steak, still steaming faintly, her fork and knife stuck in the meat, stuck in her hands not moving, not even trying.

Like Dracula?" she says, when she finally unsticks and risks looking at me again.

"That's the general idea," I say, "but they get a lot of stuff wrong."

Her eyes keep glancing down when she thinks I'm not looking. There's a knife where she's looking, and I wonder if she's planning to stab me—if she thinks she needs to defend herself against her own son. And then I get it. I place my hand over the knife's shiny blade. "Like that," I say. I pick up the knife and hold it so she can see me and my reflection in the blade. "How do you think Bela keeps his hair so neat if he can't see himself in a mirror?"

My mother smiles and I smile, too, but lips only. No fangs. As Kenny Rogers would say, years later, you got to know when to hold 'em, know when to fold 'em. Maybe I am a gambler, after all.

"How?" she asks, and I tell her.

She asks me what the world looks like through eyes that are all dilated pupil, what it feels like to have skin that's so cold.

"Holy," I say. "The world looks and feels *holy*. Everything's haloed. Everything glows. And everything feels connected to everything else, and you're connected to it, too. Just like everything, and everything else."

"Sounds Buddhist," my mother says, with no little bit of ire. Somehow, I get the feeling that given the choice of what to have for a son—a vampire or a Buddhist—my mother would pick fangs over yin-yangs any day. "Mrs. Thompson's son Billy came back a Buddhist," she says.

"No," I assure her. "No, I just drink blood."

"That's good," she says. "Because, you know, they *act* all peace and love, but really they're kind of pushy. Mrs. Thompson's son Billy won't even eat *meat* anymore."

"I can't eat meat anymore," I say. "Or corn on the cob, either, for that matter."

"That's different," she says. "You *can't*. Billy Thompson *won't*." She pauses. "You know what he calls chicken soup?"

I shrug.

" 'Corpse tea,' " my mother says. "He made his own mother cry with that one. Honestly, I never knew Buddhists could be so mean."

It occurs to me that it's probably more a Billy Thompson thing than a Buddhist thing, and I almost say so, but then don't. Because, really, it's not a Billy *or* a Buddhist thing; it's a not-talking-about-me-being-a-vampire thing. That's what's going on. It's all about not talking about where the blood I drink comes from, or what I do with the empties.

"Mom?" I say.

"Yes, dear?"

"Do you miss Dad?"

The look on her face is the look of someone who didn't know vampires could be so mean. Not that I mean to be.

"What kind of a question is *that*?"

"I . . ."

"Of *course* I miss your father."

"I . . ."

"It wasn't *me* who didn't cry at his funeral, Marty."

Now it's my turn to be surprised by the meanness of others.

"I . . ."

"He was your *father*. Even Billy Thompson cried at *his* father's funeral."

Billy Thompson again. I'm really getting to hate that name. And something tells me—a little bird, a little bat, maybe—I'll be craving Eastern cuisine in the not-too-distant future.

Meanness was not the reason I mentioned my father, by the way. Death was. Death, and dying, and *not*-dying. Because when I came back from Europe and all that death—and all that relived grief—I came back with a plan. And the plan was good. The plan was symmetrical. The plan was so good, and so symmetrical, failure was not an option. My mother had given me my mortal life, and now it was my turn to repay her with immortality. She wouldn't have to die like my dad did, and I wouldn't have to watch her die. She could *be* and I could *be,* and we could talk on the phone when either one of us got lonely—about nothing, or the weather—and we could live forever knowing that the other would always be there.

That was the plan.

I just mentioned my dad as a way to work up to it. After all, you don't just plunk immortality down in front of somebody. You ease up to it.

"What do you mean, no?" I say, staring at this woman to whom I've just offered life everlasting.

"It's sweet of you to think of me, dear," she says. But then she scrunches up her face like she's bitten into something awful. She shakes her head. "No. I don't think so."

Let me translate. Let me paint you a picture. Here I am, sitting in our old dining room, sitting in front of a cold Delmonico steak, my ears practically still ringing from World War II, my brain still spinning from being a vampire myself, and here my own mother is, saying Thanks, but no thanks. To immortality. No. Death is fine. Death will do. Given the choice between dying or hanging around with me, her son, forever, she's picking *death*.

It was the choice between the lady and the tiger. I was the lady, and my mom was going with the tiger. And I don't mind telling you, I felt a little insulted. It was like my own mom was telling me she'd rather commit suicide than be around me.

"Why the fuck not?" I shout.

And my mom? My mom's still my mom, and I've already gotten away with one in-vain usage of the Lord's name this evening. She probably figured I was owed a freebie, what with the war and all, but honestly, there's really no call for using the F-word under her roof.

"Language, Martin!" she snaps, slapping me across the face and catching me with her nails. I can feel the blood coming, and then I can see it, a long spurt hitting the Sunday tablecloth she's laid out for the occasion of my return. We both watch as the red bull's-eye grows. And when she looks up—to apologize, maybe—it's just in time to see the last nail swipe on my cheek close like a tiny mouth keeping its secrets mum.

And that, more than the pointy teeth, the onyx eyes, the cemetery skin, *that* is the clincher. Her little Marty has come home from the war a vampire. A *real* one. A dishonest-to-God *bloodsucker.*

God?

I can almost see the light go on. She jerks her head toward one of the many pictures of Jesus we have hanging around the house, one of the flaming-heart ones. She jerks a look back at me, panicked.

"Oh my God," she says. "Should I . . . ?"

She's already out of her chair, turning it over in her rush. She's already got her napkin stretched overhead, preparing to drape the picture, not at all prepared to watch her son go up in flames.

"Mom," I call after her. "Mom, it's okay. They got that part wrong, too."

She stops. She stops and just stands there, the napkin held over her head between her clenched hands, like a white flag of surrender. She doesn't turn. She doesn't lower the napkin. She barely moves. Just her shoulders, going slightly up, going slightly down, again and again.

I'm too old to live forever."

That's her first crack at giving me a reason for abandoning me.

"I can't . . ." She waves her hands over the word she's left out, which is "kill."

I tell her she can, that it's all about picking the right—killable—people. I tell her about the Nazis I've killed. I tell her there's a whole world full of people you can feel good about killing. Rapists. Murderers. Child molesters. Wife beaters. It's practically the Lord's work. All strictly eye-for-an-eye stuff.

She shakes her head. "Marty," she says. She pushes two fingers into her mouth, one on either side of her smile. And when she pulls them out, her smile comes along with them. "The otha vampithers will make thun uv me," she lisps.

I tell her about what they don't show you in the movies—how it takes several nights for your fangs to come in. I tell her how they push the old ones out along the way, and how painful that can be. "You've just got a head start, that's all," I assure her.

And still she shakes her head. "Marty," she says, tears in her eyes. "Don't make me choose."

"You don't have to *chew* anything," I say. "You puncture and suck."

"*O-O-S*," she spells. "Choose. As in 'choice.' Don't make me *choose.*"

"Choose what?" I ask, but then I know.

She still believes.

Me, I'm in between things at the moment, re the whole God and religion thing. But she still believes, and not dying means not seeing my dad again. My gift—the thing I've brought her all the way from Europe—my gift is the gift of *not* going to heaven. My gift is the gift of forcing her to choose between her husband and her son.

I cover my face with my hands. I try to imagine loving anyone that much. I try to imagine anyone loving *me* that much.

I can't, so I stop pushing. I decide to wait for her to change her mind.

S he doesn't.
Didn't.

T hat time feels like a PBS nature documentary to me now, the days compressed into seconds, time itself crumpling my poor mother in its fist. She bent, and then she drooped, and then she wilted. She became a miser of space, spending less and less of it on herself. And then the air just went out of her, as her skin pulled itself in, clinging more fiercely to her bones. Her hair began falling away, one white feather at a time.

She got old; that's all she was doing. It was the project she was working on, the fate she'd decided. She had help, of course. She had her friends, all dying right along with her. It was just me. I was the lone holdout; I was the only one playing hooky from his mortality.

On her deathbed, my mother forgave me, and I wish I could say vice versa, but it damaged me, watching my mother die for the love of my father.

I didn't date much after my mother died. *Couldn't*. Couldn't really *believe* in it. Oh sure, I arranged to have sex when the need arose, but dating? Putting myself out there in hopes of finding *true love*? Sorry, but the bar had been set pretty high.

Oh, I tried. I tried dating Lizzy, the pope's sister; I tried dating a few of my other benevolent vamplings. But it always turned out the same. I resented their inability to die for me like my mother had died for my father. Without death, without grief, it was all just so much fucking around.

And so I did—I fucked around, until fucking around became boring. I fucked around until driving too fast in the rain seemed like a good idea.

-20-

NIGHT PERSON SEEKS SAME

I begin my search for Isuzu's new mom by returning to an old haunt from my benevolent days—a strip club a few blocks from the Detroit River, called Teezers. I'm not really expecting to find maternal material here; I'm not expecting to find true love. I *am* hoping to find a familiar face, however. I need to talk. I need to get used to talking to adult women about adult things again. And I don't mind paying for the privilege. Here, conversation is just another thing that gets sold, and as the buyer of said conversation, the pressure on me is blessedly low. As long as I've got the cash, the only other thing I need is a pulse.

As luck would have it, what I find is a familiar back.

I don't actually know what her name is. I call her Tombstone. I call her that because of this outrageous tattoo she's got on her back, just above her butt, a pair of blue-green praying hands. In Gothic script, arching above, it says, "In Memory of," and underneath—I guess—the name of whoever it is she's ruined her otherwise perfect skin for. I wasn't able to read it when I first met her; the G-string got in the way.

I remember walking in that night, a thousand years ago. This was before the flip, when I was still spreading the seeds of vampirism one neck at a time. A song was playing when I entered. Tori Amos. Something powerful, and empowering, and vaguely accusatory.

I freeze right there in the doorway, handing the coat check girl my five-dollar cover, letting the bouncer point my shoulders toward one of the few empty seats at the bar. It's the music that stops me. You don't hear a lot of Tori Amos in strip clubs for pretty much the same reason you don't hear *Fiddler on the Roof* at neo-Nazi rallies. The bouncer gives my shoulders a shove to unstick me. And it works, for a step or two, but then I look up and fall into something like love.

The Tori fan onstage is dancing topless in a smoky yellow spot, five nothing minus the high heels, which are black and the real kind with spikes—not the cheater wedges a lot of the dancers use. She has small, tear-shaped breasts, upturned nipples, a gorgeous flat stomach, and a mischievous grin just this side of a smirk. Her hair's straight and midnight black and so long she wears it like a vest, flashing the customers now and then, like a fan dancer from a hundred simpler years ago.

I take my seat, order a coffee over my shoulder without turning, my vampire eyes locked on the girl onstage, clocking her every move, letting the bright light reflecting off her white, white skin pour into me through my all-pupil eyes. She glows. She seems to, at least, like most things do to my vampire eyes. But there's something else. My vampire heart tells me this one's special. Brighter than the rest. Different. Worthy.

It always started like that.

The falling in love. The targeting. The deciding: Yes. Okay. Yes.

And then she turns and my heart sinks. Ink. Blue-green tattoo ink on that perfect white skin.

Shit.

I *hate* tattoos. I hate what they symbolize, the "till death" audacity of them, as if people who can't even stick to the "one life, one marriage" plan can be trusted to choose that special something that warrants being branded into their flesh. What image, what phrase, could *possibly* weather the eventual weathering of the skin, and taste, and everything else that seems so eternal and immutable when you're—what—twenty-two, twenty-three, tops? Back then, I used to imagine every tattoo I'd see, sixty, seventy years into the future, wrinkled, illegible, being wheeled down the hall of some nursing home, the smart-ass attendant smirking all the way.

"Okay, Mr. Born-to-Lose, time to empty your colostomy bag."

It's when I see that tattoo that the falling in love stops. The targeting looks for new coordinates. The deciding decides:

No.

I swing around and look at my own face in the mirror behind the bar. Over my head, I can see my tattooed lady just hanging there, incandescent, like a bright idea.

Looking for some other distraction, I slide a few quarters from my change across the bar and drop them into a trivia game sitting next to me. I warm my hands on the cup of coffee so my answers will register when I touch the video screen, there and there.

What planet is named for the goddess of love?

Who wrote To Kill a Mockingbird?

The questions are no-brainers and I win speed points, not to mention extra no-brainer questions. I'm well on my way to becoming the top scorer in general trivia when, suddenly, the No sits down next to me, and I forget all about what I will or won't let into the future I'm building, one neck at a time.

"Hi," she says, sticking out her casually warm and mortal hand. "Pink Floyd."

"Excuse me?" I say, squeezing the coffee cup hard before sliding my hand into hers. We shake. Let go.

"Who recorded *Dark Side of the Moon*?" she says, pointing at the video screen, and then reaching past me to hit the answer button. A flurry of numbers scrolls up; congratulatory music chimes. "Woohoo," she says, pumping her arm into the air, pulling an imaginary train whistle with ironic enthusiasm.

"I knew that," I say, both because it's true and because I don't want to seem like the kind of old fart who'd miss a question like that. This was back when I worried about matching the age of my face out in public.

My "I knew that" gets an "uh-huh" look in return, heavy on the skepticism and mascara. Trying to strengthen my case, I resort to the always-effective strategy of repeating myself.

"I *did*," I insist.

"Whatever," the No says, exhaling an "I'm bored" plume of smoke.

"So," I say, trying to regroup. "Tori Amos?"

The No just smiles, taps her cigarette ash into an ashtray, blows a needle of smoke with surgical precision just past my face. She cracks her neck to the right, the left, and then draws her gaze level with my midnight eyes.

"So?" the Maybe says.

"Interesting choice."

"Yeah. Well. You know." She shoots a snake of smoke from the corner of her smirk. "I tried being boring once." Studied pause; another squirt of smoke. "Sucks."

"Yeah. Well. You know," I say, smiling a smile nearly as evil as the one on my companion's face. "Lots of things do," I add, because it's true and getting truer, one Yes at a time.

When she wakes the following night, she won't remember how she got home. She won't remember who undressed her, tucked her in, did to her apartment what's been done to her apartment. She won't remember brushing my thigh with her cigarette-free hand, or inviting me to the VIP room for a lap dance. She won't remember slithering out of her terry cloth one-piece, or my suggestion that her tattoo makes her look like a dancing tombstone. She won't remember laughing nervously, or my insistence that a dancing tombstone's not a bad thing, not a bad thing at all.

She won't even remember why her neck is so sore.

She's been too busy, sleeping the sleep of the dead.

It's not until she reaches behind to massage a knot in her neck that she finds my souvenir—two little holes, suckling at the yellowed skin of her fingertips like tiny mouths.

"What the . . . ," I imagine her saying—it's what they always said—before opening her eyes and then shutting them again, just as suddenly, shocked by the flashbulb intensity of everything. She stumbles to the dresser, shields her eyes with a hand cupping her forehead, opens one experimentally. The eye looking back from the mirror isn't hers. It's her face, yes, un-made-up, bleached out, over-exposed, but the eye . . . It's all black, as if it's been swallowed by its own pupil. She opens the other one. Same story.

"What the . . . ," she begins to say again, but stops. There's a red blur in the middle of her face. In the middle of the reflection of her face. She steps back. There's writing on the mirror in lipstick. *Her* lipstick.

"Welcome," it says.

"Hang up the phone," it says. She turns and finds the receiver lying on the nightstand bleating plaintively. Next to it are a pair of sunglasses, an empty tube from a roll of aluminum foil, and a pint-sized liquor bottle filled with something red, bearing a Post-it note that reads: "Drink me."

She puts on the sunglasses, hangs up the phone, and looks about her apartment. All the windows have been blocked out with aluminum foil, even the blurry ones in the bathroom. Her purse has been spilled out and gone through; her money—all the sad ones and twenties from last night—is scattered about like so many dead leaves. Drawers have been opened and sloppily closed. The light in the kitchen is on. The cabinets and refrigerator are open, and empty. She looks back at the "Drink me" bottle, uncaps it, smells its rusty-smelling insides, puts the cap back on.

And then the phone rings.

"Sleep well?" I ask.

"Who is this?"

"Did you drink me?" I ask.

"Who *is* this?"

"Open the door," I say.

"Not until you tell me who you are."

"Open the door," I repeat, twisting the knob I didn't bother to lock the night before.

"Who . . ."

"Your future," I say, stepping inside and flipping my cell phone closed.

•   •

Her hair's cut short now, and her taste in music has grown to include Eminem, but her face hasn't changed and the praying hands on her back still hold the memory of whomever. I never bothered to ask. An oversight I now regret, but only slightly, seeing as it gives me an excuse for starting up where we left off.

"Hey, Tombstone," I say, waving casually as if it's been a matter of days since we've last seen each other, as opposed to decades.

"Jesus H. Christ!" T calls out, shielding her crow eyes from the glare of the stage. "Marty? Is that you?"

I nod.

"Jesus," she repeats. "It's been a shit-ass long time, ya ol' blood-sucker you."

"That it has, that it has," I say, chatting my last piece of chit before getting down to business. "So, anyway," I begin, "about that tattoo."

"You like it?"

"Hate it," I admit. "Always have. I almost let the worms get you, it turned me off so bad."

T pulls an exaggerated pout. "Over a little ink? Jeez, Marty. Way to cheer a girl up."

I love the way she keeps saying my name. I was hoping I'd find someone who'd remember me, and wasn't sure what I'd do if I didn't. She keeps on talking.

" 'Course, if it wasn't you, some other sucker would've come along to do the job," she says. "Know how I know?"

"How?"

" 'Cause I'm a hot patootie," she says, smiling the same smart-ass smile that made me fall in love with her all those years ago. "A hot patootie, and cute to boot."

Confidence *and* sarcasm—I love that in a stripper. I also love the way she talks, her like-I-give-a-shit use of out-of-date slang. It's like she's going back in time, just for me. I nod my head and point at it. "This is me," I say, "rogering that."

"So, what brings you back to our fair establishment after forever?"

I look point-blank into the black holes of her eyes. "I believe the French word is," I say, pausing for effect, *"toi."*

T snorts out a laugh. "Yeah, right." She points at the black marbles I gave her for her rebirthday. "This is *moi*," she says, "rolling my eyes."

I tell her I love her laugh, and she does it some more.

"Marty, Marty, Marty," she says, patting her cold hand against my cold arm, once for each "Marty." She stops with the last one and leaves it there.

I place my own hand on top of hers, look in her eyes again, and finally ask who's memory she's got immortalized back there.

T pulls her hand out from under mine. She mimes a cigarette drag. "Mom," she says, blowing out a plume of imaginary smoke. "Throat cancer," she answers before I even get a chance to ask.

"Dad," I say, touching my heart. "Lungs."

"You couldn't . . . ?"

"Too late."

"Me too."

"I'm sorry," we say, over each other, and then freeze. We'd been shouting before, just to be heard over the background music. But it's the silence between songs into which we shout our mutual sympathy, followed by every glassy black eye in the place, turning to stare at us.

"I *hate* when that happens," I say, once the music resumes. T shrugs.

She sips her blood. I sip mine.

"So," I finally say. "How old were you?"

"When she died," T asks, "or when I got the tattoo?"

"Both."

"Thirteen," she says, "and then sixteen."

I look at T's hands, both of which are on the table. The fingers of one cross the fingers of the other, as if the hands on her back have been taken apart and put back together wrong. She taps the bottom one very nearly in time to the music that's playing.

I wait for the silence between songs. "You wanna talk about it?" I ask, barely more than a whisper.

T points at her head, letting it drop heavily to her chest. Letting it struggle back up. Letting it fix just opposite me, whiteless eye to whiteless eye.

"This is me," she says, "rogering that."

Here's something you may not appreciate: the teller at your bank wasn't always a teller. Telling—or whatever it's called—was not her calling. Making change was not what her growing up was about. Banking was not the thing that filled her heart and made it beat. Things just happened along the way, like the setup of a joke, and telling just turned out to be the punch line.

The same goes for your car dealer. The gas station guy. The factory worker. And all the other nameless, faceless people we use to do our business.

Like strippers, for instance.

It seems the woman I vamped all those years ago wasn't always a dancer. What Tombstone was, in the "always" department, was the daughter of a "for real" circus clown, one who didn't plan on being a clown any more than her daughter planned on dancing along the edge of the Detroit River at a place called Teezers. In the "always" department, Tombstone's mom was a TV weatherperson who never was.

"A love for the performing arts," T says, tapping her imaginary cigarette into an imaginary ashtray. "That's what I got from my mom."

Her mom's professional name was Rags, and she dressed in, well, her namesake. Her husband died shortly before T was born, and so it was Rags's job to put food on the table, which she did by dragging her only child from small town to small town, following the warm weather. It was a strange existence, but it worked—more or less— until T turned thirteen and Rags the Clown was diagnosed with throat cancer.

"When she died," Tombstone says, "they buried her with full circus honors." She says this like it's supposed to mean something to me.

"Meaning?" I say.

T doesn't answer at first, instead making a pair of fists at the memory.

"They cut holes in her coffin," she says, and then notices what her hands are doing. "For her clown shoes," she says, punctuating the statement with both fists, pretending she's made them for this illustration. "To poke through," she adds, before asking if I can imagine being thirteen and seeing my mother's dead feet humiliated for all eternity.

All I can think of is that magic trick—the one where the woman gets locked in a box and then sawed in half. Did her mother's feet look like that to the little girl who grew up to be a teezer? Did her heart break at even the thought of magic like mine did whenever I heard Christmas carols?

The pallbearers and all the other clowns got dressed up in their full circus regalia. But they wouldn't cry, not a goddam one of 'em, because they were afraid of smearing their makeup. Instead, they wore trick daisies, sending out arcs of slapstick grief whenever they squeezed the bulbs hidden in their too-wide, garish lapels.

"Like my mom's dying was such a knee-slapper," T says, her hands making fists again.

Tombstone was the only one around the grave wearing normal funeral clothes. She was the only one without patches, or suspenders, or some oversized something that honked. She didn't care. She was glad to stand out. She wasn't there to mourn the clown her mother had been. She was there to mourn the woman with a face so constellated with acne scars it stopped her from living her dream of doing the TV weather. Sitting in their trailer at dinnertime, T and her mom would watch the news together, each eating a TV dinner from her own TV tray, the TV itself turned down, so her mom could supply the weather report in her perky, "everything's okay" voice. Some evenings, the talk was all about the chances of rain. Others dealt with barometric pressure and fronts of various kinds. But the evenings T loved most were like little science lessons, detailing the difference between thermometer cold and the cold of exposed skin.

T looks at me now, a professional exposer of skin.

"She could have been happy," she says, having already made the connection I'm just making now, "if only she had better . . . *skin.*"

And it's the way she dwells on the word "skin"—the way she keeps on repeating it—that helps me see how the little girl in my head became the stripper sitting in front of me. This was the daughter of a woman who had to hide her dream and her skin behind greasepaint. This was a daughter who'd be damned if she'd follow in her mother's oversized footsteps. No. She hated the thought of hiding behind anything. She hated the idea of playing the fool. If fools had to be involved, it'd be her audience, not her. She'd be the one in control. There'd be no laughing at her expense. And you could bet there'd be no clowns in her future. Not after this. Not after all this was done.

"Ever notice how before, the kids always cried when the clowns showed up?" T asks. I nod.

"The clowns were supposed to be for the kids, right? That's what the parents used to think. But every kid I ever saw at any show my mom ever did, their first reaction was to cry. And who can blame 'em? The place already smells like shit, and then here comes this dead white face and this huge, bloody red mouth, making loud noises and big crazy gestures and . . ."

T pauses. "You wanna know a secret about clowns?"

I nod.

"They knew they scared kids and they did it anyway." T says she knows this for a fact, having heard her mother's coworkers talking after hours. "They'd score the little bastards in decibels, getting a real kick out of the way the parents sweated, struggling with some squirming, panicky kid." She pauses to compose a cap for her feelings, and comes up with this:

"Never underestimate the bitterness of clowns."

It was her own bitterness toward the motley profession—and her secret knowledge of her mom's true dream—that made Tombstone smile for the first and only time during the funeral. They were all standing around the grave site. The made-up pallbearers wearing their coats of many colors had set the coffin atop the canvas straps of the bier, ready to lower it when the time came. Even the priest had been coaxed into wearing a rubber nose. Out of everyone there—the sword and fire swallowers, the freaks, geeks, and barkers, the clowns, tamers, and acrobats—the priest was the only one T didn't hate. The priest was bending the rules, sacrificing his self-respect to lighten the burden for the deceased's loved ones. He didn't know that if T had her way, there wouldn't be a smudge of greasepaint or even lipstick within ten miles of the place.

"Naked," she says.

"It would have been better if we all stood there naked," she repeats, sitting across from me, at least partially there. "Funerals should be about letting go, letting out, not hiding behind a bunch of fake faces and folderol."

And that's why she smiled.

Standing next to her mother's coffin, mourning, listening to the priest, and the occasional horn honk of clown grief, T noticed the shadow of a cloud pass over her own normal-sized shoes. She looked up at the dark, rain-heavy thing, imagining that her wishing had made it so, had brought it into existence, and there, right over all those painted heads. And since it was *her* storm cloud, T closed her eyes, wishing it into doing what it was meant to do.

When the first drop splashed, big and heavy on her un-made-up cheek, T smiled and opened her eyes.

"You should have seen 'em." T smiles now, still remembering. Still remembering the clowns turtling their heads inside their motley pajamas; the others shielding their makeup with Mickey Mouse hands, or popping open their too-tiny umbrellas.

They'd been holding balloons. Balloons, instead of flowers. Instead of handkerchiefs. Or candles. Or anything else more appropriate. And when the rain came and the clowns panicked, they let go of their balloons, trying to protect their hidden selves from the judgment of heaven. Tombstone watched as the balloons rose, struggling upward against the rain, the drops drumming on their tight skins, making them beat, like wild hearts.

Good.

That's what T thought, watching the rain wipe the smiles off a dozen faces, watching all those fake grins run into all those big collars.

For you, Mom.

That's what that little girl thought—all alone then, all alone still—her clothes growing heavy with rain, her normal-sized shoes already squishy with the stuff. She imagined her mother and father both, smiling up there, where the rain came from, holding hands again. The father she knew only from pictures would be looking down at how his daughter had grown. And her mom's skin would be clear, finally, and perfect enough for TV.

Except for that one time, tracking the first of Clarissa's killers, I haven't been in one of these places since Isuzu came into my life. The thought of missing even a minute of her growing up, staring at some stranger's tits—no. But then Ebola struck the Kowalski household. And suddenly, an additional pair of mammary glands seemed like a good idea. And so I'm back. I'm back, and doing the falling-in-love thing all over again.

But I'll tell you this right now:

I don't know if I believe Tombstone.

I don't know if I believe the pink tear she's just shed.

People who don't come to these sorts of places probably think these sorts of places are all about lap dances, hard-ons, and stuffing money down G-strings. And those *are* a big part of it, but not the only part. There's the talking, too. The storytelling. The customers making up better jobs and lives to impress the dancers, the dancers making up traumas to pry a few more bills free. T could be full of grief, or full of shit—I don't honestly know.

I don't honestly care, either.

I love them both. All of a sudden. And just like that. I love the little girl, defiantly mourning her mother the clown. And I love the conniving stripper who could make up a story like that. I even love that once-scary tattoo, now that I *might* know what it's all about.

And so I keep trying not to put my foot in my mouth. I go clever.

Cute. Charming. I make connections that demonstrate I have a brain, and am not like the other defectives she's probably used to.

Tombstone smiles at me. "I like the way you . . . ," she begins. She tips the rim of her glass against the rim of mine, making them ring. ". . . *tink.*"

Something tells me she's used this joke before—perhaps as a barometer to judge the quick-wittedness of her customers. Not wanting to disappoint, I chime in with, "Tank you," and am rewarded with another smile.

By this point in the evening, we've already told our big stories. For T, it was her mom's funeral; for me, the war, my vamping, my zigzaggy stumble toward benevolence. We've talked about our jobs, music, movies, what we remember about the last sunset we ever saw.

"I was standing out back of this place, by the Dumpster, smoking a joint between sets," T says, remembering. "The sun was going down at the end of the alley, lighting up all the puddles between it and me. The sky was lavender, and the tall grass growing along the fence began sparking with all these neon green fireflies . . ."

"I just remember hoping I'd get to see it come up again," I say. "I'm in France and there's a war going on. And I'm having one of those days where death seems to be scratching closer and closer. I keep getting hit by the side effects—dirt and pebbles from a grenade going off, splinters from an exploding tree, a spray of blood from the guy I was just talking to. As it's going down, something between the sun and me is on fire, striping the sky with black ribbons of smoke . . ."

"I like mine better," T says.

"Ditto."

We pause and my eyes wander, settling finally on a reflection of Tombstone's back over her left shoulder. As I've explained before, the myth about mirrors and vampires isn't true, and you don't need much more proof than this place. There are mirrors everywhere, multiplying your viewing options, letting the shy guy stare without seeming to, letting the dancer enthralled with the trivia you're spouting check her makeup, scope out her next prospect, wink at a girlfriend onstage. Looking at the praying hands on T's back in the mirror behind her, I recall my favorite bit of recently learned trivia—the female praying mantis's habit of decapitating its mate during sex.

I share this information with the tattooed lady sitting next to me, and she says:

"Pretty slick, Slick."

"Excuse me?"

She checks her watch. "That's your second serious play to get me into bed in less than a half hour."

I blink. I really hadn't thought about the seductive potential of insect husbandry, but now that T mentions it . . . yeah, okay.

Pretty slick, Slick, I think, trying not to smile. Instead:

"I'm flummoxed," I say. "I'm flabbergasted. I'm . . ."

". . . *busted,*" T says, letting out another plume of imaginary smoke.

She takes my hand and pat-pats it, as I begin bracing myself for the Explanation re policies—official, personal—regarding the dating of customers. Or perhaps she'll introduce a convenient boyfriend or—who knows?—girlfriend, maybe. Women have so many ways of telling a guy no without driving a stake through his ego. Being a guy, of course, I've heard them all—with the possible exception of what T says next.

"So," she says, blowing an invisible snake of smoke from the corner of her mouth.

This is it, I think—the blowoff. Foreshadowed by actual blowing. Nice touch.

"This bed of yours," she goes on, sticking to the subject she's introduced like a fly to flypaper, "it's not like some old-school *coffin,* is it?"

"No . . ."

"And your shower gets plenty of hot water, right?"

I nod—perhaps a bit too eagerly. T's nice enough not to notice.

"Okie-dokie," she says, stubbing out her invisible cigarette. "I get off at two." Pause. "From work, that is." An even sexier pause. "We'll have to see about that other thing." She crosses fingers on both hands, mouthing the word "hope," comically, and twice. "Pick me up?"

"It seems I already have."

"I mean later," she says, sneaking a quick peck at my cheek. "Right now, though, I gotta skedaddle." She does a surveillance-camera pan of the room. "Got me some younguns to entertain."

"I . . . ," I begin, but she's already disappeared into munchkin land along with my heart, my head, my all.

In case you've ever wondered if it's possible to find, rent, and furnish an apartment in less than six hours, the answer is yes. The complete answer is: "Yes, provided money's no object." And you know, when you haven't been laid in several decades, it's surprising how much discretionary cash you can suddenly scare up—even after accounting for that pet mortal you've been raising in your spare time.

Speaking of which . . .

"Are we moving?" Isuzu asks, watching as I dart about the apartment, filling a garbage bag with books and assorted idiosyncratic knickknacks—"Or are you like Santa Claus's evil twin?"

"Um," I stall. How am I supposed to explain what I'm doing, what I've got planned?

Well—I imagine myself saying—*there comes a time in the life of every boy vampire when he meets someone special. But he doesn't want his new someone special to know about his other someone special (at least not yet) because, God knows, carnage could ensue— and that would not be a good thing. The boy vampire wants to get to know the new person better, and then he can introduce the Big Picture when the time seems right. If it seems right, which—cross fingers, hope, hope—it might. And that's when the first someone special gets her own someone special to talk to about special female stuff, like Ebola.*

Yeah, I could go that route. Or:

"I sold some stuff on eBay," I say, trying out the lie. "The FedEx guy is waiting." I pick up my pace, grabbing knicks, stuffing knacks. "Gotta skedaddle."

" 'Skedaddle'?" Isuzu says, cocking an eyebrow. "Since when do you use words like 'skedaddle'?"

Since it started looking like I might get laid. Do you mind?

"It's just a word," I say. "Somebody used it at work. Thought I'd try it out, see if I could get a rise out of you." Pause. "Seems to have worked."

"Uh-huh." Dubiousness, thy name is Isuzu.

"Oh," like an afterthought, like this happens all the time, "I probably won't be home tonight."

Isuzu blinks. Shakes her teenage head. "What?"

"There's this project at work. It's looking like an all-nighter."

"What are you gonna do, sleep in your cube all day?"

"I can," I say. "Might have to."

"What kind of—," she begins, but I cut her off.

"Gotta go," I say. "FedEx beckons."

"Yeah, I know," Isuzu says. "You gotta . . . 'skedaddle.' " She waits until I almost close the door before asking, "Does this all-nighter have a name?"

Which reminds me—I really need to find out what to call T other than Tombstone.

"Trust," I say back. "Family is all about *trust,*" I add, avoiding Isuzu's not terribly trusting eyes. "So, we're good here, right?"

I don't wait for an answer before pulling the door closed. The way I figure it, it's my pet food, my rent, my rules. If she doesn't like it, she can . . . Well, no, actually, she *can't.*

Kind of sweet the way that works out, I think, smiling all the way to the car.

-21-

THE SEX PART

I've been running the car heater all evening. I point this out because modesty demands I ascribe T's next comment to a thermostat-
ically enhanced libido.

"I wanted to jump your bones the first time we met," she says,
the second I close the door, sealing in our privacy with a solid Euro-
pean *thunk*. "Even before, you know, the gift that keeps on giving?"
Her voice rises at the end, like a teenage girl whose life sentence is
still a question, whose life, in general, is all about anticipation.

Not that I'm one to judge. After all, I'm the one who's too damaged to date. *I'm* the one who hasn't been laid in decades. And I'm
the one who's been driving around in a car with the heater blasting
all night.

"I wanted to jump your bones till they creaked like a frozen oak
in a windstorm."

T smiles.

"Of course, the priorities were different then," I say, changing
subjects, playing hard to get. "I was in the avant-garde in a war of
attrition and—"

"Blah, blah, blah," T says, cutting through the words, and years,
and excuses. "Been there. Done that." She pauses, a woman whose
body is still in its twenties, but whose mind has had decades to perfect its ideas about sexiness. "And now, sonny Jim," she says, prepar-

ing to name me as beneficiary to all those years of research, "it's about time *you . . . did . . . me.*"

In a different time, in a different place, after hearing a line like that, I'd *still* expect her smile to include fangs. Not that that's a *bad* thing . . .

"All in good time," I say, faking a brand of cool I don't really possess. "But before we get into all that, can you do me a favor?"

T reaches for my zipper.

"Not *that,*" I say, brushing her hand away.

"What, then?"

"Can you tell me your name?"

T flinches. Blinks.

It's one of those "oh yeah" blinks. An "oh yeah" blink laced with a little "shit" and a pinch of "fuck me."

"Rose," she says. She places the flat of her palm to her heart. Blinks again. "Rose Thorne."

It's my turn to blink. "Not your *stage* name," I say. "Your real one."

"That *is* my real name," Rose says, folding her arms over her chest and the rattling thought of us having gotten this far without my knowing her name. I look at her profile, which is all she's giving me to look at, as she stares straight out at the road ahead.

"Rose Thorne," I say aloud, just to try it out, to feel the shape of it in my mouth.

"Yep," Rose says, cinching her arms tighter. "That's my name," she adds, still talking to the windshield. "Don't wear it out."

In all honesty, I don't think I could have picked a better name. It's perfect. It sums her up as neat as can be. Beauty. Danger. Fangs. Blood red or ghost white. The all-purpose flower for weddings and funerals, love and death, Eros and Thanatos. And a little old-fashioned, too, like her way of talking.

I look at her, sitting there defiantly, making a show of *not* looking at me as the colored streetlights wash over her face and crossed arms.

Prickly. Not to be messed with.

Rose Thorne.

It's even got her job in there, by way of Gypsy Rose Lee. That, and some loftier stuff, too. Like "rose," as in the past tense for "rise." Like in resurrection. Apotheosis. Redemption.

"I like it," I say. "It's very . . . *you.*"

Rose smiles a predatory smile in the rearview mirror. "Well, ain't that a relief," she says, still playing at being angry for a few seconds longer, before unfolding her arms like the petals of her namesake. She scooches around in her seat to face me. "The name was my dad's idea," she says. "Mom says if he would've lived, there'd've been no way, but then the prick up and dies just before I get born." Pause. "Funny the things grief can make you do."

"Grief," I say, "or maybe love."

"Well, duh," Rose says. "The love part's understood. I mean, if there's no love, there's no grief, right?"

Perhaps it's the heat. Perhaps it's our mutual horniness. Perhaps it's the fact that neither of us plans on dying or being grieved. Ever. Whatever the reason, Rose's last comment strikes us both as suddenly almost unbelievably funny. The laughing starts with a giggled fuse and then explodes into howls and barks. I pull off to the side of the road and park to avoid killing us both. Rose wipes her eyes; I can feel every rib in my rib cage. The laughter subsides, but then sputters back to life. If we could, we'd be peeing our pants. Our chests heave with it. We begin to wheeze.

And then . . .

And then we're just kissing. Kissing to stop each other from laughing. And then kissing just to be kissing. Vampire tongues are porous, spongelike. Touch a finger to a vampire tongue and you can feel it sucking at the soft pad of skin like a hundred tiny mouths. And when a vampire kisses another vampire and their tongues get involved, it's like pressing Velcro together. You connect. You become like Siamese twins, joined by this one vigorous muscle pulling, pushing, needing, and being needed, so completely, so perfectly and purely, you never want it to stop.

We do. Eventually. Of course.

Stop, that is.

Have to. What with the car parked and the engine running to keep the heater going, the gas can last only so long. So we stop. Detach. Decouple. Rip the Velcro apart. I pull the car back onto the road leading to my apartment, the sequel.

We experience detours along the way. Detours of our own making. And so we park, and kiss, and thank God my car's not what you'd call a gas guzzler.

And then we laugh—mightily, fearlessly, immortally—at the irony of our fluid-driven lives.

Did you just dry clean this place?" Rose asks, covering her nose with the crook of her arm. What she means is the smell. It's been building up ever since I left to get her, and shoves back at us like a pair of invisible hands the second I open the door—the factory-fresh stink of brand-new everything.

"My blood warmer," I say, fumbling for the pieces of a good lie. "The thermostat goes nuts a couple of nights ago and . . . *boom!*" I underline the *"boom!"* by making five-fingered starbursts out of both hands. "It looked like Custer's Last Stand in here." Pause. "Just got done cleaning today."

"Uh-huh," Rose says, looking around the apartment at the other lie I'm trying to sell—the one spelled out in funky knick-knacks on loan from my *real* place. The illusion I'm going for is that someone has actually lived here for more than a few hours, the old things with personality strategically arranged to offset the glaring generic newness of everything else. That was the idea. But looking at the place now, all I can think of is a ransom note of awkwardly mixed type.

IKEA, IKEA, IKEA . . .

SS dagger from World War II.

Sharper Image, Sharper Image, Sharper Image . . .

My Bela Lugosi poster.

"I see," Rose says, registering the old-new schizophrenia I've so carefully arranged. She pauses. Smiles. Frowns. Smiles again.

Finally: "Okay," she says, accepting my explanation without really buying it. And then she just stands there, holding her purse with two hands—which is one more than strictly necessary. It's a waiting gesture. A gesture of willful disarmament. The next move is mine and she's letting me know with her body that she won't fend it off.

I should kiss her. I should take her lower lip in my teeth and bite. Oh, now she's looking around again. Away from me. Allowing the opportunity for a sneak attack. Displaying the full, incredible length of her white, white neck.

And still I hesitate. Why did it seem so much easier in the car?

"So," I say, clapping my hands over the word, startling her.

Rose turns around. "What?" she says, the word heavy with expectation.

"Is this city grimy, or what?"

That's what I say. That's what I've come up with.

"Excuse me?" Rose says, giving me the look I deserve, given the obtuse nature of my invitation.

"Grimy," I repeat. "Don't you feel, you know, *dirty*?" I mime washing my hands—a gesture that, looking back, may have come across as just a bit too Peter Lorre–ish.

Rose sets her eyes to drill.

"Listen," she says, "if that's supposed to be some crack about my job."

"No," I insist, shaking my head. "No, that's not it. I . . ."

This is me. Drowning. Slowly.

"*Yes?*" Rose says.

"I was trying to be clever," I say, suddenly fascinated by the workmanship that's gone into my shoes. "You know. Subtle?"

"Obtuse?"

"Okay," I agree. "Obtuse."

"What were you being obtuse about?"

The trouble with being immortal is the not-being-able-to-die part in situations like these.

"Nice shoes," Rose says, looking at where I'm looking. She places two fingers under my chin and pushes up. "Yes?" she repeats.

And so I just blurt it out. "The shower," I say. "I was being obtuse about the conditions under which one would feel compelled to . . ."

And then I make the mistake of listening to myself. ". . . take a shower," I whisper, running out of steam.

"Huh," Rose says.

She chucks up my chin again, smiling one of those predatory smiles. And then she turns. On one heel—like a ballerina. Like my luck, finally.

She guesses at the direction, and starts walking toward it.

Her purse is the first thing to hit the floor. Followed by the petals of her clothing, falling like autumn leaves, shed like snakeskin. And then the hands come out, pressed together forever back there, blue-green against all that white, white skin.

This is where the sex part comes in. And if this were a movie from when I was a kid, this is where the camera would lose interest in the people it's been watching, going blurry just as they're angling in for that first serious kiss. This is where they'd cut to the train, or a waterfall, or fireworks, leaving the rest up to us, alone in the dark with our overheated imaginations.

I always hated it when the camera did that.

But I understand it now. Faced with the prospect of writing a detailed account of what happened next between Rose and me, sorry, I'm afraid I'll have to pass. Some things just don't sound right when you write about them with an "I." They come across as creepy, or bragging, or both. Plus, if you don't know how sex works by now, this is no way to find out. And if you do, then you do, and there's not a lot new I can tell you. So:

[Insert fireworks here.]

-22-

3 2 - B

*M*artin *Joseph Kowalski,*" Isuzu says the second I step through the
door, looking like something the bat dragged in. A day and part of
another night have gone by since I last crossed this threshold, during which time I've apparently become the child, while Isuzu has
become the parent.

"Forget how the phone works?" she asks, her arms folded over
her almost chest. "Or did you maybe misplace the address?" she
adds, tapping her foot, pissed, pissed, and—oh yeah—pissed.

Bitch.

I've raised a bitch.

And I wasn't even trying.

"Oh, hey, Marty," I say, loosening my already loose tie. "Thanks
for working all night to put—now what was that again? oh yeah!—
food on the table." I suddenly remember the likelihood of lipstick,
and cinch my tie back up. "And paying the rent, too! Like wow! You
are, like, the *best,* man . . ."

Isuzu glares. I glare back.

"You smell like perfume," she says. "*Cheap* perfume."

"Go to your room," I snap.

"What?"

"You heard me. Quiz show's over. Time for bed."

"But . . ."

"Skat," I say.

"Don't you mean 'skedaddle'?"

"Izzy," I say, crossing my own arms, "this isn't a discussion. *Git.*"

And she does. To my utter amazement, she gits. She turns on her heel and stomps off, slamming the bedroom door behind her.

And then everything gets quiet, and it's just me.

Just me, feeling hated, feeling evil for punishing my little pet human for my own indiscretion. Feeling evil for staying out so long, having so much fun, not calling.

Feeling evil, finally, for *feeling evil* and still having to smile about it.

When I hum—which I find myself doing—it's an evil hum. A hum of pure wickedness. And when I loosen my tie and my shirt falls open—thanks to the buttons that went missing last night—my first thought is not, I'm going to need to fix that, but, I need a mirror. And there it is, the bloodred gloss of pure evil smudging my skin, bringing back the feel of Rose's mouth, her bite, the click of her teeth meeting. Standing there in the bathroom, looking at my evil face in the mirror, all I can think of is all the evil Rose and I have yet to commit.

And there's that smile again, smiling away like one of those yellow buttons popular a few years back—the ones with two dots for eyes, that simple curve of a mouth, and the two little triangles, for fangs.

After a week and a half of nearly nightly vigorous evil, I confess.

To Isuzu. Not Rose.

"I've met someone," I announce. This is in response to why it is that after nearly eight years of wearing the same thing, I've suddenly replaced everything in my closet.

"Well, duh," she says.

"That obvious, huh?"

Isuzu runs her nose across my shoulder and up my neck like a bloodhound. "Just a little," she says.

"I'm hoping you might get to meet her some night."

Isuzu says she didn't know they made suits of armor for girls her size.

"She doesn't know about you yet," I say. "I'm still feeling her out."

Isuzu rolls her eyes. "Don't you mean 'up'?"

Thank God vampires aren't big on blushing without a little thermostatic assistance.

"That was uncalled for," I say, even though the smile in my voice suggests otherwise.

"So, are you gonna, like, *marry* her or something?"

"Maybe," I say. "Like I said, I'm still exploring the situation."

More eye rolling.

"I'm doing this partly for you, you know."

"Oh yeah?" Isuzu smirks. "Which part? The one where you skip out on me every night of the week? Or the screwing-some-bimbo part?"

Smart-ass. I've raised a smart-ass without even trying.

I point at my hand. "This is me," I say, "slapping the crap out of you for what just came out of your mouth."

Isuzu blinks. She knows I'd never hit her, but knows I threaten it only when she crosses the line.

"And she's not a bimbo," I say. "You'd like her." Pause. "I think it'd be good, having a woman around here for you to—"

"Jesus," Isuzu says, spitting the word out like a cherry pit. "Is *that* what this is about? You're trying to find me a mom?"

"Is that such a bad idea?"

"I had a mom," she says. "A couple of your pals cashed her in for the deposit."

Whenever she's *really* pissed, Isuzu starts referring to vampires in general as my "pals." Linking me and my "pals" to her mother's death is as good as a "Fuck you."

I point at my hand again. She says, "Go ahead."

She says, "Go ahead, and pray I don't bleed. I wouldn't wanna be accused of being a clot tease."

I've already got one hand in the air. It'd be *so* easy. It'd be so deserved. Just a dip and torque as palm flat collides with cheeky cheek. Doing it's not a problem. It's the stopping I'm not so sure about.

And so I don't. "Truce," I say, raising my other hand, holding both out there like twin stops signs.

Isuzu starts to say something. Thinks about it. Stops. Reconsiders. Says: "I think these little heart-to-hearts are a good thing, don't you?"

"I was just gonna say this went a lot smoother than I expected."

Pause. Time to think. Me, about what I'd do without Isuzu. Isuzu, what she'd do without me. When one of us speaks again, it's the one with the most to lose.

"So," Isuzu says, "does Mom Number Two have a name?"

What do you look for when you're trying to figure out if your vampire girlfriend can be trusted around your mortal daughter?

"What do you think about kids?"

Prepared how, exactly?

Yeah, that'd be a bad sign.

On the plus side, I don't have to worry about curiosity with Rose; she already knows what blood tastes like "on tap." She was one of my early recruits, recruited to recruit others. There was no need for her to rely on the lab-grown stuff until we all had to make the switch. And it's not like she doesn't know the thrill of the hunt, the taste of fresh-squeezed adrenaline from a victim who knows his time is up. The Benevolent Vampires were mainly about preventing murder, sure, but every new recruit was offered a few justifiable homicides. To get it out of their system. To make the world a better place by getting rid of some of those people that just needed killing. Wife abusers, child abusers, rapists, Republicans—your basic scum of the earth. When skimming was called for, we let our new recruits skim.

It was a win-win situation.

If anything, what I worry about is nostalgia. Whatever you can't get anymore always seems better, more precious than whatever's freely available. That's why old junk becomes antiques and costs more used than it ever did new. That's why gas is $5 a gallon, while lab-grown blood averages about a buck fifty. I'll admit it; even *I've* had moments of longing for the old-fashioned stuff—especially the way Isuzu's been lately. But I've got my ace in the hole. All I have to do is wait until she's ready to graduate to vampirehood. Sure, it'll be willing blood, not the hunted kind, but it's way past too late for that. Even if I were to go nuts tomorrow, Isuzu wouldn't scare. Her not scaring is why she's still here. She'd just laugh at me like before, thinking it was a joke right up until it was too late. So I wait, sticking to the Plan as planned.

Except for Rose, of course. Rose wasn't part of the Plan, but she is now. And so the questions come back:

"What do you miss most about the old days?"

Killing my lovers' kids . . .

I shake my head. Listen to the broken glass and rusty nails clattering around in there. Get ready for a *very* long night.

Candlelight. That's a good start.

Candlelight, and our black marble eyes staring into each other, watching the reflections of the dancing flame. My hand reaches across the table, finds hers.

"Rose . . ."

"Yes?"

"I have something to tell you."

"Yes?"

This would be easier if she didn't keep saying "Yes" like she's been practicing, just in case I've got a ring hidden on me somewhere. "I . . ."

"Yes . . ."

". . . have a child."

There. It's said. It's out there.

"Where? Tied up in the trunk?"

Yikes! One of the *bad* responses.

"No," I say. "It's not like that. I'm raising it. I mean, 'her.' I have been for some time now."

Rose looks at me and I look at her. We're really hating the way these dead crow eyes of ours make our emotions so hard to read.

Not that emotions were a piece of cake before, but they're a bitch and a half now.

"I'm waiting for you to make a noise," I say, after she hasn't.

"I'm thinking."

"What are you thinking?"

"Hard to say," she says. "I'm still doing it."

"Maybe talking it out would help."

"Okay," she says. "Let's see. I'm trying to figure out if I should be pissed, or flattered. On the pissed side, there's you lying to me."

"I wouldn't say 'lying,' exactly," I lie. "It's not like you said, 'Marty, do you have a kid?' and I said, 'No.'"

"Being a jerk now doesn't make the thinking part go any easier," Rose points out.

"Sorry . . ."

"To continue," Rose continues. "On the flattered side, there's you trusting me enough to risk telling me now."

"If voting's allowed," I say, "I'm all for being flattered."

"Yeah. See. That's the thing," Rose says. "*You* don't get a vote."

I begin to object, but am cut off by the sound of a bottle neck clinking against the rim of an empty glass, followed by the warm glug-glugging of blood being poured. Rose drains the glass and re-fills it several times, bent not only on sating her appetite, but clubbing it to death like a baby harp seal.

"Still thinking?" I ask, after the fifth glass.

"Still thinking," she says, slamming it, and starting another.

"Still?"

"Still."

Eight. Nine. An even ten.

And then:

"So," Rose says, dabbing her chin with her napkin. "This kid got a name?"

Isuzu, Rose. Rose, Isuzu."

The two women in my life. All my bad ideas, made flesh.

There they are, squaring off like a couple of prizefighters, trying to decide what part of the other to smash first. Their eyes drill small holes into each other, and I can read both their minds, because both their minds are thinking the same thing:

"What the hell does he see in her?"

Rose is the first one to break the ice, or perhaps freeze it more solidly. "Don't the eyes freak you out?" she says, as if Isuzu's not even there. "I mean how the white part makes it so *obvious* what she's looking at."

At the moment, Isuzu is looking at a point between Rose's monotonous eyes, imagining, I'm sure, how she might arrange to drive in a six-inch spike right . . . about . . . *there.*

"Your eyes used to have a white part, too," I remind Rose. "We all did."

She flicks the comment away like a pesky fly. "Yeah, yeah, yeah," she says. "Ancient history. Just like them argument shoes."

" 'Argument shoes'?"

"You know," Rose says. "The ones that looked like they were made from a couple of beagles?"

"Hush puppies?"

"No, no. The two-tone jobbies."

"Spats?"

"Yeah. That's them."

Isuzu—who's been ping-ponging from one speaker to the next with her own two-tone jobbies—finally shoehorns her way into the conversation.

"Are those boobs for real?" she asks, zeroing in on the meanest question she can find.

Rose is a 32-B. To imagine her current bustline as the result of some form of enhancement is to imagine a former chest not only flat, but perhaps actually concave.

"Isuzu," I scold. "Is that any way to treat a guest?"

"Beats me," she says back, like a dare.

The words "Don't give me any ideas" are already on my tongue, ready for blurting when it occurs to me that Isuzu *doesn't* know how to treat a guest. In fact, *Rose* is the first company we've ever had.

And it's not exactly like there's a surplus of appropriate role models out there. As nostalgic as vampires are about the cute side of growing up, almost nobody wants to relive their teenage years, not even in period pieces on TV. To the extent that teenage-*looking* characters appear on the tube, they're invariably Screamers. And that's it. Those are my little girl's role models for growing up, a bunch of pint-size fuck-yous.

Lovely.

Rose, meanwhile, seems to have taken the whole thing in stride, and may even be affording Isuzu an inch or two more respect, for not letting the eye comment go unpaid. "Regarding my tits and their realness," she says, stepping right into the thick of it, "yes, they are. My nose, on the other hand," she adds, offering us her profile, tilting her head back slightly, "this bit of cuteness is as fake as a three-dollar bill."

"*Really?*" Isuzu practically squeals the word, showing real interest, sarcasm-free. I should probably worry about her nearly orgasmic enthusiasm for appearance-related topics, but relief gets in the way.

"Oh yeah," Rose says. "The honker I was born with—*Jesus.* Scare babies, crack mirrors, the whole nine yards. It looked like a goddam dinner roll, right there in the middle of my face. Plus, on the tip, it had a kind of butt-crack thing going."

Isuzu goes, "Disgustoid," and shakes her head, but otherwise shows every sign of—dare I say—"warming" to our guest.

" 'Course, I *was* thinking of getting a boob job, but that was years ago. Before." Rose turns to me suddenly and winks. "Before *someone* decided to lock down my looks forever."

Which is true. Cosmetic surgery just isn't done anymore. Not after the first few tries. Vampires heal too fast. The incision closes before you can stick anything inside. In a few cases, the cut actually healed around the doctor's wrists—photos of which bounced around the email joke circuit for the next couple of weeks, bearing subject lines like "What a Hoot(er)" and "Beats Mittens." Holding the wound open with a spreader didn't work, either. All that did was force the edges to heal separately, and bingo, you bought yourself a brand-new hole. With results like that, it didn't take long before the whole 32-B-or-not-to-be thing wasn't even a question anymore.

"Yep," Rose sighs. "Hair and makeup. That's pretty much it in the changing-my-looks department." Pause. "So, a word of advice, kiddo. Before Marty even gets close to vamping you, make sure it's all nailed down tight, 'cause forever's a long time to be staring at even a freckle you don't like."

The whites of Isuzu's eyes are aimed right at Rose, playing along the This and That, checking her out, confirming the truth of the wisdom just conferred. Her whites show awe. Her whites show envy. And admiration. And a grudging recognition that, yes—despite her expectations, despite her spiteful wish for it to be otherwise—*yes*, here was someone she could finally talk to about all the stuff she couldn't talk about with me.

Rose lets her look a bit longer. She's used to being looked at. It's what she does. It's what she's paid for. And then she catches Isuzu's eyes, smiling the tiniest smile, before darting a look in my direction. But it's not a look for me; it's a look *at* me. It's *for* Isuzu, whom she turns back to, and then winks.

Isuzu looks at me, too, and then back at Rose.

Winks.

So *that's* what female bonding looks like, I think; it looks like *that*.

Like trouble, that is. Like two against one.

Even though both cats are out of both bags, and have met without blowing too much fur, I decide to keep my home away from home. It's the sex mainly. The vampire sex and all the steam and hot air it calls for. I can't imagine Isuzu sleeping through it. What I can imagine, however, is her waking up drenched in sweat, the bedsheets clinging to her like a grabby ghost, her brain poached just shy of heatstroke, and needing a glass of water. What I can imagine is her stumbling about our apartment-turned-sauna only to come upon Rose and me. And let me assure you, stumbled-upon sex hasn't gotten any prettier in its vampire incarnation.

Take the practice known as "pulsing." You slice a Y incision in your palm and your partner does the same, on the opposite hand. And then you squeeze them together quick—cut to uncut, left to right—the wounds stitching you to each other as they heal. You can feel the liquid tickle of your lover's pulse, feathering the soft pad of your uncut palm. There's no mingling; vampire blood doesn't get along with vampire blood; but you share a pulse all the same, that most basic ticktock at the core of your being, synching up right along with your body temperatures. It's wild. It's almost like being able to read your partner's mind during sex, and with sex, the more synchronicity, the better. You decouple at the point of orgasm, ripping open both wounds, which then go on to reheal, separately. It's messy. It keeps the makers of bleach in business. But it's also something you wouldn't want your teenage daughter to catch you doing.

I start the car with Isuzu in bed and plenty of good darkness left in the night. My cell phone and earplug are back in the apartment, in a drawer. Isuzu's a teenager, having periods and everything. It's about time I gave her a little privacy.

"So," I say. "Whatcha think?"

"About Isuzu?" Rose closes her door and we begin heading out to find a little privacy of our own.

I nod.

"That's one fucked-up little mortal you got there, Marty."

I want to object just as much as I want "fucked-up" clarified—and now.

"What I mean is," Rose continues, "I think she's swell. A lot like me when I was—well, I was never *really* her age. Extenuating circumstances. I got matured against my will, thanks to a grabby uncle-in-quotes with detachable pants, but . . . And actually, I guess that *does* make us kinda similar, both being treated like prey from a tender age and all, but . . ." Pause. "Yeah," she concludes. "I like her. You done good. Well, as good as you could, given the extenuating circumstances."

So *that's* what she means by "fucked-up." Okay, I guess.

"So, is it true?" I ask, changing subjects.

"Is what true?"

I point at my nose.

"Shit, no." Rose laughs. "That was a—whaddayacallit?—docudrama. 'Inspired by actual events.' Only, they didn't actually happen to *me*. A friend of a cousin of a friend. Whatever. It was just something to say to get her off my tits." Pause. "Funny how she just zoomed right on in there, going for the jugular two seconds after hello."

"That's not how I raised her," I insist. "I think it's the TV."

"Hey, don't get me wrong," Rose insists right back. "I was impressed. It takes real talent to go from kid to bitch in sixty seconds. And it's not like the world's given her a lot of reasons to be Little Miss Sweetness. Come to think of it, I think she showed amazing restraint." Another pause. "Deadly accuracy, sure, but amazing restraint, too."

"By which you mean," I say, "you really *were* thinking of a boob job before I closed that door."

"Oh yeah." Rose laughs. Stops. Looks out the window at the traffic going by. "Had me a little scalpel fund going and everything." She sighs.

"Well, I'm glad you didn't," I say, grabbing her knee, giving it a reassuring squeeze.

And I mean it. I really do. Contrary to what you may have assumed, not all male vampires are breast men. There's a world of difference between "suckling" and "sucking"—a bigger world than that little *l* might suggest. For me—for example—I've never been one for imposing breasts. And the fake ones are always so obviously fake, you have to wonder who they think they're fooling. As far as I'm concerned, they're worse than tattoos. At least tattoos are upfront about what they are—no pun intended—but fake tits are just lies told in silicone.

And anyway, small-breasted women are just more interesting. Maybe that's because they think they have to be, but that's a whole other story.

"Well, I'm glad you're glad," Rose says, turning back, squeezing my knee sarcastically. "Huge load off my mind."

I turn the heater up. Rose turns it back down.

"Not just yet," she says. "We've got a little more *talking* to do."

"About?"

"The future." Pause. "What comes next."

Oh, I think.

"Oh," I say. *"That,"* I add.

"Yes," she says. *"That,"* she adds.

Martin, corner. Corner, Martin.

"Um," I say. And it's not like I don't know what I want—or what I *think* I want. It's just that my penis has decided it's a turtle, all of a sudden. And I don't know if it knows something I don't.

"Um," I say again.

"I can see you've given this lots of thought," Rose jokes, perhaps as a way to ease the tension. It doesn't work.

"I was thinking," I begin, fully prepared to *not* tell Rose what I'm *really* thinking. It's the not-dying thing. The *no* Till Death Do Us Part part. I'm thinking that every bottle of blood in my refrigerator has an expiration date, that Isuzu will grow up, get vamped, move out. I'm thinking about my mom, and my dad, and how I'm *really* not going to tell Rose about *that*.

Plus . . .

Plus, I'm thinking about staring at even a freckle I don't like— *forever.*

"Okay," Rose says. "Thinking. That's a good start."

"I was thinking that you and I . . ."

". . . yes . . ."

". . . could . . ."

"Go on."

"Yes!" I practically squeal this, just like Isuzu did with her *"Really."*

"What?"

"I was thinking," I say, "that you and I could," I roll my hand like a director telling an actor to speed it up, only with me, it means, "you know. Go on."

"Our merry ways?"

"No," I say. "Seeing each other," I add. "You and I could go on . . . seeing each other."

"Oh," Rose says. "Huh," she adds.

She turns around again and looks at the streetlights streaming by her window. She cups her chin in her uncut palm.

Sighs.

"Whatever," she says.

-23-

KELLY

So, you're in love, eh?"

That's Father Jack saying that, and me saying back: "I think so."

Me adding: "It feels like it."

We're sitting in Father Jack's den. He's got a fire going in the fireplace, not for the heat, but to look at the flames licking up the logs, to hear the crackle of things consigned to burn. Judas is curled up in the corner, sleeping.

"Must be nice," Father Jack says, looking at the flames. He's made a point of looking away from me to look at the flames, before speaking. He tightens his eyelids, narrowing the slit through which light is allowed in. The crow's-feet around his crow black eyes get deeper.

"I'm never going to see you again," he says. "Am I?" He pauses. "You're ditching me just like you ditched Trooper."

I flinch. And then I remember which Trooper he means. And it's true. This *is* my have-a-good-life, my don't-let-the-screen-door-hit-ya-on-the-way-out. It's just math. And there's only so much dead time in an evening.

"I would," I joke, trying to lighten the mood. "But I don't think the pet store would give me anything for you."

"You're probably right there." Father Jack sighs, his mood not lightened in the least. "Not a lot of call for my kind."

Oh, so it's going to be one of those talks full of hints, and evasions, and euphemisms that raise a subject just to avoid talking about it. We do this all the time, Father Jack and I, we who are made of time. But not anymore. This is good-bye. And it's as good a time as any to bring up all the stuff that can ruin everything.

"We've never really discussed that," I say, because we haven't. Because I really didn't want to know. He said he never did and I was only too happy to take him at his word. Denial—that's what I was in. I accepted his denial, and moved on to that place where I could feel superior by comparison.

"Sure we have," Father Jack says. "All my advice on your gambling? The twelve-step stuff? That was us, talking about it."

"We haven't talked about it *specifically*," I say. "I don't even know, you know *which*."

"Which?"

"Which kind," I stumble. "Boys? Girls?" Pause. "Both?"

"None of the above," Father Jack says.

I blink. I look at my empty hands, for effect. For illustration. "What's that leave?"

"Kelly," Father Jack says. "It leaves Kelly." He pauses. Looks away from the flames and back at me. "You think I'm some sort of fiend who'd go around molesting every kid that came my way, if there were any 'kids' left to come my way. But that's not how it is. It's not how it was. There was just one. Just . . . Kelly. She was a little girl in my first parish, when I was just out of the seminary." Pause. "This woman you've found. This love of your afterlife. How do you feel when you see her?"

"Like my veins are too small," I say. "Like my heart's not big enough. Like I've been poisoned and she's the antidote." I pause. Listen to myself. Deflect. "Just stop me as soon as I start sounding like an idiot, okay?"

"No. You're fine," Father Jack says, back to staring at the flames. "That's how I felt when I saw Kelly out on the playground. She looked like sunshine in a hand-me-down dress, and I wanted to buy her things. I wanted her to hug me. I wanted to feel her little arms wrapped around my neck, hear her laughter making the world okay."

I shift in my chair. I'm having trouble finding a comfortable position.

"I'd give her horsey rides around the playground. She'd hold on to my ears, my hair, my collar, always laughing that musical laugh of hers. 'Father Jack,' she'd say, tugging on my pant leg, 'can you get me God's autograph?' I didn't know what I was feeling. I just knew I didn't feel that way about the other kids, or anybody else I knew."

A log splits in the fireplace. Father Jack stops talking and watches the sparks riding shimmers of heat up the chimney.

"And then I had a dream," he says, starting again. "And then I knew."

Father Jack's chest rises, falls, waits for me to ask.

"What did you do?"

"Nothing," he says. One tick. One tock.

"No. That's not true," he confesses. Or goes on confessing. "I yelled at her. In front of everybody. I sent her to the principal's office for talking in class, even though she hadn't. I kept that up for about a week, finding things to accuse her of, anything to get her out of my classroom and into somebody else's custody."

Father Jack squeezes one hand with the other, behind his back.

"I'd see her out on the playground after that, and it was like . . . I don't know. It was like I killed something inside her. She'd wander around the playground, kicking at pebbles, not playing, not laughing. I thought I was doing the right thing, protecting her from me, but I betrayed her, instead. I . . ."

The knuckles of one hand crack in the fist of the other.

"I went to see the bishop," Father Jack says. "I sat in his office and told him I was having trouble with a child in my parish. 'Does he want money?' That's the first question he asked me. And before I can even say, no, he's sliding open a drawer. That's all I can hear, that drawer, squeaking open. Wood rubbing against wood. It sounds like the hinges on the gates of hell. I can't look at whatever's in that drawer. I get dizzy instead. And when I try standing up, I just vomit right there, in the bishop's wastebasket."

"Why didn't you just quit?"

"Oh, I tried." Father Jack laughs an utterly joyless laugh. "I tried killing myself." Pause. "I was going to be very Roman about it. I lit candles, filled the tub with warm water, turned out the lights. The razor blades were all ready and my wrists were going numb from this cream anesthetic I'd rubbed on. I wanted out, see, but I wasn't a big fan of pain. I'd already taken six aspirin, to stop the blood from clotting, but for that other thing, too. For the pain."

"What happened?"

"Seems my parish wasn't in the safest of neighborhoods," Father Jack says. "Seems a house with all the lights out during the shank of the evening was pretty much an open invitation."

"Someone broke in?"

"Someone broke in," Father Jack confirms. "He finds me unconscious and ends up calling nine-one-one. He's just a petty thief. He's no murderer. So . . . After that, I figured God just had different plans for me."

"But you never touched Kelly?" I ask.

"Never."

"And you never touched any other kids?"

I ask that just to have it confirmed. I don't know why, but I believe Father Jack. I'm not inclined to second-guess his story as I was with Rose and her mother the clown. He could be lying to make himself look good. But if that's the goal, why'd he tell me about his inclinations in the first place? Maybe I'm being stupid. Maybe I'm being naïve. Or maybe the world where it mattered just got placed in somebody else's custody.

"AA," Father Jack says, preemptively. "That's you're next question, right? What did I do, how did I cope with my impossible longings?"

I nod.

"They really didn't have a twelve-step group for my thing, so I became an 'alcoholic,'" Father Jack says. "And I went to meetings. Lots and lots of meetings. It's really comforting, surrounding yourself with the suffering of others. I'd be at a meeting and somebody'd break down crying at my table. After one of those, I'd go home happy as a clam. It was their happiness I couldn't take. Whenever too many people started getting better, started coming in with tales of personal triumph instead of tragedy, that's when I knew it was time to find a new meeting."

Another log splits, letting go more sparks and ash. Judas's head pops up, he looks around, settles back.

"That's why I'm still a priest," Father Jack says. "Confession. I'm hooked on that laundry list of everyday weaknesses. The worries of people trying to talk their way out of hell."

I smile, happy to hear that I'm not Father Jack's only dealer of vicarious thrills.

"So yeah." He sighs. "Yeah, I'm real happy for you, Marty."

"You don't sound very happy."

Father Jack turns away from the fire so I can see the weary smirk on his face. "I'm bursting at the seams," he says in the deadest dead-pan I've ever heard him use. He turns back and pokes at the fire with the poker.

"Now get your happy ass out of here," he says, "before I have Judas rip you a new one."

-24-

YOUR WORST NIGHTMARE

We'd seen too many made-for-TV movies in which somebody introduces himself as "Your worst nightmare." That's how it got started. We looked at each other, having heard the same line delivered the same way too many times, and we just started giggling.

"Hello," I said, giggling, offering my hand. "Allow me to introduce myself. I'm your nightmare."

"Would that be my *worst* nightmare?" Isuzu asked.

"Why yes, it would."

"Pleased to meet you."

"Likewise, I'm sure."

Followed by more giggling and the birth of an inside joke.

"Hello. It's me. Your worst nightmare. I'm home."

That's how I'd announce myself, returning from work, a date, whatever. And Isuzu would run up from wherever she was, give me a quick hug, and then launch into the events of her day—the fly she stalked through the apartment for over an hour, what Bobby Little was doing in his room now, how far she'd gotten in reading through the *Encyclopedia Vampirica*.

That's how it worked—right up until it didn't.

The front door and windows—that's what I worried about. How easily jimmied, how quickly smashed—and all the things that might crawl in through the holes that were left. I imagined coming home one night to splinters or shards, but never guessed that the biggest threat to our way of life was as thin as a wire. As tiny as electrons.

As untouchable as loneliness.

I should have known something was wrong when Isuzu stopped complaining about my seeing Rose and being out all night. I should have known something was up when she cheerily saw me to the door, hoped I'd have a good time, assured me she'd be fine—*fine!*—on her own.

"Reading."

That's the answer I got when I asked her what she did while I was out. And it wasn't a lie, exactly. It just wasn't the whole truth. Reading was part of it, and typing was another part. There were also digital stills, followed by "live" video feeds—none of which was covered by the answer I'd been given.

Maybe it was just tit for tat. I'd lied to her about Rose, and this was the payback.

Oh, what a tangled World Wide Web we weave.

Digital proxies. Avatars. Cyber masks. The idea's always the same—just so many pixels wrapped around an animated frame, brought in to bolster the lie of whatever online persona you've adopted. Taller? No problem. Darker, more handsome? Prettier, blonder, bigger tits, more slutty? Perhaps you've always fancied yourself another species. Go for it. Everything is negotiable. Everything's up for grabs and nothing is what it seems. And so you run into Rex_260 on Afterlife Online one night, Rex turning out to be an impeccably digitized web-surfing German shepherd.

"Are you for real?" you type, and Rex types back, "I'm a metaphor."

"You mean like that bug in Kafka?" you type, and Rex types back, "Woof!"

You can also change your age. Of course.

You don't have to be an old lech or a little squirt. Not in cyberspace. You can change your age to reflect how young you are at heart. You can change your age to seem more mature than you are.

Or you can change your age to match the age of whatever it is you're into—whatever it is you're looking for, under all these cyber rocks, in all these dark, anonymous corners.

Hell, changing your age is as easy as changing a bloodstained shirt.

Hello," I call out. "It's me. Your worst nightmare. I'm home."

Nothing.

"Hello," I repeat, only to be answered by my own echo.

Maybe she's taking a nap, I think. Or hiding as a prank, or in the bathroom, or so caught up in all that "reading" she's been doing lately that she just doesn't hear. But by the time I call out a second time, I know it's none of these.

There's a kind of silence that says "gone." You recognize it by not having heard it in so long. I haven't heard this silence, this loud, since just before bringing Isuzu home for the first time. And here it is again. And just like that, I know that the nightmare that just walked through my door is my own.

I begin checking for clues.

There's no broken glass, no sign of a forced entry. There's blood, sure, but nothing I can't explain away as just proof of my own sloppy eating habits. Rings on the coffee table, a few drops on the kitchen counter, but no Rorschachs splattering the walls, no runny asterisks footnoting some larger mess waiting to be stumbled upon.

Her bed is made.

That's the first bad sign. The last time she made her bed was a few years ago, when she'd decided to hunt down her mother's killers.

Her pillow is fluffed. The comforter is drawn up over the pillow, and the spread drawn up over the comforter.

It's just a bed.

Just a made-up bed.

So why does it look so funereal?

I rifle through her desk, her closet, her sock and underwear drawer. I peek under that neat coffin of a bed. I don't know what

I'm looking for, but I look anyway, finding nothing in particular out of place, or missing, or terribly helpful.

It's as I'm going through the desk drawer that I brush past the computer, and notice that it's still warm. Warmer than me and the rest of the room, at least. I jiggle the mouse and the screen blossoms on; the AOL icon is still ghosted over from having been used last. I try to sign on but don't know her password. Of course, I don't need a password to get into her file cabinet, which is still available offline from her last sign-in. I double click and scan the roster of emails sent, and received, and autosaved to the hard drive. There's a lot of porn spam, which is disappointing, but unavoidable if you've spent any amount of time in the online chat rooms—which it seems Isuzu has.

And then there are the emails—the real, nonjunk emails that explain the panic and echoing silence I find myself in the middle of.

From: I_Trooper
To: Farmers_daughter

There are dozens and dozens, desperate little Ping-Pong balls of need and longing and—I'm sure—absolute bald-faced lies on the part of whoever the hell this farmer's daughter *really* is. I read just enough to learn that he claims to be twelve, mortal, a farm runaway, and, of course, a girl. "Her" current living arrangements are—shall we say—vague, as is his refusal to meet with Isuzu sometime during the day, "when it'll be safe for our kind." The last email, dated from the night before, is from Isuzu to this lying online creep and includes *my* telephone number—the landline, not the cell—and the times I'm expected to be away.

I hit star 69—that self-cannibalizing bit of Zen numerology—and take down the number. It's within the area code and only an hour and some change old. I dial it, but get a busy signal. Of course. They've probably taken the phone off the hook. They wouldn't want to be interrupted—at least one of them wouldn't. On a hunch, I replace the last three digits of the number with zeros.

"Sundown Motel," the voice on the other end says. "Front desk. How may I help you?"

I ask for the cross streets. Get them. Leave.

I've got an ax in the trunk. It's been there for the last few years, ever since Clarissa's first killer's "suicide." So I've got something. I'm ready. I've got something for whatever the fuck kind of door I find at the Sundown Motel (and abattoir). I've got something that'll work just as well on whatever the fuck I find *behind* that fucking door.

I brace myself for the sight of it, diminishing my expectations to a couple of pathetic pleas.

Please . . . don't rape her. Don't make her be dead *and* raped.

Please . . . let it be quick. Don't make her suffer. Don't nurse her like a bloody bottle of beer at last call, sipping her to death and backwash.

And *please* . . . when the ax hits your neck, just *die*. Don't go *why*ing me, don't try to plead or come up with excuses. Just keep your fucking mouth shut . . .

. . . *and die*.

I don't knock.

I don't listen for a "Who's there?"

I don't offer a setup for a punch line.

I've got the punch line right here in my hands, as I swing it over my head and wedge it into one of the Sundown Motel's surprisingly sturdy doors.

Not that it matters.

Not that the door was locked to begin with.

And when the unlocked door swings open, and the ax handle slips through my hands, it's just like everything else in my world on this godforsaken night.

Air.

I'm holding . . . *air.*

And then the door hits the inside wall just hard enough to jar the ax loose, followed by the soft, heavy clunk of hardware hitting the cheesy, shag-carpeted floor.

Dolls.

That's the first thing I see, after the door does its surprise open-sesame routine.

Dolls, scattered like they might be scattered in a careless teenage girl's bedroom—kid stuff treated with just enough disrespect to hide the love still felt. Among the dolls are yellowing copies of *16 Magazine*, *Tiger Beat*, *Betty and Veronica* comics.

In the center of the room, a little table is set up for tea, and something involving cosmetics. The hostess and her guest are dressed up in dresses that are too big for them, wearing sunglasses and rouge that stands out quite a bit more on one set of cheeks than it does the other. The two little girls—the little girl and the "little girl"—sit cross-legged next to the table, their pinkies raised along with their empty teacups, stuck, frozen, *in medias* . . . sip.

Their four dark lenses are pointed right at me. Me, bent and fumbling for my ax. Me, fumbling to apologize for the ax hole in the door, and feeling like an ax hole myself.

The four dark lenses raise together as if choreographed, revealing eyes—Isuzu's human pair, her friend's far darker set.

"Marty," Isuzu says. "Meet Twit."

"Twit?"

"Short for Antoinette," Twit says.

"People don't call you Toni?" I ask, which is not the first question I was expecting to ask. Of course, my expectations have been batting zero all evening.

"Yeah," Twit sighs, a weary, much older person's "yeah."

"You see," Twit goes on, "it's like this. After a while, you stop trying to change what people call you, 'cause the harder you try, the harder they laugh, and the only way to get anything back is to just embrace your stupid nickname until it's just the sound of what people call you." Twit taps her ear, smiles some fang, shrugs. "Just air ripples tickling those tiny bones we got inside us, right about here."

"Some of us have tinier bones than others," I say, baiting our little Screamer to reveal herself for what she really is. "So, how old a Twit *are* you, anyway?"

"How old do I look?" she says, propping her little girl's chin on top of her little girl's fingertips, batting her fake big-girl lashes.

"You know what I mean," I say, "and I'm not gonna play that game."

"So what kinda game *are* you playing, if you don't mind me asking?" Twit looks me in the eye, then back at Isuzu, and back to me. "I don't notice much of a family resemblance."

"Yeah," I say, my "yeah" as old and weary as Twit's when I asked about her name. "Yeah, see. We're not going there, either."

"Okay," Twit says. "Guess that just leaves tea and makeup." She smiles again, showing a bit more fang this time. "Care to join us, Marty?" she asks, already handing me an empty cup.

The story of Twit's and Isuzu's relationship is all there in the emails—if I'd had the luxury of wading through them before tearing into the night, heart in my throat, ax in my trunk. It started as I had assumed with lies on both sides, including digital proxies. Isuzu began by passing herself off as a much older vampire, with a face age of about twenty-one and a history very much like mine. Twit, on the other hand, looked almost exactly like she really does, with the exception that her fangs had been digitally removed, and her eyes rehumanized.

Like a lot of Screamers, Twit had gone online posing as a mortal child, looking for an adult vampire "with a taste for veal." Not all Screamers became Screamers to save them from dying too young; some were Peter Panned to serve as sex toys for vampiric pedophiles. I haven't talked to Father Jack about that, either. He didn't do it. That's all that matters.

Twit wasn't a sex toy Screamer, by the way, but she *was* karmic payback for those that made them. This is as close as we get to a silver lining on this one. You see, after the change, the tables turned for those pedophiles stalking innocence online. Now the stalkers are stalked, some by their victims, some by horny, run-of-the-mill Screamers desperately needing to be needed. That was Twit's story, and hers is just one sad case in a thousand. Just read the personals:

"Shirley Temple seeks Bloody Mary."

"Thumb-sucker ISO bloodsucker."

"Me: Lolita; you: Lestat."

Isuzu's reasons for being online are screamingly obvious in their own way. I abandoned her—just like the puppy I'd given her name to, just like Father Jack. And so she became me and went online, perhaps looking for a replacement, or maybe insight into what made the Martin she knew tick. That she modeled herself after me isn't so surprising. The only safe way for her to be online was as a vampire, and I was the only vampire she really knew. I can just imagine her little heart beating when she saw Twit's screen name, made that "farm" connection, sent her first, tentative email. The charade continued for a week or so, Isuzu playing the maybe-pedophile, while Twit filled her messages with girly mortality.

Eventually, though, slips occurred and confidences were gained. Eventually, both confessed to their fakery, followed by their whole, ugly, honest-to-God truths. It was all online, that anonymous nowhere where lies and truth are both somehow easier than either is, face-to-face. So, Twit confessed her Screamer status and Isuzu her real age, sex, and expiration-datedness.

It was Twit who asked if friendship was possible. Isuzu, to her credit, took a lot of convincing. There were apparently Instant Messaging sessions that went on for hours and would read like the transcript of a hostile witness's cross-examination—if the IMs had been saved, that is, which they weren't. But both sides swear to the substance, and that I'd be proud of the precautions Isuzu took before agreeing to meet.

"First, I've gotta email her a picture of me standing next to a yardstick to show I'm really shorter than her," Twit testifies. "Then it's the scale, to show she's got the weight advantage, too. Followed by the webcam of me downing like a gallon of blood with the TV tuned to the news in the background, so she knows it's happening live, and still—*still*—she shows up with . . ." Twit pauses. "Show him what you showed up with."

Isuzu pulls out the same bread knife she used on me, all those years ago. The same one she planned on using against Clarissa's killers. The serrated edge has the same swoop-swoop-swoop as a cartoon bat wing, but done in stainless steel. My reflection in the blade is the same as before—stretched Giacometti thin, almost to the breaking point—though the blade itself looks like it may have seen some action since then.

I should probably worry about that. I should probably say something. But I'm tired, and relieved, and I've reached my paranoid quota for the evening.

And so I keep quiet, instead. Smile. Nod. Hold out my pinky, tip back my teacup.

Sip air.

-25-

OUT

Hey, Killer," Rose says as I get dressed. She's moved out of her apartment and into the one where Isuzu isn't. Our sex place.

"Hey, Demon Bitch Goddess," I say back. You gotta have pet names, right?

She's still naked, and lying on her stomach in bed, her legs crooked back and ticking—just like Isuzu when she's coloring. I shake my head. Erase that image. The comparison is getting dangerously apt. Rose's face age is in its early twenties, and she looks even younger than that. Isuzu's real age is sixteen, and she looks older. A few more ticks, and they're taking the same classes in college.

Rose is holding a coffee cup with both hands. She sips. Ticktocks. I focus on the cup—her least Isuzu-like trait at the moment.

"You know what I was thinking?" she asks.

What she's been thinking about for the last few years. Getting married. Hitched. Till-Death-Do-Us-Parted. "What?" I say, tightening my belt before tucking in my shirt.

"I was thinking . . ."

"Shit," I say.

"What?"

I lift my shirttail, showing my buckled belt. "Why am I always doing that?" I ask, unbuckling, tucking, rebuckling.

"I blame the shirt," Rose says. "It wants to be free."

"I knew I loved this shirt."

"It doesn't want to be pinned down."

"Damn fine shirt," I say. "But you were saying?"

"I was just saying the shirt suits you," Rose says, rolling over on her back, sprawling her full, vengeful nakedness at me. She stares at the ceiling. "It matches your . . ."

She trails off. She lets it hang, what it is of mine that my shirt matches.

Instead: "Tell Isuzu to be ready by ten," she says. "And the same goes for the munchkin."

Isuzu, Rose, and Twit.

Not everyone knows the first names of their Fates, so I guess I'm lucky in that regard. In no other way, sure, but you take what you can get. Me, knowing the trio that'll do me in—that's what I get, and, well, okay.

The Weird Sisters have decided to "bond," you see. Do "chick shit." "Gyno stuff." In other words:

Make my life a living hell.

"Where you off to?" I ask, watching the three of them heading doorward.

"Out," they chime, in stereo plus one.

Requesting details, specifics, bad influences to be encountered along the way there, wherever *there* is? Wasted breath. Talking to the walls. If details were part of the agenda, "Out" would *not* have been the answer. "Out" translated into English is:

You do not *want to know, boy-with-dick.*

"When . . . ?" I hazard.

"When*ever*," they chime back, their giggles echoing up the long hallway leading out.

Isuzu, Rose, and Twit.

And a place called Midnight Cowboys.

Cowboys aren't the only thing they've got. They've also got firemen, and policemen, loinclothed and business-suited men, football players, and even one priest—though he works only Wednesdays, when the women who are into that sort of thing know they can find it. The stereotypes are worn. Literally. Clothes make the man, after all. They also make the muscles bulge when worn too tightly, and the audience gasp, when shed to the quick ripping of Velcro.

Rose had gotten free passes as a professional courtesy and figured Isuzu could use the education, while Twit could use about 150 couch dances. Isuzu still had her fake fangs from our Fairbanks adventure, Rose still had her mom's clown makeup to help tweak down my little girl's blush, and all three wore sunglasses so no one of them stood out. Isuzu's just sixteen, but looks older. Not that apparent age is any barrier, not with Twit in tow.

There have been several field trips such as this already, all scheduled around the spring and fall, when it isn't hot enough to sweat or cold enough to see your breath. The intention is to provide crash courses in Girlese to help turn Isuzu into the young woman she's becoming. To help make sure Isuzu turns into something other than—as Rose puts it—"a mini Martin."

"But I thought you liked me," I said, my voice feigning the wound.

"Yeah," Rose said back. "See. It's like this. You, but smaller, with tits and no dick. It's not a look with a lot of future."

"I see."

"More like ICU," Rose said. "Fashion intensive care. But I think we can save her."

And so I let her try. At sixteen, Isuzu is no longer a hostage to the Screamer department. Taking her hand, Rose has led her away from the ironic Pooh bears, the tongue-in-cheek Tiggers, and headed straight for the aisles of adult womanhood, the two of them like a couple of sailors in Bangkok on leave. I supply the credit card and then just sit back as the boxes and bags are unpacked to the expensive ssshhh of rustling tissue paper.

"Stunning."

"Beautiful."

"Yes!"

The vocabulary of not-getting-grief-later is easy to learn, and I did. Eventually, I got it down to a simple appreciative "Mmm-hmm," dispensed with a nod, perhaps a fingertip tapping at my smiling lips.

"Mmm-hmm."

The rest of this is secondhand.

Hearsay.

Inadmissable in court.

Has to be. I wasn't there. And it'll be embellished, too—by me, filling in the gaps with what my tortured imagination imagines it was like. I've never been to Midnight Cowboys, but I've been to places like it—places where the cowboys are smaller, and cuter, with tits and no dicks. It's just a matter of translation, when you come right down to it. A kind of drag, in reverse.

Of course, I also have the accounts of Isuzu, and Rose, and Twit to go by.

That—and what they showed on TV.

You never think about the things you don't think about, the things that are just there, part of the background, part of the routine. Rose still dances a couple of nights a week. Dance bars are part of her background, her routine. The way they operate, the way they are—those are just some of the things she doesn't think about.

The other things you don't think about are the opposite things, the things that *aren't* part of your background, that fall so far outside your personal experience that you don't give them a second thought. For Rose, for instance, having a body temperature that's anything other than room temperature—that falls into this second class of unthinkables. Just like the room temperature of dance bars falls into the first.

These are excuses I'm giving her for what happened and why she let it. These are the excuses I'm using because of the third kind of thing we don't think about—the things the thinking of which just plain scares us. The things the thinking of which would change everything.

Things like: She knew it. She planned it. She wanted it to happen.

Things like: She's jealous of Isuzu. She wants her gone. She wants her out of the picture.

Things like: Think of something else. Think of something else. Think of something else.

*S*o, *two vampires and a mortal walk into a bar . . .*

It's still early in the evening and the thermostat's just warming up. There's a fireman wearing just his helmet and boots and a lot of body oil, sliding down a pole onstage. Isuzu catches her breath, staring at the other pole onstage, dangling there, longer than average, even in its professionally flaccid state. Rose and Twit laugh, elbow each other, and then push my little girl a few inches closer to womanhood.

"Git a move on, Buffalo Gal," Rose says.

"Giddy-up," Twit adds.

A round of giggles, on the house.

They get a table near the stage, three sets of dark lenses craning upward, three sets of fangs holding on to their nether lips. Certainly nothing newsworthy. Not yet. Other dancers come and go, the lineup working its way from one Village Person to the next. Meanwhile, in the background, ever so subtly, the temperature starts crawling skyward, along with the decibel level and the general enthusiasm of the customers and dancers both.

"It was like shadows when the full moon sets," Twit says later, when the Weird Sisters take turns filling me in. "They just kept getting longer and longer."

Isuzu's distracting eyes—the eyes you can always tell where they're looking—are very busy *not* looking at mine.

"I guess we should have known something was up," Rose confesses.

"So to speak," I add.

"So to speak," Rose agrees.

Eventually it happened, the betrayal of mortal biology once you turn up the heat. Isuzu began to do something vampires don't; she began to perspire. To sweat, really. And to stink. She began stinking like only a stinking human can. Twit noticed it first, perhaps because her nose and Isuzu's armpits were at roughly the same level. Her nostrils flared—"What the hell?"—and her little Screamer head turned. And there they were—full moons rising darkly under both arms. Beads of sweat dotted Isuzu's upper lip like so much glitter, while a trickle squiggled from under her hairline, ran down her cheek, and then fell to the tablecloth. The first drop was silent, but the second made a little noise—a little *plish*—falling squarely on top of the damp spot made by the first. Rose noticed the stain and then everything else, all at once, and only seconds before the table next to them, and the table next to that.

And there my little Isuzu is, sweating in a room full of vampires, giving off her human stink, surrounded by bloodsuckers who are already overamped from the adrenaline-laced blood they've been sucking back, already horny as hell because of the heat that's put Isuzu in this predicament. It's only a matter of seconds before the first patron grabs Isuzu by the arm.

"She's burning up," the patron coos, followed by the naked fireman, grabbing the other arm.

"She's . . . *mine,*" he demands, a voice full of ice and steel.

And there Isuzu is, the center of a tug-of-war, her arms the opposing halves of a wishbone. Pandemonium ensues. Chaos reigns. The TV crew, already there—"just letting off steam"—switches on the red eye of its camera, and turns Isuzu's face into a wanted poster. There she is—click, snap, whir—public *victim* number one.

I'm seeing it, you understand, watching it beamed live into vampire TVs all over the country. At home, killing time alone on girls' night out, switching on the tube for a little distraction . . . *bam!* I'm watching my daughter "live," but who knows for how much longer.

This isn't a sitcom; it's real. It's real, and happening in front of my eyes, and I don't have the luxury of knowing that main characters never die.

And so I pray.

After dropping the remote, and the glass of blood I've warmed, I drop to my knees and pray. I pray to the God that giveth and the one that taketh away to please, please, please—just this once—*please* giveth back.

Sweat.

Sweat started it. Sweat ended it.

Acne-triggering, just slightly oily, teenage sweat.

That, and the two-handed groin pull, compliments of Twit, followed by a bitch slap from Rose for the bitch clinging to Isuzu's other arm. Taken together, they were just enough to slip the bonds of the immortals coiling in for the kill. You can actually see it on the tape—the wishbone vampires looking at their suddenly empty hands, rubbing their fingers, feeling the grease, looking disappointed and disgusted, both at once.

And me, I'm still watching while my three Fates are still "out," their fates not at all clear from what's been shown so far. Sure, there's been one escape—luck, just luck—but God only knows how much more it's going to take to get them from my screen, to my door, to my arms.

And then something strange happens. Or, I guess, stranger.

It's the weirdest thing I've ever seen on TV—and that includes the mortal variety during its so-called reality phase. The wishbone vampires are no longer interesting, despite the nudity the networks have blurred over. And so the camera starts sweeping the general chaos chaotically, looking for the escapee, jiggling and jostling and otherwise looking very Zapruder-meets-Kent-State. But then the camera goes still, as if straining to hear something. Which you do, suddenly—a voice over the PA system. It's frail, and faint, a little quaky, and definitely *not* prerecorded.

It's singing.

At first, you can't really make out the words, just a voice melodically modulated. And then the words come.

"You are my sunshine . . .

"My only sunshine . . ."

Everything is still. Everything goes quiet, except for that one voice, those tiny words—so careful, so scared, so desperate.

And then the voice is joined by other voices. And the camera picks up the pink tears, glistening on dozens of vampire cheeks, the whole room singing about what makes it happy when skies are gray.

God-motherfucking-dammit!"

That's the unscripted part of my speech, when the three of them finally come tumbling in through the door, holding their sides, laughing.

"How was 'out'?" I demand. "Was 'out' out there? Was it everything you hoped and dreamed?" *These* words I've practiced, along with dozens of alternatives.

All three stop laughing at once, look at me, mark the anger making my face twitch, and start laughing again.

"Marty," Rose says, "you shoulda been there."

"I *was*," I say, and this takes them all by surprise. Perhaps they thought they could sell the agreed-upon lie, and had been prepared to launch into it.

"Me and a few million others," I add. I toss Rose the remote. "Give it a shot. I'm sure one of the networks is rerunning it. They've been doing it all night."

Isuzu and Twit look at the remote in Rose's hands as if it's a revolver loaded for Russian roulette and their turn is next.

"It hasn't made the talk show monologues, yet," I go on. "I'm figuring that'll be tomorrow night." I'm about to say something especially nasty when I notice Isuzu's face collapse in on itself. Just a moment ago, she'd been laughing, still high from the adrenaline rush of beating death and getting away. Laughing because the others were, because sometimes laughing is its own excuse, and you just can't stop until you do.

And then you do that thing you shouldn't. You look back at all the things that almost happened. That's when your adrenaline tanks. And there you are, drained of almost everything, except these clear tears leaking suddenly from so deep inside, just one good sob takes your breath away. And there you are, gulping for air, your "I'm so sorry" a strangled little thing, all but dead on arrival.

I look at Twit looking at Rose, Rose looking at Twit. Both looking at their hands. Their feet. Doing a little gulping of their own.

I don't say anything else. It seems meaner, somehow, to *not* say anything else. And so I don't. That way, we can all hear Isuzu better. Just in case any of us missed it.

Just in case any of us thought laughing was a good idea.

-26-

BULL-SOMETHING

Give it time."

That's a line you hear a lot in vampire counseling. It's the kind of talk that leads one to conclude that talk itself is cheap. After all, what's *time* to a vampire? We're made of the stuff. We've got nothing but. Hell, if time really *were* money, we'd all be rich.

"Give it time . . ."

Give me a break!

Not that it doesn't work, now and then. Take the thing with me, Rose, and Twit. I guess you could say I got a little angry with them, seeing as they almost got Isuzu killed on national television. I guess you could say there was a little while there where I was—oh, I don't know—*emotionally radioactive.* They knew this. They accepted it. They kept their distance.

They—*we*—gave it time.

So I went back to helping Father Jack walk his new dog, Judas the Second. Or should it be Third? Quibbling about that was our first argument. It was like riding a bike.

And Isuzu went back to wearing pajamas all the time, watching *Anne Frank,* naming the dust balls under her bed. She walked around the apartment like her feet weighed a ton, and became real big on shrugging.

"How you doing?"

Shrug.

"Wanna eat something?"

Shrug.

Plus, there was a new symptom I hadn't noticed before, back when I was busy dating Rose. But now, it seemed like every month, Isuzu developed a split personality. For a few days every month, questions that usually warranted a shrug got a "Go fuck yourself" instead.

Gradually, I started seeing the whole almost-getting-killed thing in a different light. When you thought about it, Rose and Twit did me a favor. They scared my little shit factory shitless. And in so doing, they brought a whole new level of serenity to my tortured mind.

Ever since coming home that first evening to find Isuzu missing, I'd been wary about her, imagining what I didn't know, wondering what clues I was missing. My dates with Rose definitely felt the strain, what with me going back to listening in. I didn't do it constantly. But every hour or so, I had to take a listen. To keep tabs. To check in.

"I heard you can get electrocuted that way, dialing a cell phone with wet hands," Rose said one evening, stepping out of the shower to catch me with the phone pressed to my ear.

"Huh?"

"Never mind . . ."

The field trips were Rose's idea. I think part of the reason was just to get away from me and my paranoia.

But now, it was obvious to everybody that Isuzu couldn't leave the apartment. Ever. She was a known mortal. The whole vampire world was looking for her. The little girl I raised just wasn't that stupid. Twit could come to our place to baby-sit, and I could go back to paying a proper level of attention to Rose. And vice versa.

So, I stopped by Teezers one night.

"Hey," Rose says.

"What's up?" I say back.

"Nothin'."

"You wanna . . . ?"

"Yeah."

And the next night, I stopped by the rectory.

"You happy again?" Father Jack asks.

"Yeah."

"Then piss off, already."

And so, for the next few years, I was pretty content. I had a teenage daughter who was a prisoner in her own home, but not because of anything *I* did. I had a girlfriend who loved me, even though I was still having trouble remembering when to tuck, when to buckle. And I had a baby-sitter who worked for free. Whether through dumb luck or it's just being time, I was convinced that I had finally stumbled upon the best of all possible worlds.

Yeah. Right . . .

Your little Trooper's got a problem," Rose says, and even though this strikes me as the understatement of the millennium, I'm the new, relaxed me.

"Only one?" I ask. "That's progress."

"A new one," Rose says. "On top of all the old ones. One you haven't noticed."

I make the "Ew" face. "Is this a female thing?"

Rose stops cold. She makes the "Huh?" face. My little question apparently isn't so little. There are sociopolitical implications, geothermal and tectonic forces at work. There are mines and toes everywhere. The whole of civilization hangs in the balance.

"Not *necessarily*," she concludes.

Meaning, yeah, mainly, except for a few tortured statistical anomalies—anecdotes, really—hauled out in the name of political correctness. Meaning, yeah, except for that hermaphrodite in Boise, it pretty much *is* a female thing.

"Not that it matters," I offer. "What matters is that it's an *Isuzu* thing, one I haven't been paying attention to, but really need to. Right?"

"Right."

"So . . . ?"

"She's got bull-something," Rose says.

"Bull-something?"

"Yeah. I've been trying to think of the word, and I know it starts with 'bull,' but I keep drawing a blank. It's not like it's something we deal with anymore."

By "we" she means vampires, meaning this bull-something has something to do with death, disease, aging, sunlight, body temperature, the white part of the eye, visible breathing this far from the Arctic Circle, reproductive sex, shitting, eating, or having periods.

"Can you at least describe what it is, without naming it by name?"

Rose considers this. "Yeah," she says. "I guess so. It's like this. She's puking a lot."

"You mean she's sick," I say. "Like a stomach flu or something?"

"No . . ."

"She's not," I begin, and then tip my thumb to my lips, mime taking a pull. I thought we were through all that a year ago. That's when she learned my disinfectant—the one I made from potatoes grown in a tub in the closet—had multiple uses. At the time, I figured saturation was the best strategy, and so we stayed up all night, doing shots in the kitchen—Xtreme Unction for me, pure alcohol for her. It was a study in contrasts, me talking faster and faster as her speech slowed to a slurred crawl.

"I luff you, Daaaad," she said, holding on to the table with both hands. "I'mmmm," she added, getting lost in the hum. "What am I? Oh yeah. I'm . . . sorry . . . if . . . I . . ."

"Yeah-yeah-yeah," I streamed right along, rubbing the lengths of both arms like a junky on empty. "Cheers. Click-click. Down the hatch." I paused just long enough to pull my bottle out of firing range. "Oops. Make that *up* the hatch . . ."

"No," Rose assures me now. "It's not that again." She pauses. "It's . . ." She inserts her index finger as far as she can into her open mouth.

"She's *making* herself throw up," I say, translating the gesture. Rose nods. "Why?"

"She wants to keep her girlish figure, but doesn't want to give up food until she has to," Rose explains. "Haven't you noticed how she eats and eats, but never puts on any weight? And what about the bathroom? She's practically camped out in there."

The truth is, I actively avoid watching what Isuzu eats. On the one hand, the sight disgusts me, and on the other, it makes my heart hurt like almost nothing else can, except for maybe the thought of a loved one who's gone forever, for no reason other than lousy timing. As for the bathroom, she's been living there since she was thirteen. Being a guy, I just figured it was a girl thing. Hearing that Rose finds it excessive has me worried.

And as far as me noticing whether or not she's gained weight, that would involve my paying attention to the shape of her body, which, rumor has it, is the body of a very fetching eighteen-year-old woman. I try not to pay that kind of attention, not only because it's creepy, but . . . Well, yeah, *mainly* because it *is* creepy, but it's dangerous, too. Emotionally, for starters, and maybe physically, too. And I'm not talking incest or six-toed babies; Isuzu's not a blood relative. And it's not like what comes out down there on my part is going to be making babies anytime soon. It's just that sex between mortals and vampires is so old, it's new again. We've gotten out of practice and learned bad habits along the way. Vampire-to-vampire sex usually involves a lot of fang play, which, when you spurt and then heal back up, is fine, but mortals don't patch up so easily. Plus, for vampires, it's all about the feeling of being bled, the vein tug and spasm, the breeze of a closed system suddenly opening and then closing back up.

A cool, premeditated, straight-out vamping is one thing, but complicate that with the kind of sex you haven't tried in decades and all bets are off. I imagine it like trying to keep two different languages straight—except, in this case, if you slip into French, somebody dies.

So:

"No, you're right," I say in English, our shared tongue. "I haven't noticed," I add, keeping the laundry list of *whys* to myself.

The bull-something was bulimia, of course—the good ol' binge-and-purge, brought to you by *Vogue, Glamour,* and Madison Avenue. The plague of middle-class white girls from way back when,

when the zombie paleness of heroin chic was about style, as opposed to simply being a side effect of living the rest of forever in the dark. It was a serious condition, taken seriously, way back when, and if I were a parent from that time with a daughter with these symptoms, I'm sure I'd have her knee-deep in therapists and Happy Meals quicker than rainy days and Mondays could get me down.

But times have changed. Isuzu knows that as well as any of us, because she's about to change, too. She's just getting ready. And frankly, it makes sense. If I knew what I know now before *I* got vamped, I'd do the same thing. I'd scarf down as much of the tastable world as I could. But there's no way I'd be taking all that extra baggage along with me into eternity. Your body's your greatest entertainment value; it only makes sense to get it in the best shape you can before setting it in stone. Rose herself gave Isuzu that same advice when they first met. Me, I got lucky in the body department. I'd been whipped into shape during basic training, and there weren't a lot of KFCs or Dunkin' Donuts waiting for me in Europe during World War II. Not that I haven't wondered what the big fuss was about. Not that I haven't wondered what culinary alchemy made Big Macs worth destroying a good chunk of the rain forest over.

Vomiting, it should be stressed, is *not* the recommended way to stay slim. Diet and exercise—that's the preferred method. Finger swallowing might be quicker, but diet and exercise won't ruin your teeth like regurgitated stomach acid will. Maybe *that's* why those sultry models from before tended to show more breastbone than anything resembling a smile.

Before, when vampirism was my secret, I liked to think the reason those cover girls never smiled was because they shared my secret. That's why they looked out at the world as if they could swallow it whole; that's why they took such pains to keep their fangs hidden. But then Farrah Fawcett came along with that poster and her grin full of big horse teeth and I started recruiting as many pretty girls to our side as I could find.

Right now, I'm looking across the kitchen table of my home away from home, into the show-nothing eyes of one of my better recruits.

I've got my hands wrapped around a warm cup of blood and she does, too. We're wearing white bathrobes, bull's-eyed and polka dotted with drying blood, our wounds underneath pink and still healing.

"Is it really so . . . ," I begin. Or continue. This conversation has been joined, already in progress.

"Yes," Rose says. "Yes, it is."

"You didn't let me finish."

"Didn't need to," she says. "You were going to ask if it was really so bad for Isuzu to be doing this, once we take dying out of the equation."

"Well, yeah . . ."

"And my answer is still yes."

"But why? I mean, I know about the teeth thing. They're just going to fall out when her fangs come in."

Rose points at her forehead. *"This,"* she says. "This is the part that doesn't change."

I don't get it. I say so.

"The puking's just a symptom of some really fucked-up ideas," Rose says. "And right at the top is that things—you, yourself, your body—can be *willed* into perfection."

I chew on that a bit.

"Okay," I say. "So it sets the hurdle a little high. Maybe a little unrealistic, but eventually . . ."

"Eventually, you either got help or you died," Rose says. "I had a friend who . . ."

And just like that, I know there's no friend. Just like that, I know Rose's acting like she forgot the word is a different kind of bull-something.

". . . who by any other name would smell as sweet?" I say, filling in what is now, to me, obvious.

Rose blinks those "Don't ask, don't tell" eyes. Her shoulders slump, their strings cut. "Yeah," she says. Sighs. She nods over her cup of blood, staring at her reflection staring back. "Gotta love the irony, huh?"

•　　•

Isuzu is in the bathroom. Again. Still. She doesn't know I've sawed partway through the bolts in the hinges, that what looks solid from the outside is really hanging on by a thread. She doesn't know that her entire world is waiting for her on the other side of the door—me, Rose, Twit—all crouching, ready to pounce, to intervene, to save her from whatever thread she's hanging by.

Rose is the one with her ear to the door and her finger in the air, instructing us to hold back. She's waiting for the sound of the faucet because she's guessing Isuzu's using the sink. The rule on toilets is the same as it's been since I brought Isuzu home—no flushing after dark. It hasn't been a problem; Isuzu's the only one who uses the thing, and she's always been good about making sure the lid's down and the window's open just a crack. But Rose says even as bad a noticer as me would have noticed a toilet routinely filling up with vomit. And so here we crouch, straining to hear the sound of another borrowed meal swirling down the drain.

Isuzu doesn't hum, doesn't sing. Never has. If it weren't for the occasional cabinet door opening, or the tick of a bottle being placed back on something porcelain, you'd hardly know anyone was in there. And then . . .

A squeak. A gush.

Rose drops her finger. I yank the door free from its breakaway hinges . . .

And there's my little girl, bent over the sink, finger halfway down her throat, looking for that magical Reset button. She turns and sees us, all ganged up and waiting for her in a suddenly open doorway. And whether it's the shock or the sight, I don't know, but Isuzu begins vomiting right then and there. It spills through the impromptu cage of her fingers, all over the floor, a veritable cornucopia of exotic foods that must have cost a small fortune.

But . . . *whose? How?*

These are rhetorical questions. Unfortunately.

Unfortunately, I know everything I need to know within seconds of seeing Isuzu. She wasn't expecting us to barge in and was naked when we did. To check herself in the mirror, I guess—to weigh herself without having to subtract clothing. She was naked and I saw it all, but most important, I saw her legs. Her thighs. And the constellation of scar tissue dotting them, the dots always coming in pairs, one dot always just a hungry grin away from its partner.

My little Isuzu, my little binge-and-purging little girl.

Apparently, there were vampire friends neither I, nor Rose, nor Twit knew anything about.

Yeah. Right. "Friends."

Or clients. Nibblers. Dabblers. Pay-per-sippers. They didn't drain. They didn't vamp. They *sampled*—merely, politely—and with more restraint than I would have thought possible. I'd heard of such things—such practices—but didn't really believe them. It seemed vaguely un-American. Some inexplicable Asian fad, like karaoke, maybe, or seafood dishes that'd kill you if the chef got them just the tiniest bit wrong. Something that's as much about philosophy as it is eating.

Well, I guess there are a lot more vampires with a lot more self-control than I was willing to give them credit for. Not counting myself, of course—or the two other abstainers standing next to me, ready to deal with a whole other crisis than the one I've just found.

Twit and Rose haven't noticed Isuzu's thighs, by the way. Not yet. Instead, their attention has been captured by all the half-chewed nostalgia puddling at their feet.

"Is that a . . . ?"

"My God, I haven't . . ."

"Where the hell did you . . . ?"

"When I was a kid—I mean a *real* kid—those used to be . . ."

All of us, it seems, have managed to get ourselves off point. We were supposed to be confronting Isuzu about her bulimia. That's what I was prepared for. That's what I was thinking about, prying up the bolts, sawing through them, tapping them back.

Now I'd give anything for something as simple as an eating disorder.

I'm not prepared to deal with a daughter whose been selling her blood by the pint.

"Where'd you find pineapple?" I say, joining Twit and Rose on their wade down memory lane while Isuzu pulls a towel around herself.

"Well I'll be . . ."

"Sure, it's a little gross, but . . ."

"What I wouldn't give," I begin, and then regret it immediately. I can't stop my brain from doing the math. Everywhere I look, the ticker in my head ticks, tallying up what this mess must have cost, translating it into fangs nipping at those tender young thighs, hidden now by terry cloth, but still klieg-lit in my imagination. How did she charge? By the ounce? By the second?

Vampires—as a rule—do not blush.

Vampires—as a rule—do not get red in the face.

Volcanoes, of course, spend most of their geologic lives *not* erupting. It's just every now and then, when the conditions are right, when the tectonics are all pushing in the right direction and the magma begins to rise . . . well, it just can't be helped.

"Jesus, Marty, what's wrong?"

It's Twit. She's skewered something on the end of something and has turned around to gross me out, the mischievous grin already stitched on her face—when she gets a look at *my* face and stops dead. Rose and Isuzu look, too. Their faces confirm it. There's something wrong with me.

"What?" I ask.

Isuzu grabs a mirror and hands it to me.

Jesus . . .

I look like the top of an old-fashioned thermometer. Not the mercury kind, the other. The kind with the red stuff inside and a little glass bulb at the end. My face looks like that bulb.

"Marty?" Rose says, trying to catch my eyes. And I can feel each dot of that hanging ellipsis, am staring over the cliff of that dangling question mark.

Without saying a word, I flick up the minimum amount of terry cloth necessary to show this snapshot:

Thigh. Scars.

I aim my face at Rose's face and push it just a touch forward. A gesture meant to mean: *Get it. Put it together.* And—maybe—*help me with this.*

Rose's eyes say, *Oh,* followed by her mouth mouthing the same thing. And then—just in case I had any worries about Rose's feelings toward Isuzu—all the borrowed blood in her starts rising to her cheeks.

I nod.

She nods.

Okay—that's what our nods mean.

Plan B.

A part of me is relieved.

Obviously, I'll have to kill the bastards who did this. And it's a relief to have an excuse for murder again. Killing is something I can do. I know how it works. I'm comfortable with it. Sure, the newer parts of my brain—the nonlizard parts—know that murder is wrong, and I've spent a lot of time forcing the rest of my nervous system to go along with that understanding. Usually. For the most part. There *was* that one time-out to dispose of Clarissa's killers, but . . .

But domestication doesn't come free.

Before the change, there was a theory about where allergies come from, and why, despite advances in health care and pollution control, allergies and asthma were on the rise. The theory was, absent anything better to do, the immune system turns on itself. I think that's what it's been like with me and murder. When I'm not hunting, my brain goes after itself, making me paranoid, anxious, overprotective. And what has this paranoia, anxiety, and overprotectiveness gotten me? A daughter who's a blood whore.

So maybe this will all work out. A few murders will do us all a world of good. All I need now is some names.

But back to Plan B.

What, you may wonder, *is* Plan B?

According to Rose, this:

Take my little angel and knock her to the bathroom floor. Take my little darling and sit on her chest. Pull a switchblade dipped in some industrial-strength anti-coagulant, and mutter, "Fess up, bitch," followed by what the switchblade already implies, ". . . or die."

Rose apparently has been looking for an excuse to let the lizard off the leash, too. And though I don't think Dr. Spock would approve of her methods, I do have to admit their effectiveness.

"It's not how it looks," Isuzu blurts.

Yeah, right. Pull the other one.

Rose teases out just a bead of blood. Isuzu winces.

"Fuck," Isuzu says, biting into the word with her blunt human teeth. "You," she adds, followed by, "I'm no blood tramp. I love him. He loves me. He does me favors. It's . . ."

It's not a cash business, she wants to say. And in her position, I'd want to say the same thing. Except I don't know the fanged dick owner behind that tiny little pronoun "him." I don't know if certain "favors" have a fixed cash value.

I nod. Twit agrees. Rose does, too.

And another bead of blood gets teased out, after which Isuzu becomes a string of numbers. Phone. Pager. Address. Email. License plate. Whatever. ID. Identification. The collection of unique letters and numbers that sum up to this so-called him.

"Call him," Isuzu demands. "He's cool. We're cool. We have an . . ."

And we're all waiting for it. I, as would-be parent. Rose, as would-be parent's would-be partner. And Twit, as would-be friend, the one excluded from the tightest, most important circle, the friend lied to by not being confided in.

". . . *understanding*," Isuzu concludes.

And that's all it takes to squash a little bug named Antoinette.

Twit's face crumples and she throws something invisible down. She mutters a "Fuck you," and then runs away as fast as her stubby little legs will take her.

I look at Rose, and she looks at Isuzu. Shrug. Shrug.

We all look at the Twit-shaped hole left where Twit used to be.

•   •

My first thought is that Isuzu has become one of those people who think soap operas are real, and treat the characters like members of their own family. My second thought is that it serves me right, making her a prisoner, limiting her contact with others to this claustrophobic little circle of ours. My third thought is that the scars are self-inflicted. If I recall correctly, the same middle-class white girls who used to starve themselves to death also had a tendency to cut themselves, even before it was sexy—little test cuts, to get attention, or to get ready for that last, big cut.

I'm thinking all this, by the way, because Isuzu has just led Rose and me into the living room and switched on the TV as a way of introducing us to this boyfriend she has an understanding with. Little Bobby Little of *The Little Bobby Little Show*. The word "live" floats in the upper right-hand corner, and, below it, Little Bobby Little— six, maybe seven—working so hard at being cute, it's like his life depends on it. Which, according to Isuzu, it does.

Or *did*.

Isuzu points at the word "live," says, "Bullshit."

Little Bobby Little is all grown up now. Bobby—*Robert*—was vamped when he turned twenty, and they've got tape of his whole life right up until that point, though they'll probably never broadcast anything past his thirteenth birthday. Not on network TV, at least.

"Too much jerking off," she explains, before going on to explain that the masturbation tapes *are* available—for pay, online, under the title *Crankin' It Big Time with Jimmy Biggs*. They've also got tapes devoted to his bowel movements, in which he's known as Gomer Pyles, and footage in which acne is the unifying theme, where he's credited as Johnny Zitz.

" 'Fetishistic nostalgia,' " Isuzu says, quoting her multiple-personality boyfriend. "His life's been edited down to smaller and smaller subcategories of vampire porn."

Yeah, yeah. Right. Boo-hoo. That still doesn't change the fact that this swinging dick's been bleeding my little girl. Literally.

And then there was Billy "the Bull" Lima.

"They were going to call him Andy Rexia, or maybe Benji Purger, but . . ."

"Purger" sounded too much like "perjure," and allusions to anorexia were not strictly accurate. It was the binging part of the tapes that appealed to those vampires nursing that particular sense of loss. And they ate it up, watching "Billy" shoveling it in, saying their bon voyages to the gustatory world by proxy. The purging scenes were implied in the cut made for this audience, just like the sex scenes from my childhood, replaced with waterfalls, fireworks, trains barreling through tunnels.

It was *Billy* that Isuzu met online. *Billy* who knew what it was like to know about all the losses that were coming. *Billy* who'd been there, done that, could sympathize, facilitate, and advise.

And it was Bobby who knew what it was like to live in a world as both pet and meat, to be held captive for your own good, to play at playing, to simulate childhood in self-defense.

It's both of them—Billy, Bobby—I feel like killing now, for what they're making me, in retrospect.

"How?" I begin. "When?"

"Twit," Isuzu says.

I don't understand and say so. Isuzu explains.

"I'd say Twit was coming over while you were, you know," she says. "And it was true, every other time. And then two for every one, and then three. The true part just kept getting smaller until it kinda disappeared."

Just like Twit, just now. It seems my little girl is taking after her father, after all—at least in the disposable friendship department.

"Did Twit know she was your cover?" I ask, already knowing the answer, or at least thinking I do.

"I don't think so," Isuzu says, honestly puzzling over it. "She *did* start getting suspicious, though."

"Wanting to know why you weren't seeing her anymore," I say, guessing aloud.

"More like why was it always the *left* leg with us," Isuzu says. She inches up a bit of terry cloth, exposing the leg in question. More paired puncture wounds, just a grin apart. Just a *smaller* grin apart . . .

And just like that, my heart wraps itself around the axle, and the brakes won't work. I turn toward Rose, looking for help from my intended, my anchor, my beloved, my . . .

. . . *God!*

She just looked away!

My heart's pumping nothing but poison, now. Poison. And pictures. And just one question:

"You *knew*?" This is me, to Rose.

And Rose, to me: "You mean you didn't? Jeesuz, Marty. What did you think they were doing? Playing with dolls?"

Um. Well. Kinda.

"Um," I say. "Well . . ."

"Just grow up, already."

-27-

EMERGENCY SEX

Twit isn't a last-waver.

She's tasted the blood of fear, the sweet juice of mortal panic. So it isn't curiosity—at least not about that. Plus, they knew each other, and neither was in a position to terrorize the other. A threatening gesture would be viewed as a joke. Trust me; I know.

What I haven't factored in, accounted for, or even imagined is that love can flavor blood just as well as fear. Love, affection, honest, wholehearted trust, honestly felt in the face of potentially danger-ous acts—these make themselves known in the bloodstream as well as the face, the word, the casual gesture.

" 'It tastes like a kiss on the forehead,' " Rose says, quoting Twit. She does this to explain, to excuse. She doesn't know that the de-scription alone is breaking my heart all over again.

"I see," I say, biting my lip, betrayed by my own blood this time, trickling down my chin for a second or two before the wound heals.

"Don't be that way," Rose whispers, cupping the back of my neck, pulling my forehead to her forehead.

"What way's that?" I ask, pulling back.

Isuzu's gone at the moment, having left through the door I opened for her. It's cold outside and her breath will show, but I'm cold inside, too—colder than even a few minutes ago—and I'm finding it hard to care. And anyway, she's taken a cell phone. Bobby or Jimmy or Dickie—whoever the fuck he is—will be at the front door of our building, will honk twice, will hold the passenger door open as Isuzu runs, holding her breath, wearing her dark glasses. They'll drive off into the moonset.

Rose looks me in the eye and the way she's got her mouth set, I swear, it's almost as if *she's* mad at *me*.

"Listen," she says, cupping me behind the neck again, but squeezing this time. Hard. Angry. She fixes those black holes on me. "Girls have sex," she says, her teeth gritting, her hand squeezing harder. "They suck. Dick. Blood. They eat. And if they're very lucky, they're eaten in return."

"You don't have to . . ."

"No. I do," Rose insists. "I think I do." She pauses, then goes on. "They let people you know and people you've never heard of do things you don't want to know about for whatever goddam reason they feel like. Even if it's dangerous. Even if it's stupid, because, you know, it's their choice."

"You really don't . . ."

"*Shut up*," Rose snaps, before going on, talking to me like the idiot I'm starting to feel like. "But the one thing they don't do is tell their fathers about any of this. And you know why?"

"They don't want to get smacked into next Tuesday?"

"No," Rose says. "It's because they *love* their fathers. And they *understand* their fathers. And they *don't* want to *hurt* their fathers, like you're hurting now."

Where do women get this? Is it from some book? Can it be rounded up and burned?

"Remember when you asked me how many partners I've had?"

I nod.

"Remember what I said?"

"Mind my own business?"

"After that."

" 'None,' " I say. "You said, 'None . . . that matter now.' "

"Exactly," Rose says. "I'm not into torture, and neither is Isuzu. And some things are best left unsaid."

I pause. Nibble my lip. Open my mouth. Close it. Open it again.

"There were enough to torture me with?" I ask, zeroing in with deadly accuracy on what matters most—my ego. "There were *that* many?"

And I can't say for sure, but from the way the light swims over the blackness of Rose's eyes, I'd swear she's rolling them.

Rose and I have never done it in my real apartment before, but we have to now. It's emergency sex. It's the sex you have because if you don't, in twenty-four hours you start to stop being a couple. Oh, you don't fall apart all at once, but you start to. The little seeds of resentment fall into the sidewalk crack, and pretty soon, the pavement splits open, the potholes form, the bumpy ride gets going in earnest.

By the way, if someone interrupts you during emergency sex, it goddam better be an emergency.

"Did you hear that?" Rose asks, though somewhat muffled, thanks to the proximity of my neck to her mouth.

"Huh?"

But before she can repeat herself, I hear it too. A knock. A strangely bass knock, the knock of someone knocking at a particularly low point on the door.

"Twit," we say together and—perhaps because it rhymes—"*shit . . .*"

I sigh, heal, pull on a robe. Pad barefoot from the bedroom, through the living room, to the front door.

"We were fucking, Twit," I say, throwing open the door. "What do you want?"

But it's not Twit.

It's Isuzu, on all fours, a hand cupped to her neck. Blood is spilling between her fingers, tracking back down the hall, staining the walls here and there with the shape of what are really very small hands. Very delicate. Very ladylike. Very . . . *dying* . . . hands.

"Christ . . ."

"Help . . ."

"Jesus . . ."

"Me . . ."

"Tell Twit we were fucking," Rose calls from the bedroom.

"It's . . . ," I try, pulling Isuzu inside, pushing the door closed. "It's not . . . ," I try again, clicking through a half dozen dead bolts.

"It's not *what*?" Rose demands, striding into the living room, defiantly naked, displaying what our presumed rude intruder will never have. It doesn't take her long to recognize her mistake. "Holy shit!" she blurts. She's at Isuzu's side even before all the syllables have gotten out. "What the hell happened?" As if it isn't already obvious, save for the particulars of how and who.

"He wasn't home," Isuzu says. "He didn't answer his phone."

"Here," Rose says. "Squeeze here." She pinches my fingers to the gash before leaving and returns with a needle and thread. As she works to close the wound, something she's apparently done before, I notice what at first I take to be a particularly hideous broach clinging to Isuzu's sweater. Upon closer inspection, I realize my mistake. Broach, no. Ear, yes. I flick up a wing of her hair, first on the left, and then on the right. Check. Check.

"Well, at least you got yourself a souven . . ." I pause. Clear my throat. ". . . *ear*," I say, plucking the awful thing from her sweater, checking the torn edges for signs of reconstitution. It doesn't usually happen with pieces this small, but every so often you can grow something useful out of what's left. And sure enough, there's some fresh flesh spreading out from where the ear leaves off, dough white, a little clammy. It occurs to me that I should put it in a bucket with some blood, maybe grow us a little police sketch of the perpetrator.

"Can you identify him?" I ask.

"Her," Isuzu manages.

"I'll take that as a yes," I say, squeezing the damned thing in my hand until all the juice runs out.

"I'm trying to work here," Rose reminds us, tugging another stitch tight.

"Sorry . . ."

"Sorry . . ."

"Shshshsh . . ."

•   •

Her."

"What?"

"You said 'her.' The person who attacked you. She wasn't a him. She was a her."

"Did I say that?"

"Yes."

"Hmmm."

"What's *that* supposed to mean?"

"Nothing," Isuzu says. "Just hmmm."

"Can you describe her?" I ask.

"Why?"

Hmmm. I would have guessed that was a straight-up yes-or-no question. Guess not.

"What do you mean, why?"

"Why do you want to know what she looks like?"

"Because, you know," I say. "So I can . . ."

"Teach Twit a lesson," Rose says, making us both turn.

"Excuse me?"

"How'd you . . . ?"

"I'm just wondering how the little freak got anywhere near your neck."

"She caught me by surprise with a head butt to the stomach, and when I doubled over, she just sort of clamped on," Isuzu says. "But how'd you know?"

"I'm the one who sewed you up," Rose says. "And those bite marks were too small to come from a full-grown anything." Rose pauses to take a drag off an imaginary cigarette, something she hasn't done since our first few dates together. She exhales a plume of imaginary smoke.

"Plus, you did the bitch dirt. She had to get even somehow."

"I didn't mean to hurt anyone," Isuzu says. "You know that, right?"

Sure. Okay, I think, and it's like my brain's the remote control for Rose's mouth.

"Sure. Okay," she says, using the exact same "You're so full of shit" tone I was thinking.

No, really, I think, aiming this one at Isuzu, who chimes in on cue.

"No, really," she says.

I look at Rose, blink, think: *Bitch.* I look at Isuzu, blink, think: *Über bitch. Mega bitch. Bitch and a half.*

"Yeah," Rose sighs, instead. "Yeah, I know."

She gives Isuzu's shoulder a good-natured shake as Isuzu winces, and cups a hand to her freshly sewn wound.

"Human, here," she says, through gritted teeth. "Human still in pain here . . ."

"Oh jeez," Rose says, pressing her fingers to her lips. "I'm sorry."

"I keep forgetting how long you guys take to heal," she adds, making a point of looking right at me.

Isuzu's wounds are messy, but not life-threatening—or *afterlife-threatening,* for that matter. But they get me thinking. Until tonight, I always imagined that I'd be the one to vamp her when the time came—that *I'd* be the first and only one to taste her mortal blood. I imagined it tenderly, like a father-daughter moment on the daughter's wedding day. There'd be advice, the rules she already knew, the lists of things she no longer had to fear, now that she was no longer prey. I'd use the inside of her wrist—neutral territory, but territory always visible to the owner, the last scar her body would ever know, a constant reminder of yours truly, her more-or-less dad. Her father-in-blood, if not her blood father, the one she got her new eyes and smile from.

Now I found myself standing in a line I never even knew existed. If I decide not to vamp her, to let her stay mortal and run out her clock—out of spite, say, or a sense of betrayal—she's got backups ready to do the job in my place.

Well, maybe . . .

I start wondering about that, too. The opportunity has clearly presented itself, over and over again, with Twit, with Mr. Whomever, turning my little Trooper into a constellation of scar tissue. And each of those scars is a *no.*

A *not yet.*

But whose *no* is it?

Has Isuzu decided she isn't ready? Does she want to be older than the heartbreaking perfection she is now, at eighteen? Is there more of the world she wants to taste? Is there a pound or two more she needs to lose, a few hundred more sit-ups to tighten that stomach? Is there something else inside—a little ache, a little weirdness she wants to fix before fixing her body for good? Is she waiting for the perfect moment—the one she'll recognize only when it passes into a less perfect one, the one that will render all others unacceptable, thanks to the memory of the something better, now lost? Will she Catch-22 herself into the dull misery of having waited too long?

Or is the *no* coming from the other direction? Is blood that tastes like a kiss to the forehead such a revelation that you can't imagine life without it? Is it addictive, like all things having to do with love?

Or are these *noes* really *yesses* to a question I wouldn't have thought to ask until tonight? Is it something kinky, something sexual, some agreed-upon sadomasochistic thing? My mind flashes on various leather-bound nightmares:

Isuzu and . . .

Isuzu and . . .

Isuzu and . . .

And the sky is getting pink in the east. Timing. What an awful time to be heading off to dreamland. Isuzu, all messed up and nowhere to go, lies curled up on the couch, exhausted from the radical secretectomy performed this evening, without benefit of anesthesia. Rose brushes a curl away from Isuzu's sleeping forehead, and looks up at me. She's beat, worn out, ready for bed. Still, she manages to find a new smile for me. It's a for-better-or-worse smile. A through-thick-or-thin one.

It's a you-'n'-me-buddy smile. And Isuzu makes three.

Rose gets up from the couch, crosses the living room, takes my hand.

"C'mon, Dad," she says, tugging me and all my bad thoughts into the sheltering dark of the bedroom.

-28-

THE PERFECT BLUE FOR THE BLUES

My first idea is to go Joan of Arc on that Malibu Barbie car she drives—the one with the jacked-up seat and blocks on the pedals. Poking holes in fuel lines is even easier than veins, and brakes break just like they did before, when Clarissa's last killer found himself stamping at the floorboard without so much as a squeak of resistance. Snip, snip—that's all it takes, and then we can all gather round the tube to find out what Twit's middle name is.

But that's just me, thinking like a dad instead of a vampire.

Isuzu is still alive. Messed up, sure, but the little twerp left her alive enough to crawl back home to get patched up. Twit's a vampire and I'm a vampire and Isuzu's still being alive is a vampire's message. Letting her crawl away after latching on—*that* was a choice. In spite of whatever anger Twit may have been feeling, the part of her that cared for Isuzu managed to say, "Stop," and she did. Rose saw it before I did. And even Isuzu knew, protecting Twit and gritting her teeth while the needle went in, came out, went in again.

Maybe Twit's hoping I'll do something rash. Maybe her pint-sized heart has had enough, and is counting on the vengeful daddy to do its dirty work. I can understand that. I've been there; I know how being immortal can make a blue night seem like it's going to last forever. Hell, if it wasn't for that feeling, I'd never have found Isuzu in the first place.

I guess it doesn't hurt that I've always kinda liked Twit.

It's her anger. The beauty of it. The purity. No apologies. No excuses. No hemming or hawing. Piss her off, and she just lets fly. Maybe it's easier to explode when the whole world expects you to. But when you're half the size of everybody else and you're *still* the one people tiptoe around—how can you *not* love that?

Maybe there's a part of me that feels just as betrayed as Twit. Just as angry. Maybe there's a part of me that's glad she did what I can't. I'm not saying that's the case. I'm just saying I don't know—and killing someone with a Maybe that big just hanging out there . . . no.

So what I do is this: I paint her blue.

I've already mentioned how humiliation plays a big role in the vampire legal system. Stockades are popular again. Ditto, tar and feathers. Stoning, but with dildoes. Scarlet letters spelling out whole scarlet words, complete with 800 numbers to call if the troublemaker starts making trouble again.

So yeah. Blue. That's the color of Twit's future.

I got the idea from those dye packs they use to discourage bank robberies. They ran a photo in the *Free Press* the night before Twit needed killing—two clown-white wannabe crooks, their hair blown back and stuck with dried dye, their faces freckled with the stuff. Something like that should do the trick, I figure, but in spray form. Something I can aim, get a little creative with.

But when I get to the hardware store, I can't find anything as simple as plain blue spray paint. Cornflower—that's what they've got. Robin's Egg. Cerulean. Cobalt. Midnight . . .

But no Smurf. No Oompah Loompah. No Choking Victim.

"What's the project?" a helpful hardware guy asks out of the . . . well, you know. He's peering over my shoulder, just a teenager, with greasy jet black hair hanging in front of his jet black eyes. A tattooed hand reaches up from inside his shirt, its tattooed fingers permanently wrapped around his paper white neck. He wears his collar unbuttoned, displaying all that blue-green angst to a world that could care less.

I wonder whether he got it done before—or after.

"What we looking for?" he adds—still helpful, still strangling in that cartoon grip.

And so I tell him.

"Justice," I say.

The helpful hardware guy lets out a smile. It's a smile that knows—that's been there, done that. Still smiling, he reaches past me and grabs a can from the shelf. "Here you go, my man," he says. "The perfect blue for the blues." He flips the can in the air, catches it one-handed. He nudges me, one broken heart to another.

"Give 'er an extra coat for me," he says, handing over the paint like a loaded gun.

And so it is I find myself sitting on top of Twit, shaking a can of Azure Sky, the perfect blue for revenge. Twit's just about given up squirming, and I'm still listening to the ball bearing rattle, giving my little Screamer plenty of time to close whatever she doesn't want painted blue.

"Ready?"

"Fuck you . . ."

"Cool."

I hold her hair back and start with the forehead. Hsssst. Hsssst. Hsssst. The paint sounds like snakes coming out. I do the cheeks next, then one side of the nose, followed by the other. I give her an extra coat for the hardware guy. Her hands are spread out on the floor, pinned, one under each foot. I give the left a shot. The right. By the time I'm done, she'll look like a sky blue Al Jolson with fangs.

Shake. Rattle. Spray.

Still sitting on top of her, waiting for the Sky to dry, it occurs to me that this is the first time we've been alone together. It occurs to me that it's probably the last, too.

"Twit?"

"What?"

"Can I ask you something?"

" 'What was it?' " Twit guesses. "What kind of disease had to be cured by turning me into what I've been turned into?" She says this slowly, like an idiot or robot, letting me know that *my* something is the same something *everyone* asks people like her. Eventually. When they can get a word in between the screams.

I nod before realizing a nod's not the easiest thing to see, what with me sitting on top of her. And so I say, "Yeah," clearing the path for the story she's either never told anyone or told a thousand times.

"It was a nasty case of still being alive," Twit says. "That's what I had. That was my disease. This was right around the time my sister and mom caught a nasty case of being dead, which made my condition stand out all the more." She pauses, assembling the blocks of her story, or maybe just catching her breath, what with me pressing down on her tiny lungs.

"My dad had just gotten the gift from one of your vampirellas at one of his after-work watering holes," she continues. "Some downriver dive called Teezers. I think your girl Rose still works there." I wonder if Twit can feel me clenching. "Hell, could've been her for all I know," she continues, and so do I. "She'd've been Dad's type—skinny, tiny tits, a smirk so fulla fuck-you it ain't even funny."

She saying this to torture me, I'm pretty sure. What with me pinning her down, her voice is the only weapon she's got.

"I'm saying this because that's what my mom was like," Twit goes on, as if reading my mind and deciding to set it straight. "Before she got killed with my sister, that is." She pauses, moves her bones around.

"They were just doing errands," she says. "They were just coming back from the mall when some guy whose cocktail hour started at nine in the morning T-bones 'em at an intersection."

I say I'm sorry, and Twit lets me.

"None of us were night people when it happened, not that it would've helped much, the mess they ended up." Twit pauses, reconsiders. "Well, maybe they wouldn't have been driving around for that asshole to kill in broad daylight, but . . ." She pauses again, what-iffing herself into temporary silence.

"Woulda, coulda, shoulda," I whisper, to pry her loose.

"After it happened is when my dad starts acquiring after-work watering holes, and 'after work' just starts getting longer and longer. Eventually, it happens. He gets recruited. He doesn't come home all night, or the following day, and the baby-sitter starts going ape shit around midnight, calling all the hospitals just like she did when my mom and sister didn't come back. *Not again*—that's what she's thinking. Her mom and her end up doing shifts with me, until Dad finally stumbles in looking like he's seen a ghost and wearing a pair of sunglasses. The sitter gets a hundred in twenties from a wallet I don't recognize, and my dad understands when she says she's not going to be available anymore, ever.

"It's after the door closes that my dad says he's not losing anybody else," Twit says. "He says he doesn't have to, and so he's not. And that's when it happens. I was just eight. I didn't know. And my dad was a brand-new night person, so he didn't really know, either. This was before—before being short and vocal was a recognized thing. We—me and my dad and the whole rest of the world—we kinda learned together."

"So, what happened to your dad?" I ask, perhaps a bit more urgently than I should, seeing as I'm a dad in the middle of a dad thing, semiavenging my semidaughter.

"Well, you know," Twit says, as if I do.

I don't. I say so.

"He brought me stuff," Twit says, "like a momma bird. I was a virgin to the hunt, and his little girl, and he was going to keep it that way. But then I got older, and curious, and started sneaking out." She sighs. Remembers. Smiles. Stops.

"He got suspicious when I never seemed to be hungry anymore. 'Annie'—my dad never called me Twit; he always called me Annie—'Annie,' he says, 'how old are you?' And I tell him. 'Nineteen,' my eight-year-old face says. And he says he figures that's old enough. So we start hunting together. Start hunting, and stop talking. I think it was the sight of me, his little girl, killing. Sentences became phrases became one-syllable words. And then he starts leaving me notes, grounding me for one made-up crime or another. So I wrote my own note, telling him what he could do with his rules and roof."

I don't mention the pink puddles between Twit's blue hands.

"I tried going back once," she says. Sniffs. "It was just a pile of black lumber. My house. Our old house. I asked around. Got the same answer a couple of times. Some freelance Buffy. Some son of an entree, getting even."

I'm sorry, I say, and Twit lets me.

Thanks for not killing Isuzu."

I'm still sitting on top of Twit when I say this, even though she stopped squirming a long time ago. I try getting up, but she starts all over again, just enough to force me back down. And I can feel her bones welcoming it, this poor excuse for human contact. It's pressure, at least. It's the weight of a body on top of hers. There's no desire in it, just deadweight and a couple of butt cheeks, but you know what they say about beggars.

The pink puddles—by the way—have gotten a little bigger.

"You could have done a better job raising her," Twit sniffs.

"Yeah," I say, shaking the can of paint just to hear the ball bearing rattle a little more. "Woulda, coulda, shoulda."

Twit sighs and I sigh back.

I toss the can at a wastebasket and sink the shot.

"Thanks for not killing me," Twit says.

She rubs a blue hand under her blue nose before adding, "I guess."

-29-

LITTLE BOBBY LITTLE

Imagine your daughter—your angel, your sunshine—coming home one night, deflowered. Imagine that the same time you learn this, you also find out she's been having an affair with a dwarf half her size. Imagine that prior to this, your big concern vis-à-vis your daughter was that she was involved in an unhealthy relationship with food, her finger, and the toilet. Imagine that after the bloodletting (both figurative *and* literal) everybody more or less makes nice. Imagine that you—you lucky stiff you—are about to meet the boyfriend/deflorist for the first time.

Imagine really needing to vomit, but having all the wrong plumbing.

"Do I look okay?"

This is Rose, to me, but looking in the mirror. Oh yeah, there's that, too. Imagine that the rapist/future son-in-law is something of a celebrity. Several celebrities, in fact, ranging from famous to infamous and back again. Imagine that your maybe-wife has been acting all girlish and starstruck for the last two nights, preparing for your little tête-à-tête.

See *vomit, comma, inability to.*

"Is that a gray hair?"

"What?"

"Kidding. You look fine."

"Really?"

We're old-school vampires. We're all products of unnatural se-lection, survival of the cutest. We're all young and beautiful. *And we all look fine.*

On the outside, at least.

But peel away a little of that stuff we grow over our skeletons—that stuff that stands between us and every day being Halloween—peel that away, and we're all brats from hell. We all imagine ourselves immortal, and we're right. We've created a world of divas and jocks, pretty boys and pretty girls with bodies that won't quit and looks that'll never fade, immune to the vengeance of time and its lessons, too.

But don't mind me. I'm in a mood.

"So when's our creep—I mean, guest, supposed to be here?"

"Suzi says midnight, which it almost is," Rose says. "So get a move on."

Ever since the Book of Revelation, Rose has taken to calling Isuzu "Suzi"—a development I do *not* endorse.

"You mean 'Isuzu.' "

"Whatever."

"Any ideas on what the guy's moniker du jour happens to be?"

"Robert, Rob, or Bob—but not Bobby," Rose says. "And really not *Little* Bobby," she adds, still preening, still primping, still pissing me off.

"Fussy little fuck, eh?"

Rose bounces a look at me from the mirror. "You're getting it all out now—is that the plan?"

I love it when the other person comes up with the excuse you haven't been able to come up with yourself.

"Yep," I say. "That's the plan."

"Okay," Rose says, turning to face me. "Let 'er rip."

"Rip?"

"Have at it," she says. "Here. I'll even get you started. 'He's so dickless . . .'—blank."

"Okay," I say. "He's so dickless . . . even a Ken doll's better hung."

"Again."

"He's so dickless . . . he's got an inny."

"Again."

"The only way he can maintain an erection is with Popsicle sticks and duct tape."

"Okay."

"The only way he can get a woman wet is with a hose."

"I said, 'Okay.' "

"When he was born, he was so ugly, the doctor slapped his mother . . ."

"Stop. *Finito.* Cease and desist."

"You started it."

"Okay," she says, gathering breath. "He's a dickless, ball-less, gutless, spineless, goat-fucking pederast from the bad part of hell. *But.*" She aims her finger at me like a gun, like that means anything. "*Suzi* loves him, and *that's* that."

"Isuzu."

"Whatever."

He comes in wearing black leather pants, a black silk shirt, black silk tie, and black leather suit coat. He's also wearing wire-rimmed glasses with black lenses, and has a ruby stud in the earlobe I can see. He stands so his face is in three-quarter profile, the better to see the strong line of his jaw.

"Mr. Kowalski, I presume."

Yes, you do, I think. *You really fucking do.*

"You can call me Martin."

"Okay, Marty."

"No," I say. "I said, Martin."

Rose pinches me strong enough to spring a leak; I ignore it.

"Okay," Robert says. "Martin."

"Have any trouble finding the place?" Rose asks, waiting to take his coat, to no avail. She stands there a second too long with her hands out, then feigns smoothing her clothes.

"Nope," Robert says. "Been here before."

Yes, I think, *but you were actually* invited *this time.*

"Well, that's good," Rose says. "Come in. Take a load off."

"Suzi around?" Robert asks, doing a surveillance-camera sweep of the living room.

"Isuzu," I say, "is in the bathroom."

"She still doing that?"

"Urinating?" I say, feigning ignorance. "Yes. You know what pissers those mortals can be."

"Tell me about it," not–Little Bobby says. "I've got one of those new apartments? You know, like one that was built after? So, like, there's no toilet, right? So, like, the first time she's over, I gotta give Suzi a bucket she can take in the closet. And it's like she's peeing on top of a drum, it echoes so bad. She comes out and I go, like, 'Jeezus, girl,' and she goes, 'You heard?' and I'm like, 'Yeah. Duh . . .' "

I look at Rose, whose lack of being impressed is impressive. I do a little thing with my mouth out of Robert's view, a little smirk thing, and Rose does it back. Translation: *Jerk? Yep. Jerk.*

Cool. One crush down. One to go. And I didn't even have to do any heavy lifting.

"So, Robbie," I say. "Robbie" was not explicitly ruled out, and I figure I might as well exploit the loophole. "That's quite some story, first thing in the door."

And just like that, the EKG of his grin flatlines.

"Oh jeez," he goes. "That was kinda gross, wasn't it?"

Rose and I do not nod. We don't have to. Robbie keeps going on his own.

"And . . . and personal and stuff. I shouldn't . . . I don't know what . . . I'm sor . . ." He regroups. "I'm just real nervous about this whole thing. Suzi . . . I mean, Isuzu, she's told me all about you and how you found her and raised her and how you're like practically a god as far as she's concerned and . . ."

Fucker. Cheap-ass, sneak-that-compliment-in-there-so-I-go-all-warm-and-fuzzy *fucker.*

"Isuzu really said *that*?" I say. "That I'm like a god?"

"Well, like Jesus, anyway," Robert says. "You know, being her savior and all."

I smile in spite of myself. Maybe . . .

"So, Robert," Rose says, picking up the slack left by yours truly, "any idea where Suzi picked up the Karen Carpenter routine?"

"Excuse me?"

Rose—my angel, my tombstone—delicately shoves a good part of one hand down her throat in demonstration.

"Oh," Mr. Little says, apparently feeling even more like his name than just a few seconds ago. "Um," he ums. "Well," he wells.

"Um, well," Rose echoes. "Yes?"

"I guess it was kinda me, I guess."

Rose's smile is sutured in place, and I can see what I didn't see before: that she worried that maybe *she* was the source of Isuzu's bull-something. The hinge of her jawbone shifts as if chewing, and her lids drop over the black marbles of her eyes—a willed, deliberate blink, accepting the new information, sealing it away.

"And you guess that *why*?" Rose asks, opening her eyes on the last word, aiming all that shiny blackness at our little guest.

"She started it," Robbie says. "She asked what it was like, knowing in advance you're gonna be vamped. I just told her what I went through, is all."

I look at Rose; Rose looks at me. Isuzu has asked both of us similar questions over the years. Like: What would we have done if we'd known in advance? Followed by: What did we miss most about being mortal? She asked the same questions over and over—in part, I think, because our answers kept changing. I remember saying once that I missed the feel of resting my head on a cool pillow— missed being able to register that difference in temperature, no matter how fleetingly. Other times, it was sweating. Other times, it was smoking. Or a good dump, a good piss. There was food—obviously, there was food—but I mixed it up with other stuff, too, like sunshine, and birds, eyes that saved you the trouble of confessing what you couldn't put into words. Time, as something that mattered. Death, as a motivator.

"If you asked *me*," Isuzu says, suddenly appearing there in our midst, "which no one's bothered to, by the way. But if you asked me, I'd say all this talk about where I got the idea from shows a pretty low regard for my ability to think for myself." She pauses to reveal all her blunt teeth, gritted together in a forced smile. "But what the hell do I know?"

"Oh, hey there, Suzi-Q," Robbie says, slithering an arm around Isuzu's shoulder and pulling her in for a quick, fangless peck on the cheek. "We were just talking about you."

Isuzu looks at me and crosses her still-crossable eyes—it's just you and me, Marty, just you and me—before returning Robbie's perfunctory kiss.

"So I heard," she says. "Did you hear me?"

"Of course not," Robbie says, giving her a bear hug that lifts Isuzu off her feet. "You know I live to ignore you."

And then—I swear to God—he *winks*. At *me*.

"He just winked at me," I say.

"Figures," Isuzu says, still airborne in Robbie's embrace. "He winks at everybody." Pause. "He even winks in his email. You know, that semicolon followed by the parenthesis? I think he averages about two or three per message."

"I do *not*," Robbie insists, and then winks at me again. After which, Isuzu winks. And then Robbie winks. And then they kiss an inch or two deeper than a peck, Isuzu still in the air, her legs folded up and back. I get uncomfortable. Rose notices me getting uncomfortable and can't stop herself from smiling, not that she's trying very hard.

Finally, Isuzu and Robbie undock, disengage, decouple as he lowers her back to the floor. And then they just stand there in their relative youth—smiling, waiting, daring me to say something parental.

Me, I'd like to return to the subject of puking, and where the idea came from. Because, if you asked *me*—which no one has, by the way—but if you asked me, I'd say looking at that happy loving couple standing in front of me right now, yeah, that should do it. Plenty of gastrointestinal inspiration, right there.

But before I can confess to any of this, or anything else equally incriminating, I find myself in the not unwelcome position of having a tongue lodged firmly in my cheek. Not my own, of course, but

Rose's prehensile, curlable darter, squirming around, underneath and over my own. Our lips lock with our vampire suction on high, our cheeks cave in, except for here and there where our wrestling tongues push back.

Take that!

I can't usually read minds, but I can read Rose's just now, and that's what she's thinking. I know this because I'm thinking it, too.

Isuzu and Robbie clap politely, the flats of their fingers tap-tapping the opposite palm.

Robbie: "Touché."

Isuzu: "Bravo."

Tit has apparently met tat, and now it's smiles all around. Followed by bridge-partner glances, shoe inspections, the silence of nobody knowing whose turn it is, or what to say next.

Finally:

"Hey," Isuzu says, "how many vampires does it take to screw in a lightbulb?"

We of the pointy teeth shrug.

"None," she says, smiling her blunt smile. "Vampires prefer the dark."

We of the pointy teeth show our pointy teeth in polite grins that say:

Ain't that the truth . . .

One of the problems with our vampire-ruled world is we've never come up with a social catalyst that works as well as dinner used to. There's no main course to compliment, no aromas to trigger anecdotes, no seating arrangements planned for minimal or optimal mischief. Sitting around drinking blood just seems pathetic by comparison. You're finished before you even start, and then it's just a bunch of suckers, sitting around the table, excuseless, waiting for someone to suggest we take it to another room, at which point the pairing and cliquing starts and the whole "Let's all get together around a table" thing sort of falls apart.

There's cards, I suppose. A lot of vampires use poker as an ex-

cuse for getting together, but it's not the same thing. Dinner is—
was—about communal nourishment; cards are about winning and
losing. Plus, Isuzu's never really taken to card games other than her
favorite, slapjack. And the image of four adults all hovering over a
pile of cards, their right hands raised like they're getting sworn in or
something . . . well, a Norman Rockwell Thanksgiving it ain't. For
one thing, waiting on the jack is a conversation killer if there ever
was one. And without the conversation, what's the point?

The alternative I've come up with is bad movies. Bad, vampirically incorrect movies. On DVD. Bad because, well, good movies
are good for conversation only after they're done, but a bad movie
can't help but be improved by talking through it. My selection for
meet-the-parents night is *Dracula,* the Bela Lugosi version. Isuzu,
Rose, and I have laughed our way through it a dozen times already, and I'm counting on the count to give me a peek at the *real*
Robert Little.

Bad movies can act as barometers to the soul. Will the other person laugh at the same dumb things? Will they go for the easy joke?
Will they laugh when you spring the sincerity-test joke—the one
that's *not-funny* on purpose, to flush out the fakers and kiss-ups?
Will they make some inspired observation, or go inexplicably teary-
eyed, connecting some nothing moment on-screen to some something moment in their lives? Will hidden depths be revealed, or true
shallowness plumbed?

Or maybe they'll just sit politely throughout the movie, knowing
they're being watched and watching us back in return, letting out
little laughs for those things only one of us finds funny, and bigger
laughs for those moments more broadly agreed to as laughable.

Like: the little pause between "drink" and "wine."

Like: the dry-ice fog, the flip-floppy bat on a wire, the cobwebs,
candelabra, and cape.

Like: the inevitable peg-o'-my-heart moment.

And then there are the bits we've developed for ourselves, like
shouting "Renfield!" all together whenever Renfield appears on
screen.

Me: "Waiter, there's a fly in my soup."

Isuzu: "Only one? I *do* apologize . . ."

Rose: "Ba-rump bump."

Robbie flinches the first time we do it, but catches on, just like he catches on to our habit of adding "bator," sotto voce, every time Renfield uses the word "master."

And then Robbie shows me something I wasn't expecting.

"Oooo," he says, all on his own, "that's gonna leave a mark," winning giggles from Isuzu and Rose, but for me . . . For me, he's done the one thing he really shouldn't have—reminded me of those scars on my little girl's thighs. I look over at him, over there, on the other end of the couch—beaming at having scored points with two-thirds of the audience, twining his fingers between Isuzu's fingers, both their hands resting in her lap, a quick squeeze, and a quick squeeze back.

I click off the video and it goes back to regular TV. And what's this? Familiar eyes in a younger face, beaming, beaming, beaming. Is it really *that* time already? And there they go, those familiar eyes in their older face—caught, snagged, utterly wrapped up in their younger incarnation, there on the screen, coming to us "live," in quotes, from some safe somewhere, or so the story goes.

Oops.

Oops, and . . . *see?*

Not that it's premeditated—just because I thought about it in advance, this little peek into the shallow heart of Little Bobby Little. Just because I imagined his elbows propped on his knees and his chin plopped on his fists, staring into his younger mirror with undisguised affection. Just because I imagined the disgusted glance Isuzu tosses at him, and its gradual turning into a disgusted stare as the seconds tick by and my little girl gets increasingly ticked. Just because I imagined it exactly the way it really played out—that's no reason for saying I planned it.

I'm just a good imaginer.

A good imaginer who liked the way his life was going before Little Bobby Little took a big bite out of it.

"Robert?" Isuzu says. "Robert, honey, we can all leave if you'd like to whip it out for a crank."

"Huh?" Robbie says, turning reluctantly away from the screen.

"We've talked about this," Isuzu says, grabbing the remote, clicking off the object of Robbie's affection. "It's not an attractive side."

"You're right," Robbie says. "I'm sorry. It's just . . ." He pauses. "I remember this one. May I?" he asks, palm out.

Isuzu reluctantly surrenders the remote, her whole body warning that whatever he's remembering better be good.

"Thanks." Robbie clicks the TV back on. "See that shadow? See how I keep looking away from it?"

We nod.

"That's the director. It was a puppy that time. I've got my Snoopy sweater on, so that means it was a puppy."

"What was a puppy?" Rose asks.

Isuzu, I can tell, already knows—has known, in an abstract way, for a while, but hasn't put the information to the actual face, recorded as it was happening. Me, I've already skipped ahead a few moves, to the part where I lose this round.

"My incentive for being cute," Robbie says.

"They promised you a puppy for being cute?" Rose says.

"No," Robbie says, and there it goes—Isuzu's hand is already cupping his shoulder. "No," Robbie repeats, resting his hand on top of Isuzu's. "They promised me a *dead* puppy for *not* being cute." He pauses, staring into the screen, waiting.

"There," he says. "That twitch? That's me, not being cute enough."

The "again"—when it comes—comes out a little strangled. Wholly apropos—I'm guessing—under the circumstances.

Before I joined the service, I met a goofy girl named Dorothy. Dotty-Dot, the other boys called her—Dorothy LaMore-or-Less. She wore braces—*that*, apparently, was the crime that earned her the reputation for being undatable. That, and a laugh that contained no small amount of snorting. Me, I hadn't signed up yet— hadn't been whipped into shape, courtesy of the U.S. Army. Dumplingesque. Big-boned. Truth was, I was just too short for my appetite. Based on hunger alone, of course, I should have been banging my head against clouds.

Based on hunger alone, Dotty-Dot didn't seem so undatable to me.

And so we did. And we did. Our dating was a furtive, secret thing, conducted in the shadows and in-between times. Before church, after church, pressed up against shaded bark, shaded brick, my tongue scraping over all that machinery and wire work, Dorothy sniffling, her nose running like she said it always did whenever she got excited. So I was fine with it, fine with the salty taste of snot in my mouth, because for a big-boned, too-short guy like me, that was about as close to making a woman come as I was likely to get for the foreseeable future. Later, in public, Dotty-Dot wore scarves to hide the little red blossoms dotty-dotting her neck, while I wore my shirt collar open for the whole world to see.

"None of your bee's wax . . ."

"A gentleman doesn't kiss and tell . . ."

"Loose lips . . ."

"Yeah, yeah," Jackie Parisi says, sucking so hard on a bottle of Coke, it actually pops when he pulls it away. "Loose lips suck dicks. But the question on the floor is whose 'loose lips' we talkin' about? Fess up, Kowalski. Or you been playin' with your mom's 'Lectrolux again?"

I pull a zipper across my lips and shrug, after which Jackie Parisi gives me a black eye. Which I'm fine with—just like I'm fine with the purple blotches dotting my neck—because the shiner and the hickeys are all about the same thing: love, and its various price tags. Frankly, I can't wait for Dot to ask about the how and why of my black eye, because the answer—defending her honor—well, hell, I can taste the snot already.

There's another side of the black eye I don't mind—the fact that it puts off for a few more weeks the thing Dot has been pressing me on lately. The coming-over-for-dinner thing. The meeting-her-folks thing.

"You don't want 'em to think I'm some sort of juvenile delinquent, do you?" I say.

Dot's lips part and then close, over and over, letting out little silvery brace glints like somebody sending out a distress signal. You can tell she's not sure what she wants 'em to think. There's a part of her inside that's all squishy at the thought of other people knowing she's got boys fighting over her. That's the part that speaks in single-word sentences, like:

See?

Yes! (and)

Finally . . .

But there's another side, too, one that's sensibly afraid of bruises it hasn't inflicted, regardless of the supposed nobility of their acquisition. "Yeah," that side says, finally. "I guess you're right," it adds, sniffing once before pulling a sleeve across its nose.

"But once that heals," Dot warns, smiling a cold, metallic smile that finishes the sentence.

And I nod, of course, like a good, secret boyfriend—already imagining what it might take to arrange for my next beating.

I haven't thought about Dotty-Dot or the parents I never met in a decade's worth of decades. But now, sitting next to my would-be daughter's would-be beau, I can't help thinking about that Buick grille of a smile, or of all the fists it took to put an ocean between me and her parents' inevitable disapproval. Despite what I might think of him, despite what I might like to believe, the truth is, Robbie showed up. Something I never had the balls to do.

You're a better man than I was, Robert Little. That's what I should probably say, as the three of them sit there still mourning the offscreen death of some anonymous puppy, the quiet of the living room longing to be broken in some dramatic fashion.

But then I'd have to explain why, and I don't really want to. For one thing, anecdotes about extreme emotional cowardice might make good fodder for a stand-up routine, but it's really best not to share them with anyone you want to keep loving you. I know; I've tried; I've gone to bed alone.

So I decide to give the nod in a subtler way.

"Suzi, could you . . . ," I begin, and before I can finish, all three heads have turned my way.

"What did you call me?" Isuzu asks.

"Suzi," I say—all innocence.

Isuzu blinks her hold-nothing-back eyes.

"I know, I know," I say. "I'm getting used to it. Thought I'd take it out for a spin."

"Okay," Isuzu says, a little dubious.

"Change happens," I observe. "Change is good."

"Change is *good*?" Rose echoes.

"Well, it's okay," I clarify.

"Change is *okay*?" Isuzu repeats, nailing down the terms.

"Well, maybe 'inevitable' is the better word," I try.

"Huh," Rose huhs.

"Ditto," Isuzu dittos.

"Am I missing something?" Robbie asks, clearly missing everything—God bless 'im.

Isuzu leans into Robbie's shoulder and delivers a peck to his cheek. "I think you passed," she says.

"Cool," Robbie says, waiting for my nod before returning Isuzu's kiss.

-30-

GUY STUFF

So, this is where you met Rose, eh?"

That's Bobby—Robert—talking. It's been decided that we should get better acquainted. Do "guy" things. That's how the non-guy decision makers put it.

"You should go do some guy stuff together," Rose said. "Now."

"Yeah," Isuzu added, opening the door. "Skedaddle."

So we skedaddled like a couple of good boys, and this is the guy thing I came up with. Teezers.

"Yep," I say, paying the cover for both of us. "This is where I met Rose."

"Huh," he says, a tad judgmentally, it seems to me. He looks around, taking in the dancers, the munchkins, the mirrors everywhere.

"You come to these sorts of places a lot?" he asks.

"Once upon a time I used to come in, once in a while," I lie. "I wouldn't call it 'a lot.' And I don't anymore. Of course."

"Except, here we are," Robbie says, taking a seat.

"Well, yes," I admit.

"Why?"

"The womenfolk kicked us out so they could talk about us behind our backs."

"No," Robbie says. "Why here? Why this place?"

"It's a guy thing," I say. "We were told to do guy stuff and this fits the bill."

"Whose bill?" Robbie asks. "And who's paying it?" He's got both hands on the table in front of him, palms down, flat. His black headlights are aimed right for me.

"Um," I shrug. "My treat?"

Of course, I can't tell him the real reason. I can't tell him I'm still hoping for one more chance to trip him up, to expose the real creep underneath that TV-trained smile. I can't mention the recorder I grabbed on our way out, or how its tiny wheels are already turning, waiting for the crude comment that will damn him to eternal bachelorhood. The comment I'm getting less and less hopeful will ever come. At least not from Robbie.

"Listen," he says, still staring at me—just me—despite all the well-paid distractions surrounding us. "I'm not trying to be a jerk or anything, but I'm not a big fan of voyeurism." He pauses, breaks eye contact, but only to look down at his own hands.

Of course!

Of course Robert Little of *The Little Bobby Little Show* wouldn't be a big fan of voyeurism for hire. What was I thinking?

"I guess I'm like one of those tribes," Robbie goes on. "The ones that think cameras steal your soul? Only with me, they stole my whole life right up until . . ." He points his index finger at his eyes like a gun. "Until I became like everybody else. And boring."

I click off the tape recorder in my pocket. I let Robbie keep his soul, the one I find myself forced to acknowledge yet again.

Dammit.

"So," I say, eager to change the subject.

"So," Robbie says at the same time, eager for the same thing.

We laugh uncomfortably. Stop uncomfortably. Pause. Sit.

I extend my empty hand, palm up, yielding the floor to my reluctant guest.

"What was she like growing up?" Robbie asks, giving the floor back to me. "What was it like being her dad?"

They say that the Ebola virus—back when it still had victims to infect—would kill by liquefying its host's internal organs. Their hearts would bleed, and then melt, and then just give up.

I give up. Give in. Little Bobby Little's a bigger man than I am without even trying.

"Horrible," I say, making Robbie smile. "It was the most wonderful horror you can imagine."

I think I understand," Robbie says, after hearing me prattle on and on about What Being a Father Means to Me. "About these places," he adds.

I don't get the connection and so Robbie makes it for me.

"It's not about the dancers," he says. "It's them." He flicks a glance at the little kid look-alikes surrounding us. "You were looking for an Isuzu before you even knew there were any left to find."

I feel like I felt when Rose saw past my cheap excuse for playing it cool. I say now what Rose said then:

"Busted."

"So," we say together. Again. Laugh, again—perhaps a bit more comfortably this time. Robbie offers me the floor and I give it back.

"What were your parents like?" I ask.

"Dunno," Robbie says. "I didn't have any." Pause. "I mean, biologically, I had to, but I never met 'em. I had a director. I had a stage crew. I had a security staff, a tutor, and a cuteness coach. But parents? Not really. Not like you and . . ."

Robbie stops.

He's stopped looking at his hands and is looking straight ahead at something over my shoulder. I turn and there we are, the two of us, framed in one of Teezers' many mirrors.

They say that daughters look for their fathers, and you really don't need much more proof than the snapshot I'm staring at now. Robbie and me, side by side, same short dark hair, same baby skin, same through-the-wringer eyes. And the same fangs, of course, but poking out of smiles tightening with the same sudden shock of recognition.

Robbie's the first to speak. "You know any other guy places?" he asks. "Someplace without so many . . ."

". . . mirrors?"

"Yeah."

I leave my car in the lot and we walk the dozen or so blocks to the Detroit River. The sky overhead is lousy with stars just like it was when I was a kid, before the night became polluted with light. That's one good thing about vampires taking over. Our all-pupil eyes demand that we switch off the lights and let the stars back into our lives.

"When I was a kid," Robbie says, craning upward, "they never let me outside. It was too dangerous. The windows in my bedroom on the show weren't real. They were a kind of special effect. Blue screen. The outside was dubbed in, but the only time I ever saw it was when I watched the videotape. Isuzu thinks I'm watching myself when I watch those old reruns. I'm not. I'm just watching the only daylight they ever let me have."

"When I was a kid," I say, "I used to dream about being a movie star, like Fred Astaire. I thought it'd be the greatest thing in the world, to have all those people sitting in the dark looking up at you, larger than life and made of light."

"It's not all it's cracked up to be," Robbie says.

"Same goes for the outdoors and daytime," I say. "That's when the bugs are out. Bees and wasps and mosquitoes. Nasty business, being outside during the day."

Robbie smiles. "I guess we both got lucky, eh?"

"Yeah," I say. "I guess so."

-31-

THE HAPPY ENDING

Oh my God!" Isuzu squeals, seeing our little blue Twit for the first time. This is after the munchkin's called, gotten Rose, asked to speak to me, and asked me to ask Isuzu if friendship was still possible.

It was.

Is.

And there she is, standing in the doorway, wearing my blue vengeance to their first face-to-face since that little fangs-to-neck incident a few lifetimes ago. Isuzu is delighted by my fashion sense.

"It's adorable," she bubbles.

And it is. In the right light. With the right distance. The blueness of Twit's skin is just unreal enough to invite touching. And so Isuzu does, reaching out, smoothing her pink fingers against the Azure Sky of Twit's cheek.

"You look just like a Smurf," Isuzu says, cupping the cheek, confirming its reality.

"You look like the bride of Frankenstein," Twit counters, meaning Isuzu's neck, the baseball stitches.

Isuzu blinks—a cat smiling. A cat suddenly remembering something. "You have absolutely *got* to keep it," she insists. "Promise me you'll keep it for . . ."

And then Isuzu stumbles, because she hasn't really told anyone yet. Meaning me, who's been eavesdropping, and Twit, who's standing right there, already blue in the face over Isuzu and her secret life.

"Keep it for what?" Twit asks. Not Halloween. Vampires still aren't openly celebrating that one.

"Um," Isuzu ums. "Well," she wells.

"Um, well," Twit mocks. "Spit it out, shit-wit."

"I'm getting married." Isuzu winces, throwing up her hands to shield her face, her still-healing neck.

Twit purses her lips tight and puffs out her cheeks. It looks like all the "fuck yous" and "goddammits" are just piling up inside, pushing out. Finally, she lets the air out in a low whistle, like a leaking tire. "How's the popster feel about that?"

"Popster didn't know."

They both look at me. I nod. Hold steady. Steer between not altogether unexpected icebergs.

It's Rose in the kitchen who drops the vase she was filling. Broken glass. Water. The fluted heads of lilies.

"You're *what*?" she says, storming into the living room, wiping her hands, joining the conversation late.

"Getting married."

"Over his dead body," Rose says, pointing at me, helpfully.

And me? Seems everybody's channeling my anger nowadays. And so I just turn the page of my newspaper and go on acting like I'm reading.

Rose and I are sworn to secrecy and act surprised when the "official" announcement is made. When Robbie asks for her hand, I ask if I should get a meat cleaver from the kitchen.

"You still have one of those?" he asks. "I bet you could get some serious cash on eBay."

I look at Isuzu, inviting her to reconsider. Inviting her to see the error of her ways, to imagine how long forever can be without an exit strategy.

But she just points my eyes back to Robbie, who's using his to wink.

"I *got* it," he says, smiling, and then winking again.

Wedding decisions start getting made. Plans are planned. And questions arise. Isuzu's vamping, for instance, and who, how, when. Me—I can see all sorts of advantages to its being me, and its happening before the wedding. If it comes *before* the wedding, we can all breathe a sigh of relief, publish an announcement in the *Detroit Free Press*, invite friends and family, go as public as we like. If it comes *before* the wedding, we won't need to lie on the license, or check with a lawyer later to find out if we need a do-over.

But I get voted down. It'd just be so romantic for the new husband to do it, all the Weird Sisters agree.

"At the 'You may now kiss the bride' part," Twit suggests, sliding into her new role with surprising ease.

"Yes!" Isuzu agrees.

"Oh, *yes*," Rose nods, darting a quick, sharp look at yours truly for some reason.

Oh, yeah, that's right, we're still living in sin. Much to Rose's overly apparent chagrin. She hasn't said anything, hasn't brought it up. At least not lately, and not in so many words. She just uses weird adjectives when talking about Robbie. Words like: "Decisive." "Determined."

"Mature."

I look at Rose and try not to smile. Try to keep my mouth shut. Try not to spill the beans.

Concerning who should officiate over this union—me, with some mail-order license to tithe, or a *real* priest—it seems all my efforts at Catholic indoctrination have suddenly come back to complicate my life.

"It's really sweet of you to offer," Isuzu says, folding her still-warm hand over my still-cold one. "But . . . you know. It's . . . I think the church . . ."

Not that she's ever been inside one. No. Everything she knows about church is what she sees on Sundays in a webcam window, kneeling before her computer. She's asked me what it's like, the real thing, and I've told her:

"Echoey."

I lean my forehead into her forehead. "Okay," I say. "Understood." I add a faint, not-too-weary smile. "But don't blame me if it gets weird."

"By 'weird' you mean . . . ?" Isuzu says, backing her forehead away from mine, taking a good hard look.

By weird I mean the measures—prophylactic, preventative, anticipatory—that will be needed. All the just-in-cases necessary to make sure she's not murdered. When it was the price I paid for free therapy, I made sure Father Jack got his time's worth. I fed him premium vicarious vampire porn. But now I'm regretting every grisly anecdote I let slip past my fangs.

Plus, there's the other thing. And even though she's a young woman now, she's still the youngest woman on the face of the planet. At least the youngest one without a price tag at the moment, or her own TV show.

"You're too young to remember this, but . . . ," I begin, proceeding to highlight the prechange infamy of some priests vis-à-vis innocence and its corruption. I mention Father Jack by name, but only to point him out as one of the good pedophiles. One of the self-torturing, nonpracticing ones.

"And this is the person you want ushering me into marital bliss?" Isuzu says.

"Listen," I say. "Father Jack's saved your butt more times than I can count."

"How?"

"I'm not at liberty to elaborate," I say. "Let's just say raising a kid's not easy."

"Oh," Isuzu says, an unconscious hand rising to rub the back of her neck.

"Oh," she repeats. "K," she adds, quite a bit later.

D o you remember that time I told you about . . ."

That's how I start, before going on to remind Father Jack about one of my "gambling" episodes.

"Yes?"

"Um," I um. "Well," I well.

"Spit it out, Marty."

And so I spit it out as Father Jack does the same thing. In my case, what gets spat is the unveiled truth about Isuzu; for Father Jack, it's a beautifully executed spit take, thanks to his unfortunate decision to sip some nonconsecrated blood while we have our little heart-to-heart.

"You have a *what*?" Father Jack demands, fine beads of sprayed blood measling me, the desk blotter, some still hanging in the air.

"Child," I repeat, wiping my face with my sleeve. "Mortal," I add. "Grown now. Plans to get vamped and married." Pause. "Married first, vamped second," I clarify.

"Hmm," Father Jack says, blotting away at his own speckled chin. "Problematic."

"Exactly."

"And how old did you say she was?"

"Eighteen."

"And one hundred percent human?" Father Jack says. "Mortal through and through?"

"Yes."

Father Jack has a dot of blood he hasn't caught on his eye. I notice this after the fact, when it disappears as the good father rolls his eyes ecstatically, contemplating the prospects.

"And you want me to officiate?" he says, knitting his fingers together, a small, expectant smile playing across his face.

"Provided," I say, "certain conditions can be met."

$\bullet$　$\bullet$

Isuzu's dress is her something borrowed—my mother's. And Twit has agreed to be her something blue.

"In more ways than one," the little munchkin whispers to me, sadly, in spite of the good show she's otherwise making.

"Join the fucking club," I whisper back.

Rose hasn't joined the blues club. Instead, she's invented her own—the "jealous of Isuzu/pissed off at Marty" club.

"What are you two conspiring about?" she asks, inserting her head between our whispering heads.

"Murder," Twit says.

"Murder most foul," I agree.

"Can I ask whose, or is that a surprise?" Rose asks.

I look at Twit; Twit looks at me.

"Surprise," we agree.

"Lovely," Rose says, stomping off.to go check something that really doesn't need checking.

"She's had just about enough of us two," Twit says.

"I noticed," I say. "You'd think it was *her* wedding night."

"No," Twit corrects. "You'd think it *wasn't*."

"Good point," I say, checking my pocket to make sure the ring is still there. I check my other pocket, too, to make sure of the other ring.

Check, and double check.

Robbie, meanwhile, is standing in the back of the almost empty church, smelling himself, though God only knows why. Vampires don't perspire. But then again, Robbie hasn't been a vampire for all that long, which is a good thing, I guess. Isuzu and he will be evenly matched.

"Are the doors locked?" I call back.

"Roger," Robbie says, giving me the thumbs-up, but then turning and tugging on both handles before turning around again, all smiles, and both thumbs. "Roger that," he repeats.

There are no blood dots on my eyes and no one can see them when they start rolling, though most can probably guess, I guess.

"Your son-in-law," Twit says. "In T-minus . . ."

"Yeah, yeah," I say, wondering if maybe I should just "misplace" one of the rings I'm holding.

And then, all of a sudden, Rose's hand is on my shoulder.

"Show time, Daddio," she says. "You, too, Lady Blue." With a hand on each of our shoulders, she must look like a teeter-totter from behind as she leads us to our stations in the back of the church.

Up front, to the left of the altar, the door to the sacristy shudders, half opens, closes, half opens again. A black shoe emerges, followed by a black sock, a black pant leg that hooks around the door and kicks it back to reveal Father Jack, meeting the conditions I've set.

I suppose I could have had him tank off before the ceremony, as Rose did before meeting Isuzu for the first time. That would have been simple—less theatrical, less humiliating. I mentioned these "conditions" as a kind of joke between longtime friends. But Father Jack nodded and agreed.

"An ounce of prevention," he said. He looked almost eager. Eager to be punished for his inclinations, perhaps. Or maybe he just liked the idea of being treated like a dangerous character for once in his bottle-fed life.

So Father Jack's vestments for the occasion include a hockey goalie's mouth protector and a straitjacket. In case you're not sure what a goalie's mouth protector looks like, just think of Anthony Hopkins in *Silence of the Lambs*, the scene where they wheel him out, wearing that mask with the fenced-off mouth hole. The straitjacket, by the way, has been dyed a more clerically correct black, and I've added a bucktoothed collar.

The door to the women's room in the back of the church has opened. And for a moment, it's almost as if there's a crowd there with us, all whispering awed little whispers and sssshhhing each other at the same time. The whispering lasts for as long as it takes

Isuzu to squeeze my mother's hoop skirt through the bathroom door, after which it's replaced by the softer, singular ssshhh of crinoline, spreading rumors across the slate-tiled floor.

"You look beautiful," I mouth.

"Thank you," she mouths back, folding her arm into my arm, squeezing my biceps for luck. Only Isuzu knows what I've got planned. I figured it was her night; I didn't want to steal away the spotlight. But she loved the idea. "It'll be like one of those Shakespeare comedies where everybody gets married in the end," she said when I told her.

"Well, that's better than a tragedy, I guess."

" 'To be or not to be'?"

"Ah, there's the rub—whatever *that* means."

Isuzu smiled and I smiled and we spent the rest of the time between then and now, enjoying Rose's being just a little pissed at both of us, not knowing what we know.

Ahead of us, Rose takes Robbie's arm in one hand and scoots Twit up ahead with the other. As Twit begins down the aisle, reaching her little hand into her little basket, sprinkling bloodred petals along the way, Rose pulls a remote control from her purse and aims it at the back of the church.

"Suzi picked it," she says, turning, warning.

Isuzu shrugs, gives me a strained "I'm sorry" grin with her blunt teeth for maybe the last time.

The boom-box pops and hisses; whatever it is, it's old. As in pre-CD, *vinyl* old.

"You are my sunshine," it starts. "My only sunshine . . ."

"Fuck you," I mouth to Isuzu, but sweetly. Sad—oh so very, very sad—but sweetly.

She smiles a smile that says she understands completely. "You're welcome," she mouths back.

Twit has to hold Father Jack's copy of the service and Father Jack has to keep leaning down to make sure he gets the words right. You'd think after all these years, he'd have the thing memorized, but then again, I guess a lot of couples like to tinker with the language. God knows Isuzu and Robbie had to. The official service has already been changed to accommodate straight vampire-to-vampire unions, most notably, the deletion of the Till Death Do Us Part part, but it hasn't been tailored to account for when the bride-to-be is also a vampire-to-be. So the task fell to Robbie and Isuzu, who sat in my kitchen till nearly dawn one night, trying to hammer out the right language.

The sticking point is the word "kiss." *That's* pivotal; *that's* what is being changed. I think about mentioning *my* first benevolent vamping—how kissing and vamping are *not* mutually exclusive—but then decide to keep quiet. Let the kids figure it out for themselves. There are bound to be a few chuckles along the way, and who knows? Maybe they might get into an argument and call the whole thing off.

An old vampire can dream, can't he?

"Suck."

That's Robbie's first offering. "Suck."

Isuzu screws up her face. "Rhymes with 'yuck,'" she says.

"Bite?"

"Like in, 'me'?"

"Eat?"

"I won't even dignify that with a 'fuck you.'"

"Okay, 'vamp,'" Robbie says. "That's what we're talking about, right?"

"Ye-ah," Isuzu says, drawing it out, doubtfully, "but it's still a little . . . I don't know. Harsh? Blunt, maybe."

"You mean like your teeth?"

"Watch it, Fang Boy."

Robbie gives his neck a long, slow roundhouse turn, popping bones loudly. Isuzu, not to be outdone, knits her fingers together and then pushes out with both palms, letting the air rip with the bony flatulence of cracking knuckles.

And me, I just shake my head. If I wasn't convinced before, I am now. They're stuck with each other. They're going to be together until the asteroids come or the nukes fry our shadows to the walls.

"Sip?" Robbie offers, and Isuzu does a sort of hmm-hmm thing with her head.

"Maybe," she says.

Other words follow—drink, immortalize, eternalize, transfuse, imbue, imbibe, induct, partake, tipple, nibble, assimilate, mingle, supplement—followed by possible alternative phrases: Let us prey; Come and get it; Wet your whistle. And finally:

"Complement," Isuzu suggests.

"Excuse me?"

"Complement," Isuzu repeats. "'You may now complement the bride.'"

"You mean, like, 'Your hair's so pretty'?" Robbie says. "That comes off as a little needy, if you ask me."

"Not 'compliment' with an *I*," Isuzu says. "'Complement' with an *E*. To complete, make whole."

Robbie looks wounded in that grown-up-kid-actor way of his— that way which I'm starting to think may not be an act. He lets his head drop and then raises it slowly. "That's 'whole' with a *W*, right?" he says. "Not with an *A*, like I just was."

Isuzu doesn't agree or disagree, she just leans forward and kisses her fiancé on the forehead.

Yep—they're stuck with each other, all right. Till the asteroids come and the glaciers glide.

The service has just reached its official punch line—Robbie and Isuzu have been pronounced a legally bound couple—and now all that remains is the new couple's P.S. Father Jack leans forward, leans back, tilts his head to one side, suggesting Reaganesque confusion, and then leans forward again. He leans back, shrugs, and announces:

"Doesn't the bride look lovely tonight?"

Rose looks at me with a question mark on her face.

Twit turns the service around and takes a blue-faced squint.

Me, I just cover my face with my hand and wonder about the quality of education being offered in seminaries.

Robbie, meanwhile, seems to be having trouble holding back a smile.

"You're right about that, Padre," the groom says, winking at me, his—oh my God!—father-in-law. "But . . . um . . ."

Isuzu snatches the script of the service from Twit, holds it in Father Jack's hockey-masked face. Her fingernail scratches along the page. "You were supposed to *read* this," she says. "Aloud. It's *not* a stage direction."

"Oh," Father Jack says.

"Do-over," he announces. He clears his throat. Cranks his head in a circle—first clockwise, then counterclockwise. "Ready?" he asks, turning toward Robbie, turning toward Isuzu. One nod, one set of angrily folded, lace-covered arms. The sssshhhh of agitated skirts.

"You may now complement the bride," Father Jack says.

This is probably a good place to point out that there was a fair amount of debate about whether Isuzu's vamping should be incorporated into the actual ceremony or be left as a private matter between the consenting adults themselves. I was conflicted, as usual. I'd always imagined it would be me—not in a creepy way, just . . . Well, I rescued her; I avenged her; I raised her; I protected her; and I'm the vampire who's known her the longest. Why shouldn't *I* introduce her to immortality? Or, for that matter, decide not to—a threat I apparently used a few too many times while raising her. Of course she got a backup plan. At least I didn't raise her stupid.

The methods of vamping—by the way—are as various as vampires themselves. Yes, some of the methods have an erotic element—if you can bite it, you can vamp through it—but that is by no means a prerequisite. For example, when the Vatican stopped killing us and began its own, en masse, ceremonial vampings, only the most orally fixated could have found that erotic. Me, I've done it all sorts of ways—with a kiss, with a syringe, with a scalpel, with a different, more southward kiss, old-school Dracula-style, and anonymously via the blood products distribution bureaucracy—though that last one came with some mixed results.

Unfortunately, all my arguments for why it wouldn't be creepy for me to do it were also arguments for Robbie's doing it in public, as part of the ceremony.

In the end, it was Rose who talked some sense into me.

"Frankly," she said, "one more word out of you, Cowboy, and I'm gonna be powerful troubled." Pause. "And I can stay 'troubled' fer a powerful long time, pardner."

And so now here we are—the last few ticks of my little girl's mortality. And Father Jack was right. She *is* lovely. Incandescent. And not just because of how my vampire eyes take in light. No matter how neurotically she may have gotten here, she's found her perfection. Her neck's a sunflower stem—fragile and tough at the same time, and just long enough to call attention to itself. Her lips are full—bee-stung—and will only look better with her new fangs. And her eyes . . .

Her eyes never were part of a heart smart diet, not when they could break one just by blinking. I can only imagine what they'll do when they go all black, upping their mystery, their inscrutability, their flagrant disregard for all matters cardiopulmonary. Perhaps she'll have to wear sunglasses, just as a public courtesy.

My mother's old wedding dress has cleaned up nicely, too, just so much frosting, meringue, a cloud buoying her up like a pillowed, precious gift from heaven or some such place.

Robbie, the clod—the lucky, lucky clod—stands there for the sake of comparison. Beast, beauty; beauty, beast. He's smiling, showing fangs, and I try not to think about the half-moons scarring that perfect body up there. I turn, look. Twit and Rose are both smiling, wistfully mournful, forced Mona Lisas, polite, respectful, resigned.

Twit reaches a blue hand into her pocket, pulls out an ancient crumpled tube of topical anesthetic Father Jack gave me. She offers the tube to the groom. Holding Isuzu's wrist, he works the ointment in with slow, gentle circles. His eyes flicker up to meet hers—to apologize in advance, to reassure—and then return to the job at hand.

Father Jack, his mouth caged, his arms crossed over his heart and bound, looks on, past the people, toward the back of the church and the double doors, locked. He is a man of the Scotchgarded cloth, its useful life chemically extended indefinitely, spillproof, resilient, colorfast. I imagine him imagining himself as Christ on the cross, looking up toward heaven, looking down at his fickle apostles as they discreetly check their watches for the time.

The suddenness with which Robbie attaches himself to Isuzu's wrist unnerves me and my foot takes an involuntary step forward. I press down on it, freeze it in place, force down roots. I grit my teeth, a perfect reflection of Isuzu's own grimace. Her throat quivers, swallows hard; her chest rises and falls fitfully, her heart tugging, bashing, struggling. But she's a tough kid. She'll kick the ass of any asshole who says she isn't. She breathes through her nose, the breaths coming out short, sharp, and fast, chugging, whistling slightly, The Little Train That Could.

Might.

Isn't So Sure at the Moment.

The Little Train Who'd Like to Maybe Sit Down in a Support Group and Discuss Its Traumatic Railroad Experiences with Other Little Trains.

Soon—too soon—her breathing grows shallow and I stop watching her. I watch Robbie instead. This is the tricky part; this is the part that makes doing this thing in front of witnesses a good idea. This is the part that bottle-fed vampires might not be so good at controlling.

And all of a sudden, I reconsider Isuzu's scars. The Twit affair was for Isuzu's benefit, little lessons in what it felt like, little lessons in how and when to say, "When." But Robbie—that was a different kind of training. That was Isuzu teaching her future husband the self-control necessary to get this last time right.

Smart, smart girl—I think, only wishing I could take the credit.

Robbie lets go, disengages, decouples, undocks with an audible *pop!* He's done a very neat job, no spillage, no splatter. The holes in her wrist look like two puckered dents in a lump of cold dough. It takes Isuzu two or three hard, forced breaths to get them bleeding—just a drop out of each, one a little ahead of the other, racing down her translucent skin toward the lace bunched up around her elbow.

Robbie's doing some hard breathing of his own. The vein squiggling down his temple pulses. His lips move silently.

One Mississippi, two Mississippi, three . . .

His chin jerks down, and then back; he grabs where his stomach used to be; his lips stop, tighten, his cheeks puff out. He presses his lips—no teeth, no fangs—to Isuzu's wrist and holds them there, as his cheeks slowly deflate, go flat, cave in.

Isuzu's head—hanging on her chest like a junky on the nod—stirs. Her eyes open blackly, forcing her head back like a shotgun blast. She blinks several times, frantically, accepts a pair of sunglasses Twit presses into her hand.

"Thanks," she says—her first word as a vampire.

"No prob," Twit says.

Safe again behind dark lenses, Isuzu looks out at the (less painfully) beaming faces of her assembled loved ones. She smiles her old, blunt smile, but that'll change in a couple of nights. She'll have to learn a new smile then, one that doesn't inadvertently bite itself, one that makes room for fangs. But the old one's good enough for now—says what doesn't need words to be said.

We smile back, welcoming our little newcomer to forever.

Well, that's that," Father Jack says, anticlimactically. "Can someone help me out here?"

"I got it," I say, bounding up to the altar, unbuckling a series of buckles. Father Jack uncrosses his arms, stretches them out in front of him, the excess sleeves drooping emptily a foot or so past the knuckles of either hand.

"Thanks, Marty," Father Jack says, patting me on the back, his empty sleeve flopping over my shoulder like the fluke of some strange and somber fish. "Wish 'em luck for me. Him, especially."

He turns. Begins to leave.

I finger the other ring in my other pocket.

"Father Jack," I call out. "There's just one more thing."

So we get married—Rose and I. I figure, what the hell? I'm the son of a cherry pit swallower. I've swallowed snot; I've swallowed blood; I've swallowed worse-tasting things than my own silly fear. And so I ask, and she accepts, and we end the evening with a double feature—just like a comedy by Shakespeare.

"Do you?" Father Jack asks, and Rose, my sweetie, my love, says, "Yeah, sure. Why not?"

"Don't answer that," I warn Isuzu, who's still kind of light-headed from her vamping and is liable to say anything. Like the truth.

Isuzu mimes twisting a key between her lips and then stands there looking at the invisible key, wondering how she's supposed to swallow it, with her lips already locked. She decides tossing it over her shoulder is good enough. She wipes the dust from her palms, then, and gives me the big okay. She tips up her dark glasses just long enough to wink one of her new eyes.

"Do you . . . ," Father Jack begins, and I hardly let him finish before spitting out my "Hell, yes!"

The priest slaps me up the back of the head. He points at the crucifix hanging over the altar and assorted other holy things.

"Language," he warns.

"Sorry . . ."

"Get used to saying that," Robbie says, nudging me like we're buddies or something. His idea of male bonding, I guess, but more forced. Maybe "male riveting" would be the better term. "Male spot-welding."

Rose and Isuzu both let him have it, of course, applying the flats of their palms to the back of his head. Smack. Smack.

Twit, meanwhile, kicks in her two cents—*and* Robbie's shins.

He yelps, grabbing his leg in both hands, hamming it up. He's making a play for our sympathy but he's playing to the wrong crowd. It's just us vampires, after all. Now and forever.

Amen.

If I had to guess what Father Jack and Twit have in common, I guess I'd guess this:

They've both had it up to here.

Twit's *here* isn't as high as Father Jack's *here,* of course, but they've both had it, right up to and just slightly past that space over their heads. They've both been screwed by Fate, and little else. They've both been humiliated by people who claim to love them—Twit with a can of Azure Sky, Father Jack with all my precautions. And neither is crazy about happy endings that don't include them.

I'm guessing that's what they're talking about back there, at the back of the church, while Isuzu and Rose take turns taking pictures of the new couples. They're probably smirking at our smiles, making snide comments about our happiness.

They're saving the *here*s they've had it up to. That's what they'll talk about, later—over the coffee they say they're going to get. Over the "coffee" that's their excuse for not joining us in a little celebration back at my place.

"Coffee?" Isuzu says. "But I thought . . ."

"Don't be thick, kiddo," I whisper. "Smile. Wave. Wish them well."

"This is me, smiling," Isuzu calls out. "This is me, wishing you well . . ."

Twit waves back and then tugs on Father Jack's pant leg. He bends down and she whispers something in his ear. He bends down farther, and she crawls up on his back. They both laugh as he straightens, unsteadily at first, but getting his bearings quickly enough. And they continue to laugh—desperate, cynical, miraculous laughter—as Father Jack gallops out those big double doors with our little blue girl holding on tight.

I know what you're thinking—you're uncomfortable at the thought of Father Jack's getting a happy ending. Here's a little secret:

So am I.

The only problem is, it's a package deal. Father Jack's happy ending is Twit's, too. It's a complicated world, this world I helped make. I'd say it sucks, but . . .

But this is me smiling—through gritted teeth.

This is me, wishing all of us well.

ACKNOWLEDGMENTS

Thanks are due to many people who helped in many different ways to make this novel a reality. For their substantive comments and suggestions on my early drafts, I want to thank Miriam Goderich, Josie Kearns, Laura Berry, Mark Schemanske, Mary Doria Russell, Amy Scheibe, Lauren McKenna, and Liz Keenan. For the time, space, inspiration, and fellowship needed to complete the first draft of this novel (and a few others) I owe a debt of gratitude to the Ragdale Foundation. For helping to place this novel with all the right people at the right time, I want to thank everyone at Dystel & Goderich Literary Management, but most especially Jane Dystel and Miriam Goderich, as well as Steven Fisher (through the Agency for the Performing Arts). And for letting me borrow elements of their persons and lives, heartfelt thanks go out to, first, the real Rose Thorne, of whom there are several (at least according to Google), but the one I'm thanking is the one who works for the R&R Rendezvous Lounge in Taylor, Michigan—thank you for letting me use your wonderful name. As promised, I must point out that other than the name, the Rose Thorne of this book and the real Rose have nothing in common. Next, I want to thank Suzian Hall for use of her incredible tattoo. As with my previous case of borrowing, I used just the tattoo (the background and the character to which the tattoo has been applied are both utterly fictional). And lastly, I want to thank my dad, Eugene Sosnowski , for the Pit Story.

ABOUT THE AUTHOR

David Sosnowski grew up in Detroit, Michigan, and has worked as a university writing instructor and a gag writer. His fiction has appeared in numerous literary magazines, including *Passages North, River City,* and *Alaska Quarterly Review.* The author of *Rapture,* Sosnowski lives in Taylor, Michigan.